W9-CNK-320

ALSO AVAILABLE FROM ELLE KENNEDY

The Campus Diaries:

The Graham Effect

Briar U Series:

The Chase

The Risk

The Play

The Dare

Off-Campus Series:

The Deal

The Mistake

The Score

The Goal

The Legacy

A full list of Elle's contemporary and suspense print titles is available on her website, ellekennedy.com

THE
DARE

BRIAR U

ELLE KENNEDY

Bloom *books*

Content warning: This book contains some light discussion of body insecurity, dieting, and food restriction.

Copyright © 2020, 2022 by Elle Kennedy
Cover and internal design © 2022, 2024 by Sourcebooks
Cover design and illustration by Elizabeth Turner Stokes

Sourcebooks and the colophon are registered trademarks of
Sourcebooks. Bloom Books is a trademark of Sourcebooks.

All rights reserved. No part of this book may be reproduced in any form or by
any electronic or mechanical means including information storage and retrieval
systems—except in the case of brief quotations embodied in critical articles or
reviews—without permission in writing from its publisher, Sourcebooks.

The characters and events portrayed in this book are fictitious or
are used fictitiously. Any similarity to real persons, living or dead,
is purely coincidental and not intended by the author.

All brand names and product names used in this book are trademarks,
registered trademarks, or trade names of their respective holders. Sourcebooks
is not associated with any product or vendor in this book.

Published by Bloom Books, an imprint of Sourcebooks
P.O. Box 4410, Naperville, Illinois 60567-4410
(630) 961-3900
sourcebooks.com

Originally self-published in 2020 by Elle Kennedy Inc. This is an updated, edited version.

Cataloging-in-Publication Data is on file with the Library of Congress.

Printed and bound in the United States of America.
WOZ 10 9 8

1
TAYLOR

It's Friday night, and I'm watching the greatest minds of my generation get destroyed by Jell-O shots and blue concoctions served from ten-gallon paint buckets. Sweat-beaded bodies writhing half-naked, frenzied, hypnotized with subliminal waves of electronic arousal. The house is wall-to-wall psych majors acting out their parental resentment on unsuspecting future MBAs. Poli-sci students planting the seeds of the blackmail checks they'll be writing in ten years.

AKA your typical Greek Row party.

"Have you ever noticed how dance music kind of sounds like listening to drunk people having sex?" Sasha Lennox remarks. She's standing beside me in the corner, where we've wedged ourselves between the grandfather clock and a standing lamp to best blend in with the furniture.

She gets it.

It's the first weekend back from spring break, and that means the annual Spring Break Hangover party at our Kappa Chi sorority house. One of the many events Sasha and I refer to as mandatory fun. As Kappas, we're required to attend, even if that means our presence is more decorative than functional.

"Like it wouldn't be so offensive if there was a melody, at least. This…" Sasha crinkles her nose, and her head twitches to a siren wail that blares through the surround sound system before another shattering bass line thunders in. "This is some shit the CIA used on doped-out MKUltra test subjects."

I cough out a strangled laugh, almost choking on the cup of whatever YouTube party punch recipe I've been nursing for the last hour. Sasha, a music major, has an almost religious aversion to anything not performed by live instruments. She'd rather be front row at a concert in some dive bar, the reverb of a Gibson Les Paul ringing in her ears, than be caught dead under the flashing techno kaleidoscope of a dance club.

Don't get me wrong, Sasha and I certainly aren't fun-averse. We hang out at the campus bars, we do karaoke in town (well, she does, while I cheer her on from the safety of the shadows). Hell, we once got lost in Boston Common at three in the morning while stone-cold sober. It was so dark that Sasha accidentally fell into the pond and almost got molested by a swan. Trust me, we know how to hang.

But the ritualistic practice of college kids plying each other with mind-altering substances until they mistake inebriation for attraction and inhibition for personality isn't our fondest idea of a good time.

"Look out." Sasha nudges me with her elbow at the sound of shouts and whistles from the foyer. "Here comes trouble."

A wall of unabashed maleness crashes through the front door to chants of *"Briar! Briar!"*

Like Wildlings storming Castle Black, the towering goliaths of the Briar University hockey team trample through the house, all thick shoulders and broad chests.

"All hail the conquering heroes," I say sarcastically, while Sasha smothers a snide smirk with the side of her thumb.

The hockey team won their game tonight, putting them into the first round of the national championship. I know this because our Kappa sister Linley is dating a benchwarmer, so she was at the game snapchatting rather than here with us cleaning toilets, vacuuming, and mixing drinks for the party. The privileges of dating royalty.

Although a fourth-stringer ain't exactly Prince Harry, but maybe somewhere closer to the coke-addict son of someone prince-adjacent.

Sasha pulls her phone from the waistband of her skin-tight faux leather leggings and checks the time.

I peer at the screen and groan. Oh man, it's only eleven p.m.? I already feel a migraine coming on.

"No, this is good," she says. "Twenty minutes flat and those goons will have the keg killed. Then they'll blow through whatever's left of the liquor. I'd say that's quitting time for me. Half hour, tops."

Charlotte Cagney, our sorority president, didn't explicitly mandate how long we had to stay to fulfill our attendance requirement. Usually, once the drinks run dry, people go looking for the after-party at which point it's easy to sneak out unnoticed. With any luck, I'll be back in my apartment in Hastings and in my pajamas by midnight. Knowing Sasha, she'll drive into Boston and find a live show.

Together, she and I are the outcast stepsisters of Kappa Chi. We each came to be among their ranks for our own ill-conceived reasons. For Sasha, it was family. Her mother, and her mother's mother, and her mother's mother's mother, and so on, were all Kappas, so it was never a question that Sasha's academic career would include carrying on the legacy. It was either that or kiss something as "frivolous and self-indulgent" as a music major goodbye. She comes from a family of doctors, so her decisions are already heavily contested.

For me, well, I suppose I had grand designs of a college glow up. From high school loser to college It Crowd. A reinvention. Total life makeover. Thing is, joining their clubs and wearing their letters and enduring their weeks of sacramental indoctrination didn't have the desired effects. I didn't come out the other side all shiny and new. It's like everyone else drank the Kool-Aid and saw the pretty colors, but I was just left standing there in the dark with a cup of water and red food coloring.

"Hey!" a bleary-eyed guy greets us, staggering to sidle up next to Sasha while openly talking to my tits. We tend to make one perfectly desirable female when standing side-by-side. Her exquisite facial symmetry and slender figure, and my enormous rack. "You wanna drink?"

"We're good," Sasha shouts back over the pounding music. We both hold up our mostly full cups. A strategic device to keep the horny frat bros at bay.

"Wanna dance?" he then asks, leaning toward my chest like he's speaking into the box at a fast food drive-thru.

"Sorry," I retort, "they don't dance."

I don't know if he hears me or understands my contempt, but he nods and strolls away just the same.

"Your boobs have a gravitational force that only attracts douche-bags," Sasha says with a snort.

"You have no idea."

One day I woke up and it was like two massive tumors just erupted on my chest. Ever since middle school I've had to walk around with these things that arrive everywhere ten minutes before I do. I'm not sure which of us is the greater hazard to each other, me or Sasha. My boobs or her face. She causes a stir just walking into the library. Dudes stumbling over themselves to stand in her presence and forget their own names.

A loud *pop* bursts through the house, causing everyone to cringe and cover their ears. Silence ensues in the confusion while our eardrums drown in the lingering echoes of tinnitus.

"Speaker's blown!" one of our sisters yells from the next room.

Boos fill the house.

A mad scramble ensues as Kappas scurry to find a quick fix to save the party before our restless guests revolt. Sasha doesn't even try to hide her excitement. She eyes me with a look that says we may get to escape this party early after all.

Then Abigail Hobbes happens.

We see her sashay through the tightly packed crowd in a skimpy little black dress, platinum hair curled into perfect tendrils. She claps her hands, and in a voice that could cut glass, demands all attention fall on her bright red lips.

"Listen up, everybody! It's time to play Dare or Dare."

Cheers erupt in response as the living room swells with more bodies. The game is a popular Kappa tradition, and it's exactly what it sounds like. Someone dares you to do something and you do it—no truth option. Occasionally amusing and often brutal, it's resulted in more than a few arrests, at least one expulsion, and rumor has it, even a couple babies.

"Now let's see…" Our house vice president puts one manicured finger to her chin and turns in a slow circle to survey the room, deciding on her first victim. "Who shall it be?"

Of course her evil green eyes land squarely on where Sasha and I are plastered against the wall. Abigail strides up to us with pure sugary malice.

"Oh, sweetie," she says to me, with the glassy stare of a girl who's had a few too many. "Loosen up, it's a party. You look like you just found another stretch mark."

Abigail's a mean drunk, and I'm her favorite target. I'm used to it from her, but the laughs she elicits every time she uses my body as a punch line never fail to leave a scar. My curves have been the bane of my existence since I was twelve years old.

"Oh, sweetie," Sasha mimics, making a show of flashing her the bird. "How about you eff right off?"

"Aww, come on," Abigail whimpers in a mocking baby voice. "Tay-Tay knows I'm just kidding." She punctuates her statement by poking my stomach like I'm a goddamn Pillsbury Doughgirl.

"We're keeping your thinning hairline in our thoughts, Abs."

I have to chomp down on my bottom lip to stop from laughing at Sasha's retort. She knows I disintegrate amid conflict and never shies away from a chance to trade barbs in my defense.

Abigail answers with a sarcastic laugh.

"Are we playing or not?" demands Jules Munn, Abigail's sidekick.

The tall brunette saunters over to us, donning a bored look. "What's the matter? Sasha trying to back out from doing a dare again like she did at the Harvest Bash?"

"Fuck off," Sasha shoots back. "You dared me to throw a brick through the dean's window. I wasn't about to get expelled over some juvenile sorority game."

Jules arches a brow. "Did she just insult an age-old tradition, Abs? Because I think she did."

"Oh, she did. But no worries, here's your chance for redemption, Sasha," Abigail offers sweetly, then pauses. "Hmm. I dare you to…" She turns toward her spectators while contemplating the dare. She's nothing if not in it for the attention. Then she snaps back around to face Sasha. "Do the Double Double then sing the chapter symphony."

My best friend snorts and shrugs, as if to say, *Is that all?*

"Upside down and backwards," Abigail adds.

Sasha curls her lips and sort of snarls at her, which gets the guys in the room hooting in amusement. Dudes love catfights.

"Whatever." Rolling her eyes, Sasha steps forward and shakes out her arms like a boxer warming up for a fight.

The Double Double is another Kappa party tradition, which entails downing two double shots of whatever's lying around, then a ten-second beer bong followed by a ten-second keg stand. Even the sturdiest drinkers among us rarely make it through the gauntlet. Throwing a handstand on top of it while singing the house song backwards is just Abigail being a spiteful bitch.

But as long as it won't get her expelled, Sasha is never one to back down from a challenge. She ties her thick black hair in a ponytail and accepts the shot glass that materializes out of nowhere, dutifully tossing back one shot, then the next. She powers through the beer bong while a couple Theta guys hold up the funnel for her, the crowd around her screaming their encouragement. To a cacophony of cheers, she muscles her way past the keg stand with a six-three hockey player keeping her legs in the air. When she's right-side up again, everyone's impressed to see her even able to stand, much less looking mean and holding steady. That girl's a warrior.

"Stand back!" Sasha declares, clearing people from the far wall.

With a gymnast's flourish, she thrusts her arms in the air and then sort of half-cartwheels so that her backside is flush against the wall in a handstand. Loud and confident, she belts out the words to our house song in reverse while the rest of us stupidly try to keep up in our heads to make sure she's getting it right.

Then, when she's done, Sasha completes an elegant dismount back to her feet and gives the crowd a bow to resounding applause.

"You're a fucking robot," I say, laughing when she prances over to resume her spot slouching in our losers' corner. "Beautiful dismount."

"Never met a landing I couldn't stick." Freshman year Sasha was on her way to Olympic qualifiers as one of the best vaulters in the world before she busted her knee slipping on some ice, and that was it for her gymnastics career.

Not to be outshined, Abigail sets her gaze on me. "Your turn, Taylor."

I take a deep breath. My heart races. Already I feel my cheeks burning red. Abigail smiles at my discomfort like a shark alerting to the vibrations of a wriggling seal in distress. I brace myself for whatever evil endeavor she's concocting for me.

"I dare you to…" She drags her teeth across her bottom lip. I see my impending humiliation in her eyes before she even opens her mouth. "Get a guy of my choice to take you upstairs."

Bitch.

Debauched hoots and catcalls burst from the men still watching this display of female aggression play out.

"Come on, Abs. Getting date-raped isn't a party game." Sasha steps forward, shielding me with her body.

Abigail rolls her eyes. "Oh, don't be so dramatic. I'll pick someone good. Someone anybody would want to get sweaty with. Even Taylor."

God, please don't make me have to do this.

To my sheer relief, help comes in the form of Taylor Swift. "Fixed it!" a sorority sister yells, just as music once again fills the house.

T-Swift's "Blank Space" elicits a wave of excited cheers, drawing attention away from Abigail's stupid game. The crowd promptly disperses to refill their drinks and get back to the rhythmic foreplay of dancing.

Thank you, hotter and skinnier Taylor.

To my dismay, Abigail is undeterred. "Hmm, who will the lucky boy be…"

I swallow a groan. I was naïve to think she'd drop it. Once a dare has been issued, any sister who fails to complete the task to the best of her ability is punished mercilessly until some poor sap is unlucky enough to take her place. And if Abigail were to get her way, that'd be three weeks after forever. I already have a hard time fitting in with the rest of the sisters. This would make me a pariah.

She scans the room, standing on her tiptoes to peer over people's heads and get a thorough look at available options. A wide grin spreads out across her face when she turns to me again.

"I dare you to seduce Conor Edwards."

Fuck.

Fucking fuck.

Yeah, I know who Conor is. Everyone does. He's on the hockey team and a regular face at the parties on Greek Row. A regular face in the sorority beds on Greek Row, too. But his real claim to fame is being arguably the hottest new guy in the junior class. Which puts him way out of my league. A perfect choice if the goal of this dare is my utter humiliation at being resoundingly rejected by a guy laughing in my face.

"Rachel is still in Daytona," Abigail adds. "You can use her bedroom."

"Abigail, please," I say, begging she let this go. But my plea only emboldens her.

"What's wrong, Tay-Tay? I don't recall you having a problem

kissing other guys on a dare. Or is your kink just hooking up with girls' boyfriends?"

Because that's what it always comes back to with Abigail: revenge, and the mistake she's been making me pay for every single day since sophomore year. No matter how many times I apologize, or how sincerely I regret hurting her, my life is but to amuse Abigail with my suffering.

"You should see a doctor about your raging bitchitis," Sasha snaps back.

"Oh, poor Taylor, such a prude. Don't turn your back or she'll steal your dude," Abigail sings. Her mockery becomes a chorus when Jules jumps in to sing along.

Their taunting stabs at the nerves behind my eyes and makes my fingers go numb. I want to shrink into the floor. Disappear into the wall. Burst in spontaneous flames and become ash that settles in the party bowl. Anything but me, here, now. I *hate* unwanted attention, and their mocking has recaptured the eyes of several drunken faces around us. A few more seconds and the whole house will bust out in song about how I'm a prude, like a horrible scene out of my worst nightmare.

"Fine!" I burst out. Just to make it stop. Anything to shut them up. "Whatever. I'll do the dare."

Abigail smiles in triumph. She couldn't be more obvious if she were drooling. "Go get your man, then," she says, extending a gracious hand behind her.

I bite my lip and follow the line of her thin arm, finally spotting Conor by the beer pong table in the dining room.

Fuck, he's tall. And his shoulders are impossibly broad. I can't see his eyes, but I do have a clear view of his chiseled profile and longish blond hair slicked away from his forehead. It should be illegal for someone to be that good-looking.

Big-girl pants, Taylor.

On a deep breath, I steel my nerves and make my way toward an unsuspecting Conor Edwards.

2

CONOR

THE BOYS ARE GETTING ABSOLUTELY RIPPED TONIGHT. WE'VE BEEN at this sorority party all of twenty minutes and already Gavin and Alec have torn open their shirts with their bare hands and are strutting around the beer pong table like a couple of barbarians. Got to admit, though, after winning our playoff game, I'm feeling pretty primal myself. Two more victories and it's on to the Frozen Four. While no one will say it out loud for fear of jinxing the team, I feel like this is our year.

"Con, get over here, asshole." Hunter calls out to me from across the room, where he and some of the guys have lined up rows of shots. "Bring those two knuckleheads with you."

We gather with our teammates, all red-faced and high on adrenaline. Each of us hold up a shot glass while our captain, Hunter Davenport, makes a speech. He doesn't even have to shout, because the music stopped about ten minutes ago. I keep seeing panicky sorority girls darting to and from the speaker system in the living room.

Hunter's gaze sweeps over everyone. "I just want to say I'm damn proud of all of us for how we've persevered as a team this season. We've had each other's backs, and everyone has put in their maximum effort. We've got two more, boys. Two more and we're in the hunt. So enjoy tonight. Let's turn it up. And then it's time to get your heads back in it for the final push."

It still doesn't feel real sometimes. My punk ass at an Ivy school, interloping among the well-bred sons and daughters of old money and founding fathers. Even with my boys, the closest thing I've ever had to family after my mom, I can't help sometimes checking over my shoulder. Like any day now they're going to figure me out.

After a shout of "Briar hockey!" we throw back our shots. Bucky swallows and releases a guttural war cry that startles everyone until we all bust out laughing.

"Easy there, killer. Save it for the ice," I tell him.

Bucky doesn't give a shit. He's too stoked. Young, dumb, and full of bad intentions tonight. He'll make some young lady very happy, I'm sure.

Speaking of ladies, it doesn't take long for them to coalesce around the beer pong table once we get another game going. This time it's Hunter and his girlfriend Demi against me and Foster. And Hunter's girl plays dirty. She's peeled off her zip-up hoodie and is now in just a thin white tank top over a black bra, which she's using to strategic effect to push her tits up in our faces as a means of distraction. And it's fucking working. Foster goes boob blind and misses the table completely with his shot.

"Fuck, Demi," I grumble, "put those things away."

"What, these?" She grabs two handfuls and lifts them practically up to her neck while making the worst attempt at looking innocent.

Hunter lands his shot in one of our cups easily.

Demi winks at me. "Sorry not sorry."

"If your girlfriend wants to take her top off, I'll forfeit right now," Foster says, trying to get a rise out of Hunter.

He's too easy. Caveman mode activated, Hunter yanks his T-shirt over his head and pulls it down over Demi so it looks like a baggy dress on her. "Eyes on the cups, dickhead."

I swallow a laugh, deciding not to point out that Demi Davis would look hot even if she were wearing a burlap sack. There was a time I might have hit that, but even before Hunter knew it, we could see that our team captain was already stupid for that girl. Just took those two a little longer to catch on.

So far, my prospects tonight aren't great. Gorgeous girls, sure. A brunette all but tries to climb me and plant a kiss on my neck when I sink the next shot into one of Hunter and Demi's cups. But these chicks have a thirsty vibe about them and so far, no one's doing it for me.

Truth be told, all the women are starting to blur together in my mind. I've slept with a lot of 'em since I transferred to Briar this past fall. Rocking a woman's world, making her feel special, is a skill of mine. But—and I'd be mocked relentlessly if I admitted this to my boys—none of the chicks I hook up with bother to make *me* feel special. A few pretend they want to get to know me, but for the most part I'm a conquest to them, a shiny prize to wave in their friends' envious faces. Half the time they don't even attempt to make small talk. They just stick their tongues down my throat and their hands down my pants.

Buy a man flowers, at least. Or hell, lead off with a good joke. But it is what it is, I suppose.

Besides, it's not like I'm in the market for a relationship. I can show women a good time for a night or a week, maybe even a month, but both parties are wholly aware that I'm not anyone's long-term option. Which is fine. I bore easily, and relationships are the epitome of boring.

But tonight I'm equally bored with the parade of chicks that passes the beer pong table, all of them flashing the same coy smiles as they not-so-innocently graze my arm with their side boobs. Yeah, I'm not feeling any of these girls right now. I'm weary of this tired old mating ritual that always ends the same way. I don't even have to chase them anymore, and that's half the fun.

A round of cheers breaks out in the house as the music comes back on. One chick tries to take advantage by pulling me to dance, but I shake my head and try to refocus on the game. It's kinda difficult, though, because some commotion out on the front lawn has now drawn everyone's attention to the bay window. A distracted Foster completely blows his shot, and I'm about to chastise him when my peripheral vision catches a blur of motion.

I turn toward the living room to see a frightened, sort of panicked-looking blonde girl scurrying toward us. Like a rabbit bolting for the safety of its hollow after spotting a hungry fox. At first I think she's going to run to the window to look at whatever the hell is happening outside, but then something truly bizarre happens.

She comes right up, grabs my arm and yanks me down so she can speak in my ear.

"I'm so sorry for this and you're going to think I'm a total psycho, but I need your help so please just play along," she babbles, so fast I'm having a hard time keeping up. "I need you to come upstairs with me and pretend we're going to hook up, but I don't actually want to touch your penis or whatever."

Or whatever?

"It's a stupid dare and I'll owe you a major favor if you could do me this solid," she whispers rapidly. "I promise I won't be weird about it."

I must admit, I'm intrigued. "So, if I heard you right, you don't want to hook up with me?" I whisper back, unable to hide my amusement.

"I don't. I want to pretend to do it."

Well. I'm certainly not bored anymore.

Getting a good look at her, she's got a cute face. Not a drop-dead stunner like Demi, but nice. Her body, though. Fuck me. She's like a walking pinup girl. Hidden under an oversized sweater that's falling off one shoulder is a set of tits I could spend all night sliding my dick between. I steal a peek at her ass and can't help thinking about getting her bent over my bed.

But all that evaporates when I see her look up at me with these pleading turquoise eyes and something in my heart just crumbles. I'd be some kind of jackass to turn my back on a woman in such dire need of saving.

"Alec," I call out without taking my gaze off the pinup girl.

"Yo," my teammate calls back.

"I'm tagging you in. Kick the captain and his evil girlfriend's asses for me."

"On it."

I don't miss the knowing chuckles from Hunter and Foster, along with Demi's loud snort.

The blonde's uncertain eyes dart past my shoulder to the beer pong table, where Alec has taken my place. "Is that a yes?" she murmurs.

In answer, I sweep a few strands of hair behind her ear and brush my lips against her skin to speak. Because whoever is torturing this poor girl is certainly watching us right now and they can eat shit.

"Lead the way, babe."

Her eyes go huge, and for a moment I think her hard drive's crashed. Not the first time that's happened in my presence. So I take her hand, and then, leaving several shocked gasps in our wake, guide her through the maze of bodies loitering throughout the house. Fact is, I know my way around this place well enough.

As we climb the stairs, I feel the eyes following us. She grips my hand a little tighter as her brain reboots. On the second floor she pulls us into a room I've yet to visit and locks the door behind us.

"Thank you," she breathes the moment we're alone.

"No problem. Mind if I make myself comfortable?"

"Um, yeah. I mean, no. I don't mind. Sit if you want. Or—wow, okay, you're lying down."

I grin at her visible nervousness. It's cute. While I stretch out my six-foot-two frame amid the stuffed animals and decorative pillows on the bed, she remains the startled rabbit plastered against the door and breathing heavily.

"Gotta be honest," I tell her, entwining my hands behind my

head, "I've never seen a girl so unhappy to be locked in a bedroom with me."

This has the desired effect of loosening her shoulders and even eliciting a shy smile. "I have no doubt."

"I'm Conor, by the way."

She rolls her eyes. "Yeah, I know."

"What's the eyeroll for?" I ask, playing wounded.

"No, sorry, I didn't mean anything by it. Just, I know who you are. You're, like, campus famous."

The more I watch her, hands braced at her sides against the door, one knee bent, dirty-blonde hair a little messy and draped over one shoulder, I can't help picturing myself holding her arms above her head while I explore her body with my mouth. She's got very kissable skin.

"Taylor Marsh," she blurts out, and I realize I don't know how long we were silent until then.

I scoot to the far side of the bed and put a pillow beside me as a divider. "Come on. If we're going to be in here awhile, let's at least make friends."

Taylor laughs out a breath and with it she releases a bit more tension. She's got a nice smile. Bright, warm. It takes a bit more coaxing, however, to get her on the bed.

"This isn't like a move," she tells me, lining up stuffed animal guards to patrol the pillow wall between us. "I'm not some sort of weirdo who tricks men into getting in bed with her and then mauls them."

"Sure." I nod with mock seriousness. "But a little mauling would be okay."

"Nope." She shakes her head with too much animation, and I think I might have just about cracked her shell. "No mauling. I will be on my best behavior."

"So tell me then, why would someone who is presumably supposed to be your friend put you in what is clearly a nightmare scenario?"

Taylor lets out a deep sigh. She picks up a stuffed turtle and clings to it against her chest. "Because Abigail is a grade-A bitch. I hate her so much."

"Why's that? What's the story there?"

She slides a dubious look toward me, clearly debating whether to trust me.

"Cross my heart," I say. "This is a safe space."

She rolls her eyes but flashes a playful smile. "Last year. It was a party like this one. I was dared to walk up to a random guy and make out with him."

I snicker. "I'm sensing a pattern."

"Yeah, well, I wasn't any more enthusiastic about it then, either. But that's their thing. The sisters. They know I have hang-ups about approaching guys, so they love to poke at my insecurities. The bitchy ones, at least."

"Girls are fucking vicious."

"Dude, you have no clue."

I adjust myself on the bed to face her fully. "Okay, so go on. You have to make out with a guy."

"Right, thing is…" She fidgets with the turtle's little plastic eyeball, twisting it between her fingers. "I walked up to the first guy I saw who wasn't so drunk he might barf on me or something. I grabbed his face, laid one on him, and just, you know, closed my eyes and went for it."

"As one does."

"Well, when I pulled away, there was Abigail. Looking like I just cut her hair in her sleep. I mean staring daggers. Turns out, the guy I mouth-assaulted was her boyfriend."

"Damn, T. That's ice-cold."

She blinks those forlorn Caribbean-blue eyes at me with a sad pouting lip. Watching her talk, I become obsessed with the Marilyn Monroe beauty mark on her right cheek.

"I didn't know! Abigail goes through boyfriends like boxes of cereal. I wasn't keeping up with her love life."

"So she didn't take it well," I say.

"She went apocalyptic. Made a huge scene at the party. Didn't talk to me for weeks, and then only in snide remarks and insults. We've pretty much been mortal enemies ever since, and now she takes every possible opportunity to humiliate me. Hence, tonight's indecent proposal. She was banking on you turning me down in spectacular fashion."

Damn. I do feel bad for this girl. Guys are dicks, and even on the team we find all sorts of evil ways to mess with each other, but it's all in good fun. This Abigail chick is something else. Daring Taylor to pick up a stranger in the hopes that she'd be brutally rejected and embarrassed in front of the entire party…now *that's* ice-cold.

An irrational pang of protectiveness starts to throb in my gut. I don't know much about her, but Taylor doesn't strike me as the kind of girl who would betray a friend so callously.

"Worst part is, before that we were actually friends. She was my closest ally during pledge week freshman year. I almost quit a dozen times, and she's the one who helped me to stick it out. But after I moved off campus, we sort of grew apart."

Voices outside the room pull Taylor's attention. I glance over and frown when I notice shadows move under the door.

"Ugh. That's her," she mutters. By now I've come to recognize the sound of dread in her voice. She blanches and her pulse visibly thrums in her neck. "Shit, they're listening."

I resist the urge to shout for our audience to get lost. If I do that, Abigail and Co. will know that Taylor and I aren't doing the dirty, otherwise we'd be laser-focused on each other instead of the bedroom door. Still, the nosy little shits need to learn a lesson. And while I can't solve Taylor's problem with these girls, I can give her this one night.

"I hope they're paying attention," I say with an impish smile.

Then I jump to my knees and put both hands on the top of the headboard. Taylor eyes me with suspicion, to which I just grin again and start thrusting my body, driving the headboard into the wall.

Bang. Bang. Bang.

"Fuck, babe, you're so tight," I groan out too loudly.

Taylor slaps her hand over her mouth. Her dark-blonde eyebrows shoot up her forehead.

"You feel so good!"

The wall shakes with every pounding blow against the headboard. I bounce on my knees, making the bedframe squeak in protest. All the necessary noises of a good time.

"What are you doing?" she whispers in amused horror.

"Putting on a good show. Don't leave me hanging, T. They're going to think I'm fucking my hand in here."

She shakes her head. Poor terrified rabbit.

"Ah, fuck, babe, not so fast, you're gonna make me come!"

Just when I think I might have pushed her too far, Taylor throws her head back, closes her eyes, and lets out the sexiest noise I've never heard come out of a woman I wasn't balls deep inside of.

"Ugh, right there. Right there," she calls out. "Oh God, I'm so close. Don't stop. Don't stop."

I lose my rhythm, laughing hysterically. The two of us are beet-red and convulsing on the bed.

"Mmmm, that's it, babe. That feel good?"

"So good," she moans back. "Don't stop. Faster, Conor."

"You like that?"

"I love it."

"Yeah?"

"Oh, yeah, put it in my butt!" she begs.

I collapse and hit my forehead on the fucking headboard. I stare at her, dumbstruck.

"What? Too much?" she asks me, all wide-eyed innocent.

This fucking girl. She's something else. "Yeah, dial it back a little," I croak.

But we can't stop laughing as it gets harder to breathe and we struggle to keep up the lusty moans. After probably way longer than necessary, we finally relent. Still shuddering with laughter, she buries her head in the pillows, bent over with her ass in the air, and suddenly I'm having a hard time remembering why we're only faking it.

"Was it good for you?" I ask, sprawling out on my back. My hair is damp with sweat and I comb it out of my eyes with my fingers as Taylor comes to lie beside me.

She regards me with a look. One I haven't seen from her tonight—staring at me under heavy-lidded eyes her lips red and swollen from biting them as she moaned. There're fathoms behind that mask, fascinating depths I'm becoming more eager to explore. For a fleeting moment, I think she wants me to kiss her. Then she blinks, and the moment's gone.

"Conor Edwards, you're a decent guy."

I've been called worse. Doesn't mean I don't notice how totally delectable her cleavage looks when she rolls onto her side to face me. "That was the best fake sex I've ever had," I say solemnly.

She snickers.

My gaze sweeps over her flushed cheeks, her flawless, glowing skin. Then it dips to her amazing cleavage again. I know what she's going to say before I even voice the question, but it slips out of my mouth regardless.

"So, you want to fool around?"

3
TAYLOR

He isn't serious. I know he isn't. Propositioning me after our little performance is just Conor's way of making me feel better about a shit situation. Further evidence that beneath the chin-length blond hair, steely gray eyes, and chiseled body, he has a soft heart. Which is even more reason to get the hell out of here before I catch feelings. Because Conor Edwards is absolutely the guy you fall for before you learn that girls like me don't get guys like him.

"Sorry, we agreed to a strict no mauling policy," I say firmly.

He flashes a crooked half-smile that makes my heart skip a beat. "Can't blame a guy for trying."

"Anyway. It's been fun," I tell him, scooting off the bed, "but I should—"

"Hang on." Conor grabs my hand. A rush of nervous energy shoots up my arm and tingles the back of my neck. "You said you'd owe me a favor, right?"

"Yeah," I say, wary.

"Well, I'm calling in your marker. We've only been up here five minutes. I can't have people downstairs thinking I don't know how to show a lady a good time." He lifts an eyebrow. "Stay awhile. Help me keep my reputation intact."

"You don't need me to protect your ego. Don't worry, they'll assume you got bored of me."

"I do get bored easily," he agrees, "but you're in luck, T. Boredom is the last thing I'm feeling right now. You're the most interesting person I've spoken to in ages."

"You must not get out much," I crack.

"C'mon," he coaxes, "don't make me go back downstairs yet. It's too thirsty down there. All the chicks act like I'm the last steak at the meat market."

"Women clamoring for your attention? You poor thing." And although I'm trying not to think of him as a piece of meat, I can't deny he is one incredible specimen. Hands down, the most beautiful guy I've ever encountered. Not to mention the sexiest. He's still clutching my hand, and the angle of his body causes every muscle of his sculpted arm to bulge enticingly.

"C'mon, stay and talk with me."

"What about your friends?" I remind him.

"I see them every day at practice." His thumb rubs a gentle circle over the inside of my wrist, and I'm done for. "Taylor. Please stay."

This is a terrible idea. Right now is the moment I'll look back on a year from now after I've changed my name, dyed my hair, and started going by Olga in a diner in Schenectady. But his imploring eyes, his skin against mine, they won't let me leave.

"Okay." I never stood a chance against Conor Edwards. "Just to talk."

Together we settle back onto the bed, the pillow fortress between us dismantled by the bouncing and thrashing. And Conor's charm. He picks up the stuffed turtle that had migrated to the end of the bed and sets it on the nightstand. I'm not sure I've ever been in here, now that I think about it. Rachel's room is…a lot. Like a VSCO girl and a mommy blogger threw up on a Disney princess.

"Help me figure you out." Conor crosses those sexy arms over his chest. "This isn't your room, is it?"

"No, you first," I insist. If I'm going to humor him, there has to be a little reciprocation. "I feel like I've monopolized the conversation. Help me figure *you* out."

"What do you want to know?"

"Anything. Everything." *What you look like naked...* But no, I'm not allowed to ask that. I might be lying in bed with the hottest guy on campus, but our clothes are staying on. Especially mine.

"Ah, well..." Toeing his shoes off, he kicks them off the bed. I'm about to tell him we're not staying that long, but then he continues. "I play hockey, but I guess you figured that out."

I nod in answer.

"I transferred here from LA last semester."

"Oh, okay. That explains a lot."

"Does it now?" He puts on an expression of mock offense.

"Not in a bad way. I mean, you're a magazine cover definition of *surfer dude*, but it suits you."

"I'm going to choose to take that as a compliment," he says, and ribs me with his elbow.

I ignore the little shiver that happily tickles my chest. His playful demeanor is way too appealing. "How did a west coast boy wind up playing hockey of all sports?"

"People play hockey on the west coast," he says dryly. "It's not exclusively an east coast thing. I played football too, in junior high, but hockey was more fun and I was better at it."

"So what made you want to come east?" New England winters are an acquired taste. We had a sister freshman year who made it six days into knee-high snow and caught a plane back to Tampa. We had to mail her stuff home.

Something flickers across Conor's face. For a moment his gray eyes become unfocused, distant. If I knew him better, I'd think I hit a nerve. When he replies, his voice has lost some of its prior playfulness.

"I just needed a change of scenery. The opportunity to transfer to Briar came up and I took it. I was living at home, you know, and it was getting a little cramped."

"Brothers and sisters?"

"No, it was just me and Mom for a long time. Dad ran out on us when I was six."

Sympathy softens my tone. "That's awful. I'm sorry."

"Eh, don't be. I hardly remember him. My mom married this other guy Max about six years ago."

"And, what, you two don't get along?"

He sighs, sinks deeper against the pillows while staring at the ceiling. A vexed line forms on his forehead. I'm tempted to backtrack, tell him he doesn't have to talk about it and it wasn't my intention to pry. I can see the subject unsettles him, but he pushes on.

"He's alright. My mom and I were living in a shitty little rental house when they met. She was working as a hairdresser sixty hours a week to take care of us. Then this slick, rich business-man comes along and whisks us out of our misery to Huntington Beach. Like I can't even tell you how much better the air smelled. That's the first thing I noticed." With a self-deprecating smile, he shrugs. "Traded public school for private. Mom cut her hours then eventually quit her job. Changed our whole lives." There's a pause. "He's good to her. She's his whole world. He and I, though, we don't connect. She was the prize; I was the stale cereal forgotten in the cupboard."

"You're not stale cereal," I tell him. That any kid would grow up thinking of himself that way breaks my heart, and I wonder if this cool, laidback persona is how he's survived the scars of feeling otherwise abandoned. "Some people aren't good with kids, you know?"

"Yeah." He nods, his expression wry, and we both know it's a wound that won't be healed with my simple platitudes.

"It's always just been me and my mom, too," I say, changing the subject to stave off the sour mood descending over Conor like a shadow. "I was the product of a fervid little one-night stand."

"Okay." Conor's eyes light up. He turns on his side to face me and props his head up in one hand. "Now we're getting somewhere."

"Oh yeah, Iris Marsh was a nerd in the streets and freak in the sheets."

His husky laughter elicits another shiver. I need to stop being so...*aware* of him. It's like my body has locked in on his frequency and now responds to his every move, every sound.

"She's an MIT professor of nuclear science and engineering, and twenty-two years ago she met this big-shot Russian scientist at a conference in New York. They had a single romantic interlude, and then he went back to Russia and Mom went back to Cambridge. Then about six months later, she had to read about it in the *Times* when he died in a car accident."

"Holy shit." He jerks his head up. "Do you think your dad was, like, assassinated by the Russian government?"

I laugh. "What?"

"Dude, what if your dad was into some serious spy shit? And the KGB found out he was a CIA asset, so they had him whacked?"

"Whacked? I think you're confusing your euphemisms. Mobs whack people. And I'm not sure the KGB is still a thing."

"Sure, that's what they want you to think." Then his eyes go wide. "Whoa, what if you're a Russian sleeper agent?"

He has an active imagination, I'll give him that. But at least his mood's improved.

"Well," I say thoughtfully, "the way I see it, that would mean one of two things: Either by becoming self-aware I'd soon be marked for death."

"Oh fuck." With impressive agility, Conor leaps up from the bed and comically peers out the window before closing the blinds and turning off the light.

The two of us are now illuminated only by Rachel's turtle night-light and the glow of streetlamps filtering through the spaces between the blinds.

Laughing, he climbs back on the bed. "Don't worry, babe, I got you."

I crack a smile. "Or, second, I'd have to kill you for discovering my secret."

"Or, *or*, hear me out: you take me on as your muscle and handsome sidekick and we hit the road as soldiers of fortune."

"Hmm." I pretend to study him, deliberating. "Tempting offer, comrade."

"But first we should probably strip search each other to check for wires. You know, to establish trust."

He's adorable in an insatiable puppy sort of way. "Yeah, no."

"You're no fun."

I can't get a read on this guy. He's sweet, charming, funny—all those sneaky qualities of men that trick us into believing we can turn them into something civilized. But at the same time bold, raw, and completely unpretentious in a way almost no one in college ever is. All of us are just stumbling through self-discovery while putting on a brave face. So how does that square with the Conor Edwards of lore? The man with more notches on his hockey stick than snowflakes in January. Who is the real Conor Edwards?

Why do I care?

"So, uh, what's your major?" I ask, feeling like a cliché.

His head falls back and he blows out a breath. "Finance, I guess."

Okay, not what I expected. "You guess?"

"I mean, I'm not really feeling it. It wasn't my idea."

"Whose idea was it?"

"My stepdad. He got it in his head I'll go work for him after I graduate. Learn how to run his company."

"You don't sound stoked about that," I say, throwing out some west coast jargon just for him. It earns me a chuckle.

"No, not stoked," he agrees. "I'd rather get strung up by my balls than put on a suit and stare at spreadsheets all day."

"What would you rather major in?"

"That's the thing. I have no idea. I guess I ultimately caved on finance because I couldn't come up with a better excuse. Couldn't pretend I had some other great interest, so…"

"Nothing?" I press.

For me, I was torn by so many possibilities. Granted, some of them were leftover fantasies from childhood about being an archaeologist or astronaut, but still. When it came time to decide what I wanted to do for the rest of my life, I had no shortage of options.

"The way I grew up, it's not like I had any right to expect much," he says gruffly. "Figured I'd end up working minimum wage with a name tag, or in jail, rather than going to college. So I never really gave it much thought."

I can't imagine what that's like. Staring into your future and having no hope for yourself. It reminds me how privileged I am to have grown up being told I could be anything I wanted, and knowing the money and access were there to back it up.

"Jail?" I try to lighten the mood. "Give yourself more credit, buddy. With your face and body, you would've made a killing in porn."

"You like my body?" He grins, gesturing to his long, muscular frame. "All yours, T. Climb aboard."

God, I wish. I swallow hard and pretend to be unaffected by his hotness. "Pass."

"Whatever you say, *buddy*."

I roll my eyes.

"What about you?" he asks. "What's your major? No, wait. Let me guess." Conor narrows his eyes, studying me for the answer. "Art history."

I shake my head.

"Journalism."

Another shake.

"Hmm…" He stares harder, biting his lip. God, he's got the sexiest mouth. "I'd say psych major, but I know one of those and you aren't it."

"Elementary education. I want to be a teacher."

He raises one eyebrow, then scans me with a look that's almost... hungry. "That's hot."

"What's hot about it?" I demand, incredulous.

"Every guy fantasizes about banging a teacher. It's a thing."

"Boys are weird."

Conor shrugs, yet that hunger still colors his face. "Tell me something...why aren't you already here with someone?"

"What do you mean?"

"There isn't a guy in the picture somewhere?"

It's my turn to shrink away from the topic. I'd probably have more to say with regards to thirteenth-century textiles than dating. And since I've embarrassed myself enough for one evening, I'd rather not compound my humiliation by sharing the details of my non-existent love life.

"So there is a story there," Conor says, misreading my hesitation for coyness. "Let's hear it."

"What about you?" I volley back. "Haven't settled on that one special groupie yet?"

He shrugs, unbothered by my teasing jab. "Don't really do girlfriends."

"Ugh, that sounds slimy."

"No, I just mean I've never dated anyone for more than a few weeks. If it's not there, it's not there, you know?"

Oh, I know the type. Bores easy. Constantly looking over his shoulder at the next thing passing by. A walking meme in the flesh.

Figures. The pretty ones are always aching for their freedom.

"Don't think you've distracted me," he says, giving me a knowing smile. "Answer the question."

"Sorry to disappoint. No guys. No story." One unremarkable entanglement sophomore year that hardly fulfilled the definition of a relationship is too pathetic to warrant mention.

"Come on. I'm not as dumb as I look. What, did you break his heart? He spend six months sleeping on the sidewalk outside the sorority house?"

"Why do you assume I'm the kind of girl a guy would pine over in the rain and sleet?"

"You kidding?" His silvery eyes sweep over me, lingering on various parts of my body before returning to meet my gaze. Everywhere he looked is now tingling like crazy. "Babe, you've got the kind of body that boys build in their heads under the sheets after dark."

"Don't do that," I tell him, all humor draining from my voice as I start to turn away. "Don't mock me. That's not nice."

"Taylor."

I jerk when he takes my hand, keeping me in place so that we're still facing each other. As my pulse kicks into overdrive, he presses my shaky hand against his chest. His body is warm, solid. His heart beats a quick, steady rhythm beneath my palm.

I'm touching Conor Edwards' chest.

What the hell is happening right now? Never in my wildest dreams did I envision the Kappa Chi Spring Break Hangover party ending this way.

"I mean it." His voice thickens. "I've been sitting here having filthy thoughts about you all night. Don't mistake my manners for indifference."

A reluctant smile pulls at the corners of my lips. "Manners, huh?" I'm not sure I believe him. Or that a porno clip in his mind starring me qualifies as a compliment. Although I guess it's the thought that counts.

"My mother didn't raise a scoundrel, but I can be downright improper if you're into it."

"And what passes for improper on the west coast?" I ask, noting the way his top lip twitches when he's being cheeky.

"Well…" His entire demeanor shifts. Eyes narrow. Breathing slows. Conor licks his lips. "If I weren't a gentleman, I might try something like pushing your hair behind your ear." He skims his fingertips through my hair. Then down the column of my neck. Just a gentle whisper of skin-to-skin.

My neck erupts in excited little bumps and my breath catches in my throat.

"And dragging my finger across your shoulder."

He does so, quickening my pulse. An ache builds inside me.

"And skimming along until—" He reaches my bra strap. I hadn't realized it was exposed with my V-neck sweater hanging off my shoulder.

"Alright. Down, boy." Regaining my wits, I remove his hand and adjust my sleeve. Jeez, this guy should come with a warning label. "I think I get it now."

"You're ridiculously attractive, Taylor." This time when he speaks, I don't doubt his sincerity, if perhaps his sanity. I suppose someone like him doesn't get around so much by being picky. "Don't spend any more time believing otherwise."

For the next few hours, I don't. Instead, I give myself permission to pretend that someone like Conor Edwards is actually into me.

We lie there in the ridiculous cocoon of Rachel's stuffed animal collection, talking as if we've been friends for years. There's surprisingly no shortage of things to say, no lag in the conversation. We move from banal topics of favorite foods and our mutual appreciation for sci-fi movies, to more serious ones, like how out of place I feel amongst my sorority sisters, to hilarious ones, like the time his sixteen-year-old punk-ass self got drunk after a road game in San Francisco and dove into the bay with the intention of swimming to Alcatraz.

"Fucking Coast Guard showed up and—" He cuts himself off mid-sentence, yawning loudly. "Shit, I can barely keep my eyes open."

I catch his contagious yawn and cover my gaping mouth with my forearm. "Me too," I say sleepily. "But we're not leaving this room until you finish that story because holy shit, you were one stupid kid."

That triggers a wave of laughter from the Norse god beside me. "Not the first time I've heard that, and it won't be the last."

By the time he finishes the story, we're yawning on a loop, blinking rapidly to try to stay awake. The stupidest, drowsiest discussion ensues as we attempt to find the strength to get up.

"We should head downstairs," I mumble.

"Mmm-hmmm," he mumbles back.

"Like now."

"Hmmm, good idea."

"Or maybe in five minutes." I yawn. "Five minutes, yeah." He yawns.

"Okay, so we'll close our eyes for five minutes and then get up."

"Just rest our eyes. You know, eyes get tired."

"They do."

"Tired eyes," he's muttering from beneath thick lashes, "and I played a game tonight, got a bit bruised up, so let's just…"

I don't hear the rest of his sentence, because we've both fallen asleep.

4
TAYLOR

KNOCK.
Knock.
Knock!
KNOCK!

The last pound on the door jolts me upright. I squint and shield my eyes from the beams of light streaking across the room. What the hell?

It's daylight. Morning. My mouth is dry, a bitter taste thick on my tongue. I don't remember falling asleep. On a yawn I stretch my limbs, feel the muscles releasing. Then another sound stops my heart.

Snoring. Beside me.

Fucking fuckturtles.

Sprawled out on his stomach, Conor lies shirtless and in only his boxers.

"Hey! Open the door! This is my room!"

More knocking. Pounding.

Shit. Rachel's home.

"Get up." I shake Conor. He doesn't stir. "Dude, get up. You need to leave."

I don't understand how he's still here or when I fell asleep last night. A quick glance shows I'm still dressed with my shoes on, so why the hell is Conor practically naked?

"Get the hell out, assholes!" Any minute now Rachel's going to start trying to kick the door down.

"Come on, get up." I give Conor a stiff smack to the small of his back, which makes him jump in a bleary confusion.

"Mrrrmmm?" he mumbles incoherently.

"We fell asleep. My sister's home and she wants her room back," I whisper urgently. "You need to get dressed."

Conor falls out of bed. He stands a bit unevenly, still muttering nonsense under his breath. Cringing, I unlock and open the door, where an irate Rachel stands fuming in the hall. Behind her, the entire house is awake, loitering in their pajamas and bed hair with mugs of coffee and cold Pop-Tarts. Sasha is nowhere to be seen, so I assume she wound up finding a concert in Boston and crashing with her friends in the city.

"What the hell, Taylor? Why was my door locked?"

I spot Abigail's cruel smirk among the faces crowding the hall. "I'm sorry, I—"

Without letting me finish, Rachel shoves open the door and bursts inside, allowing everyone a good look at Conor shirtless, buttoning his jeans.

"Oh," she squeaks. Her ire is quelled almost instantly by the sight of Conor's immaculate body.

I don't blame her for gawking. He's exquisite. Broad shoulders and defined muscles. The perfectly smooth, inviting planes of his chest. I can't believe I slept next to that and don't remember any of it.

"G'morning," Conor says with a smirk. He nods to the other sisters outside the room. "Ladies."

"I didn't know you had company," Rachel talks to me but stares at him.

"My fault," he says easily, then pulls his shirt over his sculpted chest. He steps into his shoes. "Sorry about that." To me, he winks on his way to the door. "Call me."

And just as suddenly as we became two unlikely allies, he

departs. Every single gaze remains glued to the taut ass hugged by his jeans, until finally he's out of sight, heavy footsteps thudding down the stairs.

I gulp a few times before speaking. "Rachel, I—"

"I didn't think you had it in you, Marsh." She looks surprised, of course. But also impressed. "Next time you slay a dragon in my room, be out before breakfast. 'Kay?"

"Sure. Sorry," I say with relief. The worst is averted, I suppose. I live to fight better battles. And whether I courted it or not, whether this pries another thin sliver of my dignity from me in favor of my social standing, at least for today all these girls will live vicariously through my supposed exploits.

Then there's Abigail.

While the others return to their morning cartoons and Cinnamon Toast Crunch, she lingers at the top of the stairs waiting for me. I want to push past her, ignore her, maybe trip her a little down the steps. Instead, like a dumbass, I stand there and meet her eyes.

"You must be pretty satisfied with yourself," she says, arching one perfectly tweezed brow.

"No, Abigail, just tired."

"If you think you proved something last night, you're wrong. Conor would fuck a wet sock if it smiled at him. So don't think this makes you special, Tay-Tay."

This time I do brush past her. "I wouldn't dream of it."

"And he didn't make a single move?" Sasha demands on Sunday morning after I'm done filling her in about Friday night's exploits.

Unlike me, Sasha still lives in the Kappa Chi house, so she came to meet me for breakfast at Della's Diner in town. Usually she's too lazy to come to Hastings and coerces me into meeting at one of

Briar's dining halls, but I guess my vague text to her yesterday—"*I'll tell you when I see you*"—was insufficient in satisfying my best friend's curiosity. At least now I know what it takes to drag her lazy ass off campus: dirty details.

Or lack thereof.

"Nope," I confirm. "No moves whatsoever." I'm not worried about Sasha blabbing to any of the Kappas. I trust her implicitly, and there was no way I was going to allow my closest friend to think I'd hooked up with a notorious jock playboy. She's the only one who even knows I'm a virgin.

"He didn't try to kiss you?"

"Nope." I slowly chew a bite of whole-wheat toast. I always order the same sad breakfast items at Della's: brown toast, egg-white omelet, and a small fruit bowl. If "calorie counting" was a career option, I'd be richer than Jeff Bezos.

"I find this shocking," she announces. "I mean, his reputation precedes him."

"Well, he did flirt a bit," I admit, reaching for my water glass. "And he pretended he liked my body."

She rolls her eyes. "Taylor, I guarantee he wasn't *pretending*. I know you think men only get hard-ons from stick women, but trust me, you're wrong. Curves drive them wild."

"Yeah, curves. Not rolls."

"You don't have rolls."

Thankfully, not at the moment. I've been diligent about eating healthy since the New Year, after overindulging during the holidays and putting on nearly ten pounds. In three months I'd shed about nine of those ten, which I'm happy with, but I'd love to lose more.

My ideal body goal is somewhere between Kate Upton and Ashley Graham; I tend to fluctuate between the two, but if I could get down to Kate size I'd be thrilled. I truly believe that all body types are beautiful. It's only when I look in the mirror that I forget.

My weight has been a source of stress and insecurity my entire life, so maintaining it is a priority for me.

I swallow the last bite of my omelet, while pretending not to notice how fucking delicious Sasha's breakfast looks. A mouth-watering stack of chocolate-chip pancakes bathed in a sea of sugary syrup.

She's one of those fortunate girls who can eat anything and not gain a single pound. Meanwhile, I take one bite of a cheeseburger and gain ten pounds overnight. That's just the way my body is and I've accepted it. Cheeseburgers and pancakes taste great in the moment, but they're not worth it for me in the long run.

"Anyway," I continue, "he really was a gentleman."

"Still can't believe that," she says through a mouthful of pancakes. She chews quickly. "And he told you to call him?"

I nod. "But obviously he didn't mean it."

"Why is that obvious?"

"Because he's Conor Edwards and I'm Taylor Marsh?" I roll my eyes. "Also? He didn't give me his number."

She frowns. Ha, that shut her up fast.

"Yup, so whatever fantasy romance you were concocting in your pretty head, you can forget about it. Conor did me a favor the other night." I offer a shrug. "Nothing more to it than that."

5
CONOR

IF ANY OF US HARBORED NOTIONS THAT COACH JENSEN MIGHT take it easy on us after securing our berth into the NCAA Division One championship semi-finals, that delusion is quickly put to rest when we take the ice for Monday morning skate. From the first whistle, Coach has been on a rampage like he just found out Jake Connelly knocked up his daughter or something. We spend the first hour on speed training, skating until our toenails bleed. Then he calls a series of shooting drills and I take so many shots on net it feels like my arms might melt out of their sockets.

Whistle, skate. *Whistle*, shot. *Whistle*, kill me.

By the time Coach orders us to the media room to study game footage, I'm all but crawling off the ice. Even Hunter, who's tried his damnedest to maintain a positive attitude as team captain, is starting to look like he wants to call his mommy to come pick him up. In the tunnel we share a pitiful look. *Same, dude.*

After a bottle of Gatorade and one of those jelly nutrition tubes, I'm feeling half-alive at least. The media room offers three semi-circular rows of plush chairs, and I'm in the first row with Hunter and Bucky. Everyone is slouched over from exhaustion.

Coach walks over to stand in front of the projector screen with the static image of our game against Minnesota bleeding onto his face. Even the sound of him clearing his throat gives me the jitters.

"Some of you seem to think the hard part's over. That you're just going to coast to a championship and it's all champagne and afterparties from here on out. Well, I got news for you." He slams his hand twice against the wall and I swear the whole building shakes. We all snap upright in our seats, wide the fuck awake. "Now's when the work begins. You were running on training wheels until today. Now Daddy's dragging you to the top of the hill and giving your asses a good shove."

The footage rolls in slow motion on the screen. The D-line gets caught out of position on a breakaway and gives up a shot on net that pings off the post. That's me there on the left, and watching my dumb ass scramble to chase down the shooter puts a pit in stomach.

"Right here," Coach says. "We checked out mentally. Got caught puck watching. It only takes a second to lose focus and then *bam*, we're playing catch-up."

He fast-forwards the tape. This time it's Hunter, Foster and Jesse who can't string their passes together.

"Come on, ladies. This is basic stuff you've been doing since you were five. Soft hands. Visualize where your teammates are. Get open. Follow through."

Around the room, we're all taking hits to our overinflated egos. That's the thing about Coach; he doesn't suffer divas. For a few weeks now we've felt damn near invincible on our rise to the top. Now that we've got our fiercest opponents ahead of us, it's time to get our feet back on the ground. That means taking our licks in practice.

"Wherever that puck is, I want three guys ready to take it," Coach continues. "I don't ever want to see someone standing around looking for an open man. If we want to square up to Brown or Minnesota, we need to play our game. Quick passes. High pressure. I want to see confidence behind the stick."

My coach back in LA was a real son of a bitch. The kind of guy who burst into a room screaming and shouting, slamming doors and throwing chairs. At least twice a season he'd get ejected from a game, then come to the next practice and take it all out on us. Sometimes we deserved it. Other times, it was like he needed to exorcise forty years of shame and inadequacy on a bunch of dumb kids. No wonder the hockey program was shit.

Because of him I almost didn't bother going out for the team when I transferred to Briar, but I knew the program's reputation and had heard good things. Coach Jensen was a relief. He can be hard on us, but he's never malicious. Never so focused on sport he forgets he's coaching real people. One thing I've never doubted is that Coach Jensen cares about every one of these guys. Even busted Hunter out of jail last semester. For that, we'd follow him anywhere, toenails be damned.

"Alright, that's it for today. I want everyone to check in with the nutritionist and make sure you're clear on the meal plans for the next few weeks. We're going to be pushing ourselves harder than we have all season. That means I want you guys taking care of your bodies. If you've got bangs and bumps, get with the trainers and have them evaluated. Now's not the time to hide any issues. Every man needs to know he can count on the guy next to him. Okay?"

"Hey, Coach?" Hunter speaks up. He sighs, cringing. "The guys were wondering if we could get an update on the mascot situation."

"The pig? You idiots are still on about the damn pig?"

"Uh, yeah. In the absence of Pablo Eggscobar, some of the boys are experiencing withdrawals."

I snicker under my breath. Not gonna lie, I kinda miss our stupid egg mascot too. He was a cool dude.

"Jesus Christ. Yes, you're getting your damn pet. Sometime in August, last I heard. There is an absurd amount of paperwork involved in the acquisition of a swine for non-agricultural purposes. Okay? Satisfied, Davenport?"

"Yup yup. Thanks, Coach."

We all start getting up to leave, conversations breaking out while guys head for the doors.

"Oh, hang on," Coach booms.

Everyone halts, like good little soldiers.

"Almost forgot. Word's come down from the higher-ups that our attendance is required at some alumni grip-and-grin Saturday afternoon."

Groans and protests erupt.

"What, why?" Matt Anderson calls from the back of the room.

"Oh, come on, Coach," Foster whines.

Beside me, Gavin is pissed. "That's bullshit."

"What's a grip-and-grin?" Bucky asks. "Sounds like we're supposed to be jerking them off or something."

"Essentially," Coach replies. "Listen, I hate these things, too. But when the provost says jump, the athletic director says how high."

"But we're the ones doing the jumping," Alec protests.

"Now you're getting it. These things are all about kissing ass for cash. The university counts on these little dog-and-pony shows to support things like athletics and building you princesses fancy training facilities. So get your suits pressed, comb your hair, for fuck's sake, and be on your best behavior."

"Does this mean I'm going to be getting my ass pinched by rich cougars?"The whole room laughs when Jesse raises his hand to speak. "Because I'm cool with taking one for the team, but my girlfriend is the jealous type and I'm gonna need a note or something on letter-head if she asks me about this."

"I'd like to go on record as stating I find this premise sexist and exploitative," Bucky chimes in.

In a flat tone that suggests he's well sick of our shit, Coach digs his fingers into his eyes and recites from what I assume is Briar's code of conduct.

"It is university policy that no student shall be required to behave in an unethical or immoral manner, or that which may conflict with their sincerely held religious or spiritual beliefs. The university is an equal opportunity institution based on high academic achievement and does not discriminate on the basis of gender, sexual orientation, economic status, religion or lack thereof, or the temperament of your girlfriend. Satisfied, everyone?"

"Thanks, Coach!" Bucky says with an exaggerated thumbs-up. Dude is going to give him an aneurism one of these days.

But Jesse and Bucky aren't that off base. There's something fundamentally broken about a system that has us paying fifty grand a year to still be treated like prostitutes. Those of us who aren't here on a free ride at least, like myself.

If there's one thing I'm good at, though, it's playing the boy toy.

I'll say this much for these bunch of goons, we sure clean up nice. The team came looking sharp in our best attire on Saturday afternoon. Beards trimmed. Hair gelled. Bucky even plucked his nose hairs, as he made sure to inform us all.

The alumni luncheon is being held in Woolsey Hall on campus. So far, it's consisted of listening to a bunch of people get up and talk about how Briar made them the men and women they are today, giving back, school spirit, blah, blah, blah. The assigned seating cards have split up the athletics department, along with representatives of the Greeks, student government, and a handful of other notable student organizations, among the many tables with the alumni guests. Mostly it's been smile, nod, laugh at their bad jokes, and tell them, *yes sir, we're taking the championship this year.*

It's not all bad, though. The food's decent and there's plenty of free booze. So at least I've got a little buzz going.

No matter how good I look in a suit, though, I still feel like they can smell it on me. The stench of poverty. The hospital stink of new money. All these rich assholes who probably spent most of their college years snorting coke through hundred-dollar bills from trust funds that have been earning interest since their ancestors were involved in the slave trade.

Seven months ago I showed up at Briar a punk-ass kid from LA. Exactly the type the good folks of Ivy institutions prefer to have mopping their floors rather than attending classes. A stepfather with deep pockets, however, does wonders for one's image in the eyes of the admissions board.

Yeah, I clean up nice, but shit like this reminds me I'm not one of them. I'll never be one of them.

"Mr. Edwards." The older woman seated next to me has what looks like the entirety of the Queen's jewels hanging off her neck. She slides one boney hand over my thigh and leans into me. "Would you be a dear and see if you can rustle a lady up a gin and tonic? Wine gives me a headache." She smells like cigarettes, peppermint gum, and expensive perfume.

"Sure thing." Hoping she can't pick up on my relief, I excuse myself from the table, thankful to break away for a bit.

Outside the main ballroom I find Hunter, Foster, and Bucky at the cocktail bar, where the catering staff is packing up after the hors d'oeuvre reception.

"Can I bother you for a gin and tonic?" I ask the bartender.

"Yeah, no problem." He starts pouring the drink. "More bottles I empty, less I have to carry out of here."

"Gin and tonic? Bro, when did you become my grandmother?" Bucky jokes.

"It's not for me. It's for my cougar."

Hunter snorts and sips his beer.

"Please don't laugh. A couple more gin and tonics and she'll legit be trying to hop on my dick." I nod at the bartender for permission, then steal one of the Stellas he's got sitting in a box on the floor.

"From what I hear," Foster says, "your dick's been pretty busy this week."

I pop the cap on my beer with the ring I wear on my right middle finger. "What's that supposed to mean?"

"Way I hear it, you spent the night with a Kappa last Friday and jumped right into bed with a Tri-Delt on Thursday."

It sounds crass when he says it that way. But yeah, I suppose that's how it looks. He doesn't know, of course, that Taylor and I shared a lovely platonic evening of conversation. And I can't defend her honor without also blowing her cover. I trust these guys, but it's inevitable that anything I say gets back to their girls and, well, people talk.

"Who told you about the Delta hookup?" I ask curiously, because Natalie'd snuck me into the sorority house after midnight. Apparently the Delta house has some ridiculous rule about dudes sleeping over.

"She did," Foster answers, snickering.

I furrow my brow. "Huh?"

Bucky slides his phone from his pocket. "Oh yeah, we all saw that pic. Hold on." He taps the screen a few times. "Yeah, here it is."

I peer at Bucky's Instagram feed. And yup, there's Natalie in a selfie giving the camera a thumbs-up while I'm in the lower corner of the frame, sound asleep. Below it, the caption reads, *Look who scored. #Briarhockeyhottie #StickIt #BuzzerBeater #Gooooaalll*

Real nice.

"I give it high marks for lighting and composition," Foster says, laughing. Jackass.

"Hashtag puckbunny," Bucky adds. "Hashtag—"

I take the gin and tonic from the bartender and head back inside to deliver it, shooting a middle finger at the guys as I leave.

It's not the ribbing that bothers me. Or even the picture, really. I just feel kind of...cheap. Someone's fuck for likes. I might be a little promiscuous, but I don't treat women like conquests. A simple exchange of physical pleasure, where everyone gets what they want and no lies are told, is perfectly healthy. Why go and make the other person feel like a piece of meat?

Then again, I guess it isn't any more than I deserve. Act like a fuckboy, get treated like a fuckboy.

When I return to the ballroom, the concert jazz band is playing and the plates from lunch have been cleared. Most of the guests have taken to the dance floor now, including my bejeweled cougar. I set the drink on the table and have a seat, praying that nobody comes over to force me to dance. So far, so good. I sip my beer and people-watch. Soon, a conversation a couple tables away catches my ear.

"Oh please. Don't give her so much credit. It was a dare, okay? It's not like he was hitting on her or something."

"Trust me," a girl's voice answers, "I heard what was going on in there. He saw those porn star tits and ass and probably figured as long as he fucked her from behind, he wouldn't have to look at her butter face."

"I'd bang Taylor's body with your face," a dude responds.

My fingers tighten over the beer bottle. These asshats are talking about Taylor?

"Are you kidding me, Kevin? Say that again and I'll put your balls in my flat iron."

"Damn, Abigail, I'm kidding. Down, girl."

Abigail. Taylor's sorority sister who made her take that stupid dare?

I spare a quick peek over my shoulder. Yeah, that's her. I remember her standing in the hall at the Kappa house when I made my walk of shame that morning. She's sitting with a group of Kappas I recognize from the party, and a few other guys. Taylor was right; she's a grade-A bitch.

Assuming she must be here somewhere, I scan the room for Taylor, but I can't find her.

"You know she wants to be a teacher?" another girl says. "She'll totally end up like one of those chicks who gets pregnant banging their students."

"Oh, dude, she should do teacher porn," one of the guys responds. "Those double Ds would make mad money."

"How does anyone still make money on porn? Isn't that shit free now?"

"You should see the stuff we have on video from pledge week. It would crash your spank bank."

It isn't until the cougar returns for her gin and tonic and leaves a smudged lipstick print on my cheek that I realize my fists are clenched under the table and I've been holding my breath. I'm not entirely sure what to make of that. These people suck, yeah, but why I am getting all bent out of shape about a girl I knew for one night? My teammates always joke that nothing ever fazes me, and normally they're right—I'm very good at letting shit slide off my shoulders. Especially when it doesn't directly pertain to me.

But this entire conversation is pissing me off.

"You see that Delta's post on Insta? Conor wasn't even coming back to Taylor for seconds."

"Some girls are just made to be one-night stands. That's her place," Abigail says, her tone smug. "Landing a guy like Conor is an unattainable goal for Taylor. The sooner she realizes that, the happier she'll be. It's sad, really."

"Omigod! I bet she's already doodling *Taylor Loves Conor* on her notebooks."

"Writing *Taylor Edwards* in blood in her diary."

They laugh, rolling all over themselves. Assholes.

It crosses my mind to go over there, confront them. Taylor didn't do anything to deserve this shit. She's a cool chick. Smart, funny. It's been a long time since I've actually wanted to spend a whole night talking to a total stranger. And not because she was a pity case or I needed an alibi. I had a legit good time with her. These assholes aren't allowed to talk smack about—

Speak of the devil.

My shoulders stiffen when I catch sight of Taylor walking in my direction. Her head is bent, engrossed with her phone. She's wearing a knee-length black dress, a short pink cardigan buttoned up to her neck, and her hair in a messy bun at the nape of her neck.

I remember the way she'd lamented about her curves, and I

honestly don't get it. Taylor's body is a thousand times more appealing to me than most. Women are supposed to be soft and curvy and squeezable. I'm not sure when they were brainwashed into thinking otherwise.

My mouth goes a bit dry as Taylor approaches. She looks really fucking good tonight. Sexy. Elegant.

Undeserving of these people's scorn.

Something compels me. A sense of justice, maybe. The triumph of good over evil. I get a tickle on the back of my neck, the one that says I'm about to have a stupid idea.

As she passes the table beside mine, unaware of me sitting here, I jump to my feet to catch her.

"Taylor, hey! Why didn't you call me?" I say loud enough to draw the attention of Abigail and her group two tables away.

Taylor blinks, stunned and rightfully confused.

Come on, babe. Play along.

I implore her with my eyes as I repeat myself, my tone extra forlorn. "Why didn't you call me?"

6

TAYLOR

I'm trying to listen to what Conor is saying to me, but the sight of him in a suit is affecting my concentration. His big shoulders and broad chest fill out that navy-blue jacket like nobody's business. I'm tempted to ask him to do a little spin so I can assess the butt situation. I bet his butt looks amazing.

"Taylor," he says impatiently.

I blink, forcing my gaze back to his face. "Conor, hi. Sorry, what?"

"It's been a week," he says, with a strange eagerness about him. "You haven't called me. I thought we had a good time together at the party."

My mouth falls open. Is he serious right now? I mean, yeah, he technically said "call me" as he left Saturday morning, but that was part of the performance, right? He hadn't even provided his phone number!

"Uh, sorry again?" I wrinkle my forehead. "I guess we got our wires crossed."

"Are you avoiding me?" he demands.

"What? Of course not."

He's acting weird. And sort of whiny. Suddenly I'm wondering if this is some kind of personality disorder thing.

Or maybe he's drunk? There have been a lot of free drinks at this thing. Hence why I'd been making a beeline for the restroom before he'd lunged from out of nowhere and ambushed me.

"I can't stop thinking about you, Taylor. Can't eat, can't sleep." He rakes an agitated hand through his hair. "I thought we made a connection that night. I wanted to play it cool, you know. Not come off too aggressive. But I miss you, babe."

If this is a joke, it isn't funny.

Clenching my fists to my sides, I take a step back. "Okay, I don't know what this is, but for what it's worth, I saw that Instagram post of you in bed with some girl. So I'd say you're coping just fine."

"Because you messed with my head." He lets out an agonized groan. "Look, I know I screwed up. I'm weak. But only because I've been so hurt thinking that amazing night we spent together didn't mean anything to you."

Now I'm worried about him.

Exasperation has me stepping forward again. "Conor, you're—"

He grabs me without warning. Envelops me in his arms, digging his big hands into my waist as he dips down to bury his face in the crook of my neck. I freeze, stunned, and honestly a little scared of what's happening right now.

Until he whispers against my ear.

"I promise I'm not a weirdo, but I need your help and I won't touch your penis. Just go with it, T."

I pull back to meet his eyes, glimpsing a gleam of urgency and a twinkle of humor. I'm still not sure what's going on, though. Is he trying to get back at me for what I did to him last weekend? Is it a joke? A silly callback?

"Con, man, leave the poor girl alone," an amused voice remarks.

I turn toward the dark-haired guy who'd spoken—and that's when I notice Abigail and Jules. My sorority sisters are sitting with their boyfriends and some of the Sigma guys and this is all starting to make more sense.

My heart melts a little. The world doesn't deserve Conor Edwards.

"Get lost, Captain," Conor drawls without turning around. "I'm wooing my woman."

I swallow a laugh.

He winks at me and squeezes my hand in reassurance. Then, to my complete dismay, he drops to his knees. Oh God, everyone who wasn't staring at us before is sure as shit staring at us *now*.

My good humor comes precariously close to evaporating. With his heart-stopping face, I'm sure Conor is used to being the center of attention. Me, I'd rather have wood slivers shoved under my fingernails than be on the receiving end of it. But I can feel Abigail's eyes laser-beaming into me, which means I can't convey weakness. Can't show even a trace of the anxiety currently eating away at my stomach like battery acid.

"Please, Taylor. I'm begging. Put me out of my misery. I'm ruined without you."

"What in the actual hell is happening?" another male inquires.

"Shut up, Matty," the first guy admonishes. "I'm dying to see where this goes."

Conor continues to ignore his buddies. His gray eyes never leave my face. "Go out with me. One date."

"Um, I don't think so," I reply.

A shocked gasp sounds from the vicinity of the Kappa table.

"C'mon, T," he pleads. "Just give me a shot to prove myself."

I have to bite the inside of my cheek to keep from laughing. Hysterical tears well in my eyes. When I hesitate for a long time, it's not because I'm trying to create drama and tension. I'm worried if I open my mouth, I'll either burst into laughter or sob from embarrassment.

"Fine," I finally relent, shrugging. To appear even more aloof, I sort of gaze off toward the stage, as if I'm bored with this entire exchange. "One date. I guess."

His entire face lights up. "Thank you. I promise you won't regret it."

I already do.

———

We don't stay at the alumni banquet much longer after Conor's big performance. Considering I hadn't wanted to go in the first place, I'm more than grateful to leave.

Last year Sasha and I got tipsy and had a blast, but she couldn't attend this time because she had a last-minute rehearsal for her spring showcase. Which means I'd just spent the past several hours smiling and mingling and pretending to be BFFs with Kappas who either hate me or are just indifferent. Not to mention this stupid cardigan I'm wearing; I'd thrown it on earlier after growing weary of all the ogling being directed at my cleavage, and I've been sweating like crazy.

Conor offers to give me a lift back to my apartment since we both live in Hastings, but turns out he's some kind of sneaky mind-wizard because somehow we end up at his place instead. I don't know what compels me to agree to dinner and a movie. I decide to blame the two glasses of champagne I drank at the banquet, even though I feel completely sober.

"Fair warning," he says, as we stand outside a townhouse on a quiet tree-lined street, "my roommates can be a bit excitable."

"Like trying to hump my leg excitable, or easily startled and afraid of loud noises?"

"A bit of both. Just smack 'em on the nose if they get out of hand."

I nod and square my shoulders. "Got it."

If I can handle a classroom full of two dozen six-year-olds raging on a sugar high, I'm well up to the task of taming four hockey players. Although it'd probably be easier if I had pudding cups.

"Con, that you?" someone calls when we enter. "What do you want in your grain bowl?"

Conor takes my coat to hang on one of the hooks by the door. "Everyone put your dicks away," he announces. "We've got a guest."

"Grain bowl?" I ask, confused.

"Team nutrition rules. We're all eating like mice. No wasted calories." He sighs.

I know the feeling.

He leads me around the corner into the living room, where three men of imposing figures are spread out on the couches, two playing Xbox.

They're still in their suits from the banquet, albeit in various stages of disarray, with ties undone and shirts untucked. Together they look like a *GQ* cologne ad that ostensibly attempts to portray the aftermath of a fashionable boys' night out in Vegas or something. All that's missing is disembodied female legs in heels draped over their shoulders, and maybe a pair of lacy red underwear elegantly slung over the armrest.

"Guys, this is Taylor. Taylor, these are the guys." Conor strips out of his suit jacket and tosses it on the back of a chair.

For a moment I'm transfixed, watching the way his muscles push against the crisp white fabric of his shirt. His chest straining against the buttons. He may have just ruined me for suits.

In unison the guys reply, "Hi, Taylor," like we're all in on a joke.

"Hi, guys." I wave, now feeling awkward. All the more so because it's hot in this room and I really, really want to take off my sweater.

But the dress I'm wearing must have shrunk in the wash yesterday, because my tits have been attempting to jailbreak out of it all afternoon. It's discouraging to walk around a room full of former White House officials, Nobel laureates, and Fortune 500 CEOs, and find that they still haven't perfected looking a woman in the eyes since their fraternity days.

Men are a failed species.

"So you're the one." Hunched forward with a game controller in his hand, one of the roommates raises an eyebrow at me. He's handsome, with the kind of dimples that leave bodies in their wake.

I recognize him from the banquet as the dude standing with Conor's team captain. He'd beat Conor home, but that's my fault—I needed to hit the ladies' and the lines had been atrocious.

"What one?" I ask, playing dumb.

"The one who sent Con to his knees and turned him into a slobbering, love-professing fool?" Mr. Dimples eyes me expectantly, waiting for me to fill in the gaps.

"Oh shit, that was *you*?" another guy demands. "Can't believe we skipped out before the big show." He pins an accusing look on the guy beside him. "Told you we should've stayed for one more drink."

"No interrogating my guests, Matt," Conor grumbles. "Same rule applies to all of you."

"Are you our new mommy?" The third guy cracks open a beer, smiling with stupid puppy-dog eyes, and I can't help but laugh in return.

"Alright, that's enough." Conor kicks Matt off the smaller of the two couches and gestures for me to take a seat. "This is why you dumbasses don't get visitors."

Their house is huge compared to my little apartment. A big living room with old leather sofas and a couple of reclining chairs. A massive flat screen TV with at least four different game consoles hooked up to it. When Conor said he lived with four roommates, I expected to walk into a nightmarish cave of man smells, pizza boxes, and dirty laundry, but the place is actually pretty tidy and doesn't smell at all like feet and boy farts.

"Yo, visitor?" A fourth face appears in the doorway that separates the living room from the kitchen. "What do you want from Freshy Bowl?" he demands, a cell phone pressed to his ear.

"Grilled chicken salad, please," I call back without delay. I'm very familiar with the menu of one of Hastings' only healthy eating choices.

"On me," Conor murmurs when I reach for my purse so I can chip in.

I glance over. "Thanks. I'll get the next one."

The *next* one? As if this rare occurrence of me having dinner at Conor Edwards' house will ever fucking repeat itself? There's a better chance of Halley's comet showing up a few decades ahead of schedule.

And I'm not the only one marveling over this unforeseen turn of events. When Sasha texts a few minutes later and I inform her where I am, she accuses me of pranking her.

While Conor and his roommates debate over which movie to stream, I surreptitiously text my best friend back.

> **ME:** Not a prank, I swear.
> **HER:** You're actually at his HOUSE????
> **ME:** Swear on my signed poster of Ariana Grande.

That's the only pop star Sasha allows me to fangirl over. Usually it's "if they can't sing live without lip-syncing or using their auto tuner, then they're not a real musician, blah blah blah."

> **HER:** 50% of me still thinks you're lying to me. Is it just the two of you?
> **ME:** Six of us. Me + Con + 4 roommates.
> **HER:** Con???? WE'RE ON NICKNAME BASIS NOW?
> **ME:** No, we're on shortening his name for texting convenience basis.

I'm about to punctuate that with an eyeroll emoji when the phone is unceremoniously snatched from my hand.

"Hey, give it back," I protest, but Conor just flashes an evil grin and proceeds to read my entire text convo with Sasha *out loud* to his roommates.

"You have a signed poster of Ariana Grande?" Alec demands. At least I think it's Alec. I'm still trying to learn all their names.

"Do you kiss it good night before bedtime?" inquires Matt, which evokes a howl of laughter from the others.

I glare at Conor. "Traitor."

He winks. "Hey, like my junior high teacher Ms. Dillard always warned, if she catches you writing notes in Geography, she'll read 'em out loud to the whole class."

"Ms. Dillard sounds like a sadist. And so are you." I roll my eyes dramatically. "What if I'd been texting about my horrible period cramps?"

Next to Alec, Gavin blanches. "Give 'er the phone back, Con. Nothing good could come of this."

Conor's gray eyes dip back to the screen. "But T's friend doesn't believe we're all hanging out. Hold on, let's show receipts. Smile, boys."

Then he has the gall to snap a picture. My jaw drops when all four roommates flex their biceps for the camera.

"There," Conor says with a satisfied nod. "Sent."

I forcibly wrest the phone from his stupid hand. Sure enough, he'd sent Sasha that pic. And her response is immediate.

> **HER:** OMFG. I want to lick Matt Anderson's dimples.
> **HER:** And then suck his dick.

I burst out laughing, which prompts Conor to try to steal my phone again. This time I win the battle, and firmly shove the iPhone into my purse before anyone can get their grubby hands on it.

"See this?" I tell the room, holding up the leather purse. "This is a sacred place. Any man who dares snoop through a woman's purse will be murdered in his sleep by the Bag Butcher."

Conor snickers. "Damn, babe. Your serial killer is showing."

I just shoot him a saccharine smile. Then I finally shrug out of my cardigan, because all these big male bodies are generating a crazy amount of heat.

The moment the material slides off my shoulders, I feel more than one set of eyes travel to my chest. A flush rises in my cheeks, but I ignore it and purse my lips.

"Everything okay there?" I ask Gavin, whose brown eyes are completely glazed over.

"Um, yeah, all good. I'm...you're...ah...I like your dress."

Matt snickers from his new perch on one of the recliners. "Pick your tongue off the floor, loverboy."

That snaps Gavin out of his stupor. And despite their initial ogling, the rest of the guys go back to acting normally, which I appreciate. I wouldn't quite call them perfect gentlemen, but they're not sleazebags, either.

Once the food arrives, the guys stream *DeepStar Six*. I eat my grilled chicken salad and watch as the underwater naval station is under attack by a giant crab monster, all the while wondering how I've been hypnotized into hanging out with Conor Edwards.

Not that I mind, exactly. He's fun. Sweet, even. But I still haven't figured out his angle. When it comes to men and unprovoked friendship, I tend to lean toward skeptical. In the car I'd quizzed him about why he'd made that big show in front of Abigail and her cronies, and he'd merely shrugged and said, "Because it's fun to mess with the Greeks."

I do believe he had fun messing with them, but I also know there's more to the story. I just can't ask him in front of his roommates. Which makes me wonder if he knows that, and is therefore using them as a shield so he doesn't have to answer any questions.

"Like how does that even make sense?" Joe, who told me to call him Foster, hits a bong while reclined on the La-Z-Boy. "The pressure variance between such extreme depths would require several hours of decompression before ascent."

"Dude, there's a giant crab monster trying to eat their mini sub," Matt says. "You're thinking too much."

"Nah, man. This is preposterous. If they expect me to take their premise seriously, they have to stick to certain basic laws of physics. I mean, come on. Where's the dedication to storytelling?"

Conor's shaking his head beside me on the love seat, visibly holding in a laugh. He is so ridiculously attractive it's hard to concentrate on anything other than the chiseled cut of his jaw, the perfect symmetry of his movie-star face. Every time he glances over at me, my heart flips around like a happy dolphin, and I have to force myself to play it cool.

"I think you're taking this a bit hard," he tells Foster.

"All I'm asking for is a little pride in one's work, okay? How do you make a movie about an underwater sea station and just decide that the rules don't apply? You going to make a space movie where there's no vacuum and everyone can breathe outside without a space suit? No, because that's fucking dumb."

"Take another bong hit," Gavin advises from the couch, then shoves a forkful of food in his mouth. "You're cranky when you're sober."

"Yeah, well, I'm gonna." Foster takes a long hit, releases a plume of smoke, then goes back to sulking as he angrily eats his quinoa.

He's a weird one. Hot, though. And obviously highly intelligent— before the movie started I was informed that Foster is majoring in Molecular Biophysics. Which makes him a science geek/hockey player/stoner, the strangest of combinations.

"Aren't you guys drug-tested?" I ask Conor.

"Yeah, but as long as we keep the intake to a minimum and not too often, it doesn't pop up on the piss test," he says.

"Trust me," mumbles Alec, who's draped over the armrest and not entirely conscious. He'd fallen asleep on the couch beside Gavin pretty much as soon as the movie started. "You don't want to know Foster without weed."

"Bite my ass," Foster barks back.

"Could you jackasses try not embarrassing yourselves in front of the company?" Conor chides. "Sorry, they're not housebroken."

I grin. "I like 'em."

"See that, Con," retorts Matt. "She likes us."

"Yeah, so fuck you," Gavin says cheerfully.

I wish living in the Kappa house had been more like this. I had hoped for sisterhood and got season one of *Scream Queens* with my very own Chanel Number One instead. Not that all the girls became as unbearable as Abigail, but it was all too much. The noise, the constant commotion. Every detail of life being a group activity.

I'm an only child, and for a while I entertained the idea that having siblings would fulfill some hole in my life I hadn't known was there. Well, I learned real quick that some people are built to share a bathroom and some would sooner poop in the woods than spend one more morning waiting for ten other chicks to finish brushing their hair.

When the movie ends, the guys are gunning for a scary one next, but Conor says he doesn't feel like another film and tugs me off the sofa.

"C'mon," he drawls, and my heart does a couple more backflips. "Let's go upstairs."

.7
TAYLOR

CONOR AND I RETREAT TO HIS ROOM TO WHISTLES AND SUGGES-tive grunts from the guys. They're only a step or two on the evolu-tionary scale from feral chickens, but they're certainly not boring. I know they think we're going upstairs to have sex, but I have a different goal in mind.

"Now that I've got you alone…" I say after Conor closes the door behind us.

He has the master bedroom, which is big enough for a king bed with a dark wooden frame, a love seat across the room and an enter-tainment center with another massive TV. He's also got an en suite bathroom and a big window that takes up half the wall and overlooks a small backyard where most of the winter snow has finally melted.

"Yeah, babe, I'm game." Conor rips his tie from his shirt collar and flings it across the room.

I roll my eyes. "Not that."

"Tease."

I take a seat on his bed against the headboard and put one of his pillows between us like he did the last time we found ourselves alone in a room together. The blue plaid bed set says his mom picked out something masculine for him at Neiman Marcus. It's very soft, and smells like him—sandalwood, with the salty hint of the ocean.

"I want to know—what was that display at the banquet *really* about?"

"I already told you."

"Yeah, and I think there's more to the story. So, spill."

"Wouldn't you rather make out?" He climbs onto the mattress beside me, and suddenly the bed feels very, very tiny. Is this actually a king-size? Because he's *right there*, and one measly pillow isn't going to protect me from the heat of his athletic body and the scent of his after-shave.

I force myself not to be affected by the sexy grin he flashes me. "Conor," I say with the tone I use with my first graders when one of them won't share the crayons.

His flirtatious smile evaporates. "If I said you didn't want to know, would you just trust me and let it go?"

"No." I meet his gaze head-on. "Tell me why you did what you did at the alumni banquet."

On a deep sigh he rubs his hands over his face and combs his hair out of his eyes. "I don't want to hurt you." The confession comes out in a mumble.

"I'm a big girl. If you respect me, tell me the truth."

"Damn, T. Right in the fucking feels."

He looks at me with such pained eyes, I have to brace for the worst. That maybe Abigail put him up to the whole thing, that they planned it together. That first dare, the love-bombing at Woolsey Hall...it was all a big scheme to make me catch feelings for him. Only now he's having regrets? It's a mortifying scenario, but it also wouldn't be the worst thing Abigail's ever done.

"Fine. But keep in mind, these are their words, not mine."

He recounts overhearing Abigail and Jules talking with their boyfriends earlier about my "hook-up" with Conor. I flinch when he explains in an unhappy tone that their conversation included discussion of my potential as a porn actress, among other digs.

Lovely.

He's right, I could have lived without the gory details.

Before he's even stopped speaking, I'm feeling nauseated. My stomach twists at the thought of Conor hearing them say all that shit about me.

"I'm still twenty pounds from my goal porn star weight," I joke at my own expense.

Most of the time, if you make fun of yourself first, it takes all the wind out of the fat-shaming sails. Showing people you're self-aware softens their aversion to having a chubby friend. Because it's important to everyone that we know our place.

"Don't do that." Conor sits up to level me with narrowed eyes. "There's nothing wrong with the way you look."

"It's okay. You don't need to make me feel better. I have no delusions about how people see me." The jabs land every time, but by now the nerve endings are mostly dead. At least, that's what I tell myself. "I was a chubby kid. I was a chubby teenager." I shrug. "I've struggled with weight my whole life. This is what I am, and I've accepted that."

"No, you don't get it, Taylor." Frustration crosses his expression. "Your body isn't something you have to make excuses for. I know I've said this before, and I guess I'll keep saying it until you believe me, but you're smoking hot. I'd do you right now, in a heartbeat, six different ways if you'd let me."

"Shut up your whole face." I laugh.

He doesn't laugh with me. Rather, he gets off the bed and turns his back to me.

Oh crap. Is he mad that I told him to shut up? I thought we were kidding around. That's our thing, right? Wait. Do we know each other well enough to have a thing? *Fuck.*

"Con—"

Before I can fix whatever I've broken, Conor starts unbuttoning his shirt, then peels it off his shoulders.

Stunned, I sit in admiration of his bare back. Tan skin over long, lean muscles. God, I want to press my mouth against that spot between his shoulder blades and explore it with my tongue. The notion sends a shiver running through me. I bite my lip just to keep from making a totally unbecoming noise.

He throws the shirt across the room, then undoes his trousers. They hit the hardwood, and now he's left in nothing but black socks and boxer-briefs that cling to the tightest butt I've ever seen.

"What are you doing?" My voice comes out breathier than I intend.

"Take your clothes off." He turns around and stalks back to the bed with fierce determination.

"Excuse me?" I scurry on my knees to the far edge of the mattress.

"Get naked," Conor orders.

"I certainly will not."

"Listen, Taylor. We're going to settle this and then there'll be no more arguments."

"Settle what, exactly?"

"I'm going to fuck your brains out and prove my dick is totally into you."

Excuse me?

Even as I gape at him, my gaze unwittingly drops to his crotch. I can't tell if the bulge beneath that stretchy black fabric is a hard-on or just his normal old package. Either way, Conor's declaration is so preposterous it summons a loud, hysterical bark of laughter from deep in my gut.

Then another.

And another.

Soon I can't breathe, doubled over in a painful fit. It just won't stop. Every time I look at his face, a new wave of laughter overtakes me, and tears spill down my cheeks. He's too fucking much.

"Taylor." Conor rakes both hands through his hair. "Taylor, stop laughing at me."

"I can't!"

"You're doing irreparable harm to my ego here."

Gasping, I take deep breaths. Eventually, the laughter subsides to giggles. "Thank you," I manage to croak out. "I needed that."

"You know what?" he growls, a cranky scowl on his face. "I take it all back. You're dick kryptonite."

"Aww. Come here." I climb back on the bed and pet the spot beside me.

Instead of being a normal person, he takes it upon himself to lie down and drop his head and shoulders across my lap.

It doesn't escape me that I now have a sexy man in his boxers draped over me. And it's difficult to focus with him looking so, well, like *that*. This isn't the first time I've seen Conor half-naked, and yet the effect is no less impressive. He's what guys picture in the mirror when they're lifting weights and mugging for gym selfies. Every douchebag in a tank top thinks he's Conor Fucking Edwards.

"I can't believe you didn't get naked," he grumbles in accusation.

"I'm sorry. That was a very sweet invitation, but I respectfully decline."

"Well, that makes you my first."

Conor stares up at me with those gorgeous gray eyes, and for one fleeting moment an image flashes through my mind. Me, leaning down. Him, cupping the side of my face. Our lips meeting in the space between us...

Do not kiss him, Taylor!

My inner alarm system kicks in, causing my silly schoolgirl kissing fantasy to dissolve just as quickly as it appeared.

"I'm your first what?" I ask, trying to remember what we're talking about. Conor Edwards is *in my lap* and it's really quite distracting.

"First girl to ever reject my cock."

"Not for the first time, either," I remind him.

"Yes, thank you, Taylor. You find me unfuckable. I get it." Conor flicks up an eyebrow. "It'd be a shame, though."

His hair begs for fingers. To drag them through the soft strands.

To touch. My hand itches with the urge to fulfill that wish. "What's a shame?"

"Don't stop." It isn't until he speaks that I realize my fingers have run off on their own accord. "That feels good."

So I continue, combing my fingers through his hair. Softly pulling my nails across his scalp. "What's a shame?"

"Well, we've laid such great groundwork already. Spent a night of mind-blowing sex together. Everyone thinks you've got me pussy-tranced into falling in love with you. Seems unfortunate to let that all go to waste?"

I eye him suspiciously. "What do you propose?"

"Let's ride it out."

"Ride it out." I play with the idea in my head, turning it over. It is, of course, a terribly dishonest and immature suggestion. So, naturally, I'm intrigued. "To what end?"

"Marriage, death, or graduation," he says. "Whichever comes first."

"Okay. But why? What's in it for you?"

"A cure for my boredom." He grins up at me. "I like games, T. This feels like it'll be a fun one."

"Uh-huh. But what if my perfect man comes along to sweep me off my feet but he gets scared away by Conor Fucking Edwards sniffing around my petticoats?"

"First, yes, keep calling me that. Second, if he can't take a little healthy competition, he isn't your perfect man. Trust me on that, babe."

Every time he calls me *babe* a stab of electricity shoots through my chest. I wonder if he feels my pulse spike. Or maybe he knows all too well he has that effect on every girl and I am but a toy doll off the assembly line. Lot 251 per one billion. Wind me up and watch me go.

"Fine. What about *your* admirers?" I counter. "What if Natalie from Tri-Delt wants another go and suddenly you have a fake girlfriend?"

He shrugs. "I'm not interested in another go with her."

"Bull. Have you seen her hair? It's so shiny."

That earns me a snicker. "Shiny hair aside, I'm being serious. She posted a pic of me naked in her bed when I was asleep. That ain't cool with me. Consent, you know?"

"Bull," I say again. "Look at you." With both hands, I gesture toward his half-naked *Playgirl* physique. "You probably love flaunting it for the camera."

"Not without my consent," he repeats, and the hard look on his face tells me he *really* wasn't fond of Natalie's actions.

I suppose I can't blame him. I still have nightmares about Kappa pledge week and all the embarrassing shit the seniors filmed us doing.

"Anyway," he goes on, "maybe I need a break from the sex circuit. Take some time to regroup."

I punch him in the shoulder. "*Sex circuit?* Oh my God. Must you be so gross?"

He offers that cocky grin again. "You don't think I'm gross. Otherwise you wouldn't be letting me snuggle up in your lap."

I swallow through my suddenly dry throat. "This is not considered snuggling," I say sternly.

"Sure it is, T."

"It sure isn't, C," I mock. "And, what, you're saying you're going to abstain from sex for the foreseeable future? Because I don't buy that."

Conor looks aghast. "Abstain? Hell no. I'm gonna try to seduce you at every turn."

A laugh flies out of my mouth. "You're incorrigible."

"Why'd you stop playing with my hair? Felt nice." His tongue darts out to moisten his bottom lip, an adorable action that quickens my pulse. "So what do you say? We keep pretending for a while longer?"

"The fact that I'm entertaining this idea says I had too much to drink today," I respond.

"That was hours ago. You're not drunk. Besides, tell me the look on Abigail's face every time she's seen us together hasn't gone straight to your tingly place."

"First, don't ever call it that again. Second…" I want to tell him he's wrong. That I'm above such petty amusements. However…he's not entirely wrong about the tingle. "Maybe I enjoyed it a little," I confess.

"Ha! I knew it. You enjoy the game as much as I do."

"Just a *little*," I stress.

"Liar."

When he sits abruptly, I experience a sense of loss I'm not allowed to feel. But I feel it all the same, missing the heaviness of his warm body on me and the softness of his blond hair between my fingers.

"What are you doing?" I demand as he hops off the bed and grabs his discarded pants.

He returns with his phone, plopping down beside me. His thumb slides over the screen as he…well, I'm not sure what he's doing. Because I'm nosy, I lean closer to peek, and discover that he's pulled up MyBriar, our school's social media app.

My eyes widen as I watch him change his status to *in a relationship*.

"Hey," I chide, "I didn't say yes."

"You basically said yes."

"I was at a seventy percent at best."

"Welp, might as well prance that last thirty, because we're blowing up, babe."

Oh my effing God. The little bubble above the notification icon starts blinking. Ten, twenty, forty.

"C'mon," he coaxes. "I'm bored. This'll be good for a laugh, at least. Best case scenario—you cave to my smoldering good looks and fall into bed with me."

"You wish."

"I really do. But fine, second-best case scenario: it might get Abigail to lay off you for a while. That's worth something, right?"

That *would* be nice. Especially since there's a Kappa chapter meeting tomorrow and I just know Abigail will be all over me with her passive aggressive jabs.

"You know you want to..." He wiggles his phone in the air enticingly.

My gaze is drawn to the thick silver band around his middle finger. "Nice ring. Where'd you get it?"

"LA. And you're deflecting." He holds the phone out to me. "I dare you."

"You're incredibly persistent."

"Some would consider it one of my better qualities."

"Also completely obnoxious."

Conor flashes his self-assured grin that says "obnoxious" is just girl code for "charming" when she's about to break.

"Taylor Marsh, will you do me the incredible honor of updating your relationship status and becoming my fake girlfriend?"

And break she does. As if possessed by some supernatural being, my hand takes the phone from him. My finger logs out of his MyBri and then logs into mine. And as I change my status to match his, I'm vaguely aware of two things:

One, I could have just used my own phone, but it would have ruined the moment.

And two, whatever this is, it's bound to get messy.

8

TAYLOR

LESS THAN TWENTY-FOUR HOURS AFTER CONOR AND I MAKE IT "official," the entire Kappa membership gathers at the house while our chapter president leads the meeting. First on the agenda is the upcoming spring election for next year's president and vice president. Naturally, since Charlotte is a senior, Abigail as her VP is the heir apparent. Gag me with a dishrag.

"To ensure no undue influence on the part of myself or the vice president," Charlotte is saying, "Fiona will lead the election commission with Willow and Madison. They will host the platform dinner and coordinate the ballot committee. Anyone interested in helping out should talk with them after the meeting."

Truth is, the election is all but a formality. Every year, the outgoing senior names a junior as her VP and she is elected the following year. All pretenses that we aren't living under a dynastic system are insulting. Dani, who's running against Abigail as the lone voice of resistance, doesn't stand a chance. But she's got my vote.

"Fi?" Charlotte prompts.

The tall redhead stands up. "Yes, okay. So, both Abigail and Dani will give their final campaign speeches at the platform dinner. The format will be—"

My phone vibrates against my thigh, drawing focus away from Fiona. I peer down and hide a smile when I read Conor's text.

HIM: How's my sexy babe doing this afternoon?

I covertly type back a response, although I feel Sasha's knowing gaze on me. She's in the chair next to mine, no doubt trying to read what I'm writing.

ME: In the middle of a chapter meeting. Kill me now.
HIM: Kill you?! But then how will we ever fuck?

I fight a laugh and reply with an eyeroll emoji.

He ups the ante by sending a picture of his abs, and I try not to drool all over the dining room table.

"Are you going to share with the rest of the class, Tay-Tay?" comes Abigail's snippy voice.

My head jerks up. "Sorry," I blurt, setting my phone on the table-top. I give Fiona and then Charlotte apologetic looks. "Someone texted and I was just texting back to say I'm in the middle of a meeting."

"*Someone?*" Sasha cracks, laughing. "And does that someone's name start with a C and end with an Onor?"

I turn to glare at her.

But the remark has already snagged the interest of our president. "Conor?" she echoes. "As in Conor Edwards?"

I manage a weak nod.

"My girl Taylor's landed herself a hockey god," my best friend brags on my behalf, and I'm torn between smacking her for making me the center of attention and thanking her for hyping me up. Sasha Lennox is the best hype-woman there is. She's also well aware that the whole MyBri relationship status stuff was baloney, so now I'm praying she doesn't slip up and somehow reveal the truth.

"No shit," Charlotte says, looking impressed. "Good going, Marsh."

"They fucked in my room," Rachel boasts, as if that means she's one step away from being Conor Edwards' girlfriend herself.

"Oh, big fucking deal," Abigail speaks up, her pale green eyes cool as ice. "Who *hasn't* fucked that guy? I mean, seriously. Show of hands—who here has slept with Conor Edwards?"

After several seconds of hesitation, three hands are raised. A sheepish Willow and Taryn on the other side of the table, and a blushing Laura who's standing against the wall.

Well. Dude gets around.

I swallow the tiny lump of jealousy that rises in my throat and remind myself that I already knew he was a player. Besides, he's a grown-ass man. He's allowed to sleep with whomever he wants, my sorority sisters included.

Sensing my discomfort, Sasha turns toward Abigail, pinning the platinum blonde with an equally icy stare. "What are you saying, Abs? You implying that Taylor is, what, of lesser value because her man has a past? Like that means anything. In fact—show of hands," Sasha mimics, "who here has slept with one of Abigail's douchey ex-boyfriends?"

To my great amusement, twice the amount of hands shoot up. That's right—six Kappas, and none of them look the slightest bit sheepish this time around. I suspect they're receiving some sort of perverse pleasure in admitting it because Abigail is such a bitch.

Abigail's trusted lackey Jules sports a deep scowl. "Anyone here ever heard of the girl code?"

Sasha snickers. "You tell me, Julianne. Weren't you the one who just stole Duke Jarrett away from some Theta Beta Nu chick?"

That shuts up Jules.

Charlotte clears her throat. "Alright, we've strayed off-topic. Fiona, you were telling us about the candidate speeches?"

Just as Fiona opens her mouth to answer, my phone buzzes again, eliciting an excited shriek from Rachel, who's draping practically her entire body across the dining table to see the screen.

"He's FaceTiming you!"

My heart does a nervous flip. "I'm so sorry," I tell Charlotte. "Let me just ignore the—"

"*Ignore?*" Charlotte echoes in disbelief. "For fuck's sake, Marsh, answer it."

Oh my God. This is my worst nightmare. What on earth compelled my stupid fake boyfriend to FaceTime me when I *just* told him I was in a chapter meeting? Why would he do this to—

"Answer it!" Lisa Donaldson shrieks.

I'm pretty sure this is the only time Lisa Donaldson has ever even spoken to me.

Heart racing, I tap the *accept* button. A second later the call connects and Conor's gorgeous face fills the screen.

"Babe, hey."

His deep voice fills the Kappa Chi dining room, and I notice several of my sisters honest-to-God *shiver*.

"Sorry, I know you said you were in a meeting, but I just wanted to tell you—" He stops mid-sentence, his gray eyes narrowing with appreciation. "Mmmm, damn, T, you look good enough to eat."

I'm not sure it's humanly possible to blush harder than I currently am. I shove a hunk of hair behind my ear and grumble at the screen. "Seriously? *That's* what you interrupted my meeting to say?"

"Nah, that wasn't it."

He offers a little boy grin and anyone with a clear view of my phone sighs and swoons like Victorian maidens.

"Then what was it?"

Conor winks. "Just wanted to tell you I miss you."

"Oh my God," breathes Rachel.

Damn. Someone's laying it on thick. Before I can answer him, the phone is grabbed from his hand and a new face greets me.

"Taylor!" Matt Anderson exclaims happily. "Yo, when you coming over next? Foster found us a new movie to watch."

"It's got black holes and giant squids!" comes Foster's faint shout.

"Soon, Matty," I promise, then pray he doesn't call me out for referring to him as *Matty*. But hell, if Conor's allowed to lay it on thick, then so am I. "Anyway, I'm hanging up now. I'm busy."

I disconnect the call, set down the phone, and find an entire room of wide-eyed girls staring at me with naked envy. Even Sasha seems impressed, and she's in on the charade.

"I am *so* sorry," I say awkwardly. "I'll make sure he never interrupts during a meeting again."

"All good," Charlotte assures me. "We all know those hockey players are hard to say no to. Trust me, we know."

The rest of the meeting continues without a hiccup, although it's difficult to ignore the death stares coming from Abigail and Jules's direction. Then Charlotte dismisses us with the clap of her manicured hands, chairs are scraped back, and everyone disperses. I bump into someone during the stampede, stepping away quickly when I realize it's Rebecca Locke.

"Oh, sorry," I tell the petite girl. "Didn't see you there."

"It's fine," she replies in a tight voice, and then darts off without another word.

As I watch her hurry upstairs, I sigh and wonder if things will ever get any less awkward between me and Rebecca. I was forced to kiss her during pledge week, and needless to say it was a mortifying experience for the both of us. We've spoken only a handful of times since and never been alone in the same room together.

"Wanna get some lunch?" Sasha links her arm through mine as we head for the front door.

"Sure," I reply.

"Taylor, wait," someone calls before we can leave the house.

I glance over my shoulder. Lisa Donaldson and Olivia Ling are sashaying toward us. "What's up?" I say politely.

"You live in Hastings, right?" Lisa runs a hand through her glossy mane of hair.

"Yeah, why?" I ask, and then stand there trying to hide my shock as two chicks who've never given me the time of day explain how they're in Hastings once or twice a week for their salon appointments and would *love* to grab a bite with me if I'm free Tuesday night.

"And you too, Sasha," Olivia offers in what sounds like a genuine invitation. "Usually Beth and Robin and the boyfriends meet us at the diner too. It's nice to leave campus and get a change of scenery sometimes, you know?"

"Even nicer to live off campus," I say with a grin.

"I'd bet," murmurs Lisa. Her gaze flicks toward Abigail, who's whispering furiously with Jules in the far corner of the living room. Interesting. Maybe I'm not the only one considering voting for Dani.

After agreeing to meet the girls on Tuesday, Sasha and I exit the house. Outside, I breathe in the early spring air. Release a gust of it in a slow rush.

"Conor Fucking Edwards," I mumble.

Sasha laughs softly. "The man's good, I'll give him that."

"Too good. He even had *me* convinced he missed me, and I know that's not true." Hell, he had every Kappa in that room salivating over him. One FaceTime from him and suddenly they're inviting me to *dinner*.

Conor had told me how much he loves games—well, today proved he's highly skilled at them too. Problem is, I'm terrible at games. I always lose. And the longer this silly ruse with Conor goes on, the greater the danger of it all blowing up in my face.

9
CONOR

THERE'S AN EERIE CALM ON THE ICE TUESDAY MORNING AS THE team runs through drills. Hardly anyone says a word for two hours; only the sounds of our skates and Coach's whistle echo through the empty arena.

The tournament brackets were announced yesterday. This weekend we face Minnesota Duluth in Buffalo, New York. No one wants to say it, but I think the matchup has everyone a bit spooked. The nerves are creeping in, and we're all on edge and hyper-focused on our individual parts of the machine.

Hunter's been staying late every day since we made the playoffs. He wants it bad. I think he sees it as a reflection on his success as captain, like it's his job alone to win this for us and if he doesn't, he's a failure. Man, I could never do his job. I generally make it a rule to minimize expectations and not take on responsibility for anyone but myself.

After practice, we hit the showers. I stand under the spray and let the scalding water beat down on my aching shoulders. This tournament might just be the death of me.

My old team in LA sucked, which means we never had to worry about a post-season. Going this long at this high a competitive level is taking its toll on my body. Bruises, sore ribs, tired muscles. I honestly don't know how professionals do it. If I'm even able to stand up on skates next season it'll be a miracle. There are a lot of guys who think they want to go pro. Less than half have a legitimate shot. Me, I've never harbored any delusions that I'm NHL material. Nor do I want to be. Hockey has always just been a hobby, something to keep me out of trouble. Idle hands and all that. Soon, this part of my life will be over.

Problem is, I don't have any idea what comes next.

"Hey, Captain, I move to call the Relationship Status Inquisition into session," Bucky shouts out above the noise of the showers.

"I second that motion," Jesse calls back.

"The motion carries." Hunter stands in the stall beside me. I feel him staring at the side of my face. "This session of the Relationship Status Inquisition is now open. Bucky, call your first witness."

"I call Joe Foster to the stand."

"Present!" Foster gurgles out under the spray of his shower faucet at the opposite end of the room.

"I fucking hate you guys," I say as I grab a towel and wrap it around my waist.

"Is it true, Mr. Foster, that Conor Edwards did publicly and embarrassingly drop to his knees to profess his love to Kappa Party Girl after he was known to have hooked up with Instagram Natalie?"

"Wait, what?" Foster asks blankly. "Oh, at the banquet thing. Yeah. It was fucking gross."

"And did he subsequently bring Kappa Party Girl home that evening?"

"Yo, Bucky, I didn't know you could use four-syllable words," Gavin says, ribbing him as they leave the showers.

I head to my locker to get dressed, the guys breathing down my neck.

"Yeah, they spent a long time in his bedroom. Alone." Foster's going to find his car stuffed full of dildos sometime in the very near future.

"And they FaceTimed the other day," Matt pipes up, a big stupid grin on his face. "*He* called *her*."

A round of mock gasps travels through the room.

Guess Matt can look forward to some dildos too.

"You can all eat shit," I drawl.

"I seem to remember," Hunter says, "you conspiring to interfere in my dick affairs. Payback's a bitch."

"At least I don't need you to make out with my girlfriend to get me to fuck her."

"Ouch," Bucky laughs. "He's got you there, Cap."

"So this is a real thing?" Hunter asks, unfazed by my jab at his stupid chastity bargain. "You and..."

"Taylor. And yeah, sort of."

"Sort of?"

No, it isn't real, technically. And it kind of sucks lying to the guys.

But also, what makes it *not* real? I mean, I'm not going to sleep with other women or date, because that wouldn't be respectful to either Taylor or those potential women. She hasn't said as much out loud, but I suspect she feels the same way on the subject. So that checks the monogamy box.

And okay, yeah, we're not screwing or kissing or touching at all, but that doesn't mean I'm opposed to those things. I think if I could make Taylor see herself the way I do, make her appreciate her body the way I do—fuuuuuck, do I appreciate it—then maybe she'll loosen up a little and be open to the screwing and kissing and touching part. So that checks the attraction box.

Truth is, Taylor's fun to hang out with and I like talking to her. She's unpretentious and kinda hilarious. Best of all, she doesn't expect anything from me. I don't have to be some version of me that she's concocted in her head or meet some wild expectations that only wind up disappointing both of us. And she doesn't judge—not once has she made me feel like she looks down on me or is embarrassed by my choices or reputation. I don't need her to approve, just accept, and I get the sense that she likes me for me.

Worst case, I get a good friend out of the deal. Best case, I screw her brains out. Win-win either way.

"It is what it is," I say, pulling a hoodie over my head. "We're having fun."

Fortunately, the guys drop it, mostly because they have the attention span of fruit flies. Hunter's already texting Demi on his way out the door, while Matt and Foster start discussing the squid movie we all watched the other night.

On my way out of the hockey facility, my phone rings. "*MOM*" flashes on the screen.

"Go on ahead," I tell Matt. "I'll be right there." As my teammate ambles off toward the parking lot, I slow my gait and answer the call. "Hey, Mom."

"Hey Mister," Mom says. No matter how old I get, it's like I'm still five in her eyes. "I haven't heard from you in ages. Everything okay out there in the tundra?"

I chuckle. "Sun's actually out today, if you can believe it." I don't mention that the temperature is only fifty degrees—and it's the end of frickin' March. Spring is taking its sweet-ass time getting to New England.

"That's good. I was worried you'd finish your first east coast winter with a Vitamin D deficiency."

"Nope. All good here. What about you? What's happening with the fires?" Wildfires had been wreaking havoc on the west coast for the past few weeks. It's been making me antsy knowing my mom's out there breathing in all that crap.

"Oh, well, you know. Last couple weeks I've been putting up plastic and taping the doors and windows shut to keep the smoke out. Bought four brand new air purifiers that are supposed to suck up anything bigger than an atom. I think they're drying out my skin, though. But maybe it's just the lack of humidity lately. Anyhow, the fires down this way are out now, they said, so the smoke's mostly cleared. Which is good, because I just started a new sunrise beach yoga class."

"Yoga, Mom?"

"Oh, God, I know, right?" She laughs at herself. It's an infectious sound I hadn't realized I'd missed so much. "But Christian's partner Richie—you remember Christian from across the street—he just started teaching the class. He invited me and I didn't know how to tell him no, so..."

"So now you're a yoga lady."

"I know, right? Who woulda thunk it?"

Certainly not me. Mom used to spend sixty, seventy hours a week on her feet in a salon then came home to chase my ass all over the neighborhood. If someone had invited her to sunrise beach yoga back then, she probably would've punched them in the throat. Making the transition from LA working single mother to HBC housewife was a tough one for her. She spent a lot of energy trying to fit in with a certain idea of herself and then resenting the inadequacy as a result, at least until she figured out how to stop giving a shit.

People who say money doesn't buy happiness aren't using it right. But hey, if Mom's at the point where she can take some joy in waking up at the crack of dawn for frivolous shit, I'm happy for her.

"I told Max if he starts seeing Goop charges on the credit card statements to stage an intervention."

"How is Max?" Not that I care, but it makes Mom feel better when I act like I give a shit.

In my defense, I'm certain my stepdad only asks her about me for the same reason—to score points. Max tolerates me because he loves my mom, but he's never bothered trying to get to know me. Dude's kept his distance from day one. I suspect he was relieved when I told them I wanted to transfer to an east coast school. He was so happy to get rid of me he pulled every string possible to get me into Briar.

And I was equally relieved to go. Guilt has a way of pressing down on you until you'll do anything to escape.

"He's terrific. Out of town for work right now, but he gets back Friday morning. So we'll both be cheering you on in spirit Friday night. Any chance the game will be televised?"

"Probably not," I reply as I near the parking lot. "If we make it to the final tournament, then for sure. Anyway, Mom, I gotta go. Just finished practice and need to drive home."

"Okay, sweetie. Text or call before you leave for Buffalo this weekend."

"Will do."

We say goodbye and I hang up and approach the beat-up black Jeep I share with Matt. Technically it's mine, but he chips in for gas and pays for the oil changes, which means I don't need to dip into the account Max tops up for me every month. I hate being dependent on my stepfather, but at the moment I have no choice.

"Everything okay?" Matt asks when I hop into the passenger seat.

"Yeah, sorry. Was talking to my mom."

He looks disappointed.

"What?" I narrow my eyes.

"I was hoping you'd say it was your new girl and then I could make fun of you some more. But moms are off-limits."

I snicker. "Since when? You mock Bucky about banging his mother practically on a daily basis."

Although speaking of my "new girl," I haven't heard from her since last night, when she replied "LOL" to a hilarious video I sent her. *Just* an LOL. To a video of a surfing Chihuahua! What the hell.

As Matt pulls out of the parking lot, I shoot a quick text off to Taylor.

ME: Whatcha doing, hot stuff?

She doesn't respond for nearly thirty minutes. I'm home and in my kitchen making a smoothie when she finally gets back to me.

TAYLOR: Working. I've got co-op at Hastings Elementary.

Ah, right. She'd mentioned she was serving as a teacher's aide as part of her degree requirement.

ME: Dinner later?
HER: Can't :(
HER: Have plans with friends at the diner. Talk later?

Well, shit. Been a while since anyone turned down a date with me, and even that was only so she could get me into bed faster. Taylor's rejection hurts more than I know what to do with, but I'm very good at pretending not to care about stuff. Fake it till you make it, right?

ME: Sure thing.

10
TAYLOR

I'M NECK DEEP IN CONSTRUCTION PAPER BUTTERFLIES AND PIPE cleaner caterpillars when the end-of-day bell rings. The kids drop their scissors and glue sticks to run for their cubbies where their backpacks and coats are kept.

"Not so fast," I remind them. "Come put your supplies away and hang up your projects to dry."

"Miss Marsh?" One of the girls taps me on the arm. "I can't find my shoe."

She stands forlorn in one purple waterproof boot and one cartoon character sock.

"When's the last time you had your shoe, Katy?"

She shrugs.

"Did you and Tamara trade shoes again?"

Another shrug. This one with some bottom lip protruding and eyes cast down at her mismatched feet.

I swallow a sigh. "Go find Tamara and see where she left your shoe."

Katy scurries off. I watch her progress while picking up scraps of paper and pushing desks back into their proper arrangement. With Tamara's guidance, who herself isn't wearing any shoes, they find the missing footwear in the reading corner with the costumes Mrs. Gardner uses to have the kids act out characters while they read aloud.

The thing about first graders, they lie as easy as breathing. They're just not very good at it yet. That, and it's damn near impossible to keep all their clothes on them. Half my job is just making sure we send them home wearing only what they arrived in. Yup. It is a thankless and unending battle against the Lost & Found box.

"If there was such a thing as foot lice," Mrs. Gardner says as we see the last stragglers off, "this classroom would be quarantined by the CDC."

I grin. "At least it's still cold enough outside that they're wearing socks. I hate to see what happens when it gets warmer."

She heaves a defeated breath. "That's why I keep antifungal spray in my desk."

There's a lovely thought.

Hastings Elementary is just a ten-minute walk from my three-story apartment building. There aren't any high-rises in Hastings, only little buildings and shops, and residential streets lined with townhouses or rambling old Victorians. It's a cute town and everything is in walking distance, which I appreciate because I don't own a car.

I let myself into my tiny studio and grab a granola bar from the cupboard. As I munch on it, I text Sasha with my free hand.

ME: I don't need to dress up for dinner or anything, right??

I've never actually gone out with Lisa and those girls, so I have no idea what to expect. But we're only meeting at the diner, so, really, how fancy can it be?

SASHA: Dress up?? I'm not. Jeans + tank + leather jacket + boots = me.
ME: Ok, good. I'm keeping it cas too.
HER: You bringing C? :P
ME: Why would I be bringing C??

HER: Lisa said bf's were welcome...
ME: Haha.

Sasha knows damn well that Conor isn't really my boyfriend, but she's getting a kick out of teasing me about it. Or maybe she thinks if she refers to him as my boyfriend enough times, then it'll magically transform from pretend to real. Poor, naïve Sasha. I have no doubt Conor will get bored soon, which means the charade can't last much longer. A shame, really, because our supposed love affair continues to piss the hell out of Abigail.

Last night at a mandatory house dinner, Abigail's boyfriend wouldn't let up on all the "jock cock" I was gobbling while blatantly staring at my tits. During dessert he remarked that I looked like Marilyn Monroe only "*extra* curvy," at which point Sasha asked him what it's like living life with a micropenis. Abigail, meanwhile, kept scratching at the side of her neck every time Conor's name came up, until her skin was red and raw and flaking off her. Is it possible to contract jealousy hives?

Of course, such pettiness would be entirely beneath me.

Entirely.

ME: You don't think Lisa invited Abigail, do you?
SASHA: God I hope not. I don't have the patience for 2 dinners in a row with that witch. If she's there, we turn around and walk right out, deal?
ME: Deal.

Luckily, when Sasha and I walk into the diner later that night, Abigail and her douchebag boyfriend Kevin are nowhere to be seen. Lisa brought her boyfriend Cory, though, and Robin's sitting with some guy who introduces himself as "Shep." Olivia came solo, and I end up seated next to her, with Sasha on my other side.

I get barely a bite into my BLT before the girls start in on me.

"Okay, but, like, how is he in the sack?" Lisa asks, thoroughly ignoring her boyfriend's uneasy squirm. Clearly he'd rather be anywhere else than smack in the middle of Conor Edwards' exploits.

You and me both, brother.

"How big is he?" Olivia demands.

"Is he circumcised?"

"Grower or shower?"

"Could we not?" Sasha says, dangling a chicken finger in the air. "I don't want to hear about dicks while I'm eating."

"*Thank* you," mumbles Cory.

"Fine, but is he a good kisser?" Olivia has her phone out, openly salivating at Conor's Instagram. The boyfriends have at this point been reduced to chewing their burgers in emasculated silence. "He looks like he'd be a good kisser. Not too much mouth."

"What does too much mouth even mean?" I ask with a laugh.

"You know, when they're like trying to swallow your lips. I don't want to feel any part of the kiss on my chin." Olivia plants her elbows on the table, a fork in one fist. "Spill it, Taylor. I want filthy details."

"His kissing is..." A mystery. Unascertained. None of my business. "Apt."

"Apt, she says." Sasha shakes her head, smirking. "Only you would call kissing 'apt.'"

"I don't know, it's kissing." I shrug awkwardly.

How much is there to say on the topic? Nothing, in fact, when I'm working on entirely fabricated experience. Not that the idea doesn't hold some appeal. Conor is incredibly attractive, and he has really, really nice lips. Full, in a masculine way. He seems like the kind of guy who treats kissing as its own pursuit rather than a means to an end.

To be fair, I haven't kissed many people—only four, to be exact, and three of those four were terrible experiences. Junior year of high school was my first kiss, and we both sucked at it. Waaaay too much tongue. We made out a few times after that but it didn't get any better.

Then came freshman year of college, when I was pressured into kissing Rebecca during pledge week, and sophomore year, when I accidentally kissed Abigail's boyfriend on a dare.

My fourth go at kissing wasn't awful. Not earth-shattering, either, but at least it didn't include buckets of saliva or forced contact. I dated a guy named Andrew for four months and he was a decent kisser. We never went further than dry humping, though, which is probably why we broke up. He claimed it was because I couldn't "open up" to him, and I suppose that played a part in it too, but we both knew the no-sex part wasn't cutting it for him. I just... I didn't feel comfortable doing it with him.

Sometimes I wonder if I'll ever meet a guy who makes me feel secure enough to take all my clothes off in front of him.

"Oh my God." Olivia all but dives under the table. Beside her, Lisa chokes on her soda and begins hacking up a lung.

I turn around to see what's got them in such a fit.

Conor Fucking Edwards.

Why am I not surprised? I feel like he's got Spidey senses that alert him whenever chicks are discussing his penis.

All six feet and two inches of him comes striding through the diner toward our table. He's in his black-and-silver Briar Hockey jacket and a pair of dark-blue jeans that hug his long legs. Steely gray eyes sparkle with mischief as he combs one hand through his long blond hair. When his gaze lands on me, the excitement in his full, broad smile does a number on my head. And my pulse.

Oh Lord. Men shouldn't get to be so pretty.

"Babe, I missed you." Conor snatches me up from my chair and wraps me in his arms.

He smells so good. I don't know what kind of products he uses, but he always smells vaguely of the ocean. And coconut. I love coconut.

"What are you doing here?" I whisper.

"Having dinner with my girlfriend," he says with a sly smirk that suggests he's up to no good. "She tries to keep me locked up in her bedroom all day," Conor tells the table, "but I thought it'd be fun to meet her friends."

For one terrifying moment I think he's leaning in to kiss me and I lick my lips and inhale slowly, my entire body braced and rigid.

Instead, he presses the lightest touch of his lips to the tip of my nose. In the aftermath, I don't know whether I'm disappointed or relieved.

"So this happened fast." Olivia makes room for Conor to pull up a chair and sit between me and her. I don't miss the way her hungry gaze follows his every movement.

"Did you two know each other before the party?" Lisa asks. Her eyes aren't as ravenous—probably as to not humiliate her boyfriend any further—but she's as focused on Conor as Olivia is.

"No, we didn't," I answer for him. "We met for the first time that night."

"She blew my mind." Conor puts his arm around my shoulders, drawing tiny patterns with his fingertips. "Time is relative."

Just to fuck with him, I place my hand on his thigh and tell the group, "He's already trying to convince me to let him move in with me."

But my fuckery attempt backfires. First off, his thigh is rock hard beneath my palm. Second...well, I can't think of a second thing right now because my hand is on Conor Edwards' thigh.

Before I can snatch my hand away, Conor covers my knuckles with one big palm, effectively trapping me there. The warmth of his touch has me fighting a hot shiver.

"Obviously my girl thinks it's too soon," he says solemnly. "But I disagree. It's never too soon to show how committed you are, right?" He directs this to the boyfriends, who each blurt out clichés in a mad scramble to avoid winding up in the doghouse.

"Yeah, if it's meant to be, it's meant to be," says Cory.

"When you know, you know," agrees Shep.

Sasha snorts loudly, then takes a sip of her soda.

"Conor loves commitment," I explain. "He's been planning his wedding since he was a little boy. Right, babe?"

"Right." He sharply pinches my thumb, but his expression is all innocence.

"He even has one of those, what do you call it, Con? A love board?"

"It's just a Pinterest account, babe." He glances around the table. "How am I gonna know what kind of wedding reception center-pieces I like if I don't have some options to choose from, amiright?"

Olivia, Lisa and Robin all but rip off their panties and throw them at Conor's beautiful head. Sasha meanwhile looks like she's struggling not to laugh.

"You getting married, Con?" a new voice drawls. "What, did my invite get lost in the mail?"

I look over to see a stunning woman in all black sauntering up to the table. She lightly bumps Conor's shoulder with her hip, a wry smile playing on her full red lips.

This chick is drop-dead gorgeous. Dark hair, dark eyes, those vixen lips. And she's rocking the kind of perfect body I can only dream of—slender waist, long limbs, and perfectly proportioned breasts.

Immediately I feel self-conscious in my leggings and loose white sweater. I tend to wear oversized shirts that fall off one shoulder, because they hide the curves beneath them but still show off a bit of skin. Bare shoulders are the safe kind of skin. The rest stays hidden.

"Sorry, Bren, you're not invited," Conor drawls back. "You're too much trouble."

"Mmm-hmmm, sure. *I'm* the one who's trouble." Her gaze flicks down to mine and Conor's joined hands before locking onto my face. "And you are?"

"Taylor," Conor answers easily, and I'm glad he does because my vocal cords have frozen.

And who are YOU? I want to demand. I mean, I assume she's an ex of his—or at the very least a former lover—and the envy that coats my throat makes it difficult to maintain a neutral expression. Of course this is the kind of woman Conor would be attracted to. She's perfection.

"Babe, this is Brenna," Conor introduces. "She's my coach's daughter."

Even worse. Now I've got porn scenarios about forbidden love flashing through my head. The coach's daughter and the hunky star player. She blows him in the locker room and then they have sex on Daddy's desk.

"Wait, I know you. Brenna Jensen. You're going out with Jake Connelly!" Lisa suddenly blurts out.

The dark-haired goddess narrows her eyes. "Yeah, so?"

"So, that's…you're so lucky," breathes Lisa. "Jake Connelly is…"

"Is what?" her boyfriend Cory demands, his tone revealing he's officially fed up with the way his girl has been acting all night. "Finish that sentence, Lisa—he's what?"

I think Lisa knows she's pushed him too far, because she backpedals as if it's an Olympic event. "He's one of the best players in the NHL," she finishes.

"One of?" Brenna mocks. "No, honey, he's *the* best."

Conor chuckles softly. "Whatcha doing here, B?"

"Picking up dinner for Dad and me. He can't cook for shit and I'm tired of eating burnt food every time I visit him. Speaking of food…" Her gaze shifts to the counter, where one of the waitresses at the cash is signaling Brenna. "Enjoy the rest of your night, Con. Try not to elope without telling your coach beforehand."

Everyone watches her go, and this time it's Cory and Shep whose eyes are glazing over. Brenna is sex personified. She walks with such hip-swaying confidence that I'm once again swimming with envy, even knowing she has a boyfriend and therefore no threat to my fake relationship.

"Hey," Lisa chides, smacking Cory's arm.

"Payback's a bitch, ain't it," he murmurs, his attention still fixed on Brenna Jensen's ass.

Sasha grins at our sorority sister. "He's got you there, Lisa."

"So, back to Conor's wedding board on Pinterest," Olivia announces.

"Nah," Conor says, "those pics are just for Taylor. Although… we might need to add some dress samples for inspiration, eh, baby?"

I swallow a laugh. "Definitely, *baby*."

"Is this…" Olivia's gaze darts between us, "getting serious?"

Conor looks at me. I expect his usual giddy mischief and mirth, and it's certainly there—but this time, there's something else too. A passing intensity in the crease of his forehead and straight line of his lips.

"It's getting there," he tells Olivia. But his gaze doesn't leave mine.

11
TAYLOR

Dinner at the diner turns into drinks at Malone's, the sports bar in town. Conor invites some of the guys from the team to join us. Likewise, some of my other Kappa sisters show up. In the back room near the pool tables and dartboards, we push a few tables together to accommodate our expanding party. While Conor's teammates have playoffs to worry about and are keeping their alcohol consumption to a minimum, the girls have no such restrictions.

My fellow Kappas have become emboldened by their hormones and are well on their way to getting loaded. Except for Rebecca, who ordered a Diet Coke. She's a few seats away and hasn't looked my way once. I was surprised she even came out tonight, but I suspect she hadn't known I was here when Lisa invited her. Since pledge week she's basically run the other way any time she saw me coming.

"You're not mad, are you?" Conor sits down beside me with our drinks that he just got from the bar. There's some trepidation in his eyes. Like maybe he's just realized that crashing dinner and inviting himself to drinks is more invasive than charming.

"Not mad, no." I eye him over the rim of my drink. "Curious, though."

"Oh?" A hint of his trademark playful smile resurfaces. "About?"

"What prompted you to hunt me down and subject yourself to the rabid hungry gaze of my sorority sisters. Surely you have better things to do."

"We've got to keep up appearances, right?" He's trying to play it cute, flashing his cheeky grin and flirtatious charms, but I'm not buying it this time. Something's up with him. There's a tension in his demeanor that doesn't suit him.

"I'm serious," I insist. "I want a real answer."

We're interrupted by a loud bang on the table. Courtesy of my sorority sister Beth Bradley, who showed up only thirty minutes ago and is already tipsier than everyone else.

"We should play Dare or Dare," she announces, smacking the table until she's gotten everyone's attention. She raises an eyebrow at me, biting her lip impishly.

While Lisa and Olivia don't seem to be Abigail fangirls, I know Beth is somewhat chummy with her, which means I'm instantly on guard.

"We should get a new game," I answer dryly.

"What's Dare or Dare?" Across the table, Foster has just committed the cardinal sin of volunteering himself. Poor dumb bastard.

"Well," Beth says, "I challenge you to a dare and you must complete it upon penalty of death."

The other guys snicker.

"Sounds intense," remarks Matt.

"You don't know the half of it," I tell him.

I can't help but glance in Rebecca's direction, a tiny lump rising in my throat. Whatever potential friendship we might've had was just another casualty of this stupid game.

"Here." Sasha shoves a shot in front of me. She's just returned from her own trip to the bar, sandwiching herself between me and Matt. The two of them have looked pretty darn cozy all night.

I eye the shot glass warily. Drinking this would be a terrible idea. One, I don't shoot liquor well, and two, where Conor's concerned, I've got to keep my wits about me. There are traps and pitfalls everywhere, holes full of sharpened bamboo spears waiting to impale me.

"Go on," Sasha urges. "It'll take the edge off."

So I knock it back. It tastes like cinnamon gum and licorice, and not in a good way.

"I just wanted to see you." Conor murmurs in my ear, continuing our conversation as if it had never stopped.

The combination of liquor heating my blood and his warm breath on my neck makes my head go a bit fuzzy. I lean closer, my arm draped over his thigh to keep myself steady. "Why?" I murmur back.

This time the conversation does stop. His attention has been diverted to his teammate, who is foolishly calling Beth's bluff.

"Go on then," Foster says. "Give me your best shot."

"Careful," Conor warns. "I've seen their handiwork."

"Oh no, don't dare me to sleep with a cute blonde." Foster deadpans. "That'd be the worst thing ever."

"Alright." Beth sits up straight, narrowing her eyes at him. "I dare you to get any woman in this bar to take a shot out of your waistband."

Conor and the guys burst out laughing.

"Oh shit, dude. Let me FaceTime Gavin for this one." Matt yanks out his phone, his muscular arm sliding off Sasha's shoulder.

"Yeah, cool." Foster jumps to his feet while Lisa goes to order the necessary shot. "How 'bout it, Beth. You thirsty?"

"Nuh-uh. Can't make it that easy. Better start hunting, big boy. You've got five minutes or face the consequences."

As soon as Lisa's back with the shot, Foster's on the prowl. He starts by scanning the room for groups of girls who don't look like they have any hostile meathead boyfriends to worry about. Matt and Bucky hop out of their chairs and follow him for moral support and to record his conquest.

"Tick tock!" Olivia taunts him as we all watch his progress. "Better hurry."

In short order, Foster's got a redhead on her knees. I watch with wide, impressed eyes as the girl takes the shot and pops up with a cherry between her lips. Chick's got moves.

A few seconds later, Foster saunters back to our table with a dumb grin and his chest puffed out.

"Too easy," he says, then chugs his beer. "My turn now. Beth."

She smirks up at him. "Give me your best shot."

Foster and his teammates have a conference before daring Beth to make out with a girl of her choice while the two girls trade bras. Without the slightest hesitation Beth enlists Olivia, who, as I'm discovering tonight, possesses a wild streak as well as a pretty decent sense of humor. I don't know why we never hung out before.

Not wasting any time, the two Kappas stand up and lock lips while each tucks their arms into their shirts to undo their bras and pull them out of their sleeves then put on the new one. It happens so fast the men are left speechless and gawking.

"What just happened?" Cory asks stupidly.

"That's some kind of witchcraft right there," Conor remarks beside me.

I make the mistake of looking at Rebecca again, and this time she actually looks back. What ensues is the most awkward eye-locking in the history of mankind. I break visual contact when I hear someone say, "Taylor."

"Huh?" I turn at the sound of my name.

Olivia is fluttering her fingers together like a cartoon villain. "It's your turn. I dare you to…"

Oh, right. *That's* why we don't hang out. Because anyone who knows me well and whom I consider a friend wouldn't put me on the spot like this.

Sasha must read the panic on my face. "Oh come on. Hasn't Taylor done enough? I think she's earned her retirement."

"...To give Conor a lap dance," Olivia finishes gleefully.

Fuck my life.

Conor stiffens. His eyes meet mine, and although his expression reveals nothing, I can feel his concern. We haven't known each other long, but he's perceptive enough to know I'd rather accept the penalty of death than accept this embarrassing dare.

"Hell no," he declares, jumping to his feet. "I don't want a bunch of drunk perverts eyeing my girlfriend."

To my shock, he peels out of his hoodie. Now he's left in a tight white tank top that shows off his sculpted arms and washboard abs. Olivia audibly gasps.

He cocks his head suddenly, a slow grin spreading across his face. "Nice. Even got the music on my side," he drawls. Then he pulls my chair back a bit and stands between me and the table.

"What are you doing?" I yelp.

"Blowing your mind." He winks at me.

Dread fills my stomach when I recognize the song blasting from the bar's sound system. "Pour Some Sugar on Me" by Def Leppard. Oh fuck me.

"Don't," I beg Conor, fear trembling in my voice. "Please don't."

Rather than heed my pleas, he licks his lips, sways his hips, and launches into a raunchy performance.

Oh my fucking God.

My fake boyfriend is giving me a real lap dance.

"Work it, baby!" Beth catcalls, while Olivia and the other girls transform into the living personification of the heart-eyes emoji.

When I try to cover *my* eyes, he pulls my hands away and runs them down his abs. Then he presses them against his ass as he gyrates and undulates in front of me to cheers and whistles as the entire bar stops to watch.

As mortifying as the attention is, Conor is weirdly good at this. And after the initial terror subsides, it becomes pretty hilarious the way he's playing more goofy than sexy. I find myself laughing along with everyone else, as Foster and Bucky start shouting out the chorus of the song.

It's all fun and games until it isn't. Because then I blink and the humor on Conor's handsome turns into something headier. Heavy-lidded gray eyes fixed on me, he bends slightly and thrusts one hand through my hair. Long fingers tangle in the thick strands.

Time stops.

He's not dancing anymore. Not moving. Except, he *is* moving. He's closing in on me and I know what he's about to do. He's going to kiss me. He's going to kiss me *here*, in front of everyone at Malone's? No fucking way. He said he likes games, but this one has gotten out of hand.

Before he can press his lips to mine, I launch out of my chair so fast he nearly falls to the floor. I catch only a second of his bewildered look before I run off toward the back corridor. The door there leads out to the alley next to the parking lot, and I stumble into it, relieved to find it empty.

Heart pounding like crazy, I lean against the brick wall behind Malone's and peel out of my sweater to let the frigid air rush over my skin. My breath comes out as plumes of white, but sweat continues to bead across my chest. It's barely above freezing, yet in only a camisole I'm still burning up.

"Taylor!" The door flies open. "Taylor, you out here?"

I don't say a word, hiding in the building's shadow. I just want him to go away.

"Fuck, there you are." Conor appears in front of me with worry etched on his perfect face. "What's wrong? What happened?"

"Why would you do that?" I mutter, staring at the ground.

"What? I don't understand." He reaches for me and I step out of his grasp. "What did I do wrong? Just tell me so I can fix it."

"I can't do this. I don't want to be a game to you anymore."

"You're not a game," he protests.

"Bullshit. You told me you were bored and that you love games.

That's the reason you changed your stupid MyBri status and showed up at the diner tonight. This is some weird form of entertainment for you." I shake my head. "Well, I'm not entertained anymore."

"Taylor—"

"I'm sorry. I know this is my fault and I pulled you into it at the Kappa party, but I'm done. The game's over." I try to get around him but he blocks my path. "Conor. Move."

"No."

"Please. Just move. You don't have to pretend to be into me anymore."

"No," he repeats. "Listen to me. You're not a game. I mean, yeah, I did think it would be fun to fuck with your sorority sisters and talk about wedding vision boards and all that crazy shit, but I'm not pretending to be into you. I told you the night we met how hot I think you are."

I say nothing, avoiding his eyes.

"I didn't come out tonight because of who's watching. I came because I was sitting at home thinking about you and I couldn't stand it another minute."

I slowly lift my head. "Bullshit," I accuse again.

"Honest to God truth. I like being around you. I like talking to you."

"Then why do something so stupid and screw it all up by trying to kiss me?"

"Because I wanted to know what it felt like to kiss you and I was afraid we might never find out." The corner of his mouth quirks up. "Figured if I tried it in public, I had a better shot, 'cause then you might kiss me back for appearances."

"That's a dumb reason."

"I know." Tentatively, he takes a step toward me.

This time when he reaches out to take my hand in his, I let him.

"I thought I was helping just now," he says sheepishly. "I thought I was protecting you from having to do that ridiculous dare and we were having a laugh. I read it wrong and I'm sorry for that." His voice thickens. "But I know I'm not reading *this* wrong." His thumb rubs the inside of my palm, and I gulp. "You like me."

Ugh. This was all so simple just a few days ago. Wasn't it? A little gag between friends. Now we've crossed over and there's no going back. We don't get to pretend the sexual tension is a joke, that the casual flirting doesn't mean anything, that someone isn't going to get hurt.

In this case, "someone" means me.

"I don't know where to go from here," I start awkwardly, "except that maybe it'd be better if we didn't hang out anymore."

"No."

"No?"

"Yeah, I veto that suggestion."

"You don't get a veto. If I say I don't want to hang out with you anymore, then tough shit. That's the way it is."

"I think you should let me kiss you."

"Because you were probably dropped on your head as a child," I snap back.

At that, Conor cracks a smile. He lets out a breath and squeezes my hand, then places it against his chest. Beneath my palm, his heart is pounding hard.

"I think there's something here." There's a note of challenge in his voice. "And I think you're afraid to find out what it is. Not sure why, though. Maybe you don't think you deserve it, I dunno. But that's a fucking tragedy, because you of all people deserve to be happy. So here it is: I'm going to kiss you, unless you tell me not to. Okay?"

I'm going to regret this. Even as I lick my lips and tilt my head, I know I'm going to regret this. But the word "no" refuses to exit my mouth.

"Okay," I finally whisper.

He takes full advantage of my acquiescence, leaning in to brush his lips against mine.

At first it's the lightest of caresses, but it doesn't take long for his kiss to grow deep, urgent. When I weave my arms up his shoulders and comb my fingers into his hair, he makes the sexiest sound against my mouth. Half groan, half sigh.

I feel his entire body clench against mine. His hands go to my hips, fingers biting into my bare skin, and presses me against the wall until there's no light left between us.

His mouth, so gentle yet hungry, the heat of his body, and the feel of his muscles caging me...it's surreal, thrilling. As desire courses through my veins, I kiss him back desperately. I forget myself. I forget where we are and all the reasons we shouldn't do this.

"You taste like cinnamon," he mumbles, and then his tongue is exploring again, slicking over mine and summoning a moan from deep in my throat.

I cling to him, completely and totally addicted to the feel of his mouth against mine. I drag my teeth over his bottom lip and feel rather than hear the groan vibrate in his chest. His hands slide up my ribs, pushing beneath my shirt, until they're just beneath my breasts. I suddenly wish I didn't take off my sweater, that I had an extra layer of protection between my flesh and Conor's seductive touch.

"You get me so hot, Taylor."

His lips find my neck and then he's sucking on it, triggering a flurry of shivers. His lower body bumps mine, hips giving a slow sensual thrust that makes me moan again.

He kisses me again, his tongue teasing the seam of my lips. Then he pulls back and I see the same needy, hungry lust I'm feeling reflected back at me in his eyes.

"Come home with me tonight," Conor Fucking Edwards whispers.

And that's what breaks the spell.

Breathing hard, I drop my hands from his broad shoulders and let them dangle at my sides.

Dammit. *Dammit*, what's wrong with me? I'm no clairvoyant, but I don't need to be one to see how all this is going to play out.

I go back to his place.

I lose my virginity to him.

He rocks my world for one amazing night.

And then next week I'm just another sad sap raising my hand along with his other conquests when asked who there has hooked up with him.

"Taylor?" He's still watching me. Waiting.

I bite my lip. Easing away from the heat of his body, I slowly shake my head and say, "Will you drive me home?"

12
CONOR

I can't get a read on Taylor. Outside the bar I thought we had a connection. I might be a fucking idiot sometimes, but I know when a girl is kissing me back. She definitely felt something. But the moment we stopped, she shut down again, slammed a door in my face, and now I'm driving her home with the distinct impression she's mad at me again.

I can't figure out what she wants from me. I'd leave her alone, stay out of her life, if I believed that's what Taylor really wanted, but I don't think that's the case.

"Did I make a mistake kissing you?" I ask, glancing over at the passenger side.

She put her sweater back on, which is a damn shame. The silky top she had on before was hot as hell. My dick is still aching for her.

She's silent for a long time, looking out the window like she can't get far enough away from me. Finally, she spares me a quick look and says, "It was a nice kiss."

Nice?

Well, fuck me. That's the most lukewarm response to a kiss I've ever received. And I'm not sure it answers my question.

"Then what's wrong?" I press.

"It's just…" She lets out a sigh. "I mean, think about all those people at the bar looking at us."

Frankly, I didn't even notice anyone else. When I'm with her, I'm only watching Taylor. Something about her reels me in, and it's not just the fact that my body is primed for her. Yes, I'd love to bang her brains out, but that's not the reason I showed up at the diner uninvited earlier.

Taylor Marsh has no idea how cool she is, and that's a fucking shame.

"I'm sorry if I embarrassed you," I say gruffly. "That wasn't my intention."

"No, I know. But come on, you have to know what people would say about someone like you with someone like me."

"I'm not sure what you mean."

"Damn it, Conor, don't act like it isn't obvious. I get it, you're trying to make me feel better and that's sweet, but let's be real. People see us and they think, what is *he* doing with *her*? We're a punch line."

"Bullshit. I don't believe that."

"Oh my God, you heard it yourself at the banquet! You *heard* all the shit Abigail and her douche army were saying about us."

"So what? I don't give a shit what other people think." I don't live my life on the basis of other people's opinions or to please anyone but myself. If she'd just fucking let me, I'd like to try pleasing Taylor, too.

"Well, maybe you should. Because I can assure you, they're not thinking nice things about us."

There's ice in her voice that I've never heard from her before. Hatred, even. It's not directed at me, but I'm starting to get a sense of how deep her insecurities go.

My next breath comes out ragged, frustrated. "I'll keep saying this until it sinks in, but there's nothing wrong with you, Taylor. There isn't some arbitrary hierarchy between us. I *want* you. I've wanted you since the moment I watched you cross the room at that party."

Her turquoise eyes widen slightly.

"I mean it," I say. "I have a thousand filthy thoughts about you a day. That night in my room when you were running your fingers through my hair, I had half a hard-on just lying there."

I pull up outside Taylor's apartment building and throw the Jeep in park. I angle my body so I'm facing her, but her eyes remain fixed forward.

The frustration builds again. "I get it. You're insecure. Whatever you've experienced in your life, it's made you hate the way you look and hide yourself in leggings and baggy sweaters."

Finally she turns her head. "You have no idea what it's like to be me," she says flatly.

"I don't. But I think if you tried, just a little, to accept yourself, you might figure out that everyone else has their own insecurities too. And maybe you'll believe a guy when he tells you he's wildly attracted to you." I shrug. "Wear whatever the hell you want, Taylor. But your body is incredible and you should be able to flaunt it, not live your life in a paper bag."

She abruptly rips off her seatbelt and grabs the door handle.

"Taylor—"

"Goodnight, Conor. Thanks for the ride."

Then she's gone, slamming the door.

The fuck did I do?

I want to hop out and run after her, but I recognize the internal voice that's urging me to do that. It's that voice in the back of my head where all my really dumb ideas come from. The self-destructive, self-deprecating jackass who takes anything good and easy and pure and just fucking starts tearing at it with his teeth.

Truth is, Taylor doesn't actually know me at all. She has no idea the shithead I was back in LA or the shit I did to fit in. She has no idea that most of the time I *still* don't fit—here, there, or anywhere at all. That for years I've been trying on masks until I've almost forgotten what I look like underneath. Never satisfied with the result.

I keep trying to convince Taylor to go easy on herself, appreciate her body and who she is, but I can't even convince myself. So what the hell am I doing getting wrapped up with a girl like her—a good person who doesn't need my bullshit—when I haven't even gotten myself figured out?

Sighing, I reach for the gearshift. Instead of running after Taylor, I drive home. And I tell myself it's for the best.

13
TAYLOR

I'M RELIEVED WHEN MY MOM DRIVES IN FROM CAMBRIDGE ON Thursday to have lunch. After two days of dodging calls from Conor and questions from Sasha about what happened the other night, I need a distraction.

We hit up the new vegan place in Hastings. Partly because my mother grumbles at the idea of choking down another greasy meal at the diner and mostly because eating carbs in front of her always gives me anxiety. I look like Mom's "before" image in the Before and After shots of some European med spa commercial. Iris Marsh is tall, skinny, and utterly gorgeous. She'd given me hope during puberty that any day I'd wake up and look like her younger clone. I was sixteen before it hit me that wasn't going to happen. Guess I only got my father's genes.

"How are your classes going?" she asks, draping her coat over the back of her chair as we sit with our meals. "Are you enjoying your co-op?"

"Yeah, it's great. I definitely know elementary education is where I want to be. The kids are terrific." I shake my head in amazement. "And they learn so fast. It's incredible to watch their development over such a short period of time."

I always knew I wanted to be teacher. Mom briefly tried to convince me to pursue a professor track like her, but that was a non-starter. The idea of getting up in front of a room full of college kids every day, being dissected under their scrutiny—I'd be breaking out in hives. No, with little kids, they're engineered to see teachers as authority figures first. If you treat them fairly and with kindness and compassion, they love you. Sure, there are always the brats and bullies, but at that age, kids aren't nearly as judgmental.

"What about you?" I ask. "How's work?"

Mom offers a wry smile. "We're almost through the worst of the *Chernobyl* effect. Unfortunately, it also means the research windfall has mostly dried up. Nice while it lasted, though."

I laugh in response. The HBO series was the best and worst thing to happen to Mom's nuclear science and engineering department at MIT since Fukushima. The sudden popularity brought a renewed energy to anti-nuke demonstrators who started gathering near campus or outside conferences. It also meant the research grants came pouring in, along with every fanboy who thought he was going to save the world. Except then they realize there's a lot more money in robotics, automation, and aerospace engineering, and switch majors before their parents find out their tuition checks were feeding fantasies brought on by the guy who wrote *Scary Movie 4*. Good show, though.

"We've also finally filled Dr. Matsoukas' old position. We hired a young woman from Suriname who studied with Alexis at Michigan State."

Dr. Alexis Branchaud, or Aunt Alexis as she was known when she used to stay with us during visiting lectures at MIT, is like Mom's evil French twin. The two of them with a bottle of Bacardi 151 were a natural disaster. For a while, I wondered if maybe Aunt Alexis was the reason I rarely saw my mom date.

"It'll be the first time the department will be majority female."

"Nice. Smashing atoms and the patriarchy. And what about extra-curriculars?" I ask.

She grins. "You know, normal kids don't want to hear about their mothers' sex lives."

"And whose fault is that?"

"You have a point."

"It's big of you to say so."

"Honestly," she says, "I've been swamped with work. The department is overhauling the curriculum for the master's thesis next year and Dr. Rapp and I have been taking care of Dr. Matsoukas' advisees. Elaine set me up with her husband's racquetball partner last month, but I draw a hard line at middle-aged men who still bite their fingernails."

"I have a fake boyfriend."

I don't know why I blurt that out. Probably low blood sugar. I didn't eat breakfast this morning and only had a bowl of grapes for dinner last night while I was studying for a quiz in diagnostic and corrective reading strategies.

"Okay." My mother looks justifiably baffled. "Define fake boyfriend."

"Well, it started off as a dare, and then it sort of became a joke. Now we might not be friends anymore because I might have gotten mad at him for trying to like me for real and I keep ignoring his text messages."

"Uh-huh," is her response. Her ocean-blue eyes narrow in that way they do when she's evaluating a puzzle. My mom's always been brilliant. Easily the smartest person I know. But when it comes to me, I've never felt like we were working off the same reading material. "Have you tried liking him back?"

"Definitely not."

Okay, maybe that isn't true. I know if I let myself, I would absolutely develop feelings for Conor. I've been replaying our kiss over and over again in my head since the second he dropped me off at home. I could barely concentrate on studying last night because I can't stop thinking about the firmness of his lips, the heat of his body, the feel of his rock-hard cock pressing against my belly.

There was no denying he'd wanted me that night. He asked me

to go home with him because he wanted to fuck me, no doubt about that.

But that's the problem. I know the minute I give in, Conor will wake up from this daydream to realize he should be with someone much hotter. I've seen the girls that the guys on his team date—I'd stick out like a fat sore thumb.

I'm not interested in being the collateral damage once Conor figures that out.

"Well, what did you fight about?" Mom asks curiously.

"It's not important. It's dumb that I even brought it up." I move my fork around the remnants of cauliflower rice in my bowl and try to psyche myself up for finishing it. "We've only known each other a few weeks anyway. I blame the punch bowl at the Kappa party. I should know better than to drink out of a five-gallon paint bucket."

"Yes," she says, grinning, "I should think I raised you better than that."

As we're walking back to her car, though, something dislodges itself from the back of my mind.

"Mom?"

"Yeah?"

"Do you think I…" *Dress like a bag lady? Have the fashion sense of a literary school marm? Am doomed to live out my life as a spinster?* "Do you think the way I dress says I'm embarrassed by the way I look?"

She stops beside the car and meets my eyes with sympathy. Even with her more minimalist style, which has generally consisted of blacks, whites, and grays, she always looks so fashionable and put together. Easy, I guess, when clothes are designed for exactly your body type.

It was always difficult growing up with a mom like her. Not that she didn't try—she was my consummate cheerleader and booster of self-esteem. Constantly telling me how beautiful I was, how proud she was of me, how she *wished* she had hair as thick and lustrous as mine. But despite her efforts, I couldn't help comparing myself to her in a vicious cycle of self-defeat.

"I think your clothes say nothing about your intelligence, your kindness, your wit, and humor," Mom says tactfully. "I think you ought to dress however you feel most comfortable. With that said... if you don't feel comfortable with the way you dress, perhaps that's a conversation you need to have with your heart rather than your closet."

Well, that's one vote in the bag lady column from Mom.

On the walk up to my apartment after saying bye to my mother, I decide to bite the bullet and text Conor.

ME: You home?

A ball of anxiety coils in my gut once I hit send. After ignoring him for two days, he'd have every right to have written me off by now. I was kind of a bitch the other night, I'm well aware of this. Despite his lack of social graces, Conor hadn't meant to offend me, and there was no reason to storm off the way I did. None, except that I was feeling insecure and vulnerable and generally sick of myself, so I took it out on him rather than explaining how I felt.

The screen lights up.

CONOR: Yeah.
ME: Coming over, k?
CONOR: Yeah.

Back-to-back "yeahs" aren't exactly promising, but at least he hasn't ghosted.

When he answers the door ten minutes later, hastily yanking a T-shirt down over his bare chest, I'm hit with the same flutter of desire I felt during our kiss, like pin pricks of electricity zipping up my spine. My lips remember his. My skin buzzes with the memory of his hands sliding up my ribs. Oh boy. This is going to be much harder than I expected.

"Hey," I say, because my brain is still half in the parking lot outside Malone's.

"Hey." Conor holds the door open and nods for me to enter. His roommates are either out or hiding as he leads me upstairs to his bedroom.

Fuck. I'd even missed the way his room smells. Like his shampoo that smells like the ocean, and whatever cologne he wore Tuesday night.

"Taylor, I want—"

"No." I stop him, holding my hand out to keep some air between us. I can't think straight when he's in my bubble. "Me first."

"Okay then." Shrugging, he takes a seat on the small love seat while I gather my nerves.

"I was shitty to you the other night," I say ruefully. "And I'm sorry. You were right—I was embarrassed. I don't like attention—good or bad. So having a room full of people staring at me is like the fucking worst. But you only did that silly lap dance because you thought you were saving me from a much worse fate, and I didn't thank you or at least give you some credit for trying. That wasn't fair. And then with the…" Somehow I don't think I can say "kiss" out loud without moaning, "…the outside stuff, I panicked. That wasn't your fault."

"Well, except for when I started in with the fashion advice," he points out with a self-deprecating smile.

"Yeah, no, that one was all you, jerkface. You shoulda known better."

"Trust me, I know. I already got an earful from both Demi and Summer. Friends' girlfriends," he clarifies when he notices my blank look.

"You talked to your friends' girlfriends about our fight?" For some reason, I'm oddly touched.

"Yeah." He shrugs adorably. "Needed someone to tell me where I fucked up. Apparently the clothing critique was a crime against your womanhood."

I snort.

Conor holds up his hands in surrender. "And it wasn't even what I meant to say. My brain just short circuited after…" Mimicking me a little, he winks and says, "*the outside stuff*, and I lost all control of my better judgment or the part that stops me from making an ass of myself." He flashes that cheeky smile that never fails to make my heart race. "Forgive me?"

"You're forgiven." I pause. "Forgive me for bitching out on you?"

"You're forgiven." Tentatively, he stands, inching toward me. He towers over me with his athletic frame. "So. Friends again?"

"Friends."

Conor pulls me in for a hug and it's like I never left his arms. I don't know if I want it to stop. I don't know how he does it, makes me feel so comfortable with just a hug or a smile.

"Want a ride to campus with me? I've got class in an hour. We can grab some coffee?"

"Sounds good." I sit on his bed as he gets dressed and comes in and out of his bathroom gathering his stuff. "I was wondering something."

"Yeah?" He stops in the doorway with his toothbrush in his mouth.

"Would you want to hang out this weekend? Maybe come shopping with me in Boston?"

Conor holds up one finger and disappears. A few seconds later, he returns wiping his mouth with a washcloth. "I can't, babe. I've got a semi-final game in Buffalo."

"Oh, shit, right. I knew that. No biggie. Some other—"

"Take my Jeep." Conor tosses the washcloth in his laundry hamper.

"What?"

"Yeah, come to my game," he says, his eyes lighting up. "You drive down to Buffalo in my Jeep and I'll ask Coach for permission to skip out on the bus ride back. We can stay an extra night and go shopping, hang out, whatever."

"Are you sure? I feel like that's a big ask."

He aims his crooked smirk at me. Pulling out the heavy artillery, I see. "If we win, I want you there to celebrate with us. If we lose, you can get me drunk and help me feel better."

"Oh yeah? I don't know if I'm prepared for the kind of ego stroking that would require."

He laughs at the innuendo. It feels good being able to joke around again. All we have to do is pretend that foolish kiss never happened, and everything can just go back to the way it was before.

That is, if we both ignore the implications of spending a weekend out of town together.

"So it's a plan?" he asks.

"Wouldn't miss it," I say lightly.

"Nice." He gathers his backpack and we head downstairs to the front hall. Conor opens the door and gestures for me to exit first. "So, not that I'm not grateful for the invite, but why are we going shopping?"

I wink at him over my shoulder. "I'm giving myself a makeover."

14

CONOR

The semi-final against Minnesota is a headbanger from the first whistle. Thanks to some trash talking on social media, our team goes into the game Friday night hot and ready to eat those asshats for dinner. We're sticking to our game plan, though—high press, be physical. Minnesota is a technical team, but they won't be able to absorb our pressure for sixty minutes. We won't let them touch the puck without feeling us breathing down their necks. Every pass we'll let them know we're going to make it hurt.

We end scoreless after the first period. Then right out of the gate in the second, Hunter gets the puck on a breakaway and fires it into the net to put us on the board first.

"Atta boy!" Coach thunders from the bench, smacking his clipboard against the Plexi.

He calls for a line change, and Hunter and I heave ourselves over the wall and squirt water into our mouths from bottles brandishing the Gatorade logo. The rest of our line settles on the bench, all eyes glued to the ice. The Briar D-men are struggling to keep Minnesota out of our zone, Coach barking for them to get it together.

"Dude, you need to do that exact same move again," Bucky's saying to Hunter. "Deke that ginger-haired fuck and just book it—he's not fast enough to keep up with you."

Bucky's right. Hunter's the fastest man on the ice tonight. Nobody can stop him.

We change on the fly, substituting Alec and Gavin for me and the captain. We hit the ice hard, ready to extend our lead by another goal. But Minnesota must be seeing their life flash before their eyes, because the next time Hunter receives a pass, number nineteen for Minnesota slams him into the boards. I see fucking red watching my team captain hit the ice, and before the whistle even blows I've got that asshole against the glass.

"Get off me, pretty boy," he growls.

"Make me."

We exchange some punches and elbows. At one point I feel someone wailing on me with jabs to my ribs as both benches clear to take sides in the fight. Ultimately, nineteen and I both sit in our respective penalty boxes for the brawl. Fucking worth it.

Minnesota ties it up with a wrist shot from one of their forwards just as the second period winds down. We trudge into our locker room feeling the heavy weight of that score, 1–1, bearing down on our shoulders.

"Unacceptable!" Coach Jensen rides our D-men the moment the door swings shut. "We let them dominate us those last three minutes. Where was our defense, huh? Jerking off in the corner?"

Matt, who was the leading scorer among the defense all season, hangs his head in shame. "Sorry, Coach. That one's on me. Couldn't intercept that pass."

"We got this, Coach," Hunter says, steel in his eyes. "We'll finish 'em off in the third."

But everything goes wrong in the third period.

Gavin crumples to the ice out of nowhere with a pulled hamstring and has to exit the game. Matt then gets tossed in the sin bin on a major penalty. We manage to kill it, but with the clock winding down it seems Minnesota is picking us apart. They're catching their second wind while half of us are gassing out. Maintaining the high pressure becomes more difficult and cracks form in our defense. The offense can't find any openings to force turnovers or break away.

The game turns into an uphill, brutal battle for us. Our opponent is now faster and more aggressive, and that's when it happens. Minnesota strings together four uninterrupted passes and catches all of us a step too slow. Their left-winger slaps the puck past our goalie Boris's glove to put Minnesota up by a point.

It's one point too many.

We can't claw our way back. The buzzer goes off to signal the end of the third. The end of the game.

We've been eliminated.

Back in the locker room, it's like a fucking wake. No one says a word or even looks at each other. Gavin, with ice taped to his thigh, launches a trashcan across the room, and the resounding crash makes everyone flinch. As a senior, this was his last chance for a championship, and he couldn't even finish the game. No matter what anyone says, he'll be convinced for the rest of his life that he could've made the difference. Same for Matt, who will torture himself with the guilt that taking that penalty cost us the momentum we might've had to tie it up.

When Coach Jensen walks in, the room is silent but for the rotating fan whirring in the corner.

"This one hurts," he says flatly, rubbing his jaw. He's sweating nearly as much as the rest of us.

Negative emotions pollute the air we're breathing. Anger, frustration, disappointment. And the exhaustion of playing at such a high level for so long is slowly seeping into our bones, causing shoulders to sag and chins to drop.

"That's not how we wanted to go out," Coach continues. "For the seniors, I wanted to get you guys to the big dance—we just didn't have it tonight. For everyone else, we do it all again next year."

Next year.

Hunter and I exchange a determined look. As juniors, we have one last shot to leave a legacy at Briar. Gold and glory and all that.

Straying from his usual short-and-not-at-all-sweet style, Coach goes on to say he's encouraged by the way we played tonight, by the progress we've made since the start of the season.

I choose to believe better days are ahead, because right now the feeling in this room is miserable. A dream died tonight. And it's only now, I think, that most of us are realizing we were entirely convinced we had this title in the bag. It never occurred to us we wouldn't be playing in the final. Now we just go home and pretend it doesn't gnaw at our insides.

I fucking hate losing.

15

TAYLOR

FRIDAY NIGHT WAS ROUGH. AFTER BRIAR'S EPIC LOSS, THE GUYS hit the mini bar hard and then crashed until noon the next day.

I'm not entirely sure why Conor wanted me to drive all the way to Buffalo, seeing as how I spent the hours after his game having drinks with Brenna Jensen and Summer Di Laurentis, two of Hunter Davenport's roommates, and Demi Davis, Hunter's girlfriend. The four of us had a proper girls' night. We had a great time at the hotel bar, and I won't deny how helpful it was to sit with them during the game, as they were able to explain the rules when something happened that I didn't understand.

Although, to be honest, I still couldn't tell you what offsides means or what constitutes icing. Conor getting a time-out for tackling a guy, I figured out on my own. But the rest of the hockey lingo Brenna was throwing out like a pro went right over my head. As I understand it, hockey is basically a bunch of first graders fighting over a little black puck while the referee tries to keep them from killing each other. It's cute.

Coach Jensen gave anyone who wanted to permission to hang back in Buffalo, a consolation gift of sorts, so several of Conor's teammates paid for an extra night at the hotel. I've got my room till Sunday, on another floor than the Briar players, thankfully. I ran into Demi in the tiny hotel fitness center this morning, and according to her, the entire fifth floor was hoppin' from last night's depression binge drinking. She said she and Hunter hadn't gotten a wink of sleep.

Despite Conor saying the other day that he was going to need consoling, we barely exchanged ten words after the game. He was commiserating with his teammates, which I understand. But I'm grateful the girls were around to keep me company.

Everyone seems to be in better spirits this morning. In the hotel restaurant, I meet Conor for brunch, along with a few of the others who stayed behind.

"Where're Brenna and Summer?" I slide into the chair next to Conor's and set down the plate of food I just gathered at the buffet. And by food I mean brown toast and one hard-boiled egg. Yum. "And Demi," I add when I notice Hunter is sitting alone.

"Brenna's Skyping with her boyfriend," Bucky supplies. "She's in the room next to mine and I heard them through the wall."

"Perv," Conor says while chewing on a piece of bacon.

"Hey, not my fault this hotel has paper-thin walls."

"Summer dragged Demi on some errand," Hunter tells me. "No idea where."

"What's 'a matter?" Foster grins at me. "You don't like being the only chick at the sausage party?" To punctuate that, he picks up a greasy sausage from his plate and takes a comical chunk out of it with his teeth.

I burst out laughing. "There is so much subliminal shit going on with what you just did, I can't even begin to unpack it."

Across the table, Hunter raises his coffee cup and takes a quick sip. "So what are we doing today?"

"T and I are hitting a mall," Conor answers in that lazy drawl of his.

"Sweet. Can I come?" Bucky pipes up. "I need socks. Already lost all the ones my mom got me for Christmas."

"I'm in too," says Hunter. "My girlfriend abandoned me and I'm bored."

I slowly chew and swallow a piece of toast. "Um." Feeling awkward, I glance at Conor, then his teammates. "This isn't exactly a group activity sorta thing."

Hunter lifts a brow. "The mall isn't a suitable group activity?"

"They're going to buy sex toys," Foster announces. "Guarantee it."

"We're not buying sex toys!" I sputter, then turn redder than a beet when I notice every head at the neighboring table swivel my way. I glower at Foster. "You're the worst."

"Or am I the best?" he counters.

"No, you're the worst," Hunter confirms, grinning.

"If you must know, I need some new clothes," I reveal with a sigh. "Conor's going to help me pick some out."

"What, and we can't tag along and help too?" demands Bucky. I can't tell if the wounded look on his face is for real. "You saying we have no style?"

"Oh, I got style," Hunter declares, crossing his arms over his chest.

Foster dons the same macho posture. "I've got so much style, you don't even know."

"You're right, I don't," I say dryly, shooting a pointed look at Foster's T-shirt, which appears to feature a cartoon image of a wolf riding a dragon over a sea of fire. Whether it's dragon fire is undetermined.

Foster polishes off the rest of his sausage. "All right, crew. Let's do this shit."

———

And that's how I end up at the mall a couple miles from the hotel, with four towering, imposing men standing outside my dressing room at Bloomingdale's throwing clothes at me like it's a timed collegiate event.

I barely wiggle out of one pair of designer distressed skinny jeans before an avalanche of shirts and dresses come cascading over the door.

"I think we're reaching the singularity here, guys," I call out in dismay.

"Change faster," Conor shouts through the door.

"Foster just found a whole wall full of sequins," Hunter adds like a threat.

"I don't think I have much need in my wardrobe for—" Another tidal wave of dresses falls to the floor. "That's it. We need to lay some ground rules."

I step out of the dressing room in a long-sleeved plaid shirt that cinches under my boobs and flares at the waist and a coordinating pair of dark wash skinny jeans. It's not a bad look, managing to hide the parts I'd rather not share, without looking like I hopped out of bed wearing my duvet.

Conor pops an eyebrow at me. Hunter and Bucky give polite golf claps. The three of them are standing there in full albeit ill-fitting tuxedos.

I gawk at them, too stunned to even laugh. "Wha—why—why the hell are you wearing tuxedos?"

"Why not?" is Bucky's response, and this time I can't stop the gales of laughter that pour out. Jeez. How did these clowns even have time to change clothes while burying me in fabric?

"You're getting that outfit," Conor tells me, and there's all sorts of intention behind his eyes. It's downright indecent the way he drags his gaze over my body. With an audience, no less.

And yet, under his scrutiny, I don't feel self-conscious the way I do with others. When Conor is with me, he puts my nerves at ease.

"Yeah, I like this one," I admit. Then I frown. "With that said, I'm up to my knees in here, you maniacs. Let's try to restrict it to two outfits each, shall we?"

"Aww, come on, we haven't even discussed evening wear," Bucky pouts.

"Or scarves. How many scarves do you think you'll need?" Hunter asks.

"Is statement jewelry something we should be looking at?" Foster weaves his way to the front of the group with two armfuls of cocktail dresses.

"What's your cup size?"

Conor smacks Bucky on the back of the head. "You don't get to ask my girlfriend her cup size, dickhead."

My heart does a little flip. That's the first time he's said the G-word since our fight. I wasn't sure we were still doing this, so hearing it does confusing things to my head.

"Here." I gather up the piles at my feet and push them at the boys. "Restriction measures are in place."

I close the door to someone muttering "fascist" under his breath.

After we've done all the damage Bloomingdale's can handle, we move on through the mall, Conor carrying my two shopping bags.

It's interesting to see the difference in styles each of the guys picks out. Conor seems to know me the best, or at least our tastes fit most closely together, as he picks the more casual options. Very California. Hunter tends toward an edgier look with a lot of black. Bucky has some sort of preppy fetish that I quickly steer clear from, and I'm not sure Foster understands the assignment. What I do learn, however, is that hardly any of them agree on which looks were their favorites. Not at all what I expected in terms of engineering their ideal version of a Taylor Barbie.

At one point, Conor's teammates drag us into the toy store where they challenge a couple of middle-schoolers to a lightsaber fight before getting us kicked out for scaring customers with *IT* masks. After lunch at the food court, the guys have exhausted their enthusiasm for the mall and head out to find new trouble, leaving Conor and me alone for the first time all day.

Our first stop is a surf and skate shop. Seems only fair that I get to play dress-up with him too, so with a dozen boardshorts I shove him into a dressing room.

"What's your plan for summer?" he asks through the door.

"Back to my mom's house in Cambridge. She only has one seminar for summer semester, so we were thinking about taking a trip somewhere, maybe Europe. You going home to California?"

"For a little while, at least." There's a heavy sigh in the dressing room. "This is the farthest I've ever lived from the water. I used to go to the beach and surf just about every day. I've tried to get out to the coast a few times since I transferred to Briar, but it isn't the same."

Conor steps out in the first selection of boardshorts.

It takes every ounce of willpower not to throw myself at him. He stands there shirtless, leaning against the door of his dressing room and looking absolutely edible. The deep ravine of muscle that disappears into his waistband is doing things to me. It isn't fair.

"Not bad," I say flippantly.

"Orange isn't my color."

"Agree. Next."

He goes back inside, tossing the discarded trunks to me as he changes. "You should come."

"Where? To California?"

"Yeah. Come out for a long weekend or something. We can do tourist shit and hang out at the beach. Just chill."

"Teach me how to surf?" I tease.

He emerges in another pair of shorts. I've stopped caring about the colors and patterns of the fabric and given in to blatantly gawking at his leanly muscular physique and the way his abs clench when he talks.

Would it be inappropriate to lick him?

"You'd love it," he tells me. "Man, I wish I could go back and get stoked on my first wave all over again. It's the best feeling in the world, lining up for a wave, feeling it rise beneath your board. When you get to your feet and you're both connected—you and the power of the ocean—it's symbiosis. It's freedom, baby. Perfect alignment of energy."

"You're in love."

He laughs at himself with a boyish grin. "My first love." Again he steps back into the dressing room stall. "Last summer I spent a month with some volunteers canvasing the coast from San Diego to San Francisco."

I wrinkle my forehead. "Doing what?"

"Cleaning up the beaches and sweeping the near-shore waters for trash. It was one of the best months of my life. We hauled hundreds of pounds of garbage out of the ocean and off the sand every day, then we'd surf all night and hang out around a bonfire. Felt like we were accomplishing something."

"You're passionate about this," I say, admiring this side of him. It's the first time he's talked about his interests outside of hockey and surfing. "Is that something you want to do after college?"

"What do you mean?" He comes out in another suit.

"Well, you could make a career out of this. There are probably dozens of environmental non-profits working on the west coast on ocean cleanup efforts." I cock an eyebrow. "It might not be too late to change majors from finance to non-profit administration and still graduate on time."

"I'm sure my stepdad would love that."

"Why does it matter?"

A tired expression washes over Conor. Not just his face, but all of him. He slouches, hunching his shoulders, like the weight of the topic is wearing on him.

"Max pays for everything," he admits. "My education, hockey, rent—all of it. Without him, my mom and I would barely have two cents to rub together. So when he suggested I major in finance like he did, Mom considered the matter settled and that was it."

"Okay, I get that he holds the purse strings, but it's your life. At some point you have to advocate for what you want. No one else will."

"It felt, I don't know, ungrateful to argue with him? Like I'd be an asshole to take his money and tell him to fuck off."

"Yeah, using the words 'fuck off' might be a bit harsh, but a frank conversation about how you want to spend the rest of your life isn't out of line."

"But the thing is, we don't talk. I know he loves my mom, and he's good to her, but with me, I think he still sees a punk from LA who isn't worth his time."

"And why would he think that?" I ask quietly.

"I got into some bad stuff as a kid. I was dumb and did whatever my friends were doing, which was usually getting high, shoplifting, breaking into abandoned buildings, whatever." Conor looks at me with guilt. Shame, even. "I was a little shit back then."

It's clear in his expression he's afraid I'll view him differently, but none of this changes who he is now. "Well, seems to me you're not a little shit anymore. So I hope your stepdad doesn't think you're still like that, and I'm really sorry if he does."

Conor shrugs, and I get the sense there's more to the story than he's willing to share. His relationship with his stepfather is obviously a real source of insecurities and frustrations.

"You know what would cheer me up?" he says suddenly.

A mischievous twinkle lights in his eyes, sparking my suspicion. "What?"

He walks past me to pull a skimpy black swimsuit off the returns rack near his dressing room. "Put this on."

"No way. It won't fit me," I warn.

"I'll get naked if it'll make you feel better?"

"How would that make me feel better?"

He shrugs again, offering a devilish smirk this time. "Always seems to work on other girls."

Rolling my eyes, I take the suit from his outstretched hand and duck to the next stall. I would never, ever dream of doing this for any other guy, but I know making a joke of it and doing a little runway turn for Conor will take away the dark cloud threatening to settle over his mood. So to salvage the rest of our day, I strip out of my leggings and sweater and put on the damn one-piece.

It's cut low on my hips with a deep V in front and crisscrossed straps in the back. As predicted, it's too small. My ass cheeks are barely contained, and my tits are trying to scale the walls like an attacking enemy horde. Nevertheless, I take a deep breath and step out of the dressing room.

Conor is waiting out there for me, still clad only in a pair of boardshorts, his long blond hair swept back from his face.

His mouth falls open in shock.

"Here. Don't say I never gave you anything," I tell him.

So fast I can't hold in the yelp that escapes me, Conor lurches forward and rushes us back into the stall, locking the door.

"What the hell are—"

His mouth is on mine before I can finish. Hungry, predatory. Big palms curl around my hips as I'm pressed against the mirror. His tongue parts my lips and all trepidation evaporates as my fingers tangle in his hair. I'm overwhelmed with him. Skin against skin, so very little separating us. His body is warm and firm against mine.

"Fuck, Taylor," he whispers breathlessly. "Now do you understand how hot you are?"

He's hard against my stomach. I feel every inch of him, long and stiff, and it puts ideas in my head. Dangerous ideas. I want to slide my hand under his waistband and grip his hot, heavy erection. I want to feel his tongue in my mouth while I stroke him until he's moaning my name and thrusting his hips and—

A loud knock startles us.

We break away and I hurry to pull on my clothes over the swimsuit before Conor opens the door to the frowning saleswoman standing in the hall.

Without an ounce of shame, my fake boyfriend scratches his bare chest and says, "Sorry, ma'am. My girlfriend needed an opinion."

I choke down a wave of giggles. "Sorry," I manage to say.

"Hrmmmph," she huffs, then stands there and waits while

Conor disappears to put on his clothes. With his trademark grin, he hands her the boardshorts, while I yank the tag from the swimsuit.

Avoiding his amused gaze, I address the sales associate. "I'd like to buy this bathing suit, please," I say primly.

We're both practically in hysterics at the register as I pay for the indecent swimsuit beneath my clothes. Then we both bolt from the store like we stole something, laughing all the way back to his Jeep. After the heat and hunger I felt in that dressing room, this bit of levity is much needed. Levity, good. Hunger, bad.

Yup, hungering for Conor Edwards is very, very bad.

Because he's exactly the kind of man who will break my heart. Even if he doesn't mean to.

16
CONOR

HUNTER'S HOLDING UP A SHOT GLASS AT THE BAR, LEADING US IN what I'm sure is a moving speech about the tough loss in the semi-finals last night and wishing the seniors well while the rest of us look to better days next year. Unfortunately, I can't hear a damn thing over the music in this club. The bass is rattling the ice in the discarded glass beside me. The floor vibrating beneath my feet is sending a tickle all the way up to my balls.

When Hunter stops talking, we all down our shots and chase the sting with a beer. Man, I'm going to miss these assholes.

Foster bumps my arm and says something to me, but I still can't hear a word so I gesture to my ear and shake my head. He leans in to shout, "Where's your woman?"

Good question. When Taylor and I returned to the hotel earlier, I got a text from Summer in all caps demanding to know why she hadn't been invited on the shopping trip. I reminded her that she and Demi had skipped out on brunch to run errands, to which she informed me that "my conspiracy to keep her away from malls ends today."

Have I mentioned that Summer is banana pants?

A follow-up text quickly appeared demanding that I leave Taylor in Summer's fashionista hands to prepare for our night at the club. I think Taylor felt bad that the girls might have felt excluded, so she agreed to do the whole girl thing with them and meet me here later.

Not gonna lie—I was worried about leaving her with those chicks. Taylor's done great at adapting to the guys. Hunter's roommates, on the other hand, are a fucking handful. It was with some misgivings and a warning to call me if they tried making her cut her hair that I left her in Summer, Brenna and Demi's clutches.

Now we've been at the club an hour already and I'm starting to wonder if I should organize a search party.

This place is slammed wall-to-wall. Even some of the Minnesota players showed up, along with another team from New York City. When I spot number nineteen at the bar, he offers to buy me a shot, and I accept because my pride never gets in the way of free booze. While we're mostly relegated to communicating with hand signals and nods, I think we manage to squash the beef. Until next season, anyway.

Eventually, our teams merge around the end of the bar and take turns jabbing each other and shouting stories over the DJ's set list. As much as we want to hate them, the Minnesota guys seem cool. Though I'll feel a lot better if we're the ones buying their pity drinks next year.

As I'm checking over my shoulder toward the entrance for the fiftieth time looking for Taylor, a face catches my eye. Just for a second, but then he's gone. Hell, I'm not even sure I saw him at all among the strobing lights and pulsing bodies. Despite the knot in my stomach, the sudden bolt of adrenaline, I assure myself that my eyes were just playing tricks on me.

"Jee-*zus*," exclaims number nineteen, whose name I couldn't hear when he tried to shout it over the music.

Foster follows his gaze and releases a sharp wolf whistle. "Holy fuck, Con. You seeing this?"

My brow furrows. I turn around but can't figure out what they're gawking at. Until two blonde heads catch my attention in a sweeping beam of light.

Summer and Taylor are making their way through the crowd.

They're tailed by Brenna and Demi, but everyone whose name isn't Taylor ceases to exist for me.

I think I drop my glass. Was I even holding one? Everything else filters into the darkness until it's just Taylor, walking toward me in a tiny white dress glowing under the UV lights. Her hair curled, makeup done. That sexy beauty mark above her mouth that makes her look like a modern Marilyn Monroe. That's my girlfriend.

I must look like a total jackass striding over to her while trying to hide a hard-on, but fuck me she looks stunning.

"Dance with me," I say at her ear, wrapping an arm around her waist.

In response she bites her lip and nods. Just that little thing makes my dick twitch and I'm not sure how we're getting out of here without me ripping her dress off.

"You're welcome," I hear Summer say, but I ignore her, single-mindedly pulling Taylor toward the throng of dancers.

"I suck at dancing," Taylor tells me as I gather her into my arms.

"Don't care," I mutter. I just want to touch her, hold her. I know she can feel my erection as her body melts against me. I want to ask her what she wants to do about it but I'm not that fucking drunk yet, so I hold my tongue.

"Just don't let me look stupid," she says, finding it easier to speak in my ear now that she's wearing heels.

"Never."

I place a kiss on her neck, feel her skin erupt in goose bumps in response. Then she turns to face away from me, presses her ass against me while she dances, and I bite down so hard on the inside of my cheek I taste blood.

"You're killing me," I groan, slowly sliding my hands down her body, savoring every sexy curve.

Taylor looks over her shoulder and winks. "You started it."

Someone suddenly taps me on the shoulder, a dark-haired guy I make out from the corner of my eye. I assume he's asking to cut in, and I'm prepared to tell him to fuck off when that knot in my gut returns.

"Hey, Con," a voice from the past drawls. "Fancy meeting you here."

My stomach drops, a wave of queasiness washing over me. I shutter my eyes and paste a completely expressionless mask on my face.

"Kai," I say coolly. "What are you doing here?"

He does the same gesture I've been doing all night—signaling he can't hear me. "Let's go talk over there," he says, pointing somewhere past my shoulder.

"I'm sorry about this," I mumble in Taylor's ear.

"Sorry about what?" She looks uneasy, gripping my hand tightly as we follow Kai to the smaller bar at the back of the club. I still can't believe he's here. Goddamn Kai Turner, still scrawny and stinking of weed. I haven't seen him since I moved clear across the country to get away from what we did.

The fact that he's tracked me down, all the way to some random joint in Buffalo, tells me nothing good will come of this reunion.

I've got Taylor's hand in mine, holding on for dear life. Half because I'm afraid she might take off on me. Half because I'm not sure what I'll do to this kid if we're left alone.

"The hell are you doing here, Kai?" I demand.

He smirks. I know that look too well. It worked better when we were teenagers. Now it reads like the guy trying to sell you gold-plated watches out of a backpack.

"Good to see you, too, brother." He slaps me on the shoulder. "Ain't this a fucking coincidence."

I shrug his hand off me. "Bullshit." There are no coincidences or happy accidents where Kai is concerned. Since we were in middle school, he's always had an angle. Back then, so did I. "How'd you find me?"

His leering eyes slide to Taylor, who shrinks at my side. Everything about the way he looks at her makes me want to lay him out.

"Alright, you got me. I'm living in the Big Apple now. Some of my boys were playing in the tournament and I thought I might run into you, so I tagged along. Tried hitting you up. Weird, though." His pointed gaze slides back to me. "Your number's disconnected."

"I got a new one." To lose people like him.

Taylor grasps my arm, questioning me with her big turquoise eyes.

Christ, I want to get her away from him. I'd leave if I didn't think he'd just follow us. And frankly, I can't trust what might be waiting outside the club. I know Hunter and the guys would throw down for me in a heartbeat, but I've got no way to get their attention, which means right now I'm on my own.

"This your girl?" Kai sees my discomfort and focuses in on Taylor just to get under my skin. I can't tell if he wants a fight, or if he wants me to ditch her so there isn't a witness. "Guess you *have* gone east coast."

"The fuck's that supposed to mean?" I ask, fists clenched. At this point I don't give a damn about getting tossed out of the club. I push Taylor a step behind me to shield her.

"Nah, nothing, man. I'd hit that ass. And I'm sure she's got a great personality." He flashes a toothy grin. "You just used to have standards."

Taylor drops my hand. Shit.

"Fuck you, asshole. Get lost." I give Kai's chest a shove and then try to reach for Taylor again.

"I'm gonna go," she says hastily.

"Please. Just wait for me, T. I'll go with—"

"Aww, come on, baby, I'm just messing with him," Kai shouts after Taylor, but she's already gone.

A red haze washes over my field of vision. "Listen to me," I growl. I put one hand on Kai's shoulder and force him between the bar and the wall. "We're not friends. We aren't anything. Stay the hell away from me."

"So your fake ass got a little money now and a fancy school and you forget all about your real friends, huh? You're still a poser, Con. I know where you come from and I know who you are."

"I'm not messing around, Kai. You come near me again and see what happens."

"Nah, man." He pushes my hand away and squares up to me. At barely 5'9" he doesn't even reach my shoulders. "You and me got history. I know things, remember? Like who helped someone break into your step-daddy's mansion and trash the place. You don't get to wash your hands of me that easy."

I want to fucking hit him. For finding me. For dragging his drama back into my life. For reminding me I'm still just a punk piece of shit pretending to fit in with the fancy kids we used to make fun of.

But I go after Taylor instead.

17
TAYLOR

I FEEL LIKE SUCH A JACKASS.

Taking refuge from the throbbing music and pulsating lights down a hallway outside the restrooms, I press myself into a corner and try to take a deep breath. It's too hot in here, too crowded. This place is pulling the air from my lungs.

What the hell was I thinking letting Summer talk me into borrowing this stupid dress?

And the hair.

The makeup.

The silver stilettos.

This person isn't real. She isn't me. Sure, it seemed worth it to see the look on Conor's face when he spotted me across the room. But even a good disguise can't hide what I am: a joke. Conor's charity case.

He's just too kind to see it.

"Fuck, Taylor. I'm sorry."

Speak of the well-meaning devil. My head lifts as Conor shoves past the men stumbling toward the restroom and comes to a stop in front of me.

There's real panic in his eyes. Whether it's due to me or whoever that guy was back there, I don't know. And I'm too tired to care. I'm all out of fight. None of this is his fault, but I just can't pretend anymore.

"I want to go," I tell him frankly.

He hangs his head. "Yeah, okay. I'll get us a ride back to the hotel."

It's a quiet trip. With every minute I feel the gulf between us widening, feel myself shutting down.

My mistake was letting myself believe I didn't care—about him, and the fact that our silly arrangement was always going to be temporary. I don't know how sticking it to Abigail turned into me following him six hours to Buffalo, but it's my fault that I let it happen. My mom didn't raise me on fairy tales and I was stupid for falling for my own ill-conceived ruse.

"I'm sorry," Conor says again when we reach my hotel room. His expression reflects my own loss for words. He doesn't have to say it—we both know this whole thing blew up in our faces exactly the way it was always meant to. "Can I come in?"

I should say no and spare myself the torment of an extended "it was nice knowing you." I'm weak, though. Reluctant to lose the friendship we'd only just repaired, and disappointed that I wasn't brave enough to stand up to Abigail that very first night. If I had been, I would've saved myself the heartache and humiliation now.

"Yeah," I murmur, unlocking the door. "Sure."

Inside, I kick off my new heels, grab a six-dollar bottle of water from the mini bar and start chugging. When I turn around, Conor's on the queen-sized bed, pillows arranged to form a barrier beside him.

A smile almost springs free as I remember how I did the same thing the night we met, arranging Rachel's stuffed animal collection on the bed between us.

"Will you sit with me?" His tone is rough, lacking its usual laidback inflection.

I nod. Only because my feet hurt and I'm too self-conscious standing there on display for him.

"You're upset," he begins. "And I know why."

I stretch out on the other side of the pillow wall, my short dress riding up to reveal way too much thigh. I feel sweaty and tired and I'm sure my hair is a wild mess of tangled waves. So how is it that Conor still looks fresh as a stupid daisy in a charcoal button-down over a black T-shirt and dark jeans?

"That guy back there is a total idiot, and you shouldn't waste a second worrying about the dumb shit that comes out of his mouth," Conor says. "It wouldn't have mattered who was standing next to me, trust me. Kai would've found a way to insult them. He picked on you because he knew it would get a rise out of me." I hear him sigh. "That's not fair to you. It's fucking mean and I'm sorry it happened, but please don't let this ruin your weekend."

"He hit on the one nerve," I find myself whispering.

"I know, babe. And if you knew him like I do, you would've stabbed him in the nuts with one of those heels and gone on about your life without a second thought."

"Shit." I breathe out a sad laugh. "Why didn't I think of that?"

"Because you have tact."

I give him a sideways look.

"Most of the time," he says with a smirk. "My point is, forget about what that asshole said. You look amazing tonight."

"You always say that."

"It's always true."

A blush rises to my cheeks. I hate how easy it is for him to do that, to get a physical response out of me.

I take one of the pillows from the barrier and hug it to my chest. "Who is he to you, anyway? A friend from California, I take it?"

Conor's head falls back against the headboard as he lets out another long sigh. I wait, watching the story play out across his face, as if he's deciding how much to tell me.

"Kai was my best friend growing up," he finally reveals. "Back in my old neighborhood. We'd skateboard together, surf, smoke weed, whatever. When my mom got married and we moved to Huntington

Beach, I'd still see him now and then, meet up to surf, but it's hard when you're not attending the same school anymore, you know? So we drifted apart. By college, I'd stopped returning his texts and that was pretty much it."

I don't know Conor well, certainly not well enough to have any read on his relationship with Kai. But I think I've spent enough time with him recently to know when he's holding something back. There's a wound there, something deep. Whatever it is, it's a step too far to let me see it.

"You're not convinced he tracked you down just to say hi, huh?"

"Not a chance." There's an edge to his voice. "I've known Kai most of my life. He's never not been up to something."

"So what do you think he's up to?"

Conor chews on that, his jaw working. The muscles in his neck twitch. "You know what? Not my problem and I don't want to know." He rolls onto his side to face me. Something about his vivid gray eyes, the way his lips part when he's staring at mine, does my head in every time. "I was having a great night before we were interrupted."

I can feel myself blushing again. I bite my lip a little too hard, just to remind myself of the pain that's always waiting when I let myself pretend. And yet I can't stop myself from saying, "Me too."

"I would've really liked to see where it was headed."

"Where do you think it was headed?" Oh boy. Does that throaty voice actually belong to me?

His gaze turns molten. "I've got about a thousand ideas, if you're into it."

Am I into it?

Of course I'm into it. I'm way too into it and that's the tricky part. Because right now is when I make the decision—go all in on total emotional destruction with Conor, or make a clean break for good.

Why does he have to smell so nice?

"I have to tell you something," I say, squeezing the pillow to my chest and staring at my toes. "I'm…" A coward. I take a deep breath and try again. "I've never been with anyone. Like at all. Well, I've done a little. But not much."

"Oh," is his response.

It hangs there, that infuriating little syllable. Like a wisp of smoke growing larger as it fills the room.

Then he drawls, "I was a virgin too, once."

I jab him with an elbow.

"It's been a while since I was with a virgin."

Another jab.

"I won't tell anyone that you came too fast."

I swing the pillow at his face. "This isn't funny, asshole," I say, laughing despite myself. "I'm being incredibly vulnerable right now."

"Babe." He throws the pillows to the end of the bed and climbs on top of me, settling between my legs while crouched on his knees. We're not even touching, but the image of him above me, the heat emanating from his muscular body… I've never experienced anything so erotic in my life. "I know I've been a fuckboy in the past. But I don't want to be that guy with you."

"How do I know that?" I ask honestly.

"Because I've never lied to you. I wouldn't. Even though we haven't known each other that long, you see me better than anyone else I know." I'm startled to hear his deep voice waver. "You do know me, Taylor. Trust that."

He leans in and gently presses his lips to mine. The kiss is soft, unhurried, as if he's savoring this one perfect moment, just as I am. When he pulls away, I glimpse the lust and naked need in his eyes, the same churning in mine.

"I'll go slow," he promises. "If you'll let me."

My body wins over my better judgment. I reach for him, pulling him down for another kiss. I feel him hard against my thigh, and my core clenches in response.

I know he's as turned on as I am, and yet he stokes the

anticipation for longer than I can stand. Kissing me deeply, trapping me beneath him by planting his hands on the bed at either side of my head. I wrap my leg around his hip, trying to draw him closer, to urge him toward…I don't even know what. Something to ease this ache inside me.

"Touch me," I whisper against his mouth.

"Where do you want me to touch you?" he asks, dragging his lips down my neck.

I don't know how to be, I don't know, *sexy*. So I use my body to tell him what I need. I wrap my other leg around him and arch my hips, pressing myself against his erection.

The move elicits a groan from Conor, who buries his head in the crook of my neck and thrusts between my thighs.

"When you say you've 'done a little,' what does that mean?" His warm breath tickles my collarbone as he kisses his way down to my cleavage.

"It means a little." I rock against his thrusting groin, distracted by the flurry of sensations racing through my body.

"Anyone ever done this?" he asks, and then tugs at the low scoop neck of my dress to expose a bit more of my breasts. He cups them, his thumbs stroking gently.

"Yeah. But not *this*." I pull one spaghetti strap off my shoulder to give him greater access, which exposes my nipples.

"Jesus, Taylor." Conor licks his lips. "I need to taste you."

My hips rise again. "Please."

He licks one rigid nipple, then draws it deep in his mouth. The resulting shockwave goes straight between my legs. Holy *hell*, this feels good. His hot mouth explores my breasts, kissing and sucking and nibbling until I'm writhing with the need for more of him. For him to let me off this hook of taut desire.

He chuckles at my desperation, his hand traveling down my leg, between my thighs. Then he stops. "How about this?" he rasps. "Can I?"

I moan in response, and his fingertips skim my pussy, dancing over my clit. Only one other person has touched me there, not counting my own hand, but Conor's the first man I've let tug on the elastic of my panties and slide them off.

I'm practically naked now, top and bottom exposed, with my dress bunched up around my waist.

Conor regards me with pure hunger in his eyes. "You're so fucking hot. You have no idea."

I shift in discomfort, managing a hasty laugh. "Stop looking at me like that."

"Like what?" His tongue sweeps out to lick his bottom lip.

"Like *that*. It's making me self-conscious." I try to pull my dress down a little, but he stills my hand, his palm covering my knuckles.

"Taylor." There's an intensity in his eyes that I haven't glimpsed before. "What do you think I see when I look at you?"

A chunky girl in a too-tight dress.

"I'm not sure," I lie. "But I know you're not seeing one of those chicks you're probably used to, with their perfect, toned body." I awkwardly place a palm over my half-exposed stomach. "See, no abs."

"Who needs 'em? I've got enough abs for the both of us."

I snicker, but the sound dies when he covers my hand again, this time pushing it away so that his palm is the one on my belly.

"You're exactly what I want in a woman," he says seriously, both hands now exploring my body. "Soft and warm...your thighs...your ass...fuck, these *hips*—"

His fingers curl around said hips, which my incredibly obtuse male GP once described as "more than suitable for child-bearing."

"Your curves kill me, T."

Before I can respond, he grabs my hand and presses it directly onto his crotch. There's no mistaking his arousal.

"Feel how hard I am?" He groans softly. "That's all you. You're the stuff of my fantasies."

He's either the greatest actor on the planet...or he means every word he's saying. Either way, my body is responding to his heated gaze and the husky compliments. Cheeks scorching, breasts tingling, pussy aching. If he doesn't start touching me again, I'm liable to self-combust.

"So…now…I can keep reassuring you how sexy you are," Conor says playfully, "or I can give you an orgasm. Choose wisely."

Anticipation shudders through me. "Orgasm," I blurt out. "I choose orgasm."

He chuckles. "Good call."

I bite my lip when he slips a finger inside me. Not too deep, just a knuckle or two. Just enough to cause my entire body to clench around him.

A dirty smile curves his lips. He plays with me until I can't stand it any longer and push against his fingers, silently begging for more.

Breathing hard, he slides down my body until he's gazing up at me from between my thighs. Conor run his hands up my calves, over my knees, his lips grazing my inner thighs. He kisses his way to my pussy, sweeps his tongue over my clit, and I cry out from the bolt of pleasure he generates inside me. I grab fistfuls of the blanket and press my ass into the bed to stop from squirming.

"Feel good?" he asks, then resumes his wicked ministrations without waiting for an answer.

It's the greatest feeling in the world, his warm, wet mouth exploring my sensitive, aching body. Breathy sounds and low whimpers fill the hotel room, and it takes a while to realize they're coming from me. I'm lost in a haze, completely caught up in the pleasure he's bringing. I rock against his eager mouth, then cry in disappointment when the heat of it disappears.

"Fucking hell, hold on," he chokes out.

I feel the mattress shift, hear what sounds like a zipper. My eyelids flutter open in time to see Conor slipping one hand inside his boxers. Just as it registers that he's stroking himself, his mouth returns to my pussy and short circuits my brain again.

With his tongue and fingers, he coaxes me to the edge again, while his free hand works his cock. I want to be the one helping him do that. I want his dick in my mouth. I want to taste him. I want to make him lose control the way he's doing to me.

Conor suddenly groans against my pussy, his hips moving quicker. He sucks on my clit, panting hard, breathing out, "I'm coming."

And that's all it takes for the thread of tension inside me to snap. An orgasm, one with a level of intensity I've never experienced, shudders through my muscles. Even my toes go numb as I gasp through the pulsating heat that captures my every nerve ending.

Conor Fucking Edwards.

18
CONOR

THE WEDNESDAY AFTER OUR LOSS IN BUFFALO, THE TEAM HOLDS A meeting at the Briar arena. Our season's over, and for some of the seniors that means shifting their focus to the NHL teams that drafted them and getting in the best shape of their lives for summer training camp. For others, last weekend was likely the final time they'll ever suit up. Today, however, we're here for Coach Jensen.

Hunter stands in the center of the ice where we've gathered for a little ceremony of sorts. Coach, sensing something's up, lingers just outside our circle with a suspicious look on his face. It's an expression I've seen Brenna don on more than one occasion. It's almost scary how alike Coach and his daughter are.

"So," Hunter starts, "we brought you here today pretty much because we wanted to say thank you, Coach. This bunch of degenerates and hooligans wouldn't have made it as far as we did without you, and even though we couldn't bring home the big trophy for you, you made all of us better. Not just better hockey players, but better people. And we all owe you a lot."

"Like bail money, right, Captain?" Bucky pipes up, getting a laugh from the guys.

"Thanks, Buck." Hunter flips him off. "So anyway, thank you, from all of us. We got you a little something to show our appreciation."

Gavin and Matt all but drag Coach into the center of our circle so Hunter can present him with the custom-engraved Rolex every-one on the team chipped in to buy. Which is to say, our parents did. Mom sent me a blank check with my stepdad's name on it and I told Hunter to just write in the amount. I'd rather not know.

"Man, I, uh…" Coach admires the watch, at a loss for words. "This is real nice, guys. I, umm…" He sniffs, rubbing his face. If I didn't know better, I'd think he was about to cry. "This is a special group. I mean it when I say I've never had a better bunch of guys."

"Better than the years Garrett Graham and John Logan were on the roster?" Foster demands, naming two of Briar's most famous alumni. Graham and Logan both play for the Bruins these days.

"Let's not be crazy now," Coach replies, but there's a twinkle in his eyes. "You all worked hard for each other, and that's all I can ever ask. So thank you. This is great."

Foster brings out a cooler of beers from the bench and passes out bottles while we all take one last chance to appreciate being on this ice together. I have no doubt next year we'll be a strong team. But it'll never be this one again.

Eight months ago, I showed up on this campus with a sudden pang of regret, wondering if I'd made a rash and ill-considered decision to ship my life nearly three thousand miles across the country to start over. I feared I'd never fit in with the ivy-covered legacies of this place, that I'd choke on the Ralph Lauren polos and inbred poshness of it all. And then I met these idiots.

I couldn't have asked for better friends.

And Taylor. I've known her less than a month, yet I count her among the short list of people I trust. She makes me want to be a better person. With her, I feel like I can finally get something right, like maybe I can actually have a real relationship based on friendship rather than lust. Even if some of my friends are having a hard time believing that.

"All I'm saying is," Foster babbles in the Jeep on the ride home, "Con didn't come back to our room Saturday night. So unless he hopped in bed with you and Demi, Captain, I've got a good idea what he was up to."

"Dude, jealousy is not a good look on you," I drawl.

"For real, though." Hunter leans forward from the backseat, where he's sitting with Matt. "What's up with you two?"

Hell if I know.

I mean, I like Taylor. A lot. But I'm also pretty sure that if I bring up the matter of renegotiating the terms of our relationship, I'll scare her away. I don't think she's convinced yet that I'm reformed, and to be honest, no one is more surprised by my recent turn in favor of monogamy than I am. For the moment, though, I'm enjoying myself.

"A gentleman doesn't kiss and tell," I respond.

Foster snorts. "So then what's your excuse?"

"Con, you should make Foster pay rent if he's gonna stay on your dick this much," Hunter says with a grin.

I'm starting to have sympathy for the hell we gave Hunter over Demi and the ridiculous celibacy pact he made at the beginning of the semester. This shit's annoying. The guys are like dogs with a bone, and I can only imagine it'll get worse now that the season's over and they've got nothing else to do than hound my ass.

So when Hunter corners me when we stop to pick up some lunch at the diner, my newfound sympathy has me being a bit more forthcoming with him.

"How serious is this?" he asks while we wait by the car for Matt and Foster to grab our orders from inside.

"I don't know if it's serious. Definitely on the way to being not not-serious." I shrug. "We haven't even had sex yet," I confess, because I know Hunter can keep shit to himself. "Buffalo was the first time we fooled around."

"That's sort of the best part though, isn't it? Before sex. When all you're thinking about is having it for the first time. All the anticipation, you know? Getting each other all messed up over the tension."

I wouldn't know from experience—this is the first time sex

wasn't the first step for me. Usually it's the first and last. "I remember you being kind of crabby, actually."

"Well, yeah." He laughs. "There's that too."

"Taylor's a good girl. We get along great." I hesitate for a moment. "Honestly, I'm trying to see how long I can go before she realizes I'm a dirtbag and she's too smart for me."

Hunter shakes his head. "You know, if you didn't treat yourself like a dirtbag, maybe other people wouldn't, either."

"Thanks, Dad."

"Whatever, dickhead."

I hide a smile. Hunter and I have a different relationship than I do with the other guys. Maybe because we're both working on being better people lately. He's the only one I talk to on a more serious level, so when he comes hard with the Mr. Rogers routine, it has a way of getting under my skin. His words are still crawling around in there when I get home and return a call to my mom from this morning.

"Where've you been, Mister?" she chides. "I didn't hear from you after the game."

"Yeah, sorry about that. It was a crazy weekend and I was exhausted by the time we got back. Then I had to play catch-up on assignments for class the past couple days."

"I'm sorry you guys didn't get to play in the championship. But next year, right?"

"Yeah. I'm at peace with it." Guys who get all fucking hung up on shit like that for a whole year get on my nerves. It's like, dude, get another hobby. "How are things there? How's Max?"

Her sigh tickles my ear. "He wants to buy a sailboat. Went out to Monterey to look at one."

"Does he know how to sail?"

"Of course not, but why should that stop him, right?" She laughs again. I guess it's sort of sweet how she finds his more irrational ideas charming. "I told him, you're hardly home enough to have dinner, when are you going to learn to sail? But if he's going to have a midlife crisis, I'd rather it be with a boat than a younger woman."

"You can't go to jail for setting your own boat on fire," I inform her. "I read that somewhere."

"If it comes to that," she agrees, joking. "Anyway, I don't want to take up too much of your time. Miss you. Love you. Stay out of trouble."

"Who me?"

"Yeah, that's what I thought."

"Love you, Mom. Later."

I am glad she's happy. I'm glad Max makes her happy and she's got all the money she'll ever need to bicker about shit like buying a sailboat. Yet a sour taste forms in the back of my throat when I get off the phone.

Talking about Max brings the run-in with Kai back to the front of my mind. It was like whiplash, seeing him again, and I haven't felt right since. There's been a nagging ache in my neck that just won't go away.

Getting out of California was as much about getting away from Kai as anything else. I used to think I owed him something. For a long time he was my best friend, and when I made it out of the old neighborhood and he didn't, I felt as if I'd betrayed him somehow. But then I realized, it was never about loyalty or friendship for Kai—people are just tools in his eyes. We're only as good as what we can do for him.

When I look back on it, I recognize that Kai Turner is a rot that infects everything he touches. And I hope to hell I never have to see him again.

Feeling a foul mood creeping in, I text Taylor looking for a distraction.

ME: Can I come over and go down on you?

I'm joking, but only a little.

TAYLOR: Kappa meeting. See you later?

I don't know if I should feel rejected that she doesn't even acknowledge my offer with so much as a thinking emoji. I decide to cut her some slack, seeing as how she's in the middle of a meeting and didn't have to text me back in the first place.

ME: Cool. Text me.

I toss the phone on my bed and head to the dresser in search of some gym shorts. Guess I'll go for a run since I can't even get my fake girlfriend to let me eat her pussy. Never too early to start working on my cardio.

19
TAYLOR

I JUST ABOUT SWALLOW MY TONGUE WHEN I READ THE TEXT FROM Conor. That man has the very annoying habit of catching me off guard during Kappa meetings.

"What's so funny?" Sasha rips my phone out of my hand after I send a reply to Conor. I lunge at her, but my best friend is too quick. Former gymnast and all. Bitch.

"'Can I come over and go down on you?'" she reads aloud, jumping to her feet to get away. I chase her to a standoff around the antique coffee table in the huge living room. Everything in this room is some priceless artifact donated by an alumnus for some dumb reason. "Eggplant emoji, splash emoji, peach—"

"Shut up." I hop the table to yank the phone back. "He did not send come-on-my-ass emojis."

"It's called subtext, Taylor." Sasha winks at me with a shit-eating grin. "I'm so proud of you."

"I'd let Conor Edwards come on my stuffed turtle if he wanted to," Rachel blurts out.

"We know, Rach." Olivia mimes throwing up in her mouth. "Fucking psycho."

"You said yes, right?" Beth is jerking a straw in and out of her smoothing cup. "Please tell me you said yes."

"See?" Lisa is nodding with earnest approval. "Real men eat cooch."

"Is he good at it, though?" Fiona shoves a pillow in her lap like she's got to cover her lady boner. "I feel like he'd be good at it. I can tell that about people."

Sasha and I retake our seats at the dining room table, angling our chairs toward the living room so we have a view of the entire open-concept space. I feel someone's gaze on me, and glance over to find Rebecca sitting a few seats away. When our eyes meet, she frowns and looks away.

"Can we bring the thirsty slut meter down a little?" Abigail huffs, her face red. "I don't want to hear about Taylor's fuckboy. We have business to discuss."

"Like Abigail's anointment," Sasha whispers.

"Why even bother having an election, right?" I whisper back.

Sasha puts her fingers to her head and blows her brains out.

Our chapter president doesn't start with the election, though, instead leading with a more pressing event. "Rayna, you want to bring us up to speed on the Spring Gala?" Charlotte turns the meeting over to Rayna, another senior.

"On Monday we'll have tickets ready to pick up. This year we're asking everyone to sell twenty. All the details about the Children's Hospital charity we're sponsoring are in your email, along with the dress code. Remind people when you sell them a ticket that formal attire is required. And I'm serious when I say black tie. Period. If the men don't show up in a bow tie or a dazzling sequin gown, they aren't getting in. Stephanie, I'm talking to you."

Rayna cuts a glare at the sister barely concealing a guilty grin. Last year Steph's date arrived dressed as Goth Rock Zombie Jesus. It did not go over well with the donor alumni.

"Can we do it in Boston this year?" Jules whines. "The banquet hall smelled funny and there wasn't any parking. I bet I could get my dad to—"

"No," Rayna snaps back. "The more we spend on a venue, the less money goes to charity. We'll be in the Hastings banquet hall again, but this year we're contracting with the church across the street to use their parking lot for overflow parking, and we'll have valet on-site."

"Everyone," Charlotte chimes in, "is required to sign up for a volunteer committee for the Spring Gala. VIP planning, decorations, whatever. Rayna's got the lists. If your name isn't on one, I'm picking for you."

Sasha pokes me in the ribs. She'd committed a hostile takeover of the music committee at the last meeting and conscripted me to her campaign. Mostly that involves us going through her Spotify playlists to find the right balance between danceable and inoffensive to our distinguished guests of a certain age. Last year Sasha kicked the DJ out twenty minutes into his set and ran the whole thing from her phone.

Needless to say, we've found it's easier to let Sasha have her way.

After Charlotte dismisses the meeting, Abigail corners me on my way to the hall bathroom. She's been to her bleach dealer, it seems. Her hair is now a shade of white that somehow absorbs all natural light and reflects only blinding bitch.

"You're awfully smug these days," she says, standing between me and the door to prevent me from peeing. I should pee on her fancy Louboutins just to prove a point about the repercussions of bathroom barriers.

"I can assure you I'm not. Now if you'll excuse me—"

"You know hockey boy is going to get bored and dump you soon. He never dates anyone longer than a few weeks."

"Why do you care?"

"We're sisters, Tay-Tay," she coos, cocking her head in that way that makes her look like a broken marionette. It's fucking creepy. Or perhaps it's all the blood rushing to one side of her brain to give her the ability to form words. "I wouldn't want you to get your heart broken."

"No worries." I shove my hand out and force her to dodge it so

I can push forward. "Our relationship is solely based on having lots of sex, so…"

I brush past her and do my business, then wash my hands and step back into the hall. Where Abigail is still standing. Doesn't she have better things to do than obsess over my love life?

She tails me down the hall toward the foyer. As I'm opening the door to leave, none other than Abigail's boyfriend Kevin struts inside. Lovely. He who smells like too much body spray and Cheetos.

Every time Kevin sees me there's a brief blank stare and then his eyes drop to my chest and it's like spotting someone you know in a crowded airport. His face alights with recognition. "Taylor, hey."

"Taylor," Sasha shouts at me from the staircase. "Get your ass up here."

"Look at it this way," I chirp, sliding past Abigail and her gross boyfriend's leering stare, "when I'm done with hockey boy, you can shoot your shot."

A thrill of excited energy pours through my blood. Standing up to Abigail, even just a little, feels good. Powerful, even. Taylor Marsh, able to leap tall bitches in a single bound.

"We should talk to Charlotte about having paramedics standing by," Sasha says as we climb the stairs to her bedroom. "Abigail's liable to drop dead of jealousy any minute."

"I don't know about jealousy." In Sasha's room, I plop down in her beanbag chair and toss my hair over one shoulder. "I think what drives her crazy is that her cruelty backfired into actually making me happy."

Sasha sits on the other beanbag and fixes me with a serious look. "So this is legit then? You and Conor are a real thing now?"

"It's something," I say for lack of a better word. "I don't know what."

"But it's real."

I swallow hard. "I think so. I mean, we've kissed and whatever. Messed around a little in Buffalo."

"You drove seven hours for a booty call," Sasha says, laughing. "I hope it was more than a little."

"Six and a half hours. And fine, it was a little more than a little."

"Do you still have your V-Card?" she demands.

"I'm as yet unacquainted with his penis."

That earns me a snort. "All right. So. Where's your head at? Is this like a fine-for-now thing, or is it headed in a linear direction?"

"I don't know. I mean, I'm into it. Things are a solid A in the fooling around category. He's sweet and respectful and makes me feel comfortable."

"But," Sasha says for me.

"But I'm still hesitant. He's been nothing but wonderful to me, and yet I can't shake the idea that if I have sex with him, I'm still a number on a very long list. It feels…" I trail off, unable to find the words.

"That's the patriarchy talking. Who gives a shit how many women he's slept with? Did he cheat on them? Did he promise them a ring to get them into bed and then sneak out in the middle of the night? Is he posting sex selfies on Insta and passing trophies around to his friends?"

"Not that I'm aware of, no."

"So fuck it, then. Or him." She wiggles her tongue impishly. "If you want to. When you feel like it. If the mood strikes."

"Okay," I say, rolling my eyes. "I get it."

"Society tells boys to divide and conquer, and tells girls to save ourselves for some younger future version of our father. Just doing some quick math in my head and…yep, that comes out to a bunch of hypocritical bullshit. Your self-worth is not tied up in your vagina or how many girls came before you."

"No pun intended."

"Precisely."

20
CONOR

I HAVEN'T FINGERED A GIRL THIS MUCH SINCE HIGH SCHOOL.

Taylor lies in my bed on her side, cheeks flushed and lips parted slightly. Her bra is tossed across my desk in the corner. Her shirt is pulled up to expose her perfect tits for me, jeans pushed down only enough for me to get my hand beneath her skimpy white panties. I haven't even seen this girl fully naked yet, but she's the most erotic thing I've ever witnessed. Blonde hair splayed over my pillow and warm little body wrapped around mine while she writhes against my hand. Her eyes clench tighter every time I swipe my thumb across her clit. I could do this all day.

"Stop." Taylor pulls her mouth from mine and I freeze. Shit. Was I being too rough? It's been a while since I screwed around with a virgin.

"Am I hurting you?" I ask immediately.

"No, it feels amazing."

"Then what's wrong?"

"Nothing's wrong. I just… I think I want to go down on you."

"You think?" I clamp my teeth down on my lip to stop a laugh. That's not usually how these conversations start. I mean, honestly, it usually isn't much of a conversation at all.

She nods, appearing to grow more confident as the idea tumbles around her mind. She licks her lips, and my cock damn near tunnels through my jeans. "Yeah. I want to."

"You don't have to, you know." I lift an eyebrow. "I don't believe in transactional sex."

"No, I know." Taylor smiles at me, and there's a conspiratorial glint in her eye. A girl about to set out on an adventure. It's sort of cute, in a weird way. My babe's first dick.

"All right, then." I roll over onto my back and fold my arms behind my bed. "Make a man outta me, Taylor Marsh."

Laughing softly, she crawls down my body and unbuttons my jeans, tugs them down with my boxers. I've been hard since she walked into my bedroom an hour ago, and my cock springs up to say hello.

Taylor bites her bottom lip as she takes me in her hand and carefully strokes my shaft. She says something, but I'm not listening because all my concentration is dedicated to not blowing my load. I've yanked it to this moment so many times since we met—getting her mouth on my cock, her Caribbean-blue eyes staring up at me while she sucks me off.

"Am I hurting you?" she mimics, giving me another gentle stroke. Teasing me. "Because you look like you're in pain."

"I'm in agony," I mumble. "Don't think I can survive this."

"Good. Just don't come in my hair," she orders, and my answering laughter dies in my throat when she licks up the length of my dick.

I'm done for when she takes the head fully in between her pouty lips, her tongue working me over. I thread my fingers into her hair, encouraging her to go slower. She complies, the hot suction of her lips swallowing me up one millimeter at a time. By the time I'm buried nearly to the back of her throat, I'm sweating.

Jesus fucking Christ.

I use my free hand to swipe at the beads of sweat dotting my forehead. My breathing becomes labored when Taylor utilizes the same torturous pace to drag her mouth off my cock. Her tongue sweeps over the tip in a slow, seductive swirl, and I almost lose control right then and there.

Why did I think slow would be a better idea? Slow, fast, it doesn't matter. I'm not going to last either way. I don't know where she picked this up, but Taylor's giving me the best head I've ever gotten.

"Fuck, babe, I'm close," I grind through my teeth.

Lips glistening with moisture, Taylor releases me with a wet noise and sits up, still stroking my cock. Groaning, I grab the T-shirt hanging off my headboard and take my dick from her just as my entire body tightens and shudders. I come into the shirt, while Taylor sweetly kisses my chest, my neck, until I strain for her lips. Our tongues meet, and I kiss her hungrily as the aftershocks of release tremble through my body.

"Was that okay?" She breaks the kiss, smiling shyly. How this girl turns on a dime spins my head. From innocent virgin to dick whisperer and back again.

I let out a happy sigh. "Better than okay." Then it dawns on me. "But I didn't get you off. I can still—"

"I'm good." Taylor snuggles up beside me, resting her head on my chest. Her fingers lazily travel across my stomach. "That was fun."

"I'll get you twice next time," I say, and kiss her forehead while I toss the shirt into my hamper across the room.

Hooking up with Taylor has made foreplay fun again. Before this, either a chick was so anxious to get on my dick I'd barely get her name, or I was so amped to get her naked we wouldn't even kiss. With Taylor, I don't want to miss anything. I want to learn every inch of her body, give her every experience. I'm her first, and I want to make damn sure I do it right.

My phone vibrates on the nightstand beside Taylor. "Mind grabbing that?" I ask.

She hands it to me. An unknown number lights up onscreen, triggering a frown.

"Yeah?" I answer, continuing to run my hand through the length of Taylor's hair.

"'Sup, brother."

Every muscle in my body tenses up. Kai. That motherfucker. "How'd you get this number?" I ask coldly.

Taylor looks up at me with questioning eyes.

"Don't be mad, bro. I talked it out of one of your boys at the club in Buffalo." Bucky, I bet. That kid would give up his bank PIN if you asked nicely. "Bunch of fucking lightweights, those jocks."

"Well, lose it. I told you before—"

"Easy, brother. I come in peace. Listen, I'm gonna be in Boston this weekend. Let's meet up, talk it out. It'd be good for both of us."

Yeah, right. With Kai, there's only ever what's good for him.

"Not interested." I end the call and toss my phone to the floor. Damn it.

"Was it that guy again?" Looking concerned, Taylor unwraps herself from my side and sits up, adjusting her shirt and zipping up her jeans. "Kai?"

"It's fine. Forget about it." I say the words to her, but I'm really talking to myself. Ever since Kai reappeared that night after the tournament, I haven't been able to shake the sense of dread knotting in my stomach.

"Conor. I know you're holding something back." When Taylor turns her gaze on me—sincere, vulnerable—I feel like such an asshole. "And if you're not ready to tell me, or you don't trust me with the information, that's fine. But don't act like it isn't there."

Fuck me.

"I'm sorry." I lick my suddenly dry lips. If Taylor's going to finally realize she's too good for my dumb ass, it might as well be sooner rather than later. "I didn't want to say anything because I like the person you think I am."

A groove digs into her forehead. "What does that mean?"

It means that if Taylor knew what was good for her, she'd block my number.

"It means if you'd known me back then, you'd have been smart to run the other way."

"I doubt that's true," she says, and it absolutely guts me. This girl has so much misplaced faith in me. "Just tell me. I'm sure it's worse in my head."

Fuck it.

"I've spent the last couple years trying to get away from Kai because I used to be him," I admit. "I was in it up to my neck with him since we were kids. Letting him talk me into dumb shit, breaking into abandoned buildings, tagging, some shoplifting." *Fighting, smashing out car windows.* "By high school Kai started getting into dealing. Just pot, mostly. It's what people did, you know? Like, it didn't feel wrong at the time. Sometime during sophomore year of high school, though, his older brother got locked up for chopping cars, and after Tommy went away, it seemed like Kai started speeding down the same path. Hanging out with some of his brother's friends, missing weeks of school."

I can't read Taylor's expression as I tell her all of this. And I'm still unable to bring myself to admit the worst of it, because I'm ashamed, embarrassed of what I was. Knowing it's all still in me, under the surface. The stain that's soaked through the carpet.

"Then my mom married Max and we moved out of the neighborhood. They sent me to a private school." I shrug. "That got me away from Kai, for the most part. If it weren't for that, I probably would've been locked up by now. Gotten into the same shit Kai started in on."

Taylor stares at me for a long time. Silent, pensive. I don't know I'm holding my breath until she releases hers.

"That's it?"

No.

"Yes," I say out loud. "I mean, yeah, basically."

Christ, I'm an asshole. A coward.

"Everyone comes from somewhere, Conor. We've all screwed up, made mistakes." Her tone is soft, but ringing with conviction. "I don't care who you were before. Only who you choose to be now."

I chuckle darkly. "That's easy for you to say, though. You're from Cambridge."

"What does that have to do with anything?"

"You can't understand what it's like to be dirt poor one day and dropped off at a private school in loafers and a tie the next. I hated all those pretentious fucks driving goddamn Beamers and carrying Louis Vuitton backpacks. Every day I'd get dirty looks, hassled in the halls, and I'd be thinking to myself, man, it'd be so easy to jack their car and go joyriding, or loot all their rich kid toys they just left sitting in their gym lockers. It's why I went to a state college in California, because I was tired of not belonging." I shake my head wryly. "Then I end up here with all these East Coast old money types, and it's the same shit. They smell poverty every time I walk into a room."

"That's not true," she insists with a bit more bite in her voice. "No one who cares about you gives a damn if you grew up rich or not. Anyone who does isn't your friend anyway, so fuck 'em. You belong here just as much as anybody."

I wish I could believe that. Maybe for a little while I *did* believe it. But Kai creeping back into my life has reminded me, whether I like it or not, who I really am.

21
TAYLOR

ALTHOUGH IT'S MID-APRIL ALREADY, THE WEATHER HASN'T decided which season it wants to be. Leaving class for the day, it still feels like winter; everyone wrapped up in wool coats and gloves, clutching coffee cups and breathing out big plumes of white. But thanks to the clear blue sky and golden sunlight cutting through the bare branches of oak trees to warm the brown patches of grass across the Briar lawns, it's also starting to feel a bit like spring. Which means there's only about a month left in the semester.

Until now, that day has felt so far off. But with the Spring Gala coming up, evaluation for my co-op due, and finals to prepare for, the end of the school year is charging at me like a stampede. I suppose it all feels like a lot because the better part of my attention lately has been focused elsewhere. Namely, Conor Edwards.

We still haven't labeled our relationship in explicit terms. I'm fine with that, though. Great, even. There's far less pressure to meet expectations, or have them crushed, when things are kept loosely defined.

That said, I am starting to wonder where Conor sees this going. He invited me to California over the summer, but was he serious about that? And did he mean as friends, friends with benefits, or something else? Not that I'd hold it against him if he saw the end of the semester as the conclusion of our exclusive entanglement. I just wish there were a painless, non-awkward way of asking if he expects us to ride out the summer on the status quo.

Then again, I might not want to hear the answer.

On my way to the library, I get a call from my mother. It's been a while since we spoke, so I'm happy to hear from her. "Hey there," I answer.

"Hi, honey. Do you have a minute?"

"Yep, just got out of class. What's up?" I take a seat on one of the wrought-iron benches lining the cobblestone path.

"I'm going to be in town Friday evening. Are you free?"

"For you, of course I am. The Thai place just reopened if—"

"Actually," she says, and I don't miss the note of wariness in her voice, "I already have dinner plans. I was hoping you'd join us."

"Oh?" Mom is being unusually coy about something as benign as dinner, which gets my mind racing. "Define *us*."

"I have a date, to be specific."

"A date. With someone in Hastings?" What happened to being too busy to date?

"I'd like you to meet him."

Meet him?

Is she serious? Is *this* serious? My mother's always been more driven by her career and scientific pursuits than romantic relationships. Men rarely hold her interest long enough to develop an important role in her life.

"How did *you* meet him?" I demand.

A pause. "You sound upset."

"I'm confused," I tell her. "When did you have time to meet someone in Hastings? And why is this the first time I'm hearing of him?" It's been years since Mom brought anyone around and introduced them to me; she doesn't bother until she feels the relationship is serious. The last time she visited, she wasn't seeing anyone—which means this is a very new, very fast development.

"After we met for lunch last month, I stopped in to visit a colleague at Briar and he introduced us."

"So this guy's, what, like your boyfriend now?"

She gives an awkward laugh. "Feels like such a juvenile term for someone my age, but yes, I suppose he is."

Jesus, woman. I take my eyes off her for five minutes and she's gone and shacked up with some townie. Or worse, a professor. What if he's one of *my* professors? Eww. That feels weirdly incestuous.

"What's his name?"

"Chad."

I suppose it was ridiculous to expect her to call him Professor Somethingorother. Doctor Whoeverthefuck. But Christ in a basket I never, ever envisioned Iris Marsh knocking boots with a *Chad* of all people. Somehow, I doubt he stacks up against a woman of my mother's singular intellect.

"I'm still sensing some hostility," she says, her tone cautious.

Yeah, I guess I am a little hostile to the idea that my mother's been making clandestine trips to Hastings and hasn't once asked to see me or even called to let me know.

A clench of hurt tightens my chest. When did I become second place? For my entire life it's just been the two of us against the world. Now there's a Chad.

"Just surprised," I lie.

"I want you two to get along." There's a long pause, in which I hear her disappointment that this conversation isn't going better.

She wants me to be happy for her, excited about this. She probably thought about this conversation all day, all week, worrying whether this was the right time to bring these two parts of her life together.

Her next words confirm my suspicions. "This means a lot to me, Taylor."

I gulp down the lump of resentment clogging my throat. "Yeah, dinner sounds great." It's what she wants to hear, and I suppose I owe her that much. "As long as I can bring a date."

22

CONOR

So one thing I'm learning about Taylor—she doesn't take well to sudden change. With this business about her mom's new boyfriend, a hidden, lurking, full-blown panic type-A personality has reared its hilarious head. She's rigid and coiled beside me in the passenger seat of my Jeep, her fingernails tapping the armrest. I can sense her mashing her foot down on the imaginary gas pedal in the floorboard.

"We're not going to be late," I reassure her as I pull away from the diner on Main Street. We'd stopped at Della's to pick up a pecan pie for dessert. "Dude lives in Hastings, right?"

Her phone lights up her face and reflects off her window. She's studying the route on her map. "Yeah, turn left at the lights. We're heading toward Hampshire Lane, then making a right on—no, I said go left!" she yelps as I drive straight through the intersection.

I glance over. "This'll save us time." I happen to know for a fact that the left-turn light in the intersection we just passed lasts about .04 seconds and then you're waiting like six minutes for it to change again.

"It's seven-oh-nine," Taylor growls. "We have to be there at seven-fifteen. And that was our turn!"

"You said Hampshire. I can get us there faster by avoiding the lights and cutting through the residential streets."

Her dubious expression says she doesn't believe me. "I've lived here longer than you," she reminds me.

"And you don't have a car, babe," I say, flashing her a grin she would appreciate if she weren't so wound up. "I know these roads. Coach lives nearby. Hunter and I spent a night driving up and down every one of these streets when Foster wandered off from a team dinner to smoke a joint. He got lost for three hours. Found him in some old lady's empty above-ground pool."

"Seven-ten," she snaps back.

There's no winning with Taylor. And I don't really blame her for being a bundle of nerves. I've been in her seat.

It was just me and my mom for so long—and then suddenly this Max goofball shows up at the house in khakis and a Brooks Brothers shirt and calling me Sport or some shit, and I about lost my mind. Had to talk Kai out of boosting the rims off Max's Land Rover, although I'm pretty sure it was him who slashed Max's tire the first night he stayed over.

"If you decide you don't like the dude, just give me a signal," I tell her.

"And then what?"

"I don't know. I'll switch out his sugar with salt or something. I could also replace all his beer with piss, but then you'd have to drive us home."

"Deal. But only if he's a super douche, like he's got a portrait of himself hanging up in his dining room."

"Or endangered animal heads on his wall."

"Or he doesn't recycle," she says, giggling. "Oooh, maybe you can text the guys to show up at the windows wearing Halloween masks."

"Damn, you're dark."

But she's laughing, and some of the tension finally leaves her body. This dinner is a big deal for her. For her mother and their relationship. I get the sense that Taylor's dreaded this day for a while—this moment when someone would become the other most important person in her mother's life, and she'd have to start getting used to the idea that her mom is a person with a whole life that doesn't include Taylor. Or maybe I'm just projecting.

"What's the street name?"

"Manchester Road."

I turn right onto Manchester. The street is lined with bare trees whose branches sweep across brown lawns and skim the ground where the last snow of the season has finally melted. The old Victorian homes aren't as big as the ones a few streets over, but the houses here are nice. I know this street.

"Number forty-two," Taylor supplies.

Fuck me.

"What is it?" She stares at me, alarmed by the look on my face.

"This is Coach's house."

She blinks. "I don't understand what you mean."

"I mean this is Coach Jensen's house. Forty-two Manchester Road."

"But this is Chad's house."

A strangled laugh pops out. "Hey babe, let's play a game—"

"What are you babbling about?"

"—It's called 'Guess Coach Jensen's first name.'"

There's a beat. Then Taylor's cheeks go pale. "Oh my God. IS IT CHAD?"

"It's Chad," I choke out between hearty chuckles. I can't stop laughing. I know, I know, a total dick move, but come on—what are the fucking odds?

Taylor shoots me a glare, as if this is somehow my fault, and I can only imagine what's going through her mind. I know Coach Jensen is a stand-up guy, but Taylor doesn't know him at all. Right now she's got to be asking herself if she'd want someone like me, someone like Hunter or Foster or any of those other hockey bros sliding into her mom's DMs.

Honestly, I can't blame her. Hockey men are definitely a handful. We're animals.

The numbers on my dashboard blink from 7:13 to 7:14. I glance toward Coach's house. The curtain moves in the living room window.

"T?" I prompt.

She digs her fingers into her temples, then releases a heavy breath. "Let's get this over with," she says.

Before we even reach the porch, the front door swings open to reveal Brenna. "Oh, this is perfect!" She shakes her head with a look of amused pity. "You dumbass."

"She's talking to me," I assure Taylor.

"Obviously," my girlfriend replies.

The girls hug and compliment each other's outfits. I've already forgotten what Taylor's wearing, because I'm busy trying to figure out if her mom marrying Coach makes us brother and sister until I realize Coach and I aren't related. My brain's stuck in neutral.

"You still have time to run, Con," advises Brenna. "Go. Run free, you sexy Viking conqueror."

Taylor turns to study me.

"What?" I demand.

"You *do* look like a sexy Viking conqueror." Then she grabs my hand and grips it tightly. "And you're not going anywhere, Thor. You're my wing-man, remember?"

"I agreed to the job before we discovered your mom's banging my Chad."

"She's banging my *dad*," Brenna corrects with a snicker.

"Can we please not discuss our parents' sex life?" Taylor begs.

"Good point." Brenna opens the door wider and takes our coats, hanging them up in the front hall. "You seriously didn't know?" she asks me.

"Did you? Because a warning would've been nice." I hear voices coming from the back of the house and figure everyone else is in the kitchen.

"I knew I was meeting Dad's new girlfriend's kid, but I had no idea it was Taylor—or that she'd bring you. This is the greatest night of my life." Brenna goes running into the kitchen ahead of us like a fucking tattletale. "Hey, Dad! One of your goons is here."

Coach is already grimacing at me when we turn the corner to find him and a slender blonde standing at the counter picking at a cheese plate.

I gulp. "Uh, hey, Coach."

"What are you doing here, Edwards?" Coach growls. "If Davenport's in jail again, tell him he's spending the night. I'm not bailing him out agai—" He halts when he catches sight of Taylor.

The blonde raises an eyebrow at her daughter.

"Hey, Mom. This is Conor. Conor, this is my mom. Doctor Iris Marsh."

"Nice to meet you, Doctor Mom—I mean Doctor Marsh. Fuck."

"Language!" Brenna chides me, and it takes all my willpower not to flip up my middle finger.

After the awkward introductions, the women go to the dining room while I help Coach in the kitchen. I'm not sure how I'm ever going to recover from calling Iris Doctor Mom to her face. I haven't done the whole meet-the-parents thing since middle school. And that was just Daphne Cane's dad chasing me out of his driveway for using his trashcans as a skate ramp.

"How 'bout a beer," I say, opening the fridge.

He yanks it from my hand and shoves the door closed. "Don't be a dumbass tonight, Edwards." Man, he and Brenna are so much alike. It's scary.

"I'm twenty-one," I drawl. "You know that."

"Don't care." Coach brusquely drags a hand over his buzz cut. He's dressed in a suit and tie, with a hint of cologne and aftershave wafting off him. It's his standard uniform every time there's a stodgy campus grip-and-grin to attend. Not sure what I expected Coach on a date to look like, but it wasn't this.

"Only thing going down your throat tonight is water or juice or my fist," he warns.

"Sounds delicious."

A death glare hits me square in the eye. "Edwards. I don't know why I've been cursed with sitting through this dinner with one of you knuckleheads—I assume I ran over a unicorn or set fire to an orphanage in a past life—but if you act like an idiot tonight I'm going to have you doing bag skates every day until graduation."

There goes any hope I had of Coach being my ally in surviving this night.

I keep my mouth shut. Hell, I don't even comment on his weird unicorn murder fantasies, because I'll do anything to avoid bag skate punishment. I've never puked so much in my life as the time the team showed up late and hungover to practice after driving to Rhode Island to prank Providence College by hoisting their equipment trailer onto the roof of their arena. Coach Jensen had us on the ice until midnight skating suicides. Poor Bucky tripped and fell into our puke bin. Next time I show up at practice and there's a huge plastic garbage can in the middle of the ice, I'm just leaving the country.

For his part, Coach looks nervous while he shuffles around the kitchen hunting for serving bowls and tongs. He's got platters laid out with leafy garnishes like something out of an '80s cookbook you'd find in a used bookstore. Although I can't deny the kitchen smells good. Like smoky barbecue. I wonder if he's cooking ribs.

"What can I help with?" I ask, because he seems a little scattered.

"Grab some serving spoons. Second drawer over there."

As I wander toward the drawers, I try to make conversation. "So this thing with you and Dr. Marsh—is it serious?"

"None of your damned business," is the response.

I promptly stop making conversation.

The timer on the oven beeps.

"Get that, will ya?" he says and tosses a dishrag at me.

I open the oven and a blast of hot air smacks me across the face. I don't even have a second to consider my eyebrows may have been singed off before the fire alarm blares.

23
CONOR

"Fucking hell!" Coach thunders, lunging toward the oven.

I'm not sure what stops me from just throwing the door closed. Probably the thick cloud of smoke pouring out and distorting my field of vision.

"Oh my God! Dad! THIS IS WHY I DON'T LET YOU COOK!"

Brenna bursts into the kitchen shouting over the piercing alarm with her hands over her ears, just as Coach grabs an oven mitt and picks up the roasting dish, burning his other hand.

He jolts, tilting the tray, which splashes scalding hot juices onto the bottom of the oven that ignite on the red-hot heating element.

Flames burst out of the ferocious black mouth.

While Brenna runs her dad's hand under the cold faucet, I heroically beat the flames back with the dishrag, trying to get close enough to shut the damn door. But the heat is almost suffocating and the fire is only getting bigger.

"Babe, *move*," someone orders, and suddenly Taylor rushes in front of me and tosses a heap of mashed potatoes on the source of the flare-up.

The oven coughs out a plume of smoke and we all rush outside to the sound of the fire engine approaching and the sight of red lights bouncing off the trees.

"Who's up for Thai, am I right?"

"Not now, Brenna," growls Coach. Cradling his injured hand, he watches as firefighters run into the house to survey the situation.

The flashing lights twinkle across the worry on Iris Marsh's face. She pries Coach's hand from his chest to inspect the damage.

"Oh, Chad. You should get the EMTs to look at that."

Before he can protest, she waves her hand and a woman with a big duffel bag comes rushing over to tend to his burns.

Beside me, Taylor entwines her fingers with mine and cradles my arm for warmth. We're pathetic, a shivering and embarrassed spectacle on the front lawn of 42 Manchester Road. Neighbors peer out their windows and stand in their driveways wondering what the commotion's all about.

"I'm sorry, Coach," I tell him, wincing at his red palm. "I should've tried to close the oven door."

He barely flinches while the EMT pokes at his burn. "Not your fault, Edwards. Turns out I'm the dumbass."

"You know," Iris says, "Thai sounds great."

———

A couple hours later, we're the last ones in the Thai restaurant that just reopened a few months ago after—appropriately—a fire.

Coach has ditched his coat, Taylor let me leave my tie in the Jeep, and Brenna is still wearing the bright red lipstick she dons for all occasions.

"I appreciate the quick thinking," Coach tells Taylor while reaching for another spring roll with his good hand. The other one is now bandaged up like a boxing glove.

"I don't know what made me go for the potatoes," she says sheepishly. "I went in there thinking about looking under the sink for a fire extinguisher. That's where they always put them in apartments. But then I saw the bowl of potatoes and was, like, let's see what happens."

"I might have killed us all," he says, laughing at himself. "Good thing you were there."

The damage to the Jensen kitchen wasn't too bad, thankfully. Scorch marks being the worst of it. It'll be a hell of a mess to clean up after the firefighters went in there to make sure it didn't flare up again, but I told Coach I'd get the guys to come help out after the insurance people have their say.

"Taylor's experienced with all sorts of pyrotechnic disasters," Iris informs the group.

"Mom, please."

"Really?" I slide a glance at Taylor, who's slumping down in her seat. "Was she setting these fires?"

"There was a period of, I don't know"—Iris mulls it over— "maybe two or three years from elementary to middle school when I'd be in my office grading papers or in the living room reading, while Taylor was in her room with the door closed. A terrible sense of quiet would descend over the house just before the smoke alarm went off, and I'd rush upstairs with a fire extinguisher to find a new charred hole in the carpet and a puddle of melted Barbie dolls."

"She's exaggerating." Taylor smirks despite herself. "Mom, you're so dramatic. Change of topic, please."

"No way," I object. "I want to hear more about the pyro-anarchist of Cambridge."

Taylor smacks my arm, but Iris accepts the invitation to elaborate about the time her tiny blonde terror got sent home early from a slumber party for setting another girl's pajamas on fire.

"They were barely singed," Taylor insists.

"With her still in them," Iris finishes.

Coach starts in on a "that reminds me of the time" about Brenna, which she somehow deflects toward me and the team. But I'm not paying attention anymore. I'm too busy copping a feel of Taylor's thigh, because something about the idea of her being the menace of the quiet shady streets of Ivy Lane gets me a little hard.

"I'd like to know..." Brenna takes a performative sip of water from her glass because I guess it's been five whole minutes since she was the center of attention and if boredom sets in, she self-destructs. "What your intentions are, young man, with our dear daughter." Brenna's dark eyes take on an evil gleam as she scrutinizes me.

"Excellent question," Taylor's mom agrees. Iris and Brenna have nearly polished off their second bottle of wine and at this point have created an unholy alliance I don't believe I'm comfortable with.

"Oh, we just met tonight," I say, winking at Taylor.

"Yeah, he was my Uber driver."

"She was like, listen, this is going to sound crazy, but my incredibly rich and eccentric great-uncle died and in order to get my share of the inheritance I have to show up to this family dinner with a boyfriend."

"And at first he said no," Taylor adds, "because he's a man of honor and integrity."

Coach snorts.

"But then she started crying and it got awkward."

"So finally he agreed, but only if I'd give him a five-star review."

"What about you two crazy kids?" I say to Coach. "You being safe?"

"Don't push it, Edwards."

"No, he's right, Dad." Evil Brenna is on my side now. I prefer it this way. "I know it's been a while since we had the talk, so..."

"Don't start," he grumbles at Brenna, although Taylor laughs and Iris seems blissfully unbothered.

Taylor hadn't told me much about her mother beyond what she did for a living and that they were close. So I wasn't expecting a woman still showing glimpses of strutting through the streets of Boston in a leather jacket and *Sid and Nancy* shirt with a cigarette hanging out of her mouth. A punk rock PhD. She's very attractive, her eyes and hair the same shade as Taylor's. But her features are sharper—high cheekbones, a delicate chin. Not to mention, tall and runway-model thin. I can understand where Taylor gets some of her insecurities.

"There was this one time…" Brenna starts in again, and I tune her out, my gaze sliding to Taylor.

She has no reason to feel insecure. She's gorgeous. I don't know, sometimes I just look at her and it hits me all over again. How hot she makes me, how badly I want her.

My hand's still in her lap, and suddenly I'm acutely aware that we didn't get any time to fool around before I picked her up for dinner because we both had homework to finish and she was running a little behind getting ready.

I inch my hand up, just a little. Taylor doesn't look at me, doesn't flinch. Her thighs squeeze together. At first, I think I've overstepped, but then…she spreads them. Inviting my hand to roam higher.

Brenna is spinning some embellished bullshit about her internship at ESPN and some fight that broke out among a couple of the football commentators, keeping the parents entertained, while my fingers wander under the hem of Taylor's skirt. I'm careful, methodical. Taking care not to make myself conspicuous.

As Brenna makes grand hand gestures and rattles the table with her story, my fingertips brush the fabric of Taylor's panties. Silk and lace. Jesus, that's so hot. She shivers, just a little, under my touch.

Swallowing the saliva that suddenly fills my mouth, I slide my palm over her covered pussy and *holy fuck* I can feel how wet she is through her underwear. I want to slip my fingers inside and—

I yank my hand back when the waiter suddenly appears and places the check on the table.

As everyone jumps into the dance of fighting for the bill, I sneak a peek at Taylor to see her eyes glinting with mischief. I don't know how she does it, but this girl constantly finds ways to surprise me. Letting me feel her up under the table isn't something I thought I'd find in her playbook, but I love that this side of her exists.

"Thank you," she says after we've all said goodnight and are heading for our respective vehicles.

"For what?" My tone is a bit husky.

"Being here for me." Gripping my arm as we walk to the Jeep, she gets up on her toes to kiss me. "Now let's go back to my place and finish what you started in the restaurant."

24
TAYLOR

On Sunday morning, while Conor's out with the guys helping Coach Jensen get his kitchen in order, I do laundry and clean my own disaster of an apartment. It tends to be that the deeper into the semester it gets, the more my habitat starts to resemble the harried chaos shuffling around in my head.

When my phone rings, I drop the fitted sheet I'm struggling to fold, grinning to myself. I don't even have to check the screen to know who it is. I knew this call was coming, and I knew it would happen this morning. Because my mother is the most predictable person on the planet and basically it went down like this: after driving back to Cambridge Saturday afternoon, she would've stayed up reading and grading papers with a glass of wine, then gotten up this morning to start her own laundry and vacuum, all the while rehearsing in her head how this conversation would go.

"Hey, Mom," I say, answering the phone and plopping down on the couch.

She gets right to the point with a soft opening: "Well, that was some dinner."

And I politely laugh in agreement and say, well, it wasn't boring.

Then she agrees and says, good spring rolls, too. We'll have to go back to that place.

So for two minutes we're just stuck in a ping-pong match of

platitudes about pad thai and plum wine until Mom works up the nerve to finally ask, "What did you think of Chad?"

How did this happen to us?

"He's nice," I reply. Because it's the truth and reassuring enough. "He seems cool, I guess. And Conor says good things about him, so that's something. How's his hand?"

"Not too serious. It'll heal in a few weeks."

I hate this. Neither of us saying what we mean to say—that I don't know how to like the guy my mother is dating, and that she, in turn, will be broken-hearted if Chad and I can't find a way to be friends. Or if not friends, then at least something that looks close enough from a distance, because the alternative would be some awful feeling of incompleteness every time the three of us are in a room together.

I've never needed a father. Mom was more than enough, and if you asked her she would say the same thing—that I was enough for her, too. Yet I feel like there's this programed patriarchal voice buried deep inside her, maybe the remnants of the society that raised her, saying she's a failure as a mother and a woman if she doesn't have a man in her life or can't give her only daughter a male role model.

"Do you like him?" I ask awkwardly. "Because really, that's more important. I saw no glaring flaws in him other than maybe don't let him near an oven again."

"I do like him," she confesses. "I think he was nervous last night. Chad's a private guy. He likes simple things and not a lot of fuss. I think getting you two girls together for the first time, having all of us together, was a lot of pressure for everyone. He was worried you might hate him."

"I don't hate him. And I'm sure he and I will find a way to get along if, you know, this is going to be a thing."

Although I suppose it already *is* a thing. Wasn't that the point of last night? Why we all nearly burned to death for a pot roast or whatever that blackened mess was?

My mother has gone and gotten herself into a thing with a Chad. A hockey Chad, to boot. What the fuck is it with us and hockey?

Did my dad play hockey? Isn't it also a huge sport in Russia?

Has this been festering in my DNA this whole time like a dormant virus?

Am I going to be one of those fucking clichés who grows up to marry her dad?

Did I just insinuate I'd marry Conor?

Fuck.

"How will it work long-term, though?" I ask. "I mean, if long term is where this is headed. Are you going to keep commuting or—"

"We haven't discussed that," she cuts in. "At this point it isn't—"

It's my turn to interrupt. "Because you realize you can't leave MIT, right? For a man. I don't want to be a snob or a bitch or whatever you want to call it, and I'm not trying to be mean. But you're *not* leaving MIT for him, okay?"

"Taylor."

"Mom."

A flicker of panic tears through me, and I realize that maybe this new development is getting to me more than I've been willing to admit. It's not like MIT and Briar are that far apart. But for a moment there, I imagined Mom selling our house, my childhood home, and—another jolt of dread hits me. Yeah, I definitely haven't quite processed everything yet.

"Taylor. I need you to know something," she says firmly. "You will always come first."

"Yeah."

"Always. You're my daughter. My only child. We've been a team your whole life, and that's not going to change. I'm still here for you above anything else. And anyone else. If you decide—"

"I'm not going to tell you to stop seeing him," I blurt out, because I can see where she's going with this.

"No, I know—"

"I want you to be happy."

"I know. I'm just saying, if it came to it, I'm always going to pick my daughter over anything and anyone. It's not even a question. You know that, right?"

But there were times she didn't, and we both know it.

There were times when she was competing for tenure and promotions, writing books and touring campuses for speaking engagements. When she spent all day on campus then all night locked away in her office or hopping from one plane to another. Forgetting what time zone she was in and waking me up in the middle of the night to call me.

There were times when I wondered if I'd already lost her and that's just how it was supposed to be: your parents get you walking and talking and able to heat up your own Hot Pockets, and then they get to go back to living their own lives while you were supposed to start creating your own. I thought I wasn't supposed to need my mom anymore, and I started taking care of myself.

But then it would change. Get better. She would realize we hadn't had dinner together in months; I'd realize that I'd stopped asking when she'd be back or for permission to borrow the car. She'd notice me coming home with my own groceries while she was eating a pizza on the couch and we'd realize neither of us had even considered checking with the other one. That's when we'd realize we'd become roommates, and it would get better. We'd make an effort. She'd be my mom again and I'd be her daughter.

But to say that I have and will *always* come first for her?

"Yeah, I know," I lie.

"I know you do," she lies back. And I hear her sniffle as I'm rubbing the blur out of my eyes.

"I liked Conor," she adds, which makes me smile.

"I do too."

"Are you taking him to the Spring Gala?"

"I haven't asked him yet, but probably."

"Is this serious, or...dot, dot, dot."

That's the question everyone wants an answer to, Conor and me included. The question neither of us have wanted to look directly at, instead catching it in glimpses and flashes out of the corners of our eyes. The moving target floating in the periphery of our vision. What does serious mean and what does it look like? Do either of us have an idea or would we know it if we saw it?

I don't have a good answer, and I'm not sure Conor does, either.

"It's still new," is all I can think to say.

"It's okay to try things, remember. You're allowed to be wrong."

"I like things the way they are for now. And anyway, it's probably not a good idea to put a lot of expectations on each other right before finals, and then it's summer break, so...dot, dot, dot."

"That sounds like an exit strategy." She pauses. "Which isn't a bad thing, if that's what you need."

"Just being realistic." And reality has a way of smacking you in the face when you least expect it. So, yes, Conor and I might have something good going right now, but I haven't forgotten how this whole accidental relationship started. A dare that turned into a revenge plot that morphed into a full-blown situationship.

I have a feeling that someday, many years from now, Conor and I will cross paths at an alumni banquet and, squinting at one another from across the crowded room, remember the semester we spent in each other's pants. We'll laugh about it and share the amusing anecdote with his statuesque supermodel wife and whomever I wind up with, if anyone.

"I do like him," she repeats.

I almost tell her he invited me to California over the summer then bite it back. I feel like she'd make a big deal of it.

Granted, I already opened that stupid door when I let him meet my *mother*.

It didn't even occur to me that bringing Conor to dinner last night was crossing that major relationship threshold of introducing him to Mom. I just couldn't stomach the idea of sitting through the evening without some backup.

You've got to hand it to Conor—he didn't even flinch or fluster. He'd just shrugged and said, "Sure, if you don't mind picking out my clothes." His biggest concern was whether he had to shave, and I'd told him if I had to shave then so did he. After a week of his stubble rubbing a raw patch on my chin, I had put my foot down on the facial hair situation. Thinking about it now, that was another relationship milestone.

Mom and I chat for a while longer while I putter around my apartment. We talk about the Spring Gala and finals and whether I want to keep the apartment in Hastings over the summer or move my stuff into storage…a decision I realize I'm putting off until certain other summer plans are determined.

Later, when Conor texts to say he's coming over with takeout, I consider throwing together some elaborate high school display as a way of asking him to the Spring Gala. Like writing it across my chest in red lipstick or spelling it in underwear on the floor. Then I realize that making a big deal of the ask makes a big deal of the date and maybe that sends the wrong message. So I keep it casual and bring it up over a bowl of my favorite tomato soup and grilled cheese from the diner.

"Hey, so, there's this Kappa gala coming up. And I was going to ask my other fake boyfriend to be my date…"

Conor raises an amused eyebrow.

"He goes to another school, you wouldn't know him. Anyway, then I figured, well, since you've already met my mother and we've escaped a burning house together, maybe you'd go with me?"

"Is this one of those parties where you drag me around the room making other girls jealous and generally treating me like a dick with feet?"

"Yes."

"Then I accept."

A giddy smile threatens to break free. Conor makes everything so simple, it's no wonder I'm so comfortable with him. He makes it easy for me.

I watch as he shoves the last piece of his cheeseburger into his mouth, munching happily, and my good humor falters slightly.

No matter how comfortable I feel, there's always that whisper of doubt, fear. It's like white noise, a hum in my head when I'm falling asleep, a persistent warning that maybe we don't really know each other at all. And that at any moment, the elaborate fantasy we've designed could completely and utterly collapse.

25
TAYLOR

CONOR HAS THE ARTISTIC APTITUDE OF A GERBIL.

I learn this troubling fact when he comes over on Wednesday after his Econ class to find me already in my pajamas and elbow deep in construction paper. The kids are creating paper rainforests in Mrs. Gardner's class this week and I've got about two hundred paper flowers, birds, and other living things to cut out for them tonight. When Conor offered to help, I assumed he had at least a fifth-grade education in tracing and basic humanoid skills at operating a pair of scissors. My mistake.

"What is that supposed to be?" I ask, holding back laughter. Cartoons play in the background while we sit on the living room rug. One of the things I love about working in an elementary school is that it doesn't let you take yourself too seriously.

"A frog." He admires his genetic abomination, so sweetly proud of the grotesque creature that were it alive it would wheeze in agony before throwing itself in front of a moving car.

"It looks like a turd with warts."

"The fuck, Marsh." With a look of sincere insult, he covers where the frog's ears would be. "You're going to give him a complex."

"He needs a good mercy kill, Edwards." Giggles sputter out of me and I almost feel bad for Conor's devotion to his deformed creation.

"Do you spend your off hours poisoning all the less than conventionally attractive baby bunnies, too?"

"Here." I hand him a few sheets of colored paper where I've already traced several flowers. "Just cut these out."

He pouts. "You're going to be the meanest teacher."

"Try to stay in the lines, please."

Grumbling "whatever" under his breath, Conor retreats into the joyless task of cutting out flowers.

I can't help but cast surreptitious glances his way, admiring the adorable look of concentration on his face.

How is this real? There's six feet, two inches of solid muscle and man sprawled out on my floor. Conor constantly blows his hair off of his forehead as he works.

Sometimes I forget how attractive he is. I guess I've gotten used to him being around, taken for granted the soft shape of his lips and the masculine curve of his shoulders. The way his skin brushing against mine when we don't even mean to be touching makes my nerves jitter. The way it feels when he's on top of me.

When I imagine him inside me.

After a few minutes, I check on his progress to discover he's spent his time cutting out dicks of protest and lining them up neatly across my living room floor. When he notices me noticing, he crosses him arms and smiles proudly.

"Do you care to explain the dicks?"

"They're flowers," he says in a defiant tone, and I can easily picture a younger version of Conor rolling his eyes at high school teachers and flipping them the bird behind their backs.

"They have testicles!" I sputter.

"So? Flowers have testicles. They're called anthers. Look it up." He smirks, all full of attitude and mischief. It's not fair that he's so charming when he's being a pain in the ass. If we'd met in high school, I can only imagine the trouble he'd have gotten me into. We'd probably be fugitives by now.

"What if one of your dicks made it into the flower pile and tomorrow I had to explain to their teacher why she has two dozen six-year-olds plastering penises all over her classroom?" With an irritable sigh, I gather up the dicks and dump them in the trash.

"I thought you were using the word *rainforest* as a euphemism," Conor replies, unconvincingly and quite pleased with himself. "You know, like birds and bees."

"They're in first grade."

"When I was in first grade, Kai and I once hid in the cabinet under his kitchen sink to spy on his brother's friends watching *Girls Gone Wild* DVDs."

"That explains so much." When I go to the fridge for a soda, he comes up behind me and catches me around the waist to press his body against mine. He's hard, and that knowledge sends a current pulsating under my skin.

"Actually," he murmurs against my neck, "I was just hoping we could take a break so I could get you naked."

His palms travel up my ribs, while his lips kiss down beneath my ear and across my shoulder where my oversized cropped shirt sags low. When those firm hands cup and squeeze my breasts, I can't help but arch my back.

Groaning, he spins me around and backs me up against the fridge. His lips muffle my sound of surprise, his tongue penetrating my mouth.

There's something different about him tonight. Hungry. I reach for his T-shirt, but Conor catches my hands and lifts them above my head. Holding my wrists in one hand, he uses the other to tug free the bow on the front of my pajama shorts and lets them fall down my legs. Still kissing me, his fingers slip between my thighs, beneath my bikini underwear. The stainless steel of the refrigerator is cold against my back as he gently rubs up and down my slit, teasing my entrance.

I hold my breath, pulling away from his lips as he glides one, and then a second finger inside me. My knees bend of their own accord at the wonderful feeling of fullness and Conor's thumb rubbing over my clit.

"I love making you come," he says, his voice rough. "Will you let me?"

Excited bumps erupt over my skin as a rolling wave of arousal washes through me. My body goes a bit limp as it surrenders to Conor. My eyelids flutter closed. "Yes," I beg.

He pulls away abruptly.

I open my eyes and stare at him in a daze. "What's wrong?"

"Let me look at you."

I'm not sure what he means until I watch him cup his erect cock through his jeans. The long, thick outline protruding beneath the denim makes my heart race. He squeezes, waiting for me to comply.

We've never crossed this threshold, not with the lights on anyway. But I don't want to say no. I don't want to feel self-conscious or embarrassed in front of him anymore. Conor makes me feel safe, beautiful, desired. And right now, here in this moment, I don't want to be the thing standing between us.

Slowly, I pull my shirt over my head and drop it on the cold tile floor. Then I slide my panties down my legs and kick them aside.

His hot gaze freely roams my naked body as if he owns it. "You're gorgeous, Taylor."

Once more he hoists both my hands above my head, exposing my breasts to his lust-drenched eyes. He bends his blond head and wraps his lips around one nipple, licking and suckling until I'm squirming against him, needy for attention elsewhere.

"Con. Let's go to bed. Or at least the couch."

"Nah."

God, that California surfer-boy drawl kills me every time. I shiver as he kisses his way down my abdomen and kneels in front of me, pulling one leg over his shoulder to open me to his mouth.

I moan the moment his tongue licks my slit. He flicks it over my clit and sucks purposefully. He devours me with practiced precision, and it's all I can do to hold on to his shoulders while my hips move against his mouth.

My thighs clench as I feel the orgasm building low in my belly. "Keep doing that," I plead. "I'll kill you if you stop."

His husky chuckles vibrate against my core. But he doesn't stop. Knowing I'm close, he laves my clit with his tongue and slips one long finger inside me, thrusting slowly as he coaxes me to climax. I shatter, panting in shallow breaths, the pleasure detonating in my core and surging through my body.

Before I've completely recovered, Conor stands up and buries his face in the crook of my neck, kissing and sucking on my flesh while I continue to quiver from the orgasmic aftereffects.

"I am so fucking addicted to you, Taylor." His voice is gravel. He lifts his head, and I see his eyes gleaming with need.

Then he suddenly scoops me up in his arms, eliciting a squeal of protest from my throat.

"Put me down," I yelp, as my hands instinctively loop around his neck so I don't fall on my ass. "I'm too heavy for you."

His laughter tickles the top of my head. "Babe, I bench like twice your weight on a slow day."

I relax slightly as he carries me off to my bedroom. I don't feel light as a feather in his arms, but he doesn't seem to be struggling at all, which is encouraging. Note to self: always date someone who can bench-press twice your weight.

He lays me down in the center of the mattress, carefully placing my head against the pillows. Then he stands at the foot of the bed, his hands moving to the collar of his shirt.

"Permission to get naked?" He grins adorably.

"Permission granted." Man, now *my* voice is the one that sounds gravelly.

I watch with hooded eyes as he strips out of his T-shirt, jeans, and boxer briefs. I never get tired of staring at him. The planes of his chest, the shadows that accentuate his muscular arms. His beautiful, broad, athlete's physique robs me of breath. He's perfection.

My eyes fall to his long, thick cock and a resulting bolt of heat goes right between my legs.

This is a first for him, too. Being completely naked in front of me. And I appreciate that he does it not because it was a difficult step for him, but because he wants me to be comfortable.

Conor climbs onto the bed and covers me with his body. His lips find mine and we start kissing, tongues greedy and desperate, until we're both breathing heavily. I've never made out with anyone while we were both naked. Conor's dick lies heavy between my legs, slightly nudging my opening. It'd be so easy to just say yes, part my thighs a bit wider, grip him, and guide him inside.

His tongue teases mine again and for a moment it's all I want.

I want to say yes.

But.

"I don't think I'm…you know…there yet," I whisper against his mouth.

He lifts his head. Hazy arousal has darkened his eyes.

"I mean, I want to be."

"Okay." Conor rolls onto his side beside me. His dick is at full salute, and the pearly drop pooling at the tip makes my mouth water.

Swallowing, I sit up. "There's a big part of me that just wants to do it and get it over with, but—"

"You don't have to rush for me," he says easily. "I'm not in a hurry."

"No?" I search his expression for any signs of annoyance.

"No," he promises, sitting up too. "When you're ready, I hope it's with me. If not, I'm content right here with the way things are. I mean that."

I kiss him. Because despite all his protestations to the contrary, Conor is a good guy. He's sweet and funny and I think somehow he's even become my best friend. My best friend with dick benefits.

Releasing his lips, I take his cock in my hand. He's still hard, throbbing. His entire body tenses when I wrap my fingers around him and slide my fist up, down.

"Babe," he breathes, and I don't know what he intends by it—*babe, stop? Babe, keep going?*

If it was the former, it quickly turns into the latter when I slide to the floor and settle on my knees in front of him. His hands brace against the bed and his head drops forward at the first swipe of my tongue along his length.

Conor's legs tremble while I suck him. He breathes slow and deep, as if it's taking all his concentration.

"Don't stop," he mumbles as I take him deep in my mouth. His hips start moving, gently thrusting forward. "Please don't ever stop."

It's hard to smile when my lips are wrapped tightly around him, but I'm smiling in spirit. I love doing this to him, love driving him to the edge of blissful desperation. I know when I've almost got him there because he groans as his hands reach for my breasts and his hips lift off the bed just a little.

I don't know what makes me do it, but rather than letting him finish on his stomach, I take him in my hand and stroke him until he releases on my tits. It gives me a little thrill I didn't expect, a sharp sting of naughtiness. Once he's stopped shuddering, I peer up at his gorgeous face and see raw lust staring back at me.

"Fuck," he says, winded and brushing his sweaty hair out of his eyes.

I laugh awkwardly. "I'm just gonna get cleaned up."

As I'm getting up to go to the bathroom, his phone buzzes on the floor. He answers it while I'm waiting for the shower to heat up. I can't make out exactly what he says, but he sounds upset when he hears who's on the other end.

"I can't," I think he says. "Forget it... The answer's still no."

It's Kai again, I have no doubt of that. Whatever Conor's old friend is after, he's not letting this go.

And Conor's not offering any details. After I'm out of the shower, there's a distinct thundercloud over his mood, until he finally turns down my invitation to stay the night and heads home early.

Goddamn Kai. I wish he'd just go away. Clearly there's still something between those two, some terrible secret that's eating Conor up inside. As badly as I want him to talk to me, though, I'm not going to push him.

I just hope he finds a way to deal with it before it consumes him entirely.

26
CONOR

THE WATER IS FREEZING. EVEN THROUGH MY WETSUIT IT STILL stings my toes if I don't keep moving. I paddle in circles just to keep my body temp up, but it doesn't bother me. Nothing gets to me when I'm on my board and the swells are passing beneath me. Nothing penetrates the roar of waves crashing against the shore and the seagull cries overhead and the saltwater on my tongue. It's like being inside a snow globe. A perfect sphere of tranquility separate from everything and everyone else. Serene.

Then I feel the ocean pulling at me, the suction dragging out. I know my wave's coming and get myself lined up. Flat on my chest. Fingernails digging into the wax. Poised. And you just gotta sense it now.

I paddle to stay ahead of it just enough, until finally I pop up, vibration climbing my legs.

Find the balance.

Meet the wave.

Out here they don't last long. Only a few seconds until they break and fall and glide gently into the wash.

I get about an hour in the water before the sun has fully settled into the morning sky. I'm stripping out of my wetsuit at the Jeep when I see Hunter drive up in his Land Rover with Bucky, Foster, Matt and Gavin. Less than a minute later, a second vehicle carting

Jesse, Brodowski, Alec, and Trenton pulls into the parking lot. By nine the entire team's made it out to the beach for a cleanup with the SurfRider Foundation.

"Nice turnout," Melanie, the volunteer coordinator, tells me when I introduce the boys. They fall all over themselves to greet her as if they've never seen a woman before. "You guys local?"

"A bit up the road in Hastings," I say. "We're from Briar."

"Well, it's great to have you. We appreciate the support."

We all take a bucket, some gloves, and trash-picker poles from the tent they've got set up on the beach. Foster leers at a group of cute BU sorority girls walking by and raises his hand. "Uh, yeah, I'm new and not a good swimmer. Can I be paired with a buddy? I prefer blondes."

"Shut up, dipshit." Hunter elbows him in the ribs. "Don't worry," he assures Melanie. "I'm his chaperone."

She grins. "Thank you. Now get to work, gentlemen."

"Aye aye, captain," Matt says. He flashes a grin, and, despite being at least five years older than him, Melanie proves that no woman, of any age, is immune to Anderson's dimples.

I'd gotten involved with the foundation back in Huntington Beach, so when I saw they had a local chapter, I signed up without a second's thought. But not everyone is taking to it with a positive attitude. Only an hour into the cleanup, Bucky's already pitching a fit.

"I don't remember going to court," he grumbles, trudging through the sand with a bucket. "I feel like I'd remember that."

"Stop complaining," Hunter chides him.

"And come to think of it, I don't recall getting arrested, either."

"Shut up," Foster says.

"So someone tell me why I'm on a chain gang on my day off." Bucky bends over and starts wrestling with an item buried in the sand. As he does, the rest of us catch a whiff of something foul. Like a dead animal boiled in sewage.

"Oh damn, what is that?" Matt winces and covers his face with his shirt.

"Leave it, Buck," Hunter says. "It's probably somebody's dog."

"What if it's a body?" Jesse pulls out his phone, ready to capture the gory reveal.

"It's stuck on my stupid pole," Bucky says irritably. He proceeds to dig sand out of the way, yanking, pulling, fighting with the awful stinking thing that won't break free until finally he flies backward.

Sand sprays over our heads. Bucky's ass hits the ground at the same time that a loaded diaper tangled in a discarded volleyball net lands on top of him. What looks like more than a few discarded rotisserie chicken carcasses lie in the remnants of the hole he'd dug.

"Holy fuck, man, you're covered in baby shit!" Foster shouts as we all back away from the horror show.

"Oh fuck, I'm gonna barf."

"That's so nasty."

"It's all over you!"

"Get it off me! Get it off!" Bucky writhes around in the sand while Hunter tries to capture the diaper with his grabber thing and Foster keeps kicking more sand on him for some reason.

Matt is cackling at the scene unfolding in front of us. "Wash it off, dumbass," he tells Bucky.

I'm pretty sure Matt means for Bucky to utilize the showers up by the parking lot.

Instead, Bucky strips out of everything but his boxers and goes sprinting into the freezing surf.

Oh boy. It's fifty-four degrees on land and the wind's blowing at a good clip. But mind over matter, I suppose, because Bucky dives headfirst and swims out, furiously scrubbing and rinsing.

We all watch his progress. I'm feeling real admiration for the guy. I was out there earlier freezing my ass off in a wetsuit. I shudder to think of that frigid water tickling my bare balls.

When Bucky finally runs back out of the water, he's turned a shade of blue and is shivering like a dog in an ASPCA commercial. I swiftly take off my Henley and give it to him. Gavin's waiting for him with a towel. As for shorts, he's kind of shit out of luck.

"Go warm up in the Jeep." I hand Bucky the keys.

He snatches them. "I hate the environment."

As soon as he's out of earshot, the guys drop to their knees laughing.

"He's gonna be traumatized for life after that," Foster says, still working off the chortles.

"Dude's never coming to the beach again," Gavin agrees.

"I don't blame him." Hunter grins before sauntering off to toss all the feces-covered garbage in the dumpster.

With the exception of Bucky, the guys have been pretty good sports about giving up their Saturday morning. And honestly, it means a lot that they took an interest in something important to me. Since coming to the East Coast, I haven't had a lot of time to reconnect with my passions. Hockey and classes didn't leave any time for surfing or coming out to the coast. It was Taylor who got me thinking about looking for ways to volunteer again. She'd offered to join us today, but I thought this'd be a good way to get all the guys together. With the season over, we hardly ever get everyone in the same room anymore. Or the same beach, as it were.

I'm not gonna lie—a part of me missed them. I mean, yeah, I live with like half these assholes, but it's not the same as sweating it out on the ice together. Skating drills. Spending hours on a bus. Ninety minutes of pure nail-biting determination. I guess I didn't realize how much hockey meant to me until I played it with them. This team made me love it. These men have become my brothers.

My phone buzzes in my pocket. I expect it to be Taylor wondering what time I'll be back, but an unknown number pops up on the screen. By now I know what that means.

Kai.

I shouldn't answer it. Nothing good comes from giving him the satisfaction. There's this nagging feeling, though, that keeps me from sending him to voicemail. Because when it comes to Kai Turner, I'd rather see him coming. The worst thing I can do is let him sneak up on me again.

"What?" I bark in answer.

"Easy, bro. Simmer down."

"I'm busy."

"I can see that."

My blood runs cold. Trying not to draw attention, I look around, scanning the beach, the parking lot. In the distance I glimpse a skinny dude loitering near the restrooms. He looks like a little boy in his big brother's clothing and I don't have to see his face to know.

"How the hell did you find me out here?" I take a few steps away from Hunter and the others.

"Man, I got eyes everywhere. Don't you know that by now?"

"So you followed me." Fuck. He's getting more desperate.

Tracking me down in Buffalo was one thing. Now he's come to Massachusetts? From Hastings to this beach near Boston. Who knows how long he's been watching me or what his game is this time. I hesitate to say Kai's dangerous. I'd never known him to be violent beyond a few brawls. Just kid stuff. Black eyes and bruised egos.

Then again, I don't really know him anymore.

"I wouldn't have to if you'd just talk to me like a man," he says.

I stifle a curse. "I've got nothing to say to you."

"Yeah, but I do. So you can come up here and we can do this like friends, or I gotta come down there and embarrass you in front of your fancy new douchebags."

Fuck him.

It was like this when I first moved to Huntington Beach, too. Making me feel guilty for leaving the neighborhood, as if I had any choice in the matter. Taunting me about leaving him behind for trust-fund assholes, as if I even had any friends then. Ragging on me for my mom buying me new clothes. It took me a long time to realize what he was doing, the subtle psychological manipulation. Too long.

"Fine, asshole."

I tell Hunter I'm going to take a piss, then head up to the parking lot near the restrooms. I duck into the men's for a minute before going to the benches near my Jeep. There's no telling who he might have brought out here with him, and I'd rather not let him lure me too far from the crowds. If he's gone to all this trouble, that means he wants something pretty bad. I can't trust a desperate Kai.

"You're making this difficult," he says, sitting beside me.

"That's on you. I'd rather be left alone."

"Man, I don't get you, Con. You were my ride-or-die. Back in the day—"

"Fuck. Just stop." I turn to study him, this ghost of my childhood that becomes less a memory than a nightmare with every year that passes. "Back in the day is gone, Kai. We're not kids anymore. I'm nothing to you now."

I force myself not to tear my gaze away, but I see in him everything I hate about myself. And then I hate myself a little more for thinking that way. Because at least Kai knows who he is. Yeah, he's a screw-up, but he's not walking around with delusions, trying to cram himself into a mold that was made exclusively to keep guys like him, like *us*, out.

"Whatever you want, you're not getting it," I say in a tired voice. "I'm out, man. I'm done with your drama. Let me move on with my life."

"Can't do that, bro. Not yet." He slants his head. "You help me out, though, and I go away. You don't ever need to see me again. You can forget all about me."

Fuck. Fucking damn it.

"You're in trouble," I say flatly. Of course he is. It's in his voice. Not the usual *man, I'm in a bind, can you spot me* bullshit. He's scared.

"I screwed up, alright? I was supposed to do a thing for these guys—"

"A thing."

Kai rolls his eyes, his head wobbling in exasperation. "I was just moving a little product."

"Trafficking, Kai." Goddamn idiot. "You mean trafficking. The fuck's the matter with you?"

"It's not like that, bro. I owed a favor to some guys and they said if I picked up a package from this place and took it to that place, we were square. Easy enough."

"But?" Kai's whole life is a series of easy way outs followed by a string of critical buts. *But I didn't know anyone was home. But someone talked. But I got wasted and lost the money.*

"I did exactly what they told me," he protests. "Picked up the package from their boy, took it to the place, dropped it with a guy—"

"And now they say their guy never got it."

Kai deflates with how obvious the answer is. Because any moron would have seen this coming—and Kai never does. "That's the gist," he mutters. "I don't know who's got it out for me. Somebody's trying to fuck me up over this and I don't get the animosity."

"What do you expect me to do about it? If you're looking for a place to hide out, you gotta move along. I'm not having that kind of static around me. I've got roommates."

"Nah, nothing like that." He pauses, and the contrite droop of his shoulders says it all. "I just gotta pay them back, right, or they're getting their money's worth some other way, okay? Like I know we've been here before, Con. I get that. But these people think I stole their shit."

He rubs his face. Then, with red, urgent eyes he stares at me, imploring me. We're two kids again, making a pact in a dark room. Slicing our palms open with a pocketknife.

"Conor, they'll kill me or worse. I'm sure of it."

Damn him. Damn him for constantly finding ways to reduce

himself to the street price of a brick of coke or an envelope of pills. Damn him for letting a bunch of Scarface wannabes run his life. Damn him for holding a gun to his head and telling me if I really care about him, I'd give him more bullets.

I don't want to know the answer even as I ask the question. "How much?"

"Ten grand."

"Damn it, Kai." I can't sit still anymore. I stumble off the bench and start pacing, my blood boiling with anxious energy. I'd beat the shit out of him if it'd do any good.

"Look, I know."

"Son of a bitch." I kick a trashcan, anger and desperation bubbling in my gut.

I don't even know why I'm letting this get me so fucked up. It's Kai. He's acid. Potent, corrosive acid that eats everything it touches. Once you let it touch you, it seeps to the bone. Burns a hole right through you.

"No," I finally say.

"Bro." He grabs my arm and I shake him loose with a look that says he won't get to do that again. "You gotta help me out. I'm not kidding. They *will* come after me."

"Then run, dude. Hop a bus to Idaho or North Dakota and just fucking hide. I don't give a shit anymore."

"You're serious? You'd leave your best friend hanging—"

"We're not best friends. And maybe we never were." I shake my head a few times. "This is your problem to figure out and I don't want any part of it."

"I'm sorry, man." His demeanor shifts. His eyes harden. And now I remember why he used to scare me. "I can't let you walk away."

"You don't want to try me." I warn, squaring up to him.

There was a time I was just a skinny runt on a skateboard following him around the neighborhood. Not anymore. These days, I could bench this punk and break him over my knee. Better he remembers that before he gets any really stupid ideas. "Right now, I'm letting you walk away. Next time I see you, things might be different."

"Nah, brother." He bares his teeth in a cheerless smile. "See, you forget I still own your ass. Ten grand. Today."

"You're out of your mind. I don't have that kind of money. Even if I did, I wouldn't give it to you."

"You can get it," he says, still determined. "Go and ask stepdaddy for the money."

"Fuck off."

Kai sneers at me. "I don't think that's how you want to play this, Con. If you don't get me that money, Daddy Max finds out you're the one who gave out the alarm code to the mansion and let someone break in and trash the place." He cocks a brow. "Maybe I even tell him *you're* the one who took the missing cash from his office, how's that sound?"

"You're a piece of shit, Kai, you know that?"

"Like I said, brother. We can make this easy—just tell Max you need the money for some dumb bullshit. Make something up. You get me the cash and we're all good. I peace out and everyone's happy."

The thing you don't know as a kid, when your best friends are your whole world and every day is the first and last day of your life, when everything feels urgent and dangerous, every thought and emotion an eruption of planet-colliding force, is that the worst mistake you've ever made will outlive all of that. A brief, blinding moment of rage spirals into a lifetime of guilt and regret.

What I hate most about Kai is all the ways I'm just like him. The only difference is that he can admit it.

Dragging a shaky hand through my hair, I keep my gaze fixed on the horizon and force the words out of my tight, burning throat.

"I'll get you the money."

27
TAYLOR

I'VE BECOME ONE OF THOSE GIRLS.

Obsessively checking my phone every five seconds and jumping at the phantom vibration.

Turning the phone off and on again because maybe it's being buggy and that's why I haven't gotten a response to my last three text messages.

Texting myself to make sure they're going through and then making Sasha text me because I don't fucking know how phones work.

Hating myself the deeper I fall into this spiral of desperation and self-loathing. Dangling out on this branch above a pit of insecurities.

Yup, one of *those* girls. Every minute that goes by is another minute I can concoct a new scenario where he's cheating on me, given up on me, laughing at me. I hate myself. Or rather, I hate what I've become because I let myself believe a boy could make me happy.

"Give me your phone." Sasha, who's sitting beside me on her bedroom floor with our textbooks spread between us, holds out her hand and makes gimme fingers at me. She's got *I was fed up two hours ago* written in her cold, dark eyes.

"No."

"Now, Taylor." Oh yes, she's well past sick of my shit and quickly nearing *done with your dumb ass.*

"I'll put it away, okay?" Quickly, I stuff the phone in my back pocket and grab my notebook.

"You put it away six times already. But, weirdly, it won't seem to stay put away." She lifts a brow. "Take it out one more time and I'm confiscating, you hear me?"

"I hear you." And for the next ten minutes, I make a real effort at pretending to study.

I came to the Kappa house this afternoon when I'd run out of other means to distract myself. Conor never texted me when he got back to Hastings from the beach yesterday. We'd made tentative plans to meet up with friends at Malone's for Saturday night drinks, but afternoon turned into night turned into morning and I still hadn't heard from him.

I tried texting him again today. Twice. He replied only to say "sorry, something came up," then ghosted me again when I asked what happened.

Maybe under different circumstances I wouldn't be getting so worked up, but he'd left in a weird mood on Wednesday night, too. At the time I thought he was upset about that phone call from Kai. But then another notion crawled into my head: that night was the closest we'd come to having sex, and I'd turned him down. Every time we've hooked up after Buffalo, I've let us push the boundary a little further, but he's never tried to initiate full-on intercourse.

Until Wednesday night.

He'd been reassuring at the time. He'd said all the right things to put me at ease. But looking back, I wonder if that was only to get me to finish him off. Because once he had that, he bounced.

I let out a shaky breath.

"What?" Sasha pushes her notebook aside and questions me with concerned eyes. "Whatever's spinning around in your head, just spit it out, girl."

"Maybe this is…" My teeth dig into my lower lip. "Maybe this is what everyone saw coming?"

She hesitates to answer.

"He told me the night we met he didn't do girlfriends. That he hadn't dated anyone for more than a few weeks." I ignore the sharp clench of my heart. "We're pretty much pushing that time frame."

Her eyes soften. "Is that what you really think?"

"I think he's gotten tired of blowjobs and at this point would dump me for eight seconds of missionary sex through a sheet."

Sasha cringes. "Thanks for that visual."

I swallow my bitterness. "He wouldn't be the first guy to dump a girl because she doesn't put out."

"Never heard of a guy dumping a girl for too many BJs," she points out.

Which brings it back to the question of monogamy. "Maybe it isn't the BJs, but who's giving them…"

"Taylor. I think you'll just drive yourself crazy trying to imagine what's going on in his head," she says.

"Well, I wouldn't have to imagine if I could get him to return my texts."

"Listen." Sasha tries to mask her tone of frustration with something comforting, but it just comes out sounding impatient. She's trying, but consoling isn't her thing. "I don't know him, so I can't be your dick whisperer, but I will say this: if you really thought he was that guy, you wouldn't have been wasting your time on him. So that tells me maybe something else is going on."

"Like what?"

"I don't know, maybe he's having his guy period. My point is, whatever his deal is, it isn't you. That isn't the first place your head should go."

"No?"

"No, babe. Seems to me like he's been crazy for you since the moment you two started fake dating. So either he's dealing with some shit or he's just an asshole. And if it's the latter case, you'll be lucky to be rid of him. So stop stressing. You two will talk at some

I give her a cut-it-out glare, which she ignores. She's too busy drowning in the depths of Eric's...manners. He gives the all-clear to his buddies at a table across the room, and the two guys wind their way toward us with their beers. Their names are Joel and Danny, and the five of us get cozy and acquainted, Sasha and I craning our necks at the skyscrapers Briar's recruiting as college basketball players these days.

When Danny shuffles a bit closer to me, Sasha digs her finger-nails into my arm as a means of telling me she's not letting me flee. I nudge her a few feet away so we can talk privately.

"I have a boyfriend," I remind her. To which Sasha pops a sarcastic eyebrow. "I think."

"You don't have to jump on their dicks," she replies. "Just smile and nod and drink up. A little harmless flirting won't kill anyone."

"If I saw Conor flirting with another girl—"

"But you're not seeing him because he won't return your texts. So pretend you're alive for a few hours and enjoy yourself," she says, pushing a shot at me after Danny insists on ordering us all tequila.

"To basketball," Sasha raises her shot glass.

"To Kappa Chi," Eric answers.

"To hockey," I mutter under my breath.

After we down our shots, Sasha pulls out her phone and holds it up to grab a group selfie of the five of us.

"There," she chirps.

"There what?"

She crops the image and adds a filter before posting the pic with several choice hashtags.

#girlsnight #kappachi #briaru #fuckpucks #bigballs

"Let Conor ignore this," she says with a grin.

The thing is, I don't want revenge. I don't want to make him jealous or remind him what he's missing. I just want to understand what changed.

Later, when I'm back at my apartment, getting into bed and

trying to talk myself out of texting Conor again, I realize I missed a text from him earlier.

HIM: Sorry. Talk tomorrow. Goodnight.

Somehow, this is worse than him not responding at all.

28
CONOR

A SHRINK WOULD CLASSIFY MY BEHAVIOR OF THIS PAST WEEK AS self-destructive. Or at least that's what Hunter's girlfriend accused me of doing today, and Demi is halfway to being a shrink, so she's legit. Apparently she ran into Taylor on campus earlier, prompting her to text me something along the lines of, "The fuck did you do to her???"

Which I can only take to mean I've managed to ruin Taylor, too. It's nothing more than what I expected would happen. Exactly what I deserve. Can't keep spraying perfume on the pile of crap and pretending it doesn't stink.

I wanted to call her. I drove to Taylor's apartment after the beach last weekend but couldn't make myself go inside. I couldn't lie to her face again and tell her everything's fine. I'd rather have her think I'm just another asshole jock than know what I really am.

We've met up a couple times since then, grabbing coffee between classes on campus, but I've avoided her place and haven't asked her over to mine. The coffee dates are already awkward enough, a solid hour where I can't think of anything to say and she's afraid to scare me off. And every text she sends wondering what's wrong drives the knife a little deeper.

If I were a better person I'd tell her the truth. I'd come clean and let her look at me with those beautiful turquoise eyes full of betrayal and disgust. Let her call me a pathetic loser and watch her finally understand what I'd been too chickenshit to tell her all along: that she deserves better.

TAYLOR: You wanna come over tonight?

But I'm a coward. I keep telling myself that once I get rid of Kai, things with me and Taylor can go back to normal. I'll make an excuse and she'll reluctantly forgive me and then I can spend the next month winning her back.

Except every time I see the question mark at the end of her messages it gets harder to imagine facing her again.

Another text flashes on my screen. This time, it's from Kai.

KAI: You're wasting time...

I turn the phone over so I don't have to look at the screen anymore. It's Monday morning and I shouldn't still be lying in bed. My philosophy lecture starts in less than an hour. Although I'm doing plenty of philosophizing in my head, so maybe I should just skip. Too much introspection can't be good for the soul.

I stare up at my bedroom ceiling and draw a ragged breath. Then I drag my lazy ass out of bed and force myself to get dressed.

My phone vibrates again and I pretend not to notice. It's either Taylor or Kai. Or maybe my mom.

Right now the only person it hurts more to disappoint than Taylor is my mother. I can't call her asking for that kind of money. I thought I could muster up the balls to call Max directly, feed him some bullshit story about one of my teammates getting into trouble and not wanting to worry Mom about it. Or I could say I wrecked someone's car. But then I pictured the face he'd make.

Hitting him up for cash would only provide him with more confirmation of what he'd always believed about me: that I was trash,

He shrugs. "Cool."

Before I can blink, Hunter digs around in one of his desk drawers for a checkbook. I sit there, stunned, as he fills one out to Cash. "Here you go."

Just like that, he hands it to me. Ten grand. Four zeros.

I'm such an ass.

"I can't tell you how much you've saved me." The sense of relief is instant, the remorse even quicker. I hate myself for this. But not enough to not fold the check up and stick it in my wallet. "I'm sorry about this. You—"

"Con, it's all good. We're teammates. I've always got your back."

Emotion tightens my throat. Man, I don't deserve this. It's a complete accident I even ended up here. At Briar, on this team. I got it in my head I had to get the hell out of LA, and a couple phone calls later Max had me enrolled at his alma mater.

I didn't do anything to earn a spot on a D1 team or the friend-ship of guys like Hunter Davenport. Someone owed someone a favor and I got to walk onto the team as a junior. I'm an okay hockey player, maybe even pretty good sometimes. Less frequently I might even be better than good. But how many other guys were better than good and didn't have connections? I have no doubt that there was someone else more deserving, someone who doesn't come asking for handouts from their friends to buy off the guy blackmailing him because he robbed his own family.

That's the thing about running from yourself—you're always running straight at the problem.

After I leave Hunter's place, I just drive. I've got nowhere in mind, and I end up at the coast, sitting in the sand and watching the waves. I close my eyes to the sun setting at my back and listen to the sound that saved me once. The sound that normally centers me, connects me to whatever it is we call a soul, a conscience. But the ocean isn't helping me tonight.

I drive back to Hastings and wait for some voice inside me

to offer up a better choice, the right choice, but I'm alone in my head.

Somehow I find myself at Taylor's apartment. I park the Jeep and sit there for nearly an hour watching the texts fill my screen.

TAYLOR: Getting dinner.

TAYLOR: Going to bed early.

TAYLOR: See you tomorrow for lunch?

I lean toward the glove box and pop it open, rummaging until I find the small tin Foster shoved in there the other night. I pull out the rolled joint, find a lighter in the center console. I light up and exhale a plume of smoke out the open window. Knowing my luck, a cop'll drive by this very moment, but I don't care. My nerves need some relief.

KAI: Got it yet?

KAI: Get at me

I take another deep drag, blow out another smoke cloud. My thoughts start to get away from me, almost developing a mind of their own. I'm so deep in my own head, I don't know how to dig myself out. You hear from people who have near-death experiences that their whole life flashed before their eyes, and here I am, living and breathing, yet the same surreal phenomenon is happening to me.

Or maybe you're just fucking high, man. Yeah, maybe that.

Another text message appears.

KAI: Don't try me bro

It's almost funny, right? You see a kid across the street. Sit near him in school. Piss off the neighbors doing skateboard tricks in the middle of the street. Get bloody noses and scraped elbows. Then you're learning how to hold a joint, how to inhale. Daring each other to talk to that cute girl with the fake lip piercing. Giving each other safety pin piercings in the stairwell behind the school auditorium. Stuffing beer bottles down your pants in the 7-Eleven. Cutting through chain-link fences and wedging yourself through boarded up windows. Exploring the catacombs of a decaying city, thirty-year-old darkened shopping malls where the fountains are dry but the roofs are always leaking. Skateboarding past the hollowed-out carcasses of Radio Shacks and Wet Seals. Learning to tag. Learning to tag better. Getting jumped behind the liquor store. Joyriding. Running from the cops and hopping fences.

I take another pull of the joint, then another, as my entire childhood races through my mind. Nothing shapes us like our friends. Family, definitely. Families fuck us up by an order of magnitude. But friends, we collect them like bricks and nails and drywall. They're pieces in the blueprint, but that blueprint is always under renovation. We're all deciding who we were always meant to be, choosing, mutating, growing into ourselves. Friends are the qualities we want to absorb. What we want to be.

I exhale a cloud of smoke. The thing is, we forget that our friends have designs of their own. That we're just pieces in *their* blueprint. We're constantly at cross-purposes. They've got families of their own. Their own orders of magnitude in damage. Brothers who handed them that first joint, first swig of beer.

I look back, and it's obvious Kai and I were always going to end up here. Because a part of me needed him, wanted to be like him. But then we reached the gut check moment—that sense of survival that makes some of us afraid of heights and some of us jump out of airplanes. It kicked in for me, and it was like fight or flight. An innate animal instinct that Kai would be the death of me, if I let him.

So I ran, and I changed my life—for a time. But maybe people aren't ever capable of changing once that foundation has been laid. Maybe Kai and I were always going to be each other's destruction.

Right now I'm afraid of heights and he's stopped wearing a parachute. He's leaning out of the plane and I've got one hand on his shirt and as soon as I let go, he flies. Only, he pulls me with him, and we both plummet.

I flick the joint out the window and reach for my phone.

ME: Friday night. I'll meet you.

KAI: See you then

I don't know what happens after this or how I come back from it. If things between Hunter and I will change. What happens when I go home to California and sleep in that house and have to look my mother in the eye.

Then again, I found a way last time, so maybe I should stop kidding myself that lying doesn't come naturally and guilt is permanent. Maybe I should stop pretending that if I feel bad it means I'm not completely defective. Hell, maybe I should stop feeling bad at all and embrace indifference. Accept that I'm not, and never was, a good person.

When I get home, I head upstairs to my bedroom and text Taylor to blow off lunch tomorrow.

And the day after.

Because avoidance is easier.

29
TAYLOR

I FORGOT WHAT A HASSLE THE SPRING GALA IS EVERY YEAR. FRIDAY morning I wake up late and have to scramble out of the apartment. From then it's like the day is on fast-forward.

Spill coffee on myself sprinting to class. Didn't bring the right notebook. Pop quiz. Haul ass to another class. Vending machine eats my dollar. Starving. Rush to Kappa to meet Sasha. Run to salon; they're an hour behind. Get lunch while we wait. Get our hair done. Back to the Kappa house. She does my makeup while I do her nails. She does her makeup while I steam our dresses. And finally— collapse on the floor until Abigail starts stomping through the house shouting that the setup crew needs help at the venue.

Now Sasha and I are in the banquet hall hooking up the rented sound system with her laptop. Our heads are dropping bobby pins while we crawl around on the floor in our sweats before we have to run back to Kappa house to take a baby wipe shower and get our dresses.

"Don't we have pledges for this or something?" Sasha gripes while we haul another massive speaker inside from the loading dock because the dolly has a flat tire.

"I think the freshmen are in the kitchen folding napkins."

"Seriously?" she says. We drop the speaker in place and take a moment to catch her breath. "Shit, I'll go sit on my ass and fold fucking origami. Get that lacrosse chick out here to throw a couple of these on her back."

"I think you told Charlotte you didn't want any plebes getting their grubby hands on your gear."

"Yeah, well, I didn't mean the heavy shit."

I grin. "Come on. One more. Then I'll run the rest of the cables while you do a sound check."

Sasha takes a deep breath and blots the sweat from her hairline with her sweater. "You're a good friend, Marsh."

While we're carrying the speaker in, a familiar face appears in our path. It's Eric, the basketball boy from Malone's, carrying six large boxes of donuts. We set the speaker in place and meet him at Sasha's DJ booth with feral hungry eyes.

"Help yourselves," he says easily.

"Oh my God, you're the best." Sasha shoves a donut in her mouth and takes two more. "Thank you," she mumbles with her mouth full.

Like a swarm of locusts, the other sisters descend on the donuts. Everyone's been surviving on green juice and carrots for a week or more so they could fit into their one-size-too-small dresses tonight.

"I have to run into the city to pick up my tux," Eric tells Sasha while she's licking icing off her fingers. "Just thought you girls might need a sugar boost."

"Thank you. We really appreciate it."

"For real," I agree.

Just as quickly as they arrived, the girls pick the boxes clean. There's not a sprinkle or dab of jelly filling left as they scurry away to their tasks.

I glance around the massive room in approval. Huh. This place is starting to look halfway presentable. Tables arranged. Banners and decorations hung. We might actually pull this off.

"Meet you back here at eight?" Sasha says to Eric.

"Yes ma'am. See ya then." He gives her a kiss on the cheek and waves bye to me as he leaves.

My head swivels toward her. "Um. I didn't know he was your date," I accuse.

She shrugs. "I was gonna go stag again, but this way I have someone to get me drinks while I DJ."

We cram the empty donut boxes in a trashcan, then head off in search of the alleged cooler where supposedly there's bottled water for everyone. We try the kitchen first, where eight freshmen sit in the dark amongst piles of white cloth napkins, hunched and weary. It's like a fucking sweatshop in here and we back away quietly. Freshmen are scary.

"What about Conor?" she asks as we walk down another corridor.

What about Conor... It seems like since I met him, that question has consumed a little more of my life every day. The two of us have been caught in a constant evolving state of uncertainty.

"I don't know," I reply honestly. "He's canceled our plans for the last two days."

A frown mars her perfect lips. "Have you talked at all?"

"A little. Text messages mostly, and he doesn't say much. Just that he's busy, dealing with something, yada yada. And of course, he's always sorry."

"He wouldn't just...not show up tonight, right?" Sasha watches me closely, as if monitoring for some sign or signal that I might snap into a rage or have a total nervous breakdown.

"No way," I say firmly. "He'd never do that."

"Hey, Taylor." Olivia comes around the corner from the loading dock. "You left this outside. It was buzzing."

I take my phone from her, and relief slams into me when I notice a missed call from Conor. Finally. I need to know if he's picking me up or meeting me here.

"Speak of the devil," Sasha says.

I'm about to call him back when a text comes through.

CONOR: I'm not gonna make it tonight

I stare at the screen. Then I type a response with shaky thumbs.

ME: That's not funny.
HIM: I'm sorry

"What's wrong?"
I try calling him.
Straight to voicemail.
"He didn't," Sasha says, her voice grim as she reads my expression.
I ignore her. Call him again.
Straight to voicemail.

ME: Talk to me
ME: What the hell is going on?
ME: Fuck you Conor

I wind my arm back to hurl my phone across the room, but Sasha catches my wrist before I can let go. She grabs the phone out of my hand and fixes me with a stern look.

"Let's not make any rash decisions," she advises, before pulling me into the restroom across the hall. "Talk to me. What did he say?"

"He's not coming. No explanation. Just, sorry, bailing on you again," I say, seething, gripping the edge of the sink to stop from putting my fist through the mirror. "I mean, what in the actual fuck? He didn't just decide this today, he couldn't have. He's been blowing me off all week. Which means he *knew* he wasn't coming. He could have just told me! Instead he waits until the last second to really drive the knife in."

I let out a scream and punch the stall door instead. Not quite as satisfying when the door just flies open from the force. It still hurts, but at least I didn't shred my knuckles.

"Okay, She-Ra, settle down." Sasha corrals me in a corner with her hands up, as if she's settling a cranky rhino. "You really think he's doing this to hurt you?"

I push away from her. I can't stand still. "What other explanation is there? This is probably all part of some long con he was running on me. Maybe I was the dare all along. Some bet with his teammates. Now the game's over and they're all laughing at me. Poor pathetic fat girl."

"Hey." Sasha snaps in front of my face to stop my furious pacing. "Shut the fuck up. You are not pathetic and there's nothing wrong with the way you look or the shape of your body. You're beautiful, funny, kind, and intelligent. If Conor Edwards has some fucking malfunction, it isn't your fault. It's his loss."

I can't hear her. Not really. There's a white-hot ball of rage in my gut and it's building with every second that I don't have an answer.

"I need to borrow your car," I burst out, holding out my hand.

"I don't think you're in any condition to drive right now—"

"Keys. *Please.*"

Sasha sighs and passes the keys over.

"Thank you." I dart out the bathroom door like my ass is on fire, with Sasha hot on my heels.

"Taylor, wait," she calls after me in exasperation.

Rather than wait, I tear down the hall toward the lobby. My pace is so fast that when I skid around the corner, I slam into one of my sorority sisters. Half a dozen or so Kappas are milling in the lobby, along with a couple of Sigma guys lugging chairs.

The brunette I just bulldozed stumbles forward. With her long hair falling over her eyes, it takes a second for me to realize it's Rebecca.

"Shit, I'm sorry," I tell her. "I didn't see you there."

Regaining her balance, she instantly casts her eyes downward at the sound of my voice. I'm already so testy thanks to my anger over Conor, that Rebecca's mopey scowl triggers another rush of ire.

"For fuck's sake," I snap at her. "We made out freshman year and you felt up my boobs, Rebecca. Get over it."

"Meow," cackles Jules, who's standing a few feet away and overheard me.

At her, I snap, "Shut up, Jules," and then brush past her and Abigail's douchey Sigma boyfriend, leaving their wide eyes in my wake.

Sasha catches up to me just as I'm throwing open one of the double doors at the entrance.

"*Taylor*," she orders. "Stop."

I force myself to stop. "What is it?" I ask.

Worry playing on her face, she touches my arm and gives it a soft squeeze. "No guy is worth losing your self-respect over, okay? Just remember that. And wear a seatbelt."

30
TAYLOR

Conor's Jeep is in the driveway when I get to his townhouse. Foster answers the door, donning a big dumb grin when he sees me. He lets me in without a question, saying Con's upstairs in his room. For a moment it crosses my mind to interrogate Foster. If any one of the roommates were to crack, spill the tea for a glimpse of some cleavage, it'd be Foster. Right now, though, I just want to nail Conor to a wall.

I barge into his room to find him totally alone. I guess part of me expected there to be a naked woman in his bed, but instead, it's just him, dressed like he's going somewhere and about to leave.

He doesn't even look surprised to see me. Disappointed, maybe. "I can't talk right now, T," he says with a sigh.

"Well, you're gonna have to."

He tries to open the bedroom door behind me, but I stand in his way. "Taylor, please. I don't have time for this. I need to go." His voice is cold, indifferent. He won't look at me. I think I wanted him to be angry, annoyed. This is worse.

"You owe me some kind of explanation. Blowing off dinner plans is one thing, but the Spring Gala was important to me." My eyes are hot and stinging. I swallow hard. "Now you're bailing on me hours before the event? That's cold, even for you lately."

"I said I was sorry."

"I'm sick of sorry. I feel like we broke up only you forgot to tell me. Dammit, Con, if this"—I gesture between us—"is over, just tell me. I think I deserve that much."

He turns away from me, raking his hands through his hair and mumbling something under his breath.

"What? Just spit out," I order. "I'm right here."

"It has nothing to do with you, okay?"

"Then what? Just tell me why." Exasperation washes over me. I don't understand what he possibly has to gain from all this subterfuge, if not to drive me crazy. "What's so important that you're ditching me tonight?"

"There's just something I have to do." Frustration builds in his voice. The lines deepen across his face, and his shoulders hold more tension than I've ever seen. "I wish I didn't, but it is what it is."

"That's not an answer!" I say in frustration.

"It's the only one you're getting." He stalks past me and reaches for the jacket draped over his desk chair. "I've gotta go. You need to leave."

As he grabs the jacket, it catches on the armrest and a thick white envelope about the size of a brick tumbles out of one of the pockets. From the envelope, several bound straps of twenty-dollar bills splay on the floor.

We both stare in silence at the money until Conor swipes it up off the floor and starts shoving it back in the envelope.

"What are you doing with all that money?" I ask warily.

"It's not important," he mutters, shoving the envelope into his jacket pocket. "I have to go."

"No." I shove the door closed and plaster myself against it. "No one walks around with that kind of money unless they're up to no good. I'm not letting you walk out this door until you tell me what's wrong. If you're in some kind of trouble, let me help you."

"You don't understand," he says. "Please, just get out of my way."

"I can't. Not until you tell me the truth."

"Fuck," he grits out, yanking at his hair. "Just let me go. I don't want you involved, T. Why are you making this so difficult?"

His mask has finally failed. Gone is the aloof, indifferent face he's held in place all week while he's done his best to hide the anguish inside. Now all I see is pain, desperation. This thing has been eating him up and he looks exhausted.

"Don't you get it?" I say. "I care about you. What other reason is there?"

Conor deflates. He collapses on the edge of his bed and drops his head in his hands. He's quiet for so long I think he's given up.

But then he finally speaks.

"Last May, back home in California, Kai comes to me one day—I hadn't seen him in weeks—and says he needs money. Like a lot of money. He got in bad with a drug dealer and had to pay him back or the guy would fuck him up. I told him I don't have that kind of cash. So he says, you know, ask Max for money." Conor raises his eyes, as if checking to see whether I remember what he's told me about his relationship with his stepfather.

I nod slowly.

"Right, so I said hell no, I can't do that. Kai gets pissed, like, fuck you, I thought we were friends, all that crap, but he doesn't push it. He just says he'll find another way and leaves. At the time I thought he was exaggerating about the trouble he was in, that maybe he just wanted a new phone or some dumb shit and thought I could waltz into a giant gold vault and take whatever I wanted."

Conor takes a breath and rubs at his face. As if he's gathering energy.

"So then maybe a couple weeks later, Max and I got into some stupid argument. I hadn't declared a major yet and he was getting on my case about figuring out what I'm going to do with my life. So of course I get defensive because what he really means is that I'm a loser who's never going to amount to anything if I don't become just like him. It turns into a full-on shouting match and then I get pissed off and leave. I end up at Kai's place, tell him what happened, and he says, hey, you know, we can totally get back at him. Just say the word."

I approach the bed with timid steps and sit down, keeping several feet of space between us. "And what did you say?"

"I said fuck it. Let's do it."

He shakes his head, letting out a deep sigh. I can feel the anxiety wafting off him, how hard it is to admit all of this. How far he has to reach into himself to find the courage.

"I gave Kai the alarm code and told him Max always keeps three grand in cash in his desk drawer for emergencies. I said I didn't want to know when it's gonna happen. It'd be months before Max would even notice it was missing, and besides, that kind of money is nothing to the man. He'd spend that in a week on dinner and wine. Nobody gets hurt."

"But...?"

Conor looks at me. Finally. For the first time in a week, he really looks at me.

"So one weekend we all go to Tahoe. I wanted to stay behind but Mom gave me a guilt trip about spending quality time together. So the house is empty for a few days, and Kai makes his move. He was probably high or wasted on some shit—the kid never had a fucking dimmer switch, you know? He slips in quiet enough, but then he trashes the place. He grabs one of Max's golf clubs from the garage and smashes up Max's office and the living room. We came home a couple days later and it's obvious the place has been robbed. The messed up part is, Max blamed himself. Figured he must have forgotten to set the alarm. But whatever, no big thing, he says. Insurance will cover the damage."

My forehead wrinkles. "They didn't wonder why nothing else was stolen?"

Conor barks out a sardonic laugh. "Nope. The cops decided some teenagers probably just wanted to trash the place. They said they'd seen it a million times, a crime of opportunity, and that maybe the teens got scared off by something."

"So you got away with it."

"Yeah, but that's the thing, right? The guilt tore me up from the moment we stepped inside the house and I saw what Kai did. What I did. Somehow in my head I convinced myself that it'd feel good to see the look on Max's face. But it fucking hurt. What kind of asshole trashes his own house? My mom was terrified for weeks afterward that whoever did it would come back. She couldn't sleep." His voice cracks. "*I* did that to her."

My heart hurts for him. "And Kai?"

"He found me at the beach a couple weeks later and was asking, you know, how'd it go. I told him I couldn't hang out with him anymore, that he'd gone too far and it was a bad idea to begin with. And that was it, we were through. In his head he thought he was being a good friend, like he was sticking up for me or something. That's probably the best example anyone could give you of how his brain works."

"I'm guessing he didn't take the break-up well?"

"Nope. I think more than anything he was worried I'd rat him out. But I reminded him that doing so would be mutually assured destruction. And we went our separate ways."

"Until Buffalo."

"Buffalo," he agrees ruefully. "Then Saturday at the beach. He followed me there, gave me the same old story. He owes money to bad people and they'll kill him if he doesn't get it. Except this time he needs ten grand."

"Shit," I say under my breath.

Conor laughs sadly in response. "Right?"

"You can't give him the money."

He cocks his head at me.

"No, I'm serious, Conor. You can't give him the money. This time it's ten, next time it's fifteen, twenty, fifty. He's blackmailing you, right? That's what this is all about? Mutually assured destruction? And the contents of that envelope…I bet you didn't get the money from your family."

"I don't have a choice, Taylor." His eyes turn angry.

"Yes, you do. You can tell Max and your mom the truth. If you come clean, Kai has no more leverage. He'll leave you alone and you can finally get on with your life without worrying about the day he'll show up again to derail your whole life."

"You don't know what you're talking about. You have no—"

"I know that because of this shame and embarrassment you feel, you've blown me off, fucked your family over, and done who knows what to get that money. When's it going to stop? When is it enough?" I shake my head at him. "There's only one thing you can do to fight back, or you can be a slave to this secret forever."

"Yeah, you know…" Conor gets up. "This really doesn't concern you. I told you the truth and now I've gotta go."

I jump up and try to intercept him, but he sidesteps me with little effort on his way to the door. I grab his hand as he turns his back on me. "Please. I'll help you. Don't do this."

He snatches his hand away. When he speaks, the coldness and detachment has returned. "I don't need your help, Taylor. I don't want it. And I definitely don't need some chick telling me what to do. You were right. We shouldn't be together."

He doesn't look back. Down the hallway and out the door. Not a single hesitation.

He just leaves me there with the poisoned memories of this room, with my makeup smeared and hair falling down.

Conor Fucking Edwards.

31
CONOR

THERE WAS THIS GIRL WHEN I WAS GROWING UP. DAISY. SHE WAS around my age, lived a couple doors down in the old neighborhood, and she used to sit for hours in her driveway drawing with little rocks or broken pieces of cement because she didn't have chalk. When the sun turned the concrete slab into a griddle or the rain wrinkled her skin, she'd throw stuff at us when pre-teen Kai and I would ride past on our skateboards. Rocks, bottle caps, random trash, whatever was lying around. Her dad was mean as shit and we figured she was just like him.

Then I watched one day from my porch. I watched her getting off the school bus, knocking on her front door. Her dad's truck was in the driveway and the TV inside so loud the whole neighborhood could hear the sports highlights. She kept knocking, this scrawny girl and her backpack. Then trying the window where the bars had been torn off during a break-in and never replaced. And then finally giving up, resigned, and picking another rock from the side of the street that from some decaying part of the neighborhood eventually tumbled its way to her.

Next I watched Kai rolling down the sidewalk on his skateboard. Stopping to talk to her, to taunt her. I watched as he did donuts over her drawings, then poured a soda out on the pictures and flicked the bottle cap in her hair. And I got it then, why she threw stuff at us whenever we passed her. She was aiming for Kai.

The next time she sat alone in her driveway, I brought my own rock and joined her. Eventually we left the driveway and explored the world. We watched the highway from a tall tree, counted planes from rooftops. And one day Daisy told me she was leaving. That when the school bus dropped us off, she was just going to walk away and go somewhere else. Anywhere else. *You could walk away, too,* she'd urged.

She had this magazine picture of Yosemite and got it in her head that she would live there, at a campground or something. *Because they'd have everything you'd need and it doesn't cost anything to camp, right?* We talked about it for weeks, making plans. It's not that I truly wanted to leave, but Daisy needed so much for me to go with her. It was the loneliness she feared the most.

Then she got on the bus one day and she had purple bruises on her arms. She'd been crying and suddenly it wasn't a game anymore. It wasn't some story we were writing about a great adventure to pass the time between school and sleep. When the bus pulled up at school, she looked at me, expectant, her backpack hanging heavier on her shoulders than normal. She said, *We leave today at lunch?* I didn't know what to say to her, how to not say the wrong thing. So I did something much worse.

I walked away.

I think that was the moment I learned I wasn't any good for anyone. Sure, I was barely eleven years old, so of course I wasn't running north with nothing but a backpack and a skateboard. But I'd let Daisy believe in me. I'd let her trust me. Maybe I didn't understand at the time what was really going on in her house, but on a conceptual level I got the fucking gist and yet I didn't do anything to help her. I simply became another in a long line of letdowns.

I'll never forget her eyes. How in them I saw her heart break. I see them still. Now.

My hands shake. Gripping the steering wheel, I barely see the road. It's like tunnel vision, everything narrow and faraway.

I'm driving by memory more than sight. A tightness in my chest that's been building for days now clamps down, climbing my throat. Suddenly it hurts to breathe.

When the phone buzzes in the cup holder, I nearly swerve into oncoming traffic, startled by the sound that feels louder in my head.

I hit the speakerphone button. "Yeah," I answer, forcing my voice to work. I can't hear myself. The static in my mind makes me feel like I'm underwater.

"Making sure you're still coming," Kai says. There's noise in the background. Voices and muffled music. He's already there at the stuffy Boston college bar where we arranged to meet.

"On my way."

"Tick tock."

I end the call and toss my phone on the passenger seat. The ache in my chest becomes unbearable, clenching down so hard it feels like I might snap a rib. I cut the wheel and veer onto the shoulder, slamming on the brakes. My throat's closing as I frantically tear out of layers of clothing until I'm in just a tank top and sweating. I lower the windows to fill the Jeep with cool air.

The fuck am I doing?

Head in my hands, I can't stop seeing her face. The disappointed look in her eyes. Not Daisy, the little girl from my past. But Taylor, the woman of my present.

She expected so much better from me. Not what I'd done back then, but what I was choosing to do now. She would've let me off the hook for acting like such a jackass this week if only I were strong enough to make the right decision when she gave me the chance.

Damn it, Edwards. Grow a pair.

I promised myself I'd be better for her and try to see myself through her eyes. See myself as more than just some gutter punk kid or an aimless loser or a walking one-night stand. She found the value in me, even when I couldn't. So why the hell should I let Kai take that from me? Because he hasn't just hijacked my life, he's stolen from Taylor. I should be at a dumb dance with my girlfriend, not having a panic attack on the side of the road.

Shaking my head in disgust, I grab my discarded sweater and pull it on. Then I reach for the gearshift and put the Jeep in drive.

For the first time in my life, I find the courage to respect myself.

My first stop is Hunter's place. Demi answers the door, greeting me with an inquisitive if somewhat hostile look. I don't how much she's heard since I last spoke to Taylor or what Hunter might have said after he wrote me the check.

I kiss her on the cheek as she lets me in.

Demi kind of recoils in response. "What's that for, weirdo?"

"You were right," I say with a wink.

"Well, obviously." She pauses. "About what, though?"

"Hey man." Hunter approaches us cautiously. "Everything okay?"

"It will be." I pull out the envelope of cash and hand it to him.

Demi narrows her eyes at the handoff. "What's that?" she demands.

Hunter takes the money, confused. "But why?"

"Answer me, monk," grumbles Demi, tugging on Hunter's sleeve. "What's happening?"

I shrug and answer Hunter. "Don't need it anymore."

He appears understandably relieved, though I don't envy the interrogation he's about to endure from his girlfriend.

"Go easy on him," I tell Demi. "He's a good guy."

"You want to stay and order a pizza?" Hunter offers. "We're just chilling tonight."

"Can't. I'm late for a dance."

Leaving Hunter's place, I call Kai. Already the tightness in my chest has subsided, and my hands are steady as the phone rings.

"You here?" he says.

"I don't have your money."

"Don't fuck with me, bro. I make one phone call—"

"I'm going to tell Max it was my fault." The resolve in my voice surprises me. And I become more assured of my decision with every word. "I'll leave your name out of it. For now. But if you call me again, if I so much as feel you sniffing around, I'll out you in a heartbeat. Don't try me, Kai. This is your last chance."

I hang up on him. Then, steeling my nerves, I make another call.

32
TAYLOR

I VIOLENTLY DON'T WANT TO BE HERE.

As in, I'm considering grabbing a steak knife off the nearest table and taking a hostage on my way out a shattered window to make my escape.

Sasha and I have taken up a strategic position near a stack of speakers to deter others from trying to talk to us. She also commandeered some expensive champagne, which is dribbling down our dresses as we drink straight from the bottle while watching Charlotte run around the dance floor chastising sisters for twerking on their dates in front of concerned boomers. We had to leave the DJ booth because alumni kept asking Sasha to play Neil Diamond and ABBA and she threatened to take the next one's eye out with a fork, so I forced her to take a break.

"You should go dance with Eric," I tell her, spotting him on the floor. He seems to be having a great time despite the fact that his date's all but abandoned him to the wolves.

"And miss the chance to judge everyone condescendingly from the corner? Do you not even know me?"

"I mean it. Just because I'm resigned to wallow in self-pity doesn't mean you have to suffer with me."

"That's exactly what it means," she says. "Or, you could chug the rest of this bottle and get white girl wasted on the dance floor all over some overdressed trust-fund boy."

"Not in the mood."

"Oh come on." Sasha takes another swig of champagne and wipes her mouth with her arm, painting it with lipstick. "We got all dressed up and shaved our legs. The least we can do is have something to regret in the morning."

Ha. I already have regrets. For example, what the hell I was thinking when I picked out this ridiculous dress? The tight black fabric makes my tits look like two squished hams and every fold and lump is pouring out like toothpaste from a tube. I feel disgusting and I can't remember why I'd been so excited looking in the mirror and imagining Conor's face when he saw me.

Oh wait, I remember why—because I'd let Conor fool me into believing I was beautiful. That he didn't see a chubby girl or just a pair of breasts, but me. All of me. He made me believe I was something desirable. Worth having.

And now I'm left with the ill-fitting disappointment of what could have been.

I'm annoyed to notice tears dripping down my cheeks, and I tell Sasha I'm going to evacuate some of that champagne. The restroom is stuffed with Kappas touching up their makeup, one stall occupied by a loud vomiter who has two Kappas holding her hair back. Another stall contains Lisa Anderson, who's locked herself in with her phone and is drunk-texting her now-ex Cory over the protestations of her sisters banging on the door.

After using the toilet, I'm washing my hands at the sink when Abigail and Jules walk in laughing. My stomach knots when their malicious gazes take in me and my smudged mascara.

"Taylor," Abigail calls loud enough to make sure everyone's paying attention. "I haven't seen Conor all night. He didn't stand you up, did he?"

"Leave me alone, Abigail."

She looks perfect, of course. Shimmering silver sequin dress and perfectly curled platinum hair, not a strand out of place. No sweat beading at her hairline or makeup dripping down her neck. Barely human.

"Uh-oh." She comes to stand behind me, watching us in the mirror with a mocking pout. "What's wrong? Come on, we're your sisters, Tay-Tay. You can tell us."

"He did stand you up, didn't he?" Jules says in a condescendingly sweet voice, as if she's talking to an animal. "Oh no! And your mice slaved all day making you a pretty dress for the ball."

"Joke's on you," I snap back dryly. "We broke up."

Abigail laughs, then gives me a sarcastic grin. "Well, of course he dumped you. I mean, after a month it stops being funny and then it's just sad. You should have listened to me, Tay-Tay. Could have saved yourself the embarrassment."

"Oh my God, Abigail, fuck off." My last thread snaps. The bathroom goes deathly silent and I become aware everyone is staring at us. "We get it, okay? You're a miserable cunt who mistakes bitchiness for a personality. Get a fucking life and get off my dick."

I stride out of there, skin buzzing. A sort of delirious high overwhelms me as I return to the banquet hall. I'm dizzy from the lights pulsating to the music, the bodies thrumming on the dance floor. God, telling her off was so good I want to go back for seconds. If I'd known unleashing on Abigail would feel this amazing, I would've been doing it six times a day.

After nearly half a bottle of champagne, my taste buds feel fuzzy and maybe my head does too, so I head for the bar and ask for a club soda with lime.

"Taylor," a voice says from behind me. "Hey. I almost didn't recognize you."

A guy slides in next to me. Tilting my head back to look at him, it takes a few inches before I realize it's Danny, one of the skyscrapers from Malone's the other night. He cleans up nicely in a sharp tux.

"Do me a favor, then," I say, taking my drink from the bartender, who I think was in my elementary mathematics class last semester. "Don't blow my cover. I'm in disguise."

"Oh yeah?" Danny orders a beer and moves in a little closer. "As what?"

"Haven't figured that out yet."

He laughs for lack of anything better to say. Truthfully, I don't know either. Lately I'm not sure what's actually me and what's a role I'm trying to play to please everyone else. I feel like I'm trying to live up to some expectation that becomes a little harder to define every day. Never quite achieving the image I set for myself and having a harder time remembering where I got the idea in the first place.

People always say we come to college to find ourselves, and yet I'm becoming less recognizable each morning.

"You look nice, is what I meant," he says shyly.

"Who are you here with?" I ask him.

"Oh, no, no one," he tells me. "My parents were invited by their friends, Rachel Cohen's parents, so I kinda got told to come." He takes an awkward swig of his beer and I can almost see the moment he convinces himself to go for it. "You know, I wanted to say something the other night. I mean, I should have, but I got the impression you were seeing someone?"

Oh. "Yeah, no, it was just…a casual thing."

"So then it'd be okay if I wanted to ask you out sometime?"

Sasha and I catch each other's gaze across the room, and her eyes are alight with approval. She gives me a nod that says *you should hit that*. Then she grabs Eric and they make their way to us.

I don't know how to answer his question without sounding like I'm committing to something, so I stall and take a long sip of my drink while Sasha approaches.

"You found each other," she says with too much excitement. Then smirks at me like I'm being punished somehow. "And neither of you have dates, so it all worked out."

"Actually," I start, "I was thinking I'd go—"

"You still owe me a dance," Eric reminds Sasha as she puts an arm around me to stop me from running away.

"Taylor loves to dance."

I'm going to kill her in her sleep.

"Dance with me?" Danny. Sweet, shy Danny. He holds his arm out like they do in the movies and I know he means well. And since I can either go willingly or have Sasha make a scene, I accept his invitation.

The four of us make our way onto the dance floor. It's an up-tempo song, thankfully, so Danny doesn't feel compelled to hang on to me. We start out in a loose foursome until it becomes apparent that Eric and Sasha have been looking for an excuse to get all up on each other all night and then I'm left with the awkward moves of a skyscraper who can't judge his own foot size. To be fair, I'm not giving him much to work with.

"Dance with him," Sasha leans in to hiss at me, only halfway pulling herself from Eric's grasp.

"I am," I snap back.

She shoves me at him, which forces him to catch me. Danny's smile says he thinks it's my coy way of saying, *please, hold me closer*, to which he obliges. I tense up but he doesn't seem to notice. Sasha meets my eyes again with an insistent look that says *TRY, DAMMIT!*

But I can't. My head's stuck on wondering what's happening with Conor and Kai. Has he made the drop? Is he safe? Not that I think Conor can't handle himself, but what if something went wrong? Ten grand is a lot of money to be carrying around. He could've gotten stopped by police, or worse. There are a hundred ways tonight might have gone wrong for him, and I can't even find out if he's okay. He'd just ignore my call and then I'm right back where I started—worrying about him, afraid for him.

It occurs to me I could have done more. I should've told his roommates or Hunter to stop him. Or to watch his back at least. Damn it, why didn't I do that?

If something happens to Conor, I'd never forgive myself.

I've just decided I have to make a call when I hear a low growl of warning and Danny and I are suddenly yanked apart.

33
TAYLOR

"What the hell, man?" Danny shoots forward to confront the intruder, while I stand there blinking in confusion.

What the hell indeed. What is Conor *doing* here?

"You're done here," a tuxedo-clad Conor answers, his tone cool and efficient.

"I'm sorry, what?" Danny frowns. Takes another step. Although he stands a few inches taller, his build is slight compared to Conor's more muscular frame.

"You heard me." Tension pours off of him, and there's a barely contained fury in his eyes as they burn through mine. "Thanks very much, but you can go now."

"Hey." Eric steps beside his teammate. "I don't know who you are, but you can't be—"

"I'm her boyfriend," Conor snaps, but his intense stare remains fixed on me.

"Taylor?" Danny prompts. "He your boyfriend?"

I glance at Danny, then back at Conor, and I'm momentarily startled. Conor standing there under the flashing lights in a tailored black tuxedo, his hair combed back from his face…it's like meeting him again for the first time.

I'm struck by the pure sexual magnetism of this man. For the last week I'd been so busy being mad at him that I'd forgotten how hot he is. Enough to turn the heads of nearly every female in the room. Even a few alumni are peeking over their shoulders, while their middle-aged husbands take a turn at feeling inadequate after leering at twenty-year-olds all night.

"What are you doing here?" I finally ask, ignoring Danny's question.

Sasha grabs my hand and squeezes it. I don't know if it's for moral support or she's thinking of making a run for it with me, but I squeeze back even though I can't rip my eyes from Conor's.

"You invited me," he says thickly.

"And then you dumped me." The anger returns without warning, and I cling tighter to my best friend's hand. "Consider that your invitation revoked. It also means you don't get a say in who I dance with."

"The hell I don't," he growls. He takes my other hand and pulls me forward. Like a fool I allow my grasp to slip from Sasha's.

"What are you doing?" I demand with bitterness searing on my tongue.

He tugs me against him and holds me close, and it's like my body remembers even if my head is trying to forget. "Dancing with you."

"I don't want to dance."

And yet I melt into him. Not because he wants me to, but because despite the anger and hurt, my nerves respond to his touch. It's simply natural with him.

I look over my shoulder, seeking out Danny's gaze, and I know he reads the apology in my eyes because he nods ruefully. Sweet, shy Danny. Life would be so much easier if he was the one my heart pounded for, but he's not. Because life isn't fucking fair.

"We need to talk," Conor says.

"I have nothing to say to you."

"Good, that'll make this easier," he replies, guiding us to the beat. He moves and I move with him. Not hearing the music so much as feeling his intention. It's a charged, fervent, passionate exchange, as if our bodies are fighting to put themselves back together. "I'm sorry, Taylor. For all of it. Ignoring you and blowing off tonight. I didn't mean any of it."

"You left," I tell him, with all the repressed rage that has built inside me over the last week. "You walked out on me."

He nods sadly. "I was ashamed. I didn't know how to talk to you about what was happening."

"You broke up with me."

The accusation hangs in the air. Even while our bodies touch and our eyes meet, there's still distance between us. An electric fence of regrets and betrayals.

"You backed me into a corner. I didn't know what else to do."

"You're an asshole," I say, seething at the pain he's put me through this week. It doesn't go away just because he shows up here looking good in a tux.

"You look gorgeous tonight."

"Shut up."

"I mean it." He presses a kiss to my neck, and my mind flashes back to the last time we were together.

Lying on my bed. His mouth. His bare skin against mine.

"Stop it." I push him away, because I can't think when he's touching me. I can't breathe. "You tossed me aside and it was so easy for you. It's not just that you blew me off and broke up with me. It's what you chose to do instead of just talking to me. You'd rather lose me than tell the truth." My eyes start stinging. "You made me feel like shit, Conor."

"I know, babe. Fuck," he bites out, messing up his hair as he scrubs his hands through it.

I suddenly realize others have stopped to watch the drama unfolding, and I fight the urge to sprint under a table.

"I didn't give him the money, Taylor."

"What?"

"I was halfway to Boston and I couldn't get your face out of my head. So I turned around. Couldn't go through with it knowing what I was doing to us." His voice cracks. "Because the worst thing about all of this, the worst thing I could have possibly done, was lose your respect. Nothing else matters if you hate me."

"If that were actually true—"

"Damn it, T, I'm trying to say I'm in love with you."

And before I can blink, he kisses me, all his regret and conviction distilled into the warm, engulfing sensation of our lips meeting. In his arms, I feel steady again, finally upright after being thrown askew. Because when we aren't together, the world feels misaligned. Conor gives me balance, sets the ground flat again.

When our lips part, he cups my face with one hand, dragging his thumb across my cheek. "I mean it—I'm stupidly in love with you. I should have said it sooner. I'd blame repeated head trauma, but I was just an idiot. I'm sorry."

"I'm still mad at you," I tell him honestly, though with a little less ferocity.

"I know." He smiles. A bit sad. Still sweet. "I'm prepared to do some pretty intense groveling."

I catch movement from the corner of my eye and turn to see Charlotte making a beeline for us with scowling church lady eyes.

"Well, you've caused a scene and everyone is looking at us," I say. "So you can start earning my forgiveness if you get us the hell out of here."

Conor surveys the dance floor, his silver eyes sweeping over our audience of Kappas and their dates and the scandalized blue-blooded alumni glowering in disapproval. Then he bestows his familiar impish grin onto the crowd.

"Show's over, folks," he announces. "Goodnight."

He entwines his fingers with mine and together we make our escape.

I've always hated parties anyway.

34
CONOR

Taylor invites me into her apartment, and we take turns not knowing where to stand or how to sit. She tries the couch first, but she has too much to say and it doesn't all quite come out in the order she wants to say it until she gets some traction under her feet and starts circling the room. So I take the couch next, except my muscles are still burning off the adrenaline and the lactic acid is building up. So I paste myself into a corner trying to work out if she can love me back or if I've already lost her for good.

"I spent all this time trying to understand why you were being like this," she's saying, "and without any input from you I was left with all these worst-case scenarios."

I hang my head. "I get it."

"Like I was a bet. Or you finally saw me naked and were like, yeah, no. Or some sick part of you just liked knowing you could hurt me."

"I'd never—"

"And so you have to understand that even though it's all cleared up now, I've already lived these scenarios in my mind," Taylor says quietly. "They didn't happen, but they also did, you know? In my heart, you dumped me this week because I wouldn't fuck you, because your boys put you up to it, because you met someone else. I put myself through the wringer because you were too chickenshit to communicate with me."

"I know," I say, hands in my pockets, staring at the floor.

I realize now that the damage is done, that no matter the grand gestures and sincere apologies, sometimes you hurt people too much and push them too far. There's a limit to what you can ask someone to endure for your bullshit.

And I'm terrified Taylor has reached her limit with me.

"You have to give me more than that, Con. I believe you're sorry, but I have to know I'm not signing myself up to get run over again."

I clear my throat to rid it of the gravel lodged there. "I didn't want you to know me this way. I came to Briar to be better, and for a while I thought I'd escaped my past." I swallow. "I did such a good job convincing myself I'd made a clean getaway that I stopped looking over my shoulder. Hell, I even started to believe I was a different person. Somewhere along the way I think I forgot why I kept people at a distance. And then you happened. I mean, Taylor, I never saw you coming. It was shit timing for us, but I can't regret trying."

"What happened?" she asks.

"Huh?"

"Tonight," she clarifies. "You took the money and left me at your house. Then what?" Taylor crosses her arms, watching me.

It's difficult to completely make out her expression, because it's dark in her apartment. She turned on the hall light when we walked in, but not the lamp in the living room. It's almost like we were both afraid to look at ourselves, we needed to retreat into the shadows.

Orange lines cut across her tight black dress from the street-lights prying through the blinds. I concentrate on these lines while I lay it out for her. How I turned into a shivering sack of nerves on the side of the road, how I broke the news to Kai and took the money back to Hunter.

"And after I left Hunter's, I called my mom," I confess. "I had her put Max on the phone too. Which didn't go over great considering they're three hours behind us, so Mom thought I was in the hospital or something."

Taylor leans against the opposite wall from me. "How'd that go?"

"I told them everything. I said I was sorry, that I'd fucked up and should have come clean a long time ago but I was afraid and ashamed. We left it at that. Mom was obviously shocked and disappointed. Max didn't say a lot." I bite the inside of my cheek. "There will be fallout, for sure. But for now I think they're processing."

I don't mention the possibility that Max might stop paying my tuition or that Mom might yank me back to California. Hell, if Briar's dean knew I orchestrated a B&E of my own house, I'd probably be expelled. All this pain and suffering, and there are still a dozen ways I could lose Taylor, my family, my team, and everything I've worked for. Which would be no less than I deserve. I wouldn't be the first person to suffer from a malignant lack of consequences. I'm due.

"I have serious reservations about the fact that you lied for so long about something so big," Taylor says, and there's still an entire room between us.

"I understand."

"And it still hurts that you were willing to put me through so much pain to cover for your mistake."

"You're right."

"But I believe in partial credit." She approaches me, slow, tentative.

She's a fucking vision in that curve-hugging dress, her sultry makeup, blonde hair perfectly done. It breaks my heart she went through so much trouble for tonight, and I robbed her of possibilities.

"You made a dozen wrong choices to get here. But you eventually made the right one. That counts for something."

"So where does that leave me?" I ask, growing more nervous for the answer.

"I'd say a solid C minus."

"So..." A hopeful smirk pulls at my mouth, and I smother that shit real quick. "Still passing?"

Taylor holds up her thumb and index finger to show me the thin slice of light between them.

"I'll take it."

She finally reaches me, sliding her hands down the satin lapels of my tuxedo jacket. "You seemed a little jealous back there at the gala."

"I will break that dude's hand if he touched you," I tell her with no hesitation.

"We were broken up," she reminds me. Every time those words leave her lips, it cuts a little deeper.

"I'm a dickhead," I admit. "But he's got a death wish if he thought he'd try to hit that."

She cracks a smile, which melts the tension that's been coiled in my shoulders for days. If I can still make her laugh, maybe there's hope for us yet.

Pensive, she tips her head slightly. "It was kind of hot."

"Was it?" This is sounding less like a rejection.

"Oh, for sure. I'm not one of those super-mature people who thinks jealousy is a character flaw. I fucking eat that shit up."

My grin springs free. "I'll remember that."

"Yeah, you know, Abigail's boyfriend is constantly drooling over my tits, so if later you want to do donuts on his frat's lawn, I'm all about that petty life."

"Fuck, I love you." This girl makes me laugh like no one else, even when things are heavy. And especially when they're awkward. She finds the joy in the deepest suck.

"About that," she starts, toying with the buttons on my shirt. Hesitation creases her forehead for a moment.

"I mean it. With all my heart. I wouldn't fuck with someone like that."

"You love me."

I can't tell if it's a question or a statement, but I treat it like the former. "I love you, T. I don't even know when I figured it out. Maybe when I pulled the car over, or on the drive back. Or when my fingers were shaking so much I could barely tie this stupid bow tie. All I could think about was getting to you and how every minute you were out there thinking I didn't give a shit was fucking killing me. I just knew."

She peers up at me under thick sooty lashes. "Show me."

"I will. If you give me the chance to—"

"No." Her fingers splay across my chest, push my jacket off my shoulders and let it fall to the floor. "Show me."

I need no more encouragement than her teeth pulling at her bottom lip.

Lifting her into my arms, I bring my mouth to hers and kiss her. We may have faltered as a couple, but this part still feels right. When we kiss, I can make sense of things. With her in my arms, I can see the way ahead for what we could become.

Taylor locks her legs around my waist as I walk us to her bedroom and sit on the end of her bed. She settles in my lap, her delicate fingers tangled in my hair. Her nails gently scratch at the back of my neck and set every nerve on fire.

I'm hard as granite as she grinds on my dick. All I want to do is tear her out of this dress, but I know I have to go slow or I'll push her away. Instead I slide my hands up the outside of her thighs, pushing fabric out of my way. She shifts, encouraging me, until I find the bare skin of her ass and feel the delicate lace of her underwear. She had plans, all right.

"I missed you," I tell her. It's been too long since I really looked at her. I think a part of me was using Kai and the fear of confessing to Taylor as a crutch to not acknowledge the depth of my feelings for her. Because if they weren't real, I had nothing to lose. If she left me, I didn't have to figure out how to be good enough for her.

"I missed us." Taylor tugs my shirt out of my waistband. She starts unbuttoning it, undoing my tie. I let her discard layers until she's skimming her fingers across my bare chest. "God, you're pretty."

My muscles twitch under her touch. "You're beautiful," I tell her earnestly.

She always blushes, rolls her eyes, when I say that. I get it—she can't see herself that way any more than I was willing to believe I could still be a decent person. She just needs someone to help her believe.

"I'm not going to stop trying to convince you," I warn.

"I don't want you to." She kisses me, then climbs off my lap to stand with her back to me. "Help me."

As my pulse quickens, I slowly drag her zipper down, then watch her step out of her dress. I know she gets nervous about being so exposed, so I don't give her a moment to feel self-conscious. Wrapping her in my arms, I pull her back down to the bed to lie against the pillows, settling myself between her legs. She hooks one smooth leg around my hips as I pull her bra off to kiss across her chest, squeezing her tits. My lips travel south, from her nipples to her stomach, while my fingers slip her lacy panties down her legs and spread her pussy for my tongue.

I know she's close to orgasm when I feel her tugging at the duvet, digging her nails into the fabric. Her body trembles, back arches. I slide two fingers inside her impossibly tight channel, and rise on my knees to watch her shatter for me.

It's the hottest thing I've ever seen. With a muffled moan because she's biting her lip, she shakes and clenches around my hand.

"That's it, baby," I coax, loving the flush of her cheeks, that same rosy hue on her tits, the sexy breaths leaving her mouth.

While my fingers are still lodged inside her, Taylor tugs me down, kissing me deeply while her hands search for my zipper.

"I want you," she says, breathing hard. She gets the button open, then the zipper, then shoves my trousers down my hips.

Grinning at her impatience, I kick my pants and briefs free from my legs and send them flying across the room. The moment I'm fully naked, an urgent Taylor encourages my hips forward to meet hers and whispers the two sweetest words I've ever heard.

"I'm ready."

I search her eyes, my dick hard against her pussy. "Are you sure?" My voice is a bit hoarse. "You know you don't have to do this tonight? I meant what I said before. I'm not in a hurry."

She reaches over to her nightstand and pulls out a condom. "I'm sure."

Our mouths collide again and somehow it feels new, like learning each other for the first time. Supporting my weight on my forearm, I use my free hand to slide the condom down my shaft.

"Just go slow," she says, when I'm once again settled between her legs.

"Promise." I kiss that cute little mole over the corner of her mouth, then press my lips to hers. "Just relax."

She's so tight, her body still clenched.

"Relax, babe. I got you."

With a deep breath, she lets go. Her body softens. As slow as I can, I push inside her. I grit my teeth, allowing her to adjust before I move again. Just a little. Just enough to make us both take in a sharp breath.

"You okay?" I whisper.

Taylor nods, her turquoise eyes shining with trust, need, arousal. She sucks in another breath, then grabs my hips to bring me closer.

She's perfect. Warm and tight, squeezing my dick every time I pull back and gently, achingly, plunge back into her. More than that, though. Her nails softly drag down my back and it's like my fucking soul trembles. She licks my neck and my mind is wiped of everything but her voice, her taste. I forget where I am, who I am. There's just this moment and the space between us. Her softness and her breath against my skin.

Too quickly, though, my climax builds. I want to make it last for her, but this feels too good and every time she arches her back, I can't help but draw every ounce of pleasure I can get from her body.

"Baby," I choke out.

"Mmmm?" The pleasure swimming on her face brings me dangerously closer to the edge.

"I promise I will spend every second of this relationship fucking you so good and giving you hundreds and thousands of orgasms, but right now..." I groan against her neck, my hips flexing forward, fast and erratic. "Right now...I need...to..."

I come so hard I see stars, shuddering against the perfection that is her body. When the rush of pleasure subsides, I pull out to discard the condom in the small wastebasket under her nightstand.

Lying on my back, I bring Taylor to rest against my chest, threading my fingers through her soft hair. After a few minutes, she tilts her head up to place a kiss under the corner of my jaw.

"I love you, too."

35
TAYLOR

SASHA TEXTS ME ON MY WAY INTO MY CO-OP CLASS AT THE ELEMEN-
tary school. Something to the effect of "hey, bitch, if you get a chance,
take that hockey stick out of your mouth for five seconds and text
me." Which is her endearing way of saying she misses me.

I take full responsibility for our dwindling amount of girl time;
after patching things up with Conor, he and I have spent every day
together for the past week. Now it's May, finals are only a couple
weeks away, and I'm a little ashamed to admit that what used to be
study time with Sasha at the Kappa house has become failing to
study with Conor at my place until we give up and get naked.

Turns out sex is good. I sure do like sex. Especially sex with Conor.

Although as it *also* turns out, sex is terribly distracting. Hard as
I've tried, my reading comprehension skills tank when he's trying to
tear off my clothes.

I did make it to the Kappa house for the election, however. No
surprise there—Abigail won. Though to ask her, she was just elected
supreme leader for life. I expect she'll soon have portraits of herself
riding dolphins and shooting lasers out of her eyes hanging in every
room. Sasha and I were two of only four protest votes against her. I'm
a pessimist and even I thought the resistance had greater numbers
in the house than that. I guess we'll all have to get used to bowing
down to our new supreme leader.

The thought of spending a year under Abigail's rule turns my stomach. It might have been a secret ballot, but she knows damn well I cast one of the votes against her. And I have no doubt she'll make me pay dearly for that show of dissent. How, I'm not sure yet, but knowing Abigail it won't be pretty.

If it weren't for all the time and effort I've already contributed to Kappa Chi, I'd consider leaving the sorority. But at least I have Sasha as an ally. Besides, being a Kappa means a support network of professional connections for life. I didn't assimilate into the collective just to blow up my future capital so close to the end.

So, one more year. If Abigail really runs things off the rails, Sasha and I can mount the insurrection.

Now in Mrs. Gardner's first grade class, I'm helping the kids work on collages they're making about the books they read in class this week. The room is the quietest it's been all day. Everyone has their heads down, eyes focused. They're cutting pictures out of old magazines and gluing their creations on poster board.

Thank goodness for glue sticks. I've only had to wash glue out of one girl's hair today. Mrs. Gardner banned liquid glue after a major catastrophe led to three emergency haircuts. I'll never understand how kids manage to constantly find new ways to attach themselves to each other.

"Miss Marsh?" Ellen raises her hand at her desk.

"That's looking good," I tell her when I come around the room to her seat.

"I can't find a mouse. I looked through all these."

At her feet there's a pile of mangled magazines and torn loose pages. All month Mrs. Gardner and I scoured Hastings for unwanted magazines. Doctors' offices, libraries, used bookstores. Thankfully there's always someone trying to pawn off thirty years of *National Geographics* and *Highlights*. Trouble is, when you've got more than twenty kids all reading about a mouse, the rodent supply tends to get a bit thin.

"What if we draw a mouse on some colored paper?" I suggest.

"I'm not good at drawing." She pouts, shoving another stack of loose pages to the floor.

I know the feeling. As a kid I was a high-strung type-A perfectionist who tended toward the self-critical. I'd get a grand design in my head and then lose my shit when I couldn't materialize it into being. I've been banned from several pottery-painting places in Cambridge, in fact.

Not my greatest moment.

"Everyone can be good at drawing," I lie. "The best thing about art is that everyone's is different. There are no rules." I pull out some fresh sheets of colored paper and draw a few simple shapes as an example. "See, you can draw a triangle head, and an oval body with some little feet and ears, then cut those out and paste them together to make a collage mouse. It's called abstract—they hang stuff like that in museums."

"Can I make it a purple mouse?" Ellen, the girl wearing a purple hair scrunchie and purple overalls with matching purple shoes, asks. Shocking.

"You can make it any color you want."

Delighted, she gets to work with her crayons. I'm moving to another desk when a knock sounds on the classroom door.

I look over to see Conor peeking through the window. He's picking me up today, but he's still a few minutes early.

He pokes his head inside as I walk over. "Sorry," he says, glancing around. "I was just curious what you looked like in a classroom."

There's been a lightness to him this week. He's smiling again, always energetic and in a good mood. It's a nice side of Conor, even if I know it can't last. No one is this happy all the time. And that's okay. I don't mind grumpy Conor, either. I just can't help taking pleasure in knowing some part of his positive attitude is because of me. And sex. Maybe mostly sex.

"Am I different?" I ask him.

Conor gives me a lingering examination, from top to bottom. "I like your teacher clothes."

I won't lie, I did go a bit overboard at the start of the semester with a whole Zooey Deschanel vibe. Lots of retro skirts and primary colors. I guess in my head that was the part I wanted to play, because it's important when you walk into a room where you're outnumbered by tiny creatures twenty-to-one that you display confidence. Or they'll eat you alive.

"Yeah?" I say, doing a little twirl and curtsy.

"Mmm-hmm." He licks his lips and shoves his hands in his pockets, which I've come to learn is his way of trying to hide a semi while he's thinking dirty thoughts. "You're keeping that on when we get home."

That's another thing that's crept into our vocabulary. *Home.* His place or mine, when we're going to either one, or spending the night, it's always home. The distinction between them has blurred.

"Miss Marsh," one of the girls calls to me. "Is that your booooooyyyyyyfriend?"

The rest of the class answers with oohs and laughter. Fortunately, Mrs. Gardner is out of the room or I would've made Conor leave, asap. This close to my final evaluation I can't have her thinking I'm not focused on the kids.

"Okay," I tell him, "get out of here before Ms. Caruthers next door calls security on you."

"See you outside." He plants a kiss on my cheek and winks at the kids watching us.

"Go." I all but slam the door in his face, smothering a smile.

"Miss Marsh has a boyfriend, Miss Marsh has a boyfriend," the kids chant, growing louder and more excited in their taunting.

Dammit, if they keep this up, Ms. Caruthers will come storming in to complain about the noise. I hold my index finger to my lips and raise my other hand. One by one each student mimics the pose until they're all silent again. Just call me the kid whisperer.

"Mrs. Gardner will be back soon and the bell's about to ring," I remind the class. "You better be done with your collages or there won't be any smiley faces going on the chart today."

At that, their heads snap down and they furiously return to cutting and pasting. They're only a few days away from earning a pizza party if they maintain their positive behavior streak. And I'm only a few days from passing my co-op evaluation if I can keep them docile. We're all cogs in the system.

I don't know what's gotten into Conor today, but even on the drive to his place he can't keep his paws to himself. Driving with one hand, his other finds its way under my skirt, up my thigh, and then he's rubbing my pussy while I clench my teeth and try not to alert the dude on a motorcycle who pulls up next to us at a red light.

"Pay attention to the road," I tell him, even as I open my legs wider and slouch in my seat.

"I am." He presses his fingers against my clit, rubbing through my panties.

"Pretty sure this counts as distracted driving." I want his fingers inside me. So badly that my chest aches with the tightness growing in my muscles. My eyes fall closed as I imagine grinding on his hand while his teeth tug on my nipples.

"I'm always distracted when you're sitting there."

When we make it to his house it's a mad dash to his room. His roommates aren't home yet, so hopefully we have some time to play before they show up.

Conor barely shuts his door behind us before he's pushing me up against the wall and prying open my cardigan. He doesn't open it all the way, just leaves the last few buttons intact to spread my sweater around my cleavage.

Fine. Maybe I wore this today just because I know he likes it.

Conor licks and kisses across my collarbone, then slowly pulls down one bra cup to expose my breast, while squeezing and massaging the other. He licks my nipple, sucking. My thighs squirm with the need to feel him inside me. I wrap one leg around his hips and grind on his thick erection.

"You're so damn hot," he mutters, yanking my bra farther down to suck on my other nipple.

He presses himself against me, urgent and hungry. Then I feel him working to free himself from his jeans. He opens them just enough to pull out his cock, which he holds in one hand while rubbing the tip against my pussy.

"There's a condom in my pocket," he mumbles.

I find it and rip it open, then roll it down on his dick. Bringing his mouth to mine, he kisses me deeply as he tugs my panties to the side. A happy, relieved moan escapes my throat when he enters me.

Conor fucks me against the wall. Gently at first, letting both of us get used to this position. Then harder, deeper. My hands tangle in his hair, nails digging into the back of his neck to hold on. He wraps one arm under my leg to bring it up higher and open me wider for him. Every thrust causes a burst of pleasure to cascade through my body. I lose control of my voice, overcome by the intensity.

Suddenly he stops. He turns me around to face his bed and bends me over the edge. I'm panting, out of breath, while he flips my skirt up to expose my ass, running his hands over my bare skin and squeezing my cheeks.

"Is this okay?" he asks softly, running the head of his cock against my ass.

"Yes," I say, desperate for him to be inside me again.

He shoves my panties down and plunges deep, holding onto my hips. I moan at the sensation of fullness and push back against him. Wanting, needing him to get me off.

It occurs to me that my butt is *right there*, out in the open, impossible to be missed in the rays of late afternoon sun streaming in through the open blinds. And yet it doesn't seem to matter anymore. What I've learned during all my naked encounters with Conor is that the man doesn't care about my soft tummy and the dimples on my butt.

Hell, forget *care*—he doesn't even notice. The other night when I was complaining about cellulite on the backs of my thighs, he stood there behind me and humored me for five minutes, searching and squinting and insisting he couldn't see anything. Then he ate me out and I forgot what I was complaining about.

Great sex has a way of building your confidence, I suppose. Or maybe I'm just growing up a little.

With every stroke our voices grow louder. I fist the sheets in my hands, legs trembling, pushing back to meet his deep thrusts.

"Fuck, babe. You feel so good." Conor reaches his hand around me to rub my clit as he urges me to my orgasm.

Biting my lip, I still can't muffle the sound when I finally come, riding his dick.

"Hey!" Three loud knocks pound against the bedroom door. "Some of us are trying to study. Keep it down in there unless you're going to invite us to join!"

"Fuck off, Foster," Conor shouts back.

I stifle a laugh, which makes Conor groan through his teeth as my body clenches and shakes around him. He stands me upright at the foot of his bed, squeezing my breasts in his hands from behind, as he makes short, quick thrusts to find his own climax. Soon he's shuddering, hugging me tight as he comes inside me.

"Why does it only get better?" he croaks, dropping his chin on my shoulder.

After he's discarded the condom, we lie together in his bed recovering from the elated exhaustion.

"We should probably start doing this at your apartment more," he grumbles. "I think they're coming home earlier just to catch us."

"Yeah, you're going to have to make them leave so I can walk out of here. Hmmm. Or maybe we should get a rope ladder I can hang out your window."

I like drawing little shapes on Conor's abdomen as I lie across his chest. His muscles contract under my touch as I tickle him ever so lightly. He hates it, but tolerates it because he knows it amuses me. Then I really hit a ticklish spot and he pinches my ass as a warning not to start something I can't finish.

"Nah, don't sweat it," he says in response to my escape ideas. "It's not a walk of shame so much as a strut down the red carpet. After today, expect applause."

I laugh. "I don't know if that's better."

"Or I can threaten them." Conor kisses the top of my head. "Whatever works for you."

About an hour later, Foster bangs on the door again to ask if we want to grab a bite with them at the diner. I'm starving, so we take turns in the shower of Conor's en suite bathroom and then get dressed.

"So," I say, wrapping my hair up in a bun, "have you talked any more to your mom and Max?"

Conor sighs as he sits on the edge of the bed pulling on a fresh shirt. "No. I mean, I've spoken to my mom. And she's texted me a couple times to call Max. I've made an excuse about class or studying or whatever. Said I'd do it later."

"So you're avoiding him." I know this isn't easy for Conor. Confessing was a huge step in the right direction, but the hard work isn't over yet. Right now, though, his anxiety about talking to his stepfather is winning out over his better judgment.

"I keep thinking if I wait another day, I'll figure out how to talk to him, you know? I'll know what to say. I'm just…" He rubs his face, furiously combing his fingers through his damp hair.

"Nervous," I supply. "I get it. I would be scared, too. But eventually it's going to happen. My best advice is close your eyes and bite down."

"I'm embarrassed," he admits, leaning forward to slip on his socks. "I've always known that Max doesn't think much of me, and now I've gone and proved him right. I knew better. Back then, I mean. I just got so angry and I fucked up."

"That's all you have to say." I stand between his legs, wrapping my arms around his broad shoulders. "Tell him the truth. You made a dumb mistake that you regret, it got way out of hand, and you're sorry."

Conor draws me closer, hugging me to his chest. "You're right."

"Have they said anything about what's going to happen to Kai?"

"I didn't mention his name. I told Kai I wouldn't if he left me alone. As it is, Max doesn't want to press charges since insurance paid out. It'd be more hassle than it's worth. So that's a small victory, I guess."

"You'll do the right thing." I kiss him on the cheek. Because I have faith in him. And I know as well as anyone what a difference it makes when there are people who believe in you. "In other news, my birthday is on Thursday. I was thinking about getting people together at Malone's. Nothing big. Just hang out, have a few drinks."

"Whatever you want, babe."

"Yo! Let's go!" Foster bangs on the door again. "Or I'm coming in there and getting weird."

36
CONOR

By the time I leave campus after class on Thursday, I have two missed calls from Max. I know I can't avoid him much longer, but boy do I keep trying. When I first confessed to him and my mother, I was kind of in a blind stupor of guilt and panic. Now that my head is clearer, I realize there's no part of me that wants to have the conversation that's coming. Especially not today.

I put Taylor through hell over this bullshit with Kai. The only thing I'm worried about now is giving her a perfect birthday. I know she's never had a serious boyfriend before, and I'm taking that to mean all the usual clichés are still new to her. That means flowers.

An obnoxious number of flowers.

An ecological massacre of flowers.

At the florist in Hastings, I try to relay this request, which for some reason is more difficult than I expected.

"What's the occasion?" the middle-aged woman asks. She's got a Vermont hippie vibe about her, and the whole place smells like a head shop. A flowery head shop.

"My girlfriend's birthday." I walk around the store, studying the pre-made arrangements and bouquets in the refrigerators. "I want a lot. Something really big. Or maybe several."

"What are her favorite flowers?"

"No idea." I feel like roses would be fine, but then I'm thinking maybe something more unique. Less expected.

What says *I'm sorry I dumped you because I was afraid you wouldn't respect me anymore when you found out I was a liar and a criminal but also it turns out I love you so take me back? And sex with you is pretty fantastic and I'd like to keep having it?*

"Favorite colors?"

Hell, I don't know. She wears a lot of black, gray, blue. Except when she's teaching. Then it's the opposite. I feel like after two months of dating I should know this. The hell have I been doing this whole time? Eating her pussy, mostly.

Seemingly sensing my discomfort, the woman says, "Well, she's a Taurus, so pink and green are usually a good bet. She'll appreciate something earthy yet sophisticated and refined." Hippie Lady weaves about the store between displays of flowers, touching them all, tilting an ear to them as if she's listening for something. "Snapdragons," she declares. "Foxglove and pink roses. With succulents. Yes, that'd be perfect."

I don't have the vaguest idea what those are. But I understand the word *roses*. "Sounds great. Something big," I remind her.

The bell over the front door jingles as the hippie darts into the back room. I glance over my shoulder to see none other than Coach Jensen walk in.

"Hey Coach."

He has a nervous aura about him, like the night of the family dinner. It's odd seeing him that way, when in the locker room or on the ice he's a stone wall of confidence. I guess women do that to us.

He lets out a heavy sigh. "Edwards."

Yeah, relations haven't warmed since the infamous fire. I get it. During the off-season Coach would rather not have to deal with his unruly band of misfits. Running into him around town is a lot like seeing your teacher at the mall during summer vacation. Once the season's over and the semester ends, they don't want to know us.

"Here for Iris?" I ask. "Taylor told me she and her mom share a birthday." Which further supports my theory that Taylor is in fact the product of a Russian human engineering experiment to create some sort of super sleeper agent. She has neither confirmed nor denied.

"No," he mocks, "I just like to come in a few times a week to gather petals for my bubble bath."

I like to think sarcasm is Coach's way of showing he cares. Otherwise this guy can't fucking stand me. "You two got big plans?"

He turns his back, exploring the arrangements in the cases. "Dinner in Boston."

"Well, you two kids be safe, and don't stay out too late. Remember, arrive alive."

"Don't be cute, Edwards. I still got a trashcan with your name on it."

My asshole puckers right up when he says that. "Yes, sir."

We stand around in awkward silence for a few minutes, both of us pretending to browse the tiny shop while we wait for the florist to return. I can't imagine what it must be like for Brenna's boyfriend, Jake. He's lucky they're in a long-distance relationship while he's playing pro for Edmonton, because Coach strikes me as the kind of man who might sit polishing a gun at the kitchen table when a guy comes over for his daughter. And then Brenna struts out the door after a kiss on his cheek with a pocket full of bullets.

Iris was easy as far as meet-the-parents horror stories go. I mean, what's one little fire between family, right?

"What are your plans with Taylor?" he barks, so abruptly I wonder if I've imagined it.

"Dinner first. Just the two of us. Then meeting friends later at Malone's."

"Uh-huh," he says, then clears his throat. "Well, don't show up at the table next to us, you got that?"

"No problem, Coach."

Finally the florist returns with a heaping armful of flowers in an enormous vase. Perfect. The damn thing is almost as big as I am. I'm going to have to put a seatbelt on it.

Coach looks from the flowers to me and rolls his eyes. The arrangement is so enormous and cumbersome I end up needing his help to get it out the door and to my Jeep parked at the curb. I've just got the flowers strapped into the front seat when across the street I see a face that doesn't belong. And he sees me.

Shit.

He waits for a couple cars to pass before jogging over to us. My heart's in my throat and I'm seriously thinking of hopping in the driver's seat and peeling out.

Too late.

"Conor," he says. "Finally caught up with you."

Fuck my life.

A glance at Coach. "Hey there. Nice to meet you." He offers his hand to Coach as they both look to me for a response.

"Coach Jensen," I say, feeling like I'm going to choke on my own tongue, "this is Max Saban, my stepfather."

"Great to meet you, Coach." The thing about Max is, he's so goddamn nice all the time. I don't trust it. No one smiles that much. It's fucking weird. Anyone who's in a good mood that often is hiding something. "Conor's told his mother a lot about you. He really loves your program."

"Chad," Coach says, introducing himself. "Good to meet you." He slides me a questioning glance, which I can only take to mean he senses the awkwardness of this shitshow and wondering why the hell is he getting dragged into more of my personal drama. "Conor's a great addition to the team. We're glad to have him coming back to us next year."

Ha. If only he knew. I can't bring myself to meet Max's eyes to read his reaction.

"Well, I've got to get going," Coach says, leaving me out on this floating ice sheet alone. "Nice to meet you, Max. Have a good one." Coach strides back inside the shop, and I've got nowhere left to hide or anyone to hide behind.

"When'd you get in?" I ask Max. I keep my tone casual, because he's here now and I can't avoid him anymore. The last thing I want is for him to see me squirm.

So I tamp down the anxiety. I got good at this when I was a kid, following Kai around through abandoned buildings and dark alleys. Getting into shit that scared me, all the while knowing I couldn't show weakness or I'd get my ass kicked. It's the face I put on every time I hit the ice, lining up against a guy ready to do battle. It's nothing personal, but we mean to cause some havoc. Pain is part of the game. If we didn't want to lose some teeth, we'd stay home and knit.

"Just this morning," replies Max. "I took the red-eye."

Fuck me, he's pissed. In that quiet WASP-y way. The softer they speak, the more your life's in danger.

"Stopped by your place but you'd already left."

"I have early classes on Thursday."

"Well," he says, nodding at the diner a few storefronts away. "I was going to grab a coffee before trying you again later. Since we're here, will you join me?"

Can't very well say no, can I? "Yeah, sure."

We grab a booth by the windows and the waitress comes around right away to fill our mugs. I don't even like coffee, but I drink mine too fast, too soon, scalding my tongue because I don't know what else to do with my hands and it stops my knee from bouncing.

"Guess I should start," he says.

The second most obnoxious thing about Max is how he always looks like he just walked off the set of an early 2000s family sitcom. He's one of those perpetually cheerful dads with an upstanding gentleman haircut, plaid oxford shirt, and a vest from an expensive outdoor brand, not that you've ever seen the man hike.

Maybe that's part of it—I can't take him seriously when he looks like a character from a show I never watched as a kid because we didn't have cable. Those dads who ruined us for the real men missing from our lives. Kids like me were raised on lies told by TV writers fulfilling the fantasies of their own broken childhoods.

"Obviously, I came out here because we haven't been able to connect on the phone," Max continues. "I also thought perhaps this was a discussion we ought to have in person."

That's never good. Now I'm thinking I should have had this talk with my mom first. It's not outside the realm of possibility that given my lack of cooperation, she had no choice but to leave me to Max's mercy. Cut off financially, no more school, no more house. Set adrift on a raft of my own making.

"I know we haven't had much communication over the years, Conor. I can take my fair share of the blame for that." Not quite how I saw this beginning. "I want to start off by saying, while I certainly don't approve of the actions you took, I can understand why you made the choice you did."

What?

"I know how at that age emotions get the best of us, and sometimes when outside pressure is applied to just the right spot, we make decisions and act out in ways we might never otherwise. You made a mistake, a big one. You lied. To me, yes, but more importantly to your mother. I know from your first phone call how much that's weighed on you. And what I find encouraging is that, while it took quite a bit longer than we'd have liked, you admitted your mistake. Now comes the hard part," he says with a hesitant smile. "Taking responsibility."

"Have to say, you're taking this better than I expected," I tell him. "I wouldn't fault you for being more on the irate side of things."

"I admit my initial reaction was surprise. Maybe a little irate came later. Then I thought back to what I was up to when I was nineteen." The waitress comes back to refill our mugs and he takes a long sip of coffee, as I'm left to guess what sort of trouble Max might have found for himself at Briar in his day. "Point is, I wanted to say that we're all entitled to a few fuckups."

I crack a smile at hearing him curse. It's like the first time you realize that *Full House* dad also did the raunchiest stand-up comedy.

"I'm glad you told us the truth, Conor, and as far as I'm concerned, we can all move on from the matter."

"That's it?" Seriously?

"Well, your mother can't very well ground a twenty-one-year-old man from the other side of the country," he says with a grin.

This feels like a trap. "I thought you guys would pull me out of school or at least stop paying tuition."

"That would seem counterproductive, don't you think? How does interrupting your college education serve as a constructive punishment?"

"I assumed there'd be some instinct to cut me off. Financially." It'd be more than fair considering what I did to him. The fact is, my entire livelihood is wrapped up in Max's bank account. He supports all of us. It's not a stretch to think he might reconsider that arrangement.

"Conor, perhaps there's some kind of wisdom in telling you to go find a job and work eighty hours a week to still not make enough to pay rent and finish school—if you were someone else. But nobody needs to tell you how tough it is out there or the value of a dollar. Least of all me." He sets down his mug. "You and your mother have experienced enough hardship. It wouldn't sit well inflicting any more, and the truth is, whatever cash value your mistake cost is an insignificant sum compared to the value I place on this family."

"I don't know what to say." Max has never spoken to me like this before, either about family or the way Mom and I lived before he came along. I'm not sure we've said this many words the entire time we've known each other. "I didn't know you felt that way."

"Family is the most important thing in my life." He stares into his mug and his demeanor changes, a solemnness descending over his face. "You know, my dad died when I was at Briar. It was difficult for me, but more so for my mother. After that it was only the two of us and all the empty places where Dad wasn't. When someone dies, everything becomes a memory of them not being there. Holidays and special occasions, you know? Then Mom died while I was in graduate school and I got twice as many empty memories."

Something tightens my chest. Regret, maybe. A sense of kinship. It never occurred to me the ways in which Max and I might be similar. I mean, there's a big difference between a runaway father and a decent one who dies too early, but both of us know what it's like to watch our mothers struggle and be helpless to fix anything.

"What I'm trying to say is, when I met your mother, I had the utmost respect for how much she'd accomplished in raising you on her own. And I sympathized with how difficult it must have been for you. When Naomi and I married, I promised my first job would always be to take care of both of you. To make sure, as best I could, this family was a happy one." His voice softens slightly. "I know I haven't always lived up to that promise where you and I are concerned."

"To be fair," I say, "I never gave you much of a chance." From the start, I saw Max as some tool in suit. Someone I'd never relate to, so why bother trying. "I figured you came for my mom, and I was the unfortunate compromise. Because you were from such a different world than us, you just saw me as a loser kid who wasn't worth the effort."

"No, Conor, not at all." He pushes his coffee mug aside and sets his elbows on the table.

He's got a certain magnetism about him, I can't deny that. I feel like when he sits across a boardroom from someone, they can't help but believe whatever he's selling them will make them rich.

"Listen, I came into this thing with zero idea how to do it well. I wasn't sure if I should try to be a father to you or a friend, and I failed at accomplishing either. I was so afraid to assert myself too much in the middle of you and your mother, that maybe I didn't make enough of an effort to build a relationship with you."

"I didn't make it easy for you," I admit. "I figured if you couldn't stand me then I could be just as good at hating you. I think maybe…" I swallow hard, averting my eyes. "I didn't want to get rejected by another dad. So I rejected you first."

"Why would you think that?" He sits back, appearing genuinely surprised.

"I mean, look at us. We're nothing alike." Well, that might be a little less true now that I know we have some things in common, but still, I can't imagine he'd have much use for me if I were a stranger off the street. "I know you have this idea in your head that I should be more like you, take an interest in business and finance, work at your company and follow your path, but honestly, that bores the hell out of me. It drains the joy from my entire being to even think about it. So I'm left with this feeling that I'm never going to be good enough. I avoided your calls this week because I was embarrassed and I didn't need confirmation that everything I'd feared about myself was true."

I slouch in the booth, hands in my lap, wanting to shrink into the space between the cushions and live with the dust. At least it's out now. Whatever there is after this, it won't be as humiliating as this moment. It can't be.

Max is quiet a long time. I can't read his reaction, and in each second that passes I take his silence as agreement. I don't even blame him. It isn't his fault he estimates success differently than I do. We're just different people and trying to measure either against the other is pointless. I'd feel better if we agreed to stop trying.

"Conor," he says finally. "I should have said this a long time ago—you have *never* not been good enough. I've never seen you as anything less than a funny, charming, intelligent kid who is becoming a remarkable young man. You're right, there's a paternal part of me who likes the idea of being a mentor to you, a role model.

To bring you into the company and teach you to take over when I'm gone. If that's not where your heart lies, I respect that. I probably should have taken the hint a little sooner, huh? But whatever you choose to do with your life and career, your mother and I will support you. As a team. As a family. Because we know you'll make the right decisions for you. If I can help, I'm glad to. Otherwise," he says with a self-deprecating laugh, "I'll stay out of your way. In either case, I want you to know I'm exceedingly proud of you."

I laugh weakly. "Come on now, let's not get crazy here."

"I'm proud of you," he repeats, reaching into his pocket to pull out his phone.

I watch suspiciously as he goes to a website that has a photo of him sitting at his desk. One of those corporate PR shots. Then he places the phone on the table between us and zooms in. Behind him, beside all the awards and plaques, is a framed photograph of my mom and me.

My breath hitches slightly and I hope he doesn't hear it. The picture is from their honeymoon, a couple days after the wedding. We all went to Hawaii, and on our last night there, Max took a photo of us watching the sunset. I'd never left California before that. Never been on a plane. I was in a shit mood the whole time because they were doing couple stuff and I had no one to hang out with, but that evening on the beach with my mom was my best memory from the trip.

"I've always been proud of you," Max says gruffly, as my eyes begin to sting. "I'll always be proud of you, Conor. I love you."

"Well, shit," I say, coughing to clear the rocks from my throat. "Guess I'm the asshole."

He laughs while we both discreetly rub our eyes and make other manly guttural noises that are absolutely not crying.

"Not sure what to say now," I admit. "Sorta feels like shit that we spent all this time being weird around each other." I'm not about to be the guy's best friend or start calling him Dad, but the last few years would've been a hell of a lot easier if we'd had this conversation sooner.

"Cheesy as it sounds, I'd appreciate it if we could start over," he says. "Try to be friends?"

There are worse things. "Yeah, I could do that."

I'm about to suggest we order some grub, but then I remember I've got a large child's worth of flowers drying out in my front seat, and some more errands to run before I pick up Taylor for our date.

"How long are you staying in town?" I ask.

"Planning to head back tomorrow morning. Why, what's up?"

"Well, it's my girlfriend's birthday tonight and we've got plans with her friends. But if you don't mind sticking around a bit longer, maybe the three of us could have dinner tomorrow night? I was talking to Mom about my girl coming to visit me in California this summer."

Max's face breaks into a wide smile that he then tries to smother as he nods. "Not a problem. I can change my flight. You just let me know where and when. I'd love to meet her."

I can't help thinking Taylor would be proud of me right now.

37
TAYLOR

CONOR IS UP TO SOMETHING. THERE'S A DEFINITE SENSE OF mischief about him. Nothing he's said, exactly, just more of a vibe I'm getting. He texted this morning to wish me a happy birthday and to tell me to get dressed up this evening. Which is unusual, since lately he's been more concerned with getting me undressed. Then he dropped a hint that he wouldn't be able to meet me after class because he had "special errands to attend to."

Whatever he's got planned for our date tonight, I have a feeling he's gone completely overboard. And I can't say I'd be mad at him. Truth is, I've never had a boyfriend on my birthday before, so I'm sort of looking forward to getting the full Hallmark movie treatment television promised me. More than anything, I'm excited about the prospect of Conor and me making memories.

Of course, getting dressed up requires a consultation with my beauty advisor. I text Sasha as I'm leaving class.

ME: Hot date tonight. Do my face?

She gives good face. One of her many shifting career aspirations over the last couple years has been to work as a makeup artist. At least as a way of supporting her music interests, and if that whole supervillain thing doesn't work out.

By the time I reach my street on the walk home, she texts back.

HER: Why bother? Just going to ruin it sucking Conor's dick.

HER: JK just got home, come on over.

ME: lol you said come.

HER: Mind out of the gutter, dirty girl.

ME: You started it.

I add a string of nonsensical but contextually explicit emojis, then pick up my dress from my apartment and take an Uber to Greek Row.

I do need to get better at balancing my time. Being totally absorbed in a couple cocoon has been fun, but I don't want to neglect my friends. Sasha, especially. More than anyone else, she has supported me through the rough spots over the last few years. I probably would've had a total nervous breakdown and set my hair on fire more than once if it weren't for her. But lately I feel like I have no idea what's going on in her life, which is a sign that I've been taking more than I've given. Major friendship no-no on my part. I need to change that, asap.

The weather's finally warming up, which means the typically quiet lawns of Greek Row on a weekday afternoon are more active. Porches are dotted with people studying. A few lounge chairs in the grass contain girls working on their tans for summer vacation. At the Sigma frat house, guys are playing beer pong in the driveway. I don't pay much attention to their shouts and catcalls as I slide out of the Uber and plant my feet on the sidewalk.

The frat boys shower me with unimaginative variations on "show us your tits," the typical garbage girls get from that house. Then something catches my attention.

"Hey superstar! Can we get a picture?"

"Can I have your autograph?"

"Where do I sign up for the live cam?"

That sounds…specific. Quite oddly so.

I keep my eyes straight ahead and don't slow down as I hurry up the front path of the Kappa house. The best defense is not giving them the satisfaction of a response. Mulling it over, I chalk it up to a dumb joke. Abigail's boyfriend likes to call me a "fat Marilyn Monroe," so I assume that's what the whole *superstar gimme your autograph* junk refers to.

Well, he and his douchey Sigma brothers can fuck right off. I happen to know that *some* men like curves, particularly men named Conor Edwards.

I can barely keep the smile off my face as I walk into the house. I can't wait to see him tonight. I don't know exactly when it happened, but I'm so gone for that guy. Just the thought of him makes me want to giggle like a preteen with her first crush.

Upstairs, Sasha has a beauty station set up for me at her desk when I enter her room. I toss my bag on her bed and hang my dress on the closet door. "You're the best," I inform her.

"Obviously. Go ahead and wash your face," she says as she flips through eyeshadow palettes.

"Hey, I just want to make sure," I call out, standing at the sink in the shared bathroom that connects with the bedroom next door. "There isn't a surprise party scenario in play, right?"

"Not that I know of."

I rinse and pat my face dry with a washcloth. When I return, Sasha has me sit at her desk then proceeds to smear me with moisturizer.

"I only ask because I think Conor feels like he has something to prove. So when I said we were just going to have a low-key hang at Malone's, I wouldn't be shocked if he spun that into some major event."

"I don't think so." She hands me a tiny electric fan to dry my face.

Next comes the primer, which Sasha is always telling me to add to my makeup routine and I always tell *her* I would if I ever wore makeup except when she does it, which is why I don't need to buy makeup products because I have her. It's a perfect system. When we're old she'll live next door and I'll roll over in my wheelchair to get ready for my hot dates down at the bingo hall.

"What about you?" I ask while she starts on my foundation. "How'd things go with Eric at the gala after I left?"

"Not bad."

I wait for her to elaborate. When it becomes clear she has no intention of doing so, I know there's more to the story.

"So you banged his brains out in the walk-in freezer, didn't you?"

"That's unsanitary," she says.

"Let him eat you out under the silent auction table?"

"Those donations are for the children, you degenerate."

Sasha is a tough nut. She considers the meddling in the private dramas of others an Olympic sport, but she's fiercely private about her own life. It's one of the qualities I most respect about her. She's good at setting boundaries and standing up for herself, something I aim to get better at. However, those boundaries don't apply to me, as far as I'm concerned.

"You're in love with him and you've already eloped and gotten married in Reno," I guess.

"Actually, in my bag there's a pair of bloody stilettos. If you could dump those over a bridge the next time you head into the city, that'd be super."

"Come on. I'm not asking for the gory details. Just an update." I mock pout. "I've been feeling left out and I need a Sasha recap."

She rolls her eyes, smirking as she tells me to close my eyes while she applies shadow.

"The gala went well. We've had a few dates since then."

"Okay…" This is good. He seems like a nice guy. Attractive, charming. Sasha is famously picky and gets the ick the way some people catch colds. I can't remember the last time she went on more than two dates with anyone.

"I like him," she continues.

"Yeah..."

"I think I like his sister more."

"Damn." This is, I hate to say, not the first time that's happened. And it never ends well.

"Yep." The dilemma is evident in her voice, a sort of resignation to the injustice of her life. "I really need to start making all potential partners run through a slideshow. If they've got attractive siblings, that shit is a non-starter. I'm only fucking with the acorns falling from the ugly trees."

"Is she into girls?"

"Don't know," Sasha says. "Like a sixty-forty yes. But they live together, so..."

"Damn."

"Yep."

"So what are you going to—"

Before I can finish, Sasha's bedroom door flies open and bangs off the wall. We both jump, startled.

"Yo, what the fuck?" Sasha shouts.

"What did you do?" Rebecca is standing in the doorway, her face red and puffy, as tears stream down her face. She's shaking, teeth clenched, visibly enraged. "What the hell did you do?"

"Bitch, I have no idea what your problem is, but—"

"Not you. *Her.*" Finger pointed at me, Rebecca charges into the room holding an iPad. "Did you know about this? Why would you do this to me?"

She's hysterical. Terrifying, even. The first place my mind goes is that this has something to do with Conor.

"What have I ever done to you?" she yells. "What is wrong with you?"

I stand up, Sasha coming up behind me with a hairbrush like she might have to put her down. "Rebecca," I say evenly. "I don't know what you're talking about. If you explain—"

"*Look* at this!"

There's an audience now. Kappas are gathered in the hallway and peering out of their bedrooms to watch.

Rebecca lunges forward and holds up her iPad in front of my face. The browser's open to a porn site and a video is cued up.

Even before she hits play my stomach sinks. I can tell just by the still image on screen what she's about to show me.

The kitchen of the Kappa house. It's dark, night outside. The only illumination comes from fairy lights strung up across the ceiling, and flashlights the sisters flicker and strobe around us, meant to disorient our overtired eyes. The room is draped in tarps and plastic sheeting to protect the walls and floors, like a scene from a bad sorority row horror movie. The senior members of Kappa Chi stand in a circle around six of us dressed in nothing but white tank tops and panties.

It's Pledge Week. Freshman year. Abigail stands beside me. Both of us are shy and terrified, questioning why we'd thought any of this was a good idea. Exhausted because by then we'd been awake going on thirty hours. Time spent doing laundry for the sisters, escorting them to and from classes, cleaning the house, and being subjected to six straight hours of "character-proving," because they're not allowed to call it hazing anymore. All of which culminated in this scene.

One of the seniors orders the six of us pledges to take body shots off each other in a line, then picks up the garden hose they fed in the side door from the yard and sprays us with it. We cower and tremble, spitting up water. Soaked to the bone. Then another sister points to me.

"Dare or Dare."

Shivering, I wipe water and hair from my eyes, and say, "Dare."

She smirks. "I dare you to make out with…" Her attention first lands on Abigail. But knowing the two of us were probably the closest of this pledge class, she opts for a greater embarrassment factor. Her eyes slide to my right. "Rebecca."

With a nod of agreement to simply grin and bear the terribly unsexy episode of kissing while feeling like a couple of drowned cats, Rebecca and I turn to each other and kiss.

"No, I said make out. Like you fucking mean it, pledges. Fuck her mouth."

So we do. Because more than anything, pledge week breaks down your sense of self-preservation, your will. By that point our responses were almost automatic. They say jump, we learn to fly.

So there it is on the Internet for horny dudes to wank it to: me and Rebecca, hot and heavy, our clothes soaked through and practically transparent. Tits and vag out on full view.

And it goes on for much longer than I remember. So long I assume it must be looped, until finally it ends and I look up at Rebecca who's still sobbing. Not in anger anymore, but humiliation. The video has thousands of views in just a few hours. Already, it's spreading.

To Kappa.

To Greek Row.

The entire campus.

And the only person who could have uploaded it is in this house.

38
TAYLOR

I'M GOING TO BE SICK.

The thought reaches my brain well after my stomach spasms and vomit rises in my throat. I bolt for Sasha's bathroom and barely make it to the toilet before I choke on the hot liquid filling my mouth. I hear the bathroom door shut while I'm rinsing my mouth out and assume it's Sasha come to check on me. Instead, I turn around to see Rebecca sitting on the edge of the bathtub.

She's composed herself. Face still red, eyes puffy. Her tears have dried. In their place, a frozen image of resignation.

"So it wasn't you," she says dully.

I wipe my face, smearing the makeup Sasha had just applied. "No."

"I'm sorry I accused you like that."

Closing the lid of the toilet, I sit down, still trying to get my own heart rate under control. Hurling did a lot to temper my panic, but the longer I'm upright, the faster the thoughts rush back to the surface.

"I understand," I say.

If I'd been the first of us to see the video, I'm not sure I would have reacted any better. Maybe not charging through the house screaming, but certainly suspicious. Fact is, Rebecca and I have never been friends. She was the shyest of our pledge class back then, and after pledge week we hardly spoke again. Not for lack of trying on my part—it just always seemed when I walked into a room, she found her way to the other side.

Now, something's changed. Besides the obvious, I mean. She sits there looking at me, defeated, like all this time she's tried to outrun me and her knee's finally given out.

"My parents are going to kill me," Rebecca whispers, hanging her head. She sighs. A big burdened release, as if rather than fearing the consequences, she's almost relieved to accept them.

"They wouldn't really blame you for the video getting out, would they? They have to understand it's not your fault."

"You don't get it." Her fingernails dig into the folio cover on her iPad, leaving crescent shapes in the fake leather. "My parents are ultra conservative, Taylor. They hardly associate with anyone outside their church. My dad didn't even want me to pledge a sorority, but I convinced my mom that Kappa was basically like joining a bible study group. She said they hoped it would teach me how to be a proper young lady."

A frown touches my lips. "What does that mean?"

It's hard to imagine my own mother ever going on a parent kick, trying to tell me what to do. I think the last time she told me to clean my room was when I lost the class ferret somewhere in the month-old laundry pile.

"I had my first girlfriend in eighth grade," Rebecca says, meeting my eyes. "We were only together for a couple weeks when a girl caught us kissing in the band room and told her mom, who went to church with my parents. My dad bullied my girlfriend's parents until they finally pulled her out of band and got her transferred out of any classes we had together. We were forbidden to see each other." She shakes her head bitterly. "Every summer after that, my Dad sent me to bible camp. Started setting me up with boys from church. Usually some gay kid who was just as mortified and depressed to be forced to kiss a girl in painfully staged date pictures. By the time I graduated high school, though, I'd convinced them I was reformed. I could be trusted again. I figured living in a sorority house would at least keep my parents from dropping in whenever they felt like it to snoop through my room or hide cameras in my walls."

"Shit, Rebecca. I had no idea. I'm sorry."

She shrugs. A sad grin makes a fleeting appearance, then vanishes. "I'm sorry we never became friends."

"No, I get it." I bite my lip. "I can't pretend to know how you feel, but I get it."

A lot of us are trapped in our own lives. Told we're made wrong, deficient. As if being ourselves is somehow an affront to society. Some of us are constantly beaten with a stick of conformity until we learn to love the pain or give up altogether. I still haven't figured my way out of that trap. Yet there's nothing worse than when it's your own family on the other end of that stick. Which pretty much makes Rebecca the strongest person I know—and one hell of an ally.

"So what are we going to do?" she says quietly.

My teeth dig harder into my lip. "Only a Kappa could have shared that video."

"Agreed."

"I have a pretty good idea who."

I don't remember who was holding the phone. One of the seniors, I'd guess. Except for rituals, all pledge activities were recorded for "posterity."

The real question is, who had access to the video. I've never seen any footage from mine or another pledge week aside from the highlight reel that always runs at the first dinner after confirmations. It makes sense the person who would have control over that archive is the president.

And her VP.

Downstairs, Rebecca and I confront Charlotte in the lounge. She's alone, curled up in a high-back chair with her laptop open and her headphones on. Considering the commotion a few minutes ago, I would've expected her to have circled the wagons, as it were.

"We have to talk," I tell her.

Charlotte pushes one of her headphones off one ear, lifting an irritated eyebrow without looking up from her screen. "What?"

"We need to talk," I repeat.

"Do we?"

"Yes," Rebecca insists.

Charlotte's gaze remains on the laptop. Lately she's completely checked out. She's graduating and Abigail was named her successor, so there's not much left for Charlotte to do than hand over the keys and pose for a photo that'll hang on the wall with the other former presidents. We've all noticed the change in her attitude in that regard. Full-on senioritis.

"Charlotte," I snap.

Rolling her eyes, she slides the headphones off and shuts her laptop. "Fine. What is it?"

"This." Rebecca shoves her iPad in Charlotte's face and presses play again on the video.

At first, Charlotte appears bored, confused, glancing at us for an explanation. Then I watch the realization dawn on her. She scrolls down to read the comments. Scrolls up to look at the website name at the top of the page. Her startled eyes dart up to ours.

"Who posted this?" she demands, fire in her voice. Charlotte Cagney is a force to be reckoned with, which is why she was elected president in the first place. Everyone voted out of fear of what would happen to all those who opposed her. No one dared run against her.

"We came to ask you that," I say pointedly. "You're saying you don't know?"

"This is the first I'm seeing of this." She shoves her laptop to the side and stands. "I just got back from graduation rehearsal and was trying to study for finals. How did you find this?"

Rebecca's lips tighten. "I just got home and found Nancy and Robin watching it in the kitchen."

"Sigma has seen it, too," I add. "So you can bet it's all over campus by now."

I see the sudden change in Charlotte's eyes. From small kitchen fire to scorching inferno. She shoves the iPad at Rebecca and storms out of the room, still talking as if she hasn't left us in her dust.

"Get everyone to the blue room," she says. Then, shouting, "House meeting, motherfuckers!" Charlotte tears up to the second floor and starts banging on doors. "Everyone downstairs now!" Then back down and through every room. Beth and Olivia are with a group in the TV room, their backs turned, when Charlotte launches a banana at their heads. "Blue room. Get up."

I have no idea where she picked up the projectile banana.

Rebecca stands somewhat behind me once we've all gathered in the blue room. We wait a few minutes, everyone staring at each other, bracing for impact, while the last stragglers haul ass back to the house for the meeting. Abigail then takes the roll to confirm we're all here before Charlotte begins.

My eyes meet Abigail's from across the room. I try to read her for any hint or tell, but she's impassive.

"Alright, it's come to my attention that there's a video going around." Charlotte's glare lands on Nancy and Robin, who at least have the decency to look contrite. "And apparently none of you thought it appropriate to make your house president aware of this severe breach of trust and privacy."

Sasha works her way through the room to stand with me and Rebecca. She slips her fingers through mine, and I squeeze her hand, grateful for her presence.

"Robin, what's the first tenet of the Kappa creed?" Charlotte demands.

Chewing on her thumbnail, a nervous Robin stares at her feet. "I will protect my sister as myself."

Next Charlotte turns her blazing ire on the sister who's turning beet red. "Nancy, what's the second tenet of the Kappa creed?"

Nancy tries to speak but only air comes out. Then, voice shaking, "To act with honor and integrity."

"Yeah," Charlotte says, pacing the room like she's got a loaded pistol, "that's what I thought. But apparently some of you have forgotten that. So I want to know who the sister fucker is. Who is the selfish little shit who stole a private video from the Kappa archive and uploaded it to a porn site?"

A shocked silence crashes over the room.

It becomes evident then who had still been in the dark. Questioning eyes begin scanning the room, factions trading accusatory glances. I spot more confused faces than I expected. I guess I figured every girl in the house had already seen the video and was laughing about it behind our backs. But other than Nancy and Robin, I pick out only a few other girls who I suspect might've known.

Naturally, my examination of Abigail lasts the longest. A deep groove has cut into her forehead, but I'm not sure what it means. Is she stunned? Baffled?

Her green eyes keep sliding around to study the faces of our sisters. Searching for the culprit…or looking for allies?

"Nope, uh-uh," Charlotte says, wagging her finger. "Don't go quiet on me now. Your big-girl ass thought this was a good idea—you can't walk that shit back now. Someone's going to confess, or we will sit here all night. All day. Until the end of fucking time until one of you little brats tells the truth."

Abigail just stands there, arms crossed. Not saying a word.

I can't stand it any longer.

"Abigail," I call out, and the oxygen is sucked out of the room. "Have anything to say?"

She flinches. "What's that supposed to mean?"

"Well, I'm just checking my watch and, oh, look, it's spiteful-bitch-thirty, so maybe you have something to add to this conversation."

Sasha's eyes go wide as she turns to me in slow motion, staring at me as if I've grown a second head. And maybe I have. This one's fed the fuck up.

"You're accusing me?" Abigail's voice jumps two octaves as her face crinkles in denial. "I didn't have anything to do with it!"

"Really? Because you're the only person in this room who's made it her unending mission to ruin my life, so…"

"Only two people have the password to the server where the archive is stored," Charlotte says, her attention now trained on Abigail. "You're the other one."

"I didn't do it." She tosses her hands up, pleading. "I swear. Okay, I admit, there's a beef there, but I would never upload revenge porn of another woman."

"Even a woman you hate?" I snap back.

Abigail drops her hands. For the first time in years, she looks at me with sincerity. "Not even my worst enemy. That's not who I am."

Silence falls over the room. My gaze remains locked with the platinum blonde who's made my life miserable for so long.

Fuck me, but I believe her.

"Then who is it?" I challenge. "Who wanted to humiliate me?"

Because I know this was about me. Rebecca and I might have remained obscure to one another since freshman year, but I can't think of anyone who even mildly dislikes her enough to humiliate her like this. The target had to be me.

"I have the password saved on my phone," Abigail says, growing visibly anxious. "If someone broke into my phone…"

I'm not sure she means to do it, or is even consciously aware, when her gaze slides to Jules, who's trying to blend into a potted plant at the back of the room.

When Jules realizes she's been singled out, she reveals a panicked expression that is quickly overcome by betrayal.

"Did you hack my phone?" Abigail asks her best friend, a note of horror in her tone.

At first it appears she might deny it, but then the pretense falls. Jules huffs, rolls her eyes. "It was just a joke, okay? They both had their clothes on. What's the big deal?"

Abigail's jaw falls open. "Why?" she demands. "Why would you ever do something like that?"

Jules offers a shrug, her body language trying to downplay it all. "The other night, remember? Kev said something like, *I wonder how many views Taylor's tits would get on PornHub*. So later I was over at the Sigma house visiting Duke, and Kevin was there. He and I were talking, and I was like, well, I can totally get a video of her tits. And the next time you left your phone out, I tried a few passwords until I got it unlocked." Jules shakes her head defiantly. "Like it wasn't a big thing. Just a dumb prank. Why is everyone getting so bent out of shape?"

"Christ, Jules, would it kill you to grow a mind of your own?"

"Fuck off, Sasha. Taylor started it by kissing Abigail's ex! She's the sister fucker. And she would've left Kappa by now if she didn't have you always fighting her battles for her."

"You're a real cunt, Jules, You know that?"

My eyes widen, because that one came from Rebecca.

"Oh, stuff it up your cooch, Rebecca. If anyone wanted to yank it to a ten-year-old boy they'd become a priest."

"All of you, shut up!" Charlotte shouts. She closes her eyes, massaging her temples like a mother just before she blacks out and smothers her new baby in its crib.

"I call for an emergency vote."

I frown at Abigail's declaration. I look over to see her nudging Olivia beside her, who seconds the motion even though she hardly seems to understand why.

Charlotte gives a slow nod. "Okay, call your vote."

"All in favor of revoking Jules's membership in Kappa Chi sorority and evicting her from the house, raise your hands."

Wait.

What?

For some reason, I assumed Abigail would protect Jules, and Charlotte would protect Abigail. I'd been the sorority punchline for so long that I forgot about all my old hopes and dreams of sisterhood, of having close friends to support me and watch my back.

But Abigail's declaration brings some unexpected redemption to the Kappa house, as everyone bands together during the vote. Rebecca's hand is the first up. Followed closely by Lisa, Sasha, Olivia and Beth. More hands rise, each encouraged by the growing majority. Until finally, my hand goes up.

"Good, it's unanimous," Charlotte says with a nod. "Julianne Munn, by unanimous decision, the membership of the Briar chapter of Kappa Chi have lost faith in your commitment to our shared tenets of sisterhood, and you are hereby excommunicated and banished from the grounds." Our president pauses, staring at Jules when she doesn't respond. "Well, get the fuck out."

"Are you shitting me? This isn't fair," Jules argues, looking at Abigail to save her. She searches the room, shocked and dejected when no one comes to her rescue. "Seriously? Fine. Fuck you all. Have a nice life."

Jules storms up the stairs to her room while the rest of the sisters sit dumbfounded at what's just happened. I know the feeling.

"Taylor," a sheepish voice pipes up. It belongs to Nancy, who eyes me sadly from across the room. "I'm really sorry we were watching that crap. We were trying to figure out how to say something when Rebecca caught us."

"Shep sent me the link like five seconds before you got home," Robin adds, glancing at Rebecca. "We weren't laughing about it, I swear."

Rebecca and I each respond with a nod. I'm not quite sure I believe them, but at least they apologized.

After Charlotte dismisses everyone, Abigail gets my attention, weaving her way through the room.

"Taylor, wait up. I want to talk," she pleads.

I've got less than zero interest in what she has to say. She chose this one moment to grow a conscience and do the right thing. Good for her. But I'm not giving her a pat on the back for it. We aren't friends.

Instead, I rush up the stairs with Sasha. Rebecca disappears into her room. I wish I knew how better to comfort her, but the minute Sasha and I are alone, and I catch a glimpse of myself in the mirror, I remember it's my birthday and that Conor is on his way over.

He'll be here any minute and I'm a fucking mess from the inside out.

"I can't do this," I mutter, stumbling into Sasha's bathroom to wipe the makeup from my face.

"So let's get the hell out of here," she says, standing in the doorway. "Tell Conor to meet us at your place with some liquor and we'll stay in and get loaded."

"No, I mean I can't see him."

The idea of facing him after this has me feeling queasy again. Like the slightest nudge could send me hugging the toilet.

"Do you want me to call him, say you're sick or something?" Our eyes meet in the mirror. Reading my face, Sasha's expression sobers. "Are you going to tell him?"

Tell him what? That I'm now a trending topic on one of the world's most popular porn sites?

That when he tells his mom and stepdad about me, they can go online and see my tits?

That every one of my mom's Rate My Professor reviews will now include a link to her daughter?

Bile rises in my throat as panic once again attacks my insides.

Oh my fucking God. This is going to affect my entire life. What happens when elementary school principals and parents get a look at Ms. Marsh and her famous rack and I'm banned from every school district across the country because a woman's body is more dangerous than a hand grenade?

"Taylor—"

I push Sasha's hand off me and lunge for the toilet again, where I kneel there dry-heaving.

I didn't choose this. To be put on display. To be the object of humiliation. The thought of Conor having to deal with it too makes me want to cry again.

His teammates will see the video. Spank it under the covers then smirk every time they see me. Hang screenshots in the locker room. He doesn't deserve to have a fucking embarrassment, no, a *joke*, for a girlfriend. And then what? He'll forever have to keep defending me? Keep being infinitely patient and understanding during the numerous freak-outs I now envision in my future?

I can't live like that, constantly feeling like everyone I meet is seeing me naked and knowing I'm embarrassing my boyfriend even if he pretends otherwise. I can't. I can't see him anymore.

I fucking *can't*.

"Take me home," I say, rising on wobbly legs. "I'll text him on the way."

Sasha nods. "Whatever you need."

Once I've gathered my things, we head downstairs. But the universe hates me, so I'm not surprised to discover that Conor is early.

He's striding up the darkened driveway as we open the door. Dressed in a sharp black suit somewhere behind an enormous flower arrangement. I never get tired of seeing him all pressed and polished. He's like sex personified. A walking fantasy.

And I'm walking away.

He smiles wide when he sees me, then notices my rumpled state and gives a sheepish look. "Shit. You're not ready. I'm sorry, I should have done another couple laps." He's adorable when he's excited. And here I am about to take him out back with a shotgun. "I was getting a little overanxious. But I can wait."

"I'm sorry," I say, "I have to cancel."

The words come out in someone else's voice. Distant and strange. I feel myself shutting down even as I stand under the lights of the house. My mind is peeling away from my body, recoiling from everything.

"Why? What happened?"

He sets the huge flower arrangement on the ground and tries to reach for me, but I step out of his grasp. If I let him touch me, my resolve will crack. I'm not strong enough to withstand Conor Edwards' touch.

"Taylor, what's wrong?" The hurt in his eyes is immediate and gutting.

I can't form the words. I remember how frustrated I was last month when he wasn't communicating with me, and yet here I am, doing the same thing. But his shit was righted by the simple act of telling his family the truth, removing himself from Kai's influence.

My shit isn't going away. The truth won't help a goddamn bit, because the Internet is fucking *forever*.

How the hell do I ask him to tie himself to that bullshit long-term? He's been so patient and encouraging already, but this is too much for anyone to handle. It's too much for *me*.

I see the alarm on his face, and I know what comes next. The pain, the betrayal. I don't want to do this to him. He deserves better and probably always has. We were a mess from the start and maybe it's fitting it should be just as messy at the end. He won't understand, but he'll get over it. They always do.

"I'm sorry, Conor. It's over."

39
CONOR

THIS ISN'T FUNNY. BECAUSE SHE HAS TO BE MESSING WITH ME, right? Some sick idea of a joke. *In lieu of presents I will be scaring the shit out of you.*

"Taylor, stop."

"I'm serious," she says, looking at her feet.

I came up to the Kappa house to find her acting suspiciously, like she was making an escape. Bag slung over her shoulder. She looks worn out, ragged, and if I didn't know better, I'd think she was hung-over. Yet there's a coldness about her. Her expression hard and impassive, as if my Taylor isn't even in there anymore.

"Listen, I'm sorry, but you're just going to have to accept it. This is over." She shrugs. "I've got to go."

Like hell it is. "Talk to me," I order.

She's got Sasha with her and they start walking toward a red car parked at the side of the house. I leave the flowers behind to follow them, because she's not pulling this shit today.

"You're seriously breaking up with me? On your *birthday*? The fuck is that, Taylor?"

"I know this is shitty," she says, walking fast and refusing to look at me, "but it's the way it has to be. Just…I'm sorry."

"I don't believe you." I step in front of her, needing her to look me in the eyes and tell me the truth. I notice Sasha trying to edge away from us, but Taylor glances over in panic and Sasha stops. She stands a few feet away, but doesn't leave.

"It doesn't matter what you believe," Taylor mutters.

"I love you." And yesterday I would have said she loved me too. "Something's happened. Just tell me what it is. If someone said something to make you think—"

"It was a fling, Conor. It's run its course. You'll bounce back." Her gaze drops to the pavement. "We both got in over our heads."

"What does that even mean?" This woman is fucking infuriating. I feel like I'm losing my mind. Everything up is down and left is right. It makes no sense that yesterday she was in my bed and today she's practically running at the sight of me. "I was in this for real. I *am* in it. And I know you were too. Why are you lying?"

"I'm not lying." Her indignation is far from compelling and the more she feeds me this bullshit, the less I can remember why I'm still standing here like a jackass getting my heart stomped on. "Whatever you want to call it—"

"A relationship," I growl. "It's a fucking relationship."

"Well, not anymore." She sighs, and at this point I'd believe she didn't give a shit about me if it weren't for the fact that I know her better than she'd like to admit. "The semester is ending, anyway. You're going back to California and I'm going home to Cambridge, so. The long-distance thing never works."

"I wanted you to come stay with me. Already cleared it with Max and my mom." I shake my head in frustration. "They were excited to meet you, T. My mom was redecorating one of the spare bedrooms for you."

"Yeah, well…" She fidgets, eyes bouncing from the ground to the road. Anywhere but me. "I don't know where you got the idea I wanted to spend the summer with your parents. I never said yes."

Taylor isn't a cruel person. She doesn't treat people like this. Even me. Even when I was breaking her heart because I was too afraid to face her. She isn't this heartless.

And yet.

"Why are you doing this?" This act, this façade she's put on, is nothing like the person I've known for the past few months. "If this is about the whole thing with Kai, I'm sorry. I thought we'd—"

"Maybe you guys should take the night to sleep on it and talk again tomorrow," Sasha cuts in, her attention trained on Taylor. I don't know Sasha well, but even she is giving off a sketchy vibe.

Taylor moves to go around me so I block her path. She glares at me not with anger but something that resembles defeat.

"Just level with me, Taylor." This is exhausting and I don't know how else to get through to her, to break through this barrier she's erected between us. Even the first night we met I never felt this distant from her. As if she's looking past me. Invisible. Irrelevant. "You owe me that much. Just tell me the truth."

"I don't want *you* as a boyfriend, okay? Are you happy now?"

The gun was loaded that time. Bullet goes right through my chest.

"Like, seriously, Conor, you're a great guy and you're good looking, but what else do you have going on? You have no idea what you want to do with the rest of your life. You have no ambition. No plan or prospects. And that's fine for you. You can live in your parents' house and hang out on the beach for the rest of your life. Well, I want more for myself. It was fun, but next year we'll be seniors and I'm ready to grow up. You're not."

At that, she grabs Sasha's hand and pushes past me.

This time I let her go.

Because finally she hit the nail on the head, what I've always known and hoped she'd ignore—that we're on two different paths. Taylor is bright and motivated. She'll accomplish whatever she sets her mind to. I'm...a fuckup. A perennial drifter carried on the current with no aim or drive of my own.

Sasha's car pulls out down the driveway and disappears around the corner.

A pang of loss stabs me square in the gut. A deep, buried memory of pain breaks the surface. A child's memory of being in a darkened room, crying, alone and unconsoled. It was the first time I realized I had no father, when I was truly old enough to understand that it was something other kids had, but not me. Not because he died, but because we weren't good enough. *I* wasn't good enough. Abandoned. Disposable. Garbage.

It was bound to happen. That moment Taylor woke up and realized she was out of my league. That she'd been too quick to forgive me for running out on her over Kai. I'd kept her hanging and waited too long to figure out my feelings for her. I waited too long to make my intentions clear and define our relationship. I was selfish to think she needed me, wanted me, enough to be patient. I took her for granted because no one had ever made me feel as comfortable and accepted as she did. No one had ever given me that sense of self-worth before she did.

And now the best thing that's ever happened to me just drove away.

40
TAYLOR

I ONLY WATCH SHOWS WITH BRITISH ACCENTS NOW. IT'S LIKE going on vacation without having to put on pants. On Friday I skipped class—it was just a review anyway—turned off my phone, and dove into my to-be-watched list that has languished for months. When that failed to adequately distract me, I signed up for about a dozen streaming free trials.

My takeaway thus far is that serial killers are rampant in quaint country villages. Also, dating shows are better with accents, too. Although one thing I've noticed is the severe lack of excessive drinking on their reality programming—I mean, how are people supposed to start throwing chairs and breaking shit if they're sober all the time? They do love their lip fillers and hair extensions, though.

"I like the one who says 'fit' a lot," I tell Sasha over speakerphone while I watch a show that's essentially Tinder, except they all live together. "And they call girls *birds*. I feel like it's still the fifties in just Cuba and England."

"Uh-huh," Sasha says with boredom in her voice. "Have you showered today?"

Clearly she doesn't appreciate sophisticated television.

"It's Saturday," I tell her.

"Do we not shower on Saturdays now?" Always so judgey.

"Water doesn't grow on trees, you know."

After Sasha drove me home from the Kappa house Thursday night, I got in my sweats, went to the couch, and watched British Cottage Murder Detective Priest while eating an entire box of Cheerios before falling asleep in the same position, waking up this morning, getting more cereal delivered, and resuming my viewing schedule. This will be my life now. With Instacart and online classes, who needs to leave the house?

"It's the end of the semester," I add. "Isn't this what college students are supposed to do? Lie around in a nest of our own molting skin, watching TV and gorging on processed foods."

"Not since millennials all got startups, Taylor."

"Well, I'm an old soul."

"You're hiding," she says sharply.

"So." So what. Aren't I allowed? I was dragged out in the middle of the student union, stripped, and ogled by the entire campus. That's how it feels, anyway. So fucking sue me if all I want to do is lock myself inside and escape into other people's lives for a while.

"So you were violated," she starts, her tone softening.

"I'm aware." Thanks.

"Don't you want to do something about it? We can get the video taken down. We can go to the police. I'll help you. You shouldn't have to just accept that this happened and suffer for it."

"What am I going to do, have Jules arrested?"

"Yes," her voice bursts out of the speaker. "And Abigail's shithead boyfriend. Or, ex, I guess, based on the screaming coming from her room last night. What those two did is a crime, Taylor. It would make them sex offenders in some places."

"I don't know."

Cops mean statements. Sitting in a room with a dude staring at my tits while I recount my humiliation for him.

Or worse, a morally righteous woman who tells me this wouldn't have happened if there wasn't a video, if I hadn't put myself in that situation.

Screw that.

"If it were me, I'd be slitting throats."

"It's not you." I appreciate Sasha's venom. It's what I love about her. She's everything I'm not, vengeful and confident. I'm not built that way. "I know you're trying. Thank you. But I still need time to think. I'm not there yet."

Truth is, I've barely wrapped my head around the idea that this is happening, much less the larger implications. When my alarm went off yesterday morning for class, a fierce and immediate sense of panic erupted through my muscles. I felt sick at the thought of walking across campus to the lingering eyes and hushed conversations. Heads turning when I entered the room. Classmates with their phones in their laps, the video playing. Giggles and stares. I couldn't do it.

So I stayed home. On one of my TV breaks, I even texted Rebecca. I don't know why, I guess to share in the misery together. She didn't respond, which is probably for the best. Maybe if we just ignore this and each other, it'll just go away.

"Have you heard from Conor?" Her voice is apprehensive, as if she's concerned I might hang up on her for daring to ask.

I almost do. Because just the sound of his name sends a knife of pain to my heart. "He's texted a few times, but I'm ignoring the messages."

"Taylor."

"What? It's over," I mutter. "You were there when I dumped him."

"Yes, I was, and it was obvious you weren't thinking clearly," she says in aggravation. "You did everything you could to push him away. I get it, okay? When we're in that level of crisis, we fall back on our worst insecurities. You were worried he'd judge you or feel embarrassed on your behalf—"

"I don't need a psychology lesson right now," I interrupt. "Please. Just leave it alone."

There's a short beat of silence.

"All right, I'll leave it." Another beat, and then she somberly says, "I'm here for you. Anything you need. I'll drop everything."

"I know. You're a good friend."

With a smile in her voice, she replies, "Yes, I am."

After I hang up with Sasha, I go back to my shows and stress-eating. A few episodes later, there's a knock at the door. I'm confused for a minute, wondering if I'd forgotten I ordered something else, until I hear another knock and Abigail's voice asking me to let her in.

Fuck.

"Before you tell me to piss off," she says when I reluctantly open the door, "I come in peace. And to apologize."

"It's fine," I reply, just to get rid of her. "You apologized. Bye."

I try to close the door, but she pushes it open and slips her ass in before I can slam her foot in the doorjamb.

"Abigail," I huff, "I just want to be left alone."

"Yeah…" Scrunching her face at my never-to-be-seen-by-another-human-person sweat ensemble, she says, "I can see that."

"Why are you here, dammit?"

Being Abigail, she waltzes over to one of the stools at the tiny kitchen island and takes a seat. "I heard you broke up with Conor."

"Seriously? You want to start with that?" Fucking unbelievable.

"I didn't mean it like that," she says quickly and takes a breath before starting over. "I mean, I think you made a mistake."

Her pretenses drop. That air of permanent bitchiness. For the first time in a long time, she's regarding me without a smirk of cruelty or sarcasm. It's…sort of creepy.

Still not ready to trust her intentions, I stand against the opposite counter from her. "Why do you care?" Not that I give a shit what she thinks.

"Okay, look. I do this too." There's a chord of sympathy in her voice. "You're upset and embarrassed and you want to push everyone away. Especially the people closest to you. That way they don't see the pain you're going through. They don't see you the way you feel about yourself. I get it. I truly do."

First Sasha, now Abigail? Why can't everyone just leave me alone?

"What the hell do you know about anything?" I mutter. "You run through boys like makeup wipes."

"I have issues, too," she insists. "Just because you don't see my insecurities doesn't mean they aren't there. We all have scars on the inside."

"Yeah, well, I'm sorry about your deep personal traumas, but you're one of mine, so…"

If Abigail is feeling some remorse because her assheadedness blew up in my face, she's going to have to turn elsewhere for absolution. She might have sympathy for me, but I have none for her.

"That's exactly what I mean," she says ruefully. "I was so insecure about you kissing a guy I was dating on a stupid dare that the only way I knew how to cope with that was to take my hurt out on you. After the kiss he wouldn't shut up about *oh her huge tits* and *have you ever thought about implants* and all kinds of shit. Do you know how humiliating that is?"

A crease cuts into my forehead. I didn't know that. I mean, sure, I knew she was pissed. But if a guy I was seeing kept going on about it, comparing us, I'd have lost my shit, too.

"In high school," she confesses, drawing patterns on the countertop, "I was called pancakes. I didn't even have enough to fill out a training bra. I know you probably think that's a stupid thing to obsess about, but all I've wanted, for my entire life, was to feel good in my clothes, you know? To feel sexy. For guys to look at me the way they look at other girls."

"But you're gorgeous," I say, exasperated. "You've got a perfect body and a beautiful face. You know the last time I wore a bikini? I was still sleeping with a nightlight." I gesture to my chest. "These things are a fucking burden. They're heavy. They don't fit any apparatus known to man. I've got back problems like I'm seventy. Every guy I meet is staring at my boobs to distract him from the rest of me."

Except Conor. Which sends another pang of loneliness stabbing through my gut.

"And yet, I never feel good enough. I never feel confident in who I am," Abigail counters. "I make up for it with—"

"Being a bitch."

She smiles, rolling her eyes. "Mostly, yeah. My point is, I've felt like shit and pushed people away, too. That's what you're doing with Conor and it sucks. I don't know or care at what point you two stopped messing with me—and don't bother denying it. I saw right through that bullshit. But at some point it changed and you made it official. Yeah, I noticed that too. He obviously loves you, and if your sudden change in attitude the last couple weeks is any indication, you loved him too. So what sense does it make to lose that because someone else did a shitty thing?"

"You don't understand." Because she can't. And I don't know what else to tell her that doesn't sound like an excuse. Even the thought of facing Conor after this makes my throat close up and my legs shake. "Thanks for coming by, but—"

"Fine." She pivots, sensing I'm about to tell her to beat it so I can get back to conversations that take place exclusively in a Manchester accent. "We won't talk about Conor. Or that the flowers he left for you are now taking up the entire living room coffee table. Have you gone to the police yet?"

You've got to be kidding me. "Did Jules send you over here?" I demand.

"No," she says quickly. "Nothing like that, I promise. Just if you are going to report the video, I'll go with you. I can explain how Jules got access to it and everything. Be a witness, if you want."

This topic is getting exhausting. "You know, I'm getting a little sick of people pushing me. Everyone has their ideas of what I have to do and it's pretty damn overwhelming. Can I have like a fucking minute."

"I know this is scary, but you really should go to the police," Abigail insists. "If you don't attack this now, it will spread. What happens when one day you apply for a job or, who knows, you want to run for office or something and this video pops up? It will live with you forever." She flicks up her eyebrows. "Or you can do something about it."

"You're not the best person to be giving me advice," I remind her.

It's easy for others to say this is what must be done, tell me to suck it up. If our positions were reversed, I might say the same. Things look a whole lot different on this end, though. The last thing I want to be doing is weighing the impact of court cases and depositions, headlines and news vans, with tucking myself under my blankets and never, ever coming out again. The latter is a whole lot cozier.

"You're right. I've been terrible to you. I didn't know how to deal with my feelings." Abigail looks down at her hands, picking at her nails. "You were my best friend during pledge."

"Yeah, I remember," I say bitterly.

"I was so excited about us being sisters. Then it all went wrong. That was my fault, I should have done something about it then, talked it out or whatever, and instead it's only gotten worse. I lost a friend. But I'm trying to start making up for that. Let me help you."

"Why should I?" It's all well and good that Abigail has reached her epiphany, but it doesn't mean we're going to be besties now.

"Because with shit like this, women have to stick together," she says earnestly. "This transcends all that other bullshit. Jules was wrong. No one deserves what she did. I want her punished for you but also for all of us. Even if you never talk to me after this, I've got your back. Every single Kappa does."

I admit, she sounds sincere. Which I suppose means she isn't entirely devoid of humanity. And it did take courage to come here.

I hate myself so much.

"Feel better?" Hunter asks cheerfully, handing me a bottle of water.

"No." I take a few swigs, swish, and spit it out in the bushes. I know these bushes. I'm near my driveway. I don't remember leaving the party across town, though. And I definitely don't remember getting in Hunter's car. Where's my Jeep? "Wait. You said you've been looking for me?"

"Man, you went MIA last night."

I check my pockets and find my keys, phone, and wallet. So at least I'm good in that department.

We go back to Hunter's Rover and lean against the trunk while I take inventory of my last recollections. There was a house party at some friend of Demi's. The guys were all there. We played beer pong, the usual. I remember pounding shots with Foster and Bucky. A girl. Shit.

"Where'd you go?" Hunter asks, apparently seeing the realization creep across my face.

"I made out with some chick," I say half as a question.

"Yeah, we all saw. You two were all up on each other in the kitchen. Then you disappeared."

Fuck. "She took me into one of the bedrooms. We were going at it, you know. Kissing and whatnot. Then she tried to get my pants off to blow me and I bugged out. Couldn't do it."

"Whiskey dick?"

"Limp as a piece of raw chicken." I search my brain. "I think I sort of left her there."

"Demi saw her come down, but we couldn't find you after that," Hunter tells me. "Nobody could. We all started calling. Fanned out looking for you."

It's all pretty fuzzy. There are gaps. Starts and stops of a jittery picture. "I left the house, I think, out the back. It was too crowded in the yard and I couldn't find the gate in the fence, so I think I hopped it."

I look down at my hands. They're all scratched up and my jeans have a fresh tear in them. I look like I went rolling down the side of a mountain.

"Then I think I was going to walk home, but I couldn't figure out which way I was pointed or where home was. I remember being real fucking confused about where I was, and I think my phone died, so I was like, fuck it, I'll just wait for one of you to take me home. I don't know why, but I guess I crawled in your backseat."

"Jesus, dude." Hunter shakes his head, laughing at me. Rightly so. "I left the car at the party last night after we suspended the search. Demi and I walked home because we'd both been drinking. Foster called this morning and said you never came home, so I went back for my car so I could start driving around checking ditches for you. Found you in my backseat and drove you home."

"Sorry, man." This isn't the first time I've woken up in a strange place after a night out. But it's the first time it's happened since I came to Briar. "Guess I got a little outta hand last night."

"You've been a little outta hand all week." Hunter turns to me, arms crossed. He's got his captain's face on. The *I'm not your daddy but* face. "Maybe it's time to take it down a notch with the partying. I know I was Team Drink It Out of Your System before, but now I'm calling it. Going missing for twelve hours is the limit."

He's right. I've been out every night since Taylor dumped me. Knocking back drinks like it's my job, trying to lose the memory of her in some other girl's face. Only, it doesn't work. Not for my heart and not for my dick.

I miss her. I miss only her.

"You should try talking to her again," Hunter says gruffly. "It's been a few days. Maybe she's ready to come around."

"I've texted her. She won't text me back." Probably blocked my number by now.

"Look, I can't begin to understand what went wrong there. But when she's ready I know you two can work it out. I don't know

Taylor well or anything, but anyone could see you were both happy together. She's going through something. Like you were before." He shrugs. "Maybe it's her turn to figure stuff out."

She already has. She finally figured out that she's too damn good for me. I might be making strides to better my life, but I'm not there yet and Taylor knew it and she didn't want to wait around, I guess. I almost don't even blame her. What the fuck have I ever done for her aside from giving her some orgasms and standing her up at a dance?

I choke down the rush of bitterness that fills my throat. Hey, at least it's not puke anymore.

"Anyway, whatever you need, man. You know I'm here for you." Hunter pats me on the back then gives me a shove. "Now get the hell off my car. I've gotta go wash the piss out of the backseat."

"Fuck off. There's no piss there." I pause. "Just some vomit maybe."

"Asshole."

"Thanks for the ride," I say, laughing as I back away. "See ya later."

I head into the house, where I take a ragging from the roommates about last night. Won't be living this one down for a long time. They invite me to brunch at the diner, but I'm exhausted and I've got a shit ton of packing to do before I head back to Cali in a few days. So I go take a shower, and they go out and bring me back some waffles and bacon.

About an hour into laundry and packing boxes, our doorbell rings. The guys are deep into a video game, so I wander over to the front door and answer it.

On the other side I find half a dozen of Taylor's Kappa sisters, led by the infamous Abigail.

Before I can get a word out, she says, "Truce. We're on the same side."

I blink. "Huh?"

I don't invite her in so much as she invites herself. Plus the six other girls trailing behind. They march into the house and take a stance like a troupe of angry townsfolk in the middle of the living room.

Foster gives me a wary look from the couch. "Hunter said no more parties."

"Shut up, dumbass." I focus on Abigail, who's clearly the leader of this invasion. If it has something to do with Taylor, I want to hear it. "Why are you here?"

"Listen up." She steps forward, hands on her hips. "Taylor didn't dump you because she doesn't love you anymore."

"Oh snap!" Foster exclaims then buttons his lips when I shoot a warning glare at him.

"She dumped you because there's a video going around of her from pledge week freshman year. It was never supposed to be public, but someone uploaded it to embarrass her. Now she's humiliated and scared and she didn't want you to know about it so she broke up with you first."

"What kind of video?" I demand, confused with the vagueness of it. "And if she didn't want me to know, why are you here?"

"Because," Abigail says, "if I rip the Band-Aid off for her, maybe she'll stop being afraid and fight back."

If she means what she's saying, I guess she isn't quite the enemy anymore. No telling what brought on this sudden change of heart, but that's another conversation entirely, and one I'm not sure is mine to have. I'm not ready to trust her completely, but this would be a hell of a long way to go to pull a prank.

"Fight back against what?" Matt asks from his spot in the recliner.

Good question. The other guys sit up, anxious and interested. The controllers and game are all but forgotten.

Abigail looks around awkwardly. "On the last night of pledge week, they had us in tank tops and underwear, and the seniors hosed us down while ordering Taylor and another girl to make out. They recorded it. Last week someone stole the video and posted it on a porn site. It's…graphic. As in, you can see, you know, stuff."

"Oh hell no." Foster looks at me, eyes wide.

Motherfuckers. An overwhelming urge to punch a wall flashes through my mind, but I stop just short, remembering the last time I did that I hit a stud in the wall and broke my hand.

The fury has no outlet and instead courses through my blood. Heart to fingers to toes and back up again. Hot, boiling rage accompanied by the images assaulting my mind—random guys watching her, leering at her. Jerking it to my girlfriend.

Fuck. All I want to do is start ripping heads off. I glance at Alec and Gavin, both of them hunched forward like they're about to launch out of their seats. Fists clenched, just like mine.

"How am I only hearing about this video now if you say it's been going around?" I demand.

"Honestly I'm surprised you didn't already know." She glances at her fellow Kappas with a pleased nod. "I guess our efforts are working."

"Efforts?" I frown.

"To shut it down and stop it from spreading through campus. We ordered everyone on Greek Row to shut the hell up about the video and not pass it around, but I didn't expect any of those jackasses to actually listen, especially the frats. We've been doing everything we can to try to stop this shit from going viral."

"Who?" I growl through gritted teeth. "Who uploaded it?"

"One of our Kappa sisters. Now former sister," Abigail is quick to add. "And my ex-boyfriend."

That's all the guys needed to hear—there's another dude whose ass we could kick.

They jump to their feet without delay.

"Where do we find this asshole?" Foster grunts.

"Should curb-stomp his face."

"'Bout to fuck up his whole day."

"Dude better have a will."

"No," Abigail orders, throwing her hands up like a blockade.

"We came here because you need to convince Taylor to go to the police. We tried to work on her and the other sister in the video, but they're scared. We hoped if you could get through to Taylor, she'd convince the other girl it's the right thing to do."

"Nah, fuck that," I mutter. "She can do what she wants. I'm gonna fucking shred this jackass."

"You can't. Trust me. Kevin's a sniveling little shit and he'll absolutely go to the cops if you lay a hand on him. You'll end up in jail and who's going to protect Taylor then? So simmer down, big guy, and listen."

"Taylor isn't talking to me," I tell the girls, who are all looking at me like I'm an idiot. "I've tried."

"So try harder." Abigail rolls her eyes, making a show of sighing loudly. "Duh."

"Put your back into it," another one says.

"Mind over matter." This comes from one of the chicks who was at the diner that one time. Olivia something or other.

They're right, though. Much as I'd like to drag this fucker behind my Jeep, now would be a terrible time to get arrested. As long as that video of Taylor is out there, she's a target. Who knows what kind of sick pervert might get a real dumb idea to mess with her. I've got to be here to watch her back, even if she doesn't know I am.

I'd do anything to keep her safe.

"I'll try," I promise Taylor's sorority sisters. My voice sounds raspy, so I clear my throat. "I'll head over to her place now."

If Abigail's story about why Taylor broke it off is true, I've got to get her back. Up until this point, I hadn't wanted to push Taylor too hard. Yeah, I probably blew up her phone too much the night she ended it, but I didn't stand outside her window with a portable speaker or wait outside her classes with a banner. I didn't want to be overbearing and wind up driving her further away.

But now I realize I was hiding too. The things she'd said that night had really hurt. She stirred up all my insecurities, and I've been nursing my pride ever since. I didn't chase her or beg her to take me back because I didn't think there was any reason for her to do that. Because I wasn't worthy of her.

More than that, I think I was afraid of a final rejection there'd be no return from. If I avoided the subject, I could keep believing there was a chance, at some distant time, where we'd come back to each other. If I didn't look in the box, the cat was both alive and dead.

This changes everything.

42
TAYLOR

I FEEL LIKE I'VE PUT ON FIVE POUNDS THIS WEEK AND I CAN'T FIND IT in me to care. After the first shower I've taken in two days, I throw on a peasant top and a pair of jeans. My mom called yesterday to invite me to another family dinner with Chad and Brenna Jensen, so I have no choice but to make an effort. That means brushing my hair, too. Ugh.

This time they're making the safe play to eat out at the Italian place in town rather than risk another cooking catastrophe. I'd tried to make an excuse to decline, but Mom wasn't having it.

And then, of course, I had to dodge on the topic of Conor when she told me to invite him. I told her he was busy, and besides, whatever Coach might have said, he'd probably appreciate not having one of his players tagging along on all his dates. She bought it, albeit skeptically. Mom can read me like a book—I'm sure she's guessed the relationship has fizzled out, but she's gracefully declining to press for details.

As much as I'm dreading tonight, I suppose it offers a distraction from the obvious, a commercial break in my infinite binge and self-pity party.

I've just got my hair up in a ponytail when there's knocking on the door. I check my phone for the time. They're early. Whatever. I didn't feel like putting on makeup anyway.

"Just give me a second to find my shoes," I say as I fling open the door.

It isn't my mom.

Not Brenna either.

Conor stands in my doorway. "Hey," he says roughly.

I'm momentarily struck by him. It's like my heart had forgotten his face. His aura. His magnetism and spirit. I've forgotten the electric air that crackles around us whenever we're in the same space, my body still a slave to its baser instincts.

"You can't be here," I blurt out.

"Are you going somewhere?" He examines me, taken aback.

"I have plans." As badly as I want to throw my arms around him, I force myself to stick to my guns. Bite down and bear it. "You can't be here, Conor."

Already the nerves are tightening my chest, butterflies taking flight in my stomach. The strong urge to slam the door in his face and hide rears its head, as shame and embarrassment join the tangle of emotions I'm already feeling. I'm a war within a war, at odds with myself and losing.

"We need to talk." Conor takes up the entire doorway, all broad shoulders and wide chest. Tension pounds off him like a palpable drumbeat.

"Now's not a good time." I try to shut the door on him. Instead, he muscles his way through like I'm not even standing here.

"Yeah, I'm sorry," he says, barging in, "but this can't wait."

"What the hell is the matter with you?" I charge into the living room after him.

His tone is flat, unhappy. "I know everything, T. Abigail came to my house and explained it all. The video, why you broke up with me. I know."

Shock flies into me. Is he serious? And here I thought Abigail and I had an understanding. We're really going to have to work on our communication.

"Well, I'm sorry she involved you," I mutter, "but it's really none of your concern, so—"

"I'm not sorry," he cuts in. "Not one bit. What would ever make you think I wouldn't want to stand beside you through this? That I wouldn't want to be here to protect you?"

I ignore the sharp clench of my heart, avoid his imploring eyes. "I don't want to talk about it."

"Come on, Taylor. This is me. You dragged my deepest, darkest secrets out of me because it almost cost us all of this," he says, gesturing between us. "You can talk to me. Nothing changes how I feel about you." His deep voice shakes slightly. "Let me help."

"I don't have time for this." Or the emotional bandwidth. I'm strung out, exhausted. There's no fight left in me this time. All I want is to close my eyes and make it all go away. "My mom is on her way over with Chad and Brenna for dinner."

"So cancel. Let's go to the police station. I promise, I'll be right there beside you."

"You don't understand, Conor. I *can't*. As humiliated as you were to talk to your mom and Max about Kai and the break-in, this is a hundred times worse."

"But you didn't do anything wrong," he counters. "You're not the one who messed up."

"It's humiliating!" I shout back.

Oh my God, I'm at my fucking wit's end having to explain this to everyone else. Don't they get it? Don't they see?

"I go in there, make a report—then that's another dozen people who see the video," I say desperately, starting to pace. "They file a case, go to court—that's another dozen, two dozen. Every move I make invites more people to see me like that."

"So what?" he snaps. "You've got to be getting sick of me telling you that you're hot as hell, Taylor. Some poor suckers get a few seconds of joy watching you do nothing more than kiss a girl."

"And you don't care if a bunch of strangers see me practically naked?"

"I fucking care," he growls. "And if you want me to beat the shit

out of every dude in a twenty-mile radius who looks at you funny,
I will. But there's nothing about this that you should be ashamed
of. You did nothing wrong. *You're* the victim. When Abigail came
by and told me and the guys, every one of them was ready to throw
down in your honor. Nobody was cracking jokes or grabbing their
phones. We're only concerned for you. You're all I care about, Taylor."

My heart is breaking. Not for me, but for everything we almost
were. How good it could have been if Jules hadn't thrown a grenade
in the middle of our relationship.

"You don't know how it feels," I whisper. "I can't just get over it."

"No one's asking you to. Just to stick up for yourself."

"And maybe for me, that means waiting for it to blow over and
trying to trick myself into forgetting. You don't know what it's like
to feel like the whole world has seen you naked."

"You're right." He pauses for a beat. "Maybe I should."

I blink and suddenly Conor is yanking off his shirt.

"What do you think you're doing?"

"Empathizing." He kicks off his shoes.

"Stop it," I order.

"No." His socks go next. Then he drops his pants in the middle
of my living room and pushes his boxers down his legs.

"Conor, put your fucking pants back on." And yet my eyes can't
pry themselves from his dick. It's just so…there.

Without another word, he strides out the front door.

"Get back here, you lunatic."

When I hear his footsteps on the stairs, I grab his discarded
clothing and chase after him. But the jackass is fast. I don't catch
up to him until he's across the parking lot and standing on the grass
that abuts the road.

"Get your phones out, people," Conor shouts into the air, his
muscular arms spread wide. "Don't see this every day."

"You've lost your damn mind." I watch him twirling, gorgeous
and ridiculous. He has a body you only see in airbrushed fantasies,

but it isn't supposed to be wiggling around on the front lawn. "Oh my God, Conor, stop. Someone's going to call the cops on you."

"I'll plead temporary insanity due to a broken heart," he says.

Fortunately, this is exclusively a college student-infested street. For at least five blocks in every direction from campus, no townies dare to tread. Families long ago escaped the midweek parties and drunks passed out in the bushes, so that means no traumatized children, either.

Doors start opening up and down the street. Window blinds are separating. He's got an audience now. Shouts and whistles ring out, an eruption of horny banter.

"Stop encouraging him," I yell back at the spectators. I refocus my attention on Conor and his amazing, swinging penis and groan in frustration. "Will you please stop!"

"Never. I've gone completely mad for you, Taylor Antonia Marsh."

"That's not even my middle name!"

"It's *a* middle name and I don't care, if this is what I have to do to take away your embarrassment, I'll do it. I'll do anything."

"You need to be hospitalized," I declare, all the while smothering the laughter threatening to spill over.

This man is…ridiculous. I've never met anyone like Conor Edwards, this sexy crazy handful who's flashing the entire neighborhood just to prove a point and make me feel not as alone.

"Edwards!" someone thunders.

A car rolls up, and from the driver's side window Chad Jensen pokes his head out. "What the hell are you doing running around with no pants on? Put your damn cock away!"

Conor glances over at the car, completely unfazed. "Hey Coach," he drawls. "What's up?" When he realizes my mother is in the passenger side, he offers a sheepish smile. "Doctor Mom, good to see you again."

Unbelievable. I shove Conor's clothes at him. As he covers his junk, I glance over at my mother and see that her lips are shaking with the effort not to laugh and her eyes are watering. Brenna, on the other hand, is hysterical in the back seat, so loud her laughter is echoing off the buildings.

"Are you quite finished?" I ask this big dumb idiot with a heart of gold.

"Only if you're ready to go to the police."

"The police?" My mother leans toward the window, visibly alarmed. "What's wrong?"

I shoot Conor a glare.

I could lie. Make up some innocuous story my mom wouldn't buy but might accept as an alternative to the clear indication that I don't want to discuss it. I could say Conor was just chasing away a creeper who had been hanging around. Fight dick with dick, or whatever. Mom understands boundaries—she trusts my judgment and doesn't push me to make uncomfortable decisions.

And maybe that's why I don't, and never have. Nobody has ever encouraged me to make the hard choices, and I never pushed myself to do it. My whole life I simply retreated into myself, allowed an ever-growing chasm to build between me and anything that could cause me pain. Anything that could reject me.

I created my own safe space and avoided drawing attention to myself. No one can point fingers if they can't see me. There's nothing for them to laugh at if I'm not there. I stayed inside my bubble, safe and alone.

No, I don't especially like my friends and enemies and lovers joining forces to press my hand. It's not how I operate. And yet... maybe it was exactly what I needed. A good kick in the ass. Not because they're right or I'm wrong, but because I wasn't serving myself. I was serving my fears. I've been feeding them and allowing them to take up more space inside me until I'm no longer myself and can't remember a time I was anything else.

This is how people grow up to be old and bitter. Jaded and

spiteful. When they let the world and the bad actors in it strip them of joy and replace it with doubt and insecurities.

I'm too young to be this unhappy, and too loved to be this alone. I owe myself better.

My gaze drifts to Conor, whose earnest gray eyes tell me he won't leave my side if I allow him to stand beside me. Then I turn toward my mom, whose concern is visible and whose support is mine for the taking. There are people who want to fight for me. I should want to fight for myself.

I meet Mom's gaze and give her a reassuring smile. "I'll tell you on the way to the police station."

43
TAYLOR

IT'S LATE WHEN CONOR AND I GET BACK TO MY APARTMENT. I leave him on the couch watching TV while I take a long, hot bath. I put on my relaxation playlist and turn off the lights except for a couple of candles on the bathroom counter, and for the first time in a week, I feel some of the tension leaving my body.

It was mortifying explaining the situation to my mom while Conor drove the three of us in his Jeep tonight. I was sorry I was the reason she called off dinner with Chad and Brenna, but when I tried to apologize for spoiling her plans she wouldn't have it.

"My daughter comes *first*," she'd said firmly, and it was as if all the times she'd neglected me in the past had just disappeared. Today I was her first priority, her only concern. Everything had ceased to exist for her but me, and for that I was grateful.

After a chain of text messages, Abigail, Sasha, and Rebecca met us at the police station. I had a good conversation with Rebecca before we made the decision to go through with filing a report. Both of us were hesitant. Her because of what her parents might think; me because of the added exposure. Eventually, we came around to the idea that we could turn this into an opportunity for something positive. We didn't ask for this, but rather than hiding, ashamed, we could take our power back. So with the beginnings of a plan in mind, we walked in there together. Stronger.

As Abigail's mother explained to us over the phone, Massachusetts doesn't have a specific revenge porn law. If Abigail herself, for instance, had uploaded the video, it might not have been a crime. However, Jules and Abigail's ex Kevin can be charged under other state laws for the unauthorized access to Abigail's phone, the Kappa cloud server, copying the video, and uploading it without consent. Mrs. Hobbes believes, and the officer we spoke to agreed, that there's a strong case.

I didn't ask what would happen to Jules and Kevin, or when. I don't particularly care, as long as they're punished. My mother, however, called Briar's dean of students at home and scheduled a meeting with him first thing tomorrow morning. By the end of the day, I suspect Briar will begin the process of expelling those two.

My brain is still spinning. Dominoes in my mind have yet to fall. Just the *click, click, click* of a thousand consequences rapidly colliding toward an eventual conclusion at some distant time, in some future place.

The panic has subsided, though. The overwhelming cord of dread around my neck has loosened. Instead, I'm bursting with ideas, surging with adrenaline. I'm sure the chemical stimulation will fade soon and I'll crash a few days from now to sleep for a week. Until then, dot, dot, dot.

After I get out of the bath and put on my pajamas, I stand in the hall for a moment watching Conor on the couch. His eyes are closed, head lolled to one shoulder. His chest rises and falls on deep, restful breaths.

He's remarkable. Not many guys would have reacted to the situation the way he did, appreciated the gravity of the violation rather than making light of my humiliation.

But that's Conor. He has an instinct toward empathy that most guys don't. He'd rather make people around him feel good about themselves, even when it provides no personal gain for himself. More than anything, that's what I fell in love with.

I was foolish to think I needed to protect him. He's the strongest, most resilient person I know.

I'm tempted to let him sleep a while longer, but as if he senses me watching him, his eyes blink open and find me in the shadows.

"Sorry," he says huskily. "Didn't mean to crash on you."

"No, it's fine. It's been a long day."

A nervous silence ensues. Conor shifts around collecting his phone and keys from between the couch cushions.

"Anyway, I'll get out of your way. Just wanted to make sure you were okay after everything." He gets up to leave, coming around the couch.

"No," I say, stopping him. "Stay. You want anything? Are you hungry?" I catch his arm and then release it like it bit me.

I don't know how to be around him now. The ease between us isn't here right now. It feels stilted and forced. But there's also this indefinable urge to be near him that grows stronger the longer he's here.

"Not really," he says.

"Yeah, me neither."

Shit. This is awkward. As far as I can tell, we're still broken up. Despite everything we'd been through with each other over the past few weeks, I don't know how to approach the subject. I mean, I stood outside the Kappa house and shoved a knife through his chest. He came back to help me in a time of need, but that doesn't mean all is forgiven.

"We can, um, watch a movie?" I suggest. Baby steps.

Conor nods. Then an almost imperceptible smirk dances across his lips. "You inviting me to Netflix and chill?"

"Damn, you're easy. I mean, jeez, Conor, have some respect for yourself. You'll never find a good woman if you're always giving the milk away for free."

He sighs dramatically. "My mom keeps saying the same thing, but I never learn."

We laugh, still standing all stupid and nervous in the middle of my apartment. Then his expression sobers.

"We should talk," he says.

"Yeah."

He leads me over to the couch to sit. Facing me but staring at his hands in his lap, he struggles to find a place to start.

"I don't know where your head's at or what your expectations are. I don't have any, I want you to know. You're going through something, I get it, and I want to be here for you, but only as much as you want me to." He shrugs awkwardly. "Whatever that looks like."

I open my mouth to interject, but he holds a hand up to say he isn't finished yet.

After a deep breath, he continues. "I made out with another girl last night at a party."

I briefly close my eyes. "All right."

His throat dips as he swallows. "I got hammered and it happened. She took me to a bedroom to do more, but I couldn't go through with it—physically or emotionally. Honestly, though, it was more of a physical impairment. I might've gone through with it if the equipment was working."

I nod slowly.

"I wasn't thinking straight. Then afterward, I felt sick about it. It wasn't like I set out to find a revenge lay or to get over you with someone else. I was hurt, confused, pissed off, so all I wanted to do was drink my feelings. Shit got out of control."

"We were broken up," I tell him sincerely. "You don't have to explain."

"I do. I want to. Because I don't want any more secrets. Not mine, anyway. I don't want you to ever have a reason to doubt or mistrust me."

"I do trust you."

He looks up, and in his cool gray eyes I see the wounds I've inflicted. The insecurity I've instilled. A month ago I would have said Conor Fucking Edwards was impervious to everyone and everything. Completely immune to heartache.

I was wrong.

"Then why?" he asks roughly. "Why did breaking up seem like the only solution?"

"Because it's what I've always done. I hide." Shame clamps around my throat. "Hiding felt like the safer option, the path of least embarrassment. Just cut ties and escape and everything will be okay."

"I wish you'd trusted that I would be there for you."

My eyes widen. "God, no, you don't get it—I had no doubt you'd be there. That was the one thing I *knew* I could trust. But I didn't want to put you through all that."

I swallow hard because suddenly my throat feels too tight and dry.

"I need you to know something," I start. Gulp again. "I didn't mean any of those awful things I said to you. I only said them because I needed you to accept the breakup. It was wrong and hurtful and I'm so sorry I didn't have the nerve to tell you the truth." Tears sting my eyelids. "I was afraid of what you'd think of me, that you'd be embarrassed by me. It was humiliating enough to deal with all this myself. I didn't want to make it your problem, too. Didn't want you to see me differently."

"I only see you." He takes my hand, rubbing his thumb over the inside of my wrist. "Just as you are. I don't imagine you as some impossible ideal. To me you're…real." His lips quirk in a half-smile. "Stubborn, opinionated, pushy, funny, intelligent, kind, too hard on herself, snarky, sarcastic, jaded, yet somehow a closeted optimist. I fell in love with you for you, T. Nothing you could say or do would embarrass me. Ever."

"Considering how we met, right?" I say, smiling.

"I knew you were nervous. Scared shitless, even." His thumb continues its soft caresses across my skin, lulling me into a calm I haven't felt in days. "Still, you were brave and so refreshingly honest.

I was having dirty thoughts about you right away, but my favorite thing about you that first night was that you were completely unpretentious."

"Yeah, it was pretty much the hair for me," I say solemnly. "Oh, and the abs. The abs are good too."

Conor laughs, shaking his head. "You're such a brat."

"For real, though, I'm sorry. For all of it. I freaked out and made a rash decision. It just seemed like the only thing I could do at the time." I put on a firm tone. "I need you to know that I'm on board with whatever career path you choose. You *do* have prospects, and whatever you decide will *always* be good enough for me. That bullshit I fed you when I ended it was just that—bullshit. I didn't mean a single word of it."

He laces his fingers through mine, squeezing. "I get it. We both made mistakes."

"Thank you for sticking by my side even though I was pushing you away. For not turning your back on me."

"Never."

Leaning in, I place a kiss on his lips.

He hesitates, just for a beat. Then, as if he's suddenly convinced it's really happening, his hands go to my ribs and pull my body against his. His kiss is soft but greedy. Sweet hunger and gentle need.

"I still love you," he whispers against my mouth.

"I still love you," I whisper back.

Getting to my knees, I straddle his lap as he slides to lie back against the armrest. My fingers tangle in the long, silky strands of hair at the base of his neck.

"Is it too late to plead temporary insanity?" I ask.

"I thought we were going to pretend the whole breakup was a vivid fever dream." Conor's thumbs drag slow, agonizing strokes under my breasts.

"I could go along with that."

I kiss along his jaw, his neck. In response, his fingers dig into my skin. He's hard between my legs, hips rising to meet me. I pull his shirt over his head and toss it aside. Then, with unhurried attention, I explore his bare chest with my mouth. I kiss those glorious abs, nip at the skin just above the waistband of his jeans until he shudders and his sinewy muscles contract.

"Can I?" I murmur, tugging at his belt.

Conor nods tightly, jaw clenched, as if it's taking all his effort to lie still. It's that coiled, kinetic strength of him that's always attracted and intrigued me. A man so at once peaceful and dynamic.

I free his erection from his jeans, stroking the thick length as his hands reach above his head to grip a throw pillow. He watches me with anticipation, rapt and eager. "Fuck, Taylor, you're the most beautiful thing I've ever seen."

My sweet-talking man. Smiling, I take him in my mouth. Slowly, at first, then with more intent. I moan at the masculine taste of him, the heat of his cock as it slides through my lips.

"So beautiful," he mumbles, sliding his fingers down to cup my head, play with my hair.

I suck and lick and tease until he's panting and groaning. I could do this forever, but it's not long before his hand brushes the side of my face and his hips pull away to signal I have to stop unless I want this to be over quickly.

So I straddle him again, pressing myself against his hard cock, grinding on his shaft. Conor grabs my ass with both hands, urging my movements.

I tug my shirt over my head, and his attention moves to my breasts. He cups them, kneading them in both hands, his thumbs playing with my nipples. Then he adjusts his position and sits up, one arm wrapped behind my back to support us both. He lowers his head and sucks one nipple into his mouth, while his fingers tease the other. Within seconds my insides are twisted tight, my clit is throbbing, and I can't stand the teasing any longer.

"I want to be inside you," he breathes.

"Condoms are in the bedroom."

With no warning he stands us up and carries me to the bed. He puts a condom on while I shimmy out of my pajama shorts. We're both naked now, breathing hard, gazes locked.

Then he growls, "C'mere," and I smile and climb on top of him.

I lean down and press my lips to his, and just as he parts them to let my tongue slide into his mouth, I deliberately come down on his dick. We both moan, delighting in the sensation. He fills me completely, his body satiating my every aching need.

He doesn't rush me. Hands resting loosely on my hips, he lets me set the pace. Find my own perfect rhythm where every plunge sends pleasure skittering across my nerve endings. Soon I quicken my movements, riding him with greater insistence.

Conor bites down on his lip but can't stop the low, quiet groans that build in his chest. And when he can't control his body, he grabs my tits with both hands and thrusts his hips into me. Harder, faster. Both of us sprinting toward magnificent release.

He knows my body, sometimes even better than I do. Sensing my need, he presses his thumb to my clit and starts rubbing. Gentle at first, then applying more pressure as I rock forward and back on his dick, finding that perfect angle where he's deep inside and hitting the sweetest spot.

"Oh, fucking fuckturtles, I'm coming," I choke out, and his answering laughter heats the air around us.

I'm too mindless with orgasm to laugh back. My muscles clench in a cascade of pure bliss, and I collapse on top of him as my body trembles wildly. He chases his own orgasm, pumping into me until he finds his own release a moment later, moaning my name.

Afterward, we're hot and sweaty and clinging to one another.

"I missed you," he says, breathless.

"I missed us."

"Let's stop breaking up, deal?"

I'm not sure how I got lucky enough to meet Conor Edwards.

Like all the times the world took a shit on my shoes were leading up to this one big *I'm sorry* gift. Sometimes we make all the wrong decisions, end up in all the wrong places, and still find exactly where we're supposed to be. Conor's my happy accident. My wrong place, wrong time, exactly right guy. He taught me how to love myself against my best efforts, showed me an image of myself I'd never believed was there. Strong. Beautiful. Confident.

And I'll never take that for granted again.

Rising up on my elbow, I peer into his sated, heavy-lidded eyes and smile. "Deal."

EPILOGUE
CONOR

WELL, IT TOOK A FEW BRUISES AND A HELL OF A LOT OF PATIENCE, but I finally got Taylor to stand up on a surfboard.

From just beyond the swells, I straddle my board and watch as she rides the end of a wave into the shallow foam. Her stance is still a bit awkward and uncertain, but I think she's getting a feel for it. When she pops out of the water after her ride into shore, she's got a big shiny grin on her face. She waves, ecstatic, making sure I saw her. Then she hops up and down a couple times and forms a victory sign with her arms.

Fuck, she's adorable.

Having her here in Huntington Beach the last three weeks has been such a relief, for both of us. Zero stress. Just sleeping in, chilling at the beach, showing her the sights. It's the perfect antidote for the headaches back on campus.

My mom and Max love her. So much so they're already making plans for Thanksgiving and Christmas. She's my future now, and I'm hers.

Coach is totally going to kick my ass when he realizes he's stuck with me at another family dinner with Iris.

I had hoped I could keep Taylor's mind off anything that wasn't the beach or us doing naked stuff, but a few times now I've caught her on the phone or with her laptop open, hard at work. Apparently, when she and Rebecca made the decision to file the police report, they hatched a plan first. With Abigail and Kappa's help, they're petitioning the Greek Council on campus to host a seminar on consent, sexual assault, and sexual harassment. They're inviting several guest speakers to host talks and want to promote a month of outreach and awareness ahead of pledge week in the fall.

I've never seen Taylor so passionate and engaged on anything. Not gonna lie, at first I was worried the project might start to have a negative effect on her mood—dragging all of those feelings to the surface again—but it's done just the opposite. She's never looked happier since they got the ball rolling on this. It's like having a mission is finally giving her some real peace of mind.

"Hey," Taylor calls as she paddles up alongside me, a little out of breath but smiling wide.

"You're getting better, babe. That was almost not atrocious."

Laughing, she slaps a handful of water at me. "Dick."

"Brat."

She gets herself turned around so we're both facing the shore. "Your phone was ringing when I went back to our stuff for a drink. Screen said Devin."

"Oh, nice. That's the guy from the non-profit I was telling you about."

"Yeah? A call is a good sign, right?"

Taylor is returning to Boston in a few days, and I'm not heading back till mid-August, so we won't see each other for a while. Figured I'd better find something to keep me out of trouble for the month and a half we'll be apart.

"I think so," I say. "Seems like if it was a no, they'd just send an email or something."

After a bit of research, I found out there were some available summer internships with the local chapter of another environmental protection group. It's mostly a community outreach kind of thing, working booths at farmers markets and festivals, signing up volunteers. They're focused on clean oceans and beaches, and educating the public about sustainable ways to enjoy marine recreation. After giving it a lot of thought over the last month—and having a lot of long talks with my super-smart girlfriend—I've decided that's where my passion lies. This internship seemed like as good a step as any to figuring out how to make a career out of it.

I know Taylor didn't mean the things she said on the Kappa lawn when she dumped me, but she wasn't wrong. For the last few years, I haven't had a direction outside of hockey and just going along with the path Max had set out for me. I know he only wanted to help, but I'm not him. I can't follow in his footsteps.

I needed to find my own path, and finally, I feel like I have a purpose. Like I can be a man Taylor would be proud of.

"I got an email from Abigail's mom this morning," she says, dragging her fingers through the water as we bob on the tide. "Jules is pleading down to a lesser charge. I guess the prosecutor scared the shit out of her with some threat about felony hacking charges. But it sounds like Kevin's parents have hired some expensive bulldog lawyer to fight the case. So it might end up going to trial."

"Think you're up for that?"

She's been so brave through this whole ordeal. I really hoped it could end quickly for her, but no, apparently that dickwad intends to make her suffer just so he can avoid taking responsibility. I keep telling myself bashing his face in would not help Taylor's side of things. It's a struggle.

"I'll have to be," she says. "Really, the more he pushes me, the more I want to get involved. Like this dude is going to wish he never fucked with me."

A grin tugs on my lips. "That's my girl."

Man, I couldn't be more impressed with how she's handled the pressure. Taylor's my fucking hero. With every new development in the case, she rises to the challenge, more committed now than ever to defy the people who wanted to bring her down.

Every day, I'm falling more in love with her. Which only makes the knot in my stomach that much tighter.

"So," I say, pausing as a swell tumbles beneath us. "You know Alec, Matt, and Gavin graduated, right? So, since it was just going to be the two of us, Foster and I didn't bother renewing our lease on the house."

"Yeah, I still have a couple weeks before I need to decide if I'm keeping mine or looking for something else."

"Well, I was talking to Hunter, and it looks like he and Demi are thinking about their arrangements, too. Brenna and Summer are both leaving to live with their boyfriends, and Mike Hollis is married now, so…yeah…"

She raises an eyebrow at me. Fuck, I didn't think this would be so hard.

I gulp. "Anyway, I don't remember how we got on the topic, but someone mentioned, you know, maybe the four of us, could, like, get a place."

"A place," she repeats.

"Together."

"You're asking me to move in with you."

"I mean, no. But yeah, sorta."

"Huh." Taylor stares at me. Unmoving. Not even a lip twitch. It's sort of scary how still she is. "But won't that be awkward for you and Demi?"

My eyebrows fly up. "What? No. Not even a little. I mean, she kissed me once, but that was just to make Hunter jealous. There's no *thing* there."

"No," Taylor corrects, deadpan, "I meant with all the super-obvious sexual tension between me and Hunter. We've kept it quiet all this time, but—"

"Fuck off," I say, laughing and launching a splash at her. "You're such an asshole."

"I have to confess," she continues, "I've got the mega hots for your best friend. I mean, he is the captain, after all."

I narrow my eyes. "I'll break his legs in his sleep."

"You can watch, if you want." She flashes this self-impressed grin at me, and I can't help myself. I'm stupid for this girl.

"Come here." I pull her board closer and kiss her. Deeply and with purpose. "You're a pain in my ass."

"Love you, too."

If someone had asked me to describe my perfect match, I wouldn't have been able to do it. I probably would have spit out a bunch of clichés that would have amounted to every one-night stand I've ever had. Yet somehow, life put Taylor right in front of me anyway. She's made me a better person. Taught me to be true to myself. Helped me see the value in me as a person. Hell, she put my family back together.

She and I found every possible way to try to sabotage our happiness, each of us falling back on old habits and insecurities. But what gives me faith in us is that we always managed to end up right back here. Together. I guess there's hope for a couple of hopeless fuckups after all.

"So is that a yes?" I ask her.

Taylor looks over her shoulder at the incoming swell. She lines up her board and prepares to catch it. Then, with a mischievous grin, she starts paddling.

"Race you for it."

The End

Discover the world of Briar U with a sneak peek into *The Chase*, the first book in the bestselling Briar U series

1
SUMMER

"Is this a joke?" I gape at the five girls who are holding me in judgment. They have various hair, skin, and eye colors, and yet I can't tell them apart because their expressions are identical. There's a whole lot of *smug* peeking through the phony remorse they're trying to convey, as if they're truly devastated by the news.

Ha. They're enjoying this.

"I'm sorry, Summer, but it's not a joke." Kaya offers a pitying smile. "As the Standards Committee, we take Kappa Beta Nu's reputation very seriously. We received word from Nationals this morning—"

"Oh really? You received word? Did they send a telegram?"

"No, it was an email," she says, completely missing the sarcasm. She flips her glossy hair over one shoulder. "They reminded the committee that every member of this sorority must uphold the behavior standards set by them, otherwise our chapter will lose its good standing with Nationals."

"We *have* to remain in good standing," Bianca pipes up pleading at me with her eyes. Of the five bi-otches in front of me, she seems like the most reasonable.

"Especially after what happened to Daphne Kettleman," adds a girl whose name I can't remember.

Curiosity gets the better of me. "What happened to Daphne Kettleman?"

"Alcohol poisoning." The fourth girl—I think her name's Hailey—lowers her voice to a whisper and quickly glances around, as if there might be a bug or two hidden in the antique furnishings that fill the living room of the Kappa mansion.

"She had to get her stomach pumped," the no-name girl reveals gleefully. Which makes me question whether she's actually thrilled that Daphne Kettleman almost died.

Kaya speaks up in a curt voice. "Enough about Daphne. You shouldn't have even brought her up, Coral—"

Coral! Right. That's her name. And it sounds as stupid now as it did when she introduced herself fifteen minutes ago.

"We don't speak Daphne's name in this house," Kaya explains to me.

Jee-zus. One measly stomach pumping and poor Daphne gets Voldemorted? The Kappa Beta Nu chapter of Briar University is evidently a lot stricter than the Brown chapter.

Case in point—they're kicking me out before I'd even moved in.

"This isn't personal," Kaya continues, giving me another fake consolatory smile. "Our reputation is very important to us, and although you're a legacy—"

"A presidential legacy," I point out. *So ha! In your face, Kaya!* My mom was president of a Kappa chapter during her junior and senior years, and so was my grandmother. Heyward women and Kappa Beta Nu go together like abs and any male Hemsworth.

"A *legacy*," she repeats, "but we don't adhere as strictly to those ancestral bonds the way we used to."

Ancestral bonds? Who says that? Did she time-travel from the olden days?

"As I said, we have rules and policies. And you didn't leave the Brown chapter on the best of terms."

"I didn't get kicked out of Kappa," I argue. "I got kicked out of school in general."

Kaya stares at me in disbelief. "Is this a point of pride for you? Getting expelled from one of the best colleges in the country?"

I answer through clenched teeth. "No, I'm not proud of it. I'm just saying, technically speaking, I'm still a member of this sorority."

"Maybe so, but that doesn't mean you're entitled to live in this house." Kaya crosses her arms over the front of her white mohair sweater.

"I see." I mimic her pose, except I cross my legs too.

Kaya's envious gaze lands on my black suede Prada boots, a gift from my grandmother to celebrate my admission to Briar. I had a good chuckle when I opened the package last night—I'm not sure Nana Celeste understands that I'm only attending Briar because I was expelled from my other school. Actually, I bet she does, and just doesn't care. Nana will find any excuse to get her Prada on. She's my soulmate.

"And you didn't think," I go on, an edge creeping into my voice, "to let me know this until *after* I packed up my stuff, drove all the way down here from Manhattan, and walked through the front door?"

Bianca is the only one who has the decency to look guilty. "We're really sorry, Summer. But like Kaya said, Nationals didn't get in touch until this morning, and then we had to vote, and…" She shrugs weakly. "Sorry," she says again.

"So you voted and decided I'm not allowed to live here."

"Yes," Kaya says.

I glance at the others. "Hailey?"

"Halley," she corrects icily.

Oh, whatever. Like I'm supposed to remember their names? We literally just met. "Halley." I look to the next girl. "Coral." And then the next girl. Crap. I legit don't know this one. "Laura?"

"Tawny," she bites out.

Swing and a miss! "Tawny," I repeat apologetically. "You guys are sure about this?"

I get three nods.

"Cool. Thanks for wasting my time." I stand up, push my hair over one shoulder, and start wrapping my red cashmere scarf around my neck. A bit too vigorously maybe, because it seems to annoy Kaya.

"Stop being so dramatic," she orders in a snarky voice. "And don't act like *we're* to blame for the fact that you burned down your former house. Excuse us if we don't want to live with an *arsonist*."

I struggle to keep my temper in check. "I didn't burn anything down."

"That's not what our Brown sisters said." She tightens her lips. "Anyway, we have a house meeting in ten minutes. It's time for you to go."

"Another meeting? Look at you! A packed schedule today!"

"We're organizing a New Year's Eve charity event tonight to raise money," Kaya says stiffly.

Ah, my bad. "What's the charity?"

"Oh." Bianca looks sheepish. "We're raising money to renovate the basement here in the mansion."

Oh my God. *They're* the charity? "You better get to it, then." With a mocking smile, I flutter my fingers in a careless wave and march out of the room.

In the hall, I feel the first sting of tears.

Fuck these girls. I don't need them or their dumb sorority.

"Summer, wait."

Bianca catches up to me at the front doors. I quickly paste on a smile and blink away the tears that had begun to well up. I won't let them see me cry, and I'm so frigging glad I left all my suitcases in the car and only came in with my oversized purse. How mortifying would it have been to lug my bags back to the car? It would've taken multiple trips too, because I don't travel light.

"Listen," Bianca says, her voice so quiet I strain to hear her. "You should consider yourself lucky."

I raise my eyebrows. "For being homeless? Sure, I feel blessed."

She cracks a smile. "Your last name is Heyward-Di Laurentis. You are not, and will never be, homeless."

I grin sheepishly. Can't argue with that.

"But I'm serious," she whispers. "You don't want to live here." Her almond-shaped eyes dart toward the doorway. "Kaya is like a drill sergeant. It's her first year as Kappa president, and she's on some crazy power trip."

"I've noticed," I say dryly.

"You should've seen what she did to Daphne! She acted like it was the alcohol thing, but really she was just jealous because Daph slept with her ex-boyfriend Chris, so she made Daph's life miserable. One weekend when Daphne was away, Kaya 'accidentally'"—Bianca uses air quotes—"donated every piece of her clothing to these freshmen who were collecting stuff for the annual clothes drive. Daph eventually quit the sorority and moved out."

I'm starting to think that alcohol poisoning was the best thing that could've ever happened to Daphne Kettleman, if it got her out of this hellhole.

"Whatever. I don't care if I live here or not. Like you said, I'll be just fine." I put on the cavalier, nothing-in-life-ever-*ever*-gets-to-me voice that I've perfected over the years.

It's my armor. I pretend that my life is a beautiful Victorian house and hope that nobody peers close enough to see the cracks in my facade.

But no matter how convincing I am in front of Bianca, there's no stopping the massive wave of anxiety that hits me the moment I slide into my car five minutes later. It stilts my breathing and quickens my pulse, making it hard to think clearly.

What am I supposed to do?

Where am I supposed to go?

I inhale deeply. *It's okay. It's fine.* I take another breath. Yes, I'll figure it out. I always do, right? I'm constantly screwing up, and I always find a way to unscrew myself. I just have to buckle down and think—

My phone blares out its ringtone rendition of Sia's "Cheap Thrills." Thank God.

I waste no time answering the call. "Hey," I greet my brother Dean, grateful for the interruption.

"Hey, Boogers. Just checking that you made it to campus in one piece."

"Why wouldn't I?"

"Gosh, who knows. You might've run off to Miami with some hitchhiking wannabe rapper you picked up on the interstate—or what I like to call a recipe for becoming a serial killer's skin-suit. Oh wait! You already fucking did that."

"Oh my God. First of all, Jasper was an aspiring *country singer*, not a rapper. Second, I was with two other girls and we were driving to Daytona Beach, not Miami. Third, he didn't even try to touch me, let alone murder me." I sigh. "Lacey did hook up with him, though, and he gave her herpes."

Incredulous silence meets my ears.

"Dicky?" That's my childhood nickname for Dean. He hates it. "You there?"

"I'm trying to understand how you think your version of the story is in *any way* more palatable than mine." He suddenly curses. "Aw fuck, didn't I hook up with Lacey at your eighteenth birthday party?" A pause. "The herpes trip would've happened *before* that party. Dammit, Summer! I mean, I used protection, but a warning would've been nice!"

"No, you didn't hook up with Lacey. You're thinking of Laney, with an 'N.' I stopped being her friend after that."

"How come?"

"Because she slept with my brother when she was supposed to be hanging out with me at *my* party. That's not cool."

"Truth. Selfish move."

"Yup."

There's a sudden blast of noise on the line—what sounds like wind, car engines, and then a barrage of honking. "Sorry," Dean says. "Just leaving the apartment. My Uber's here."

"Where are you off to?"

"Picking up our dry-cleaning. The place Allie and I go to is in Tribeca, but they're awesome, so worth the trek. Highly recommend."

Dean and his girlfriend Allie live in the West Village in Manhattan. Allie admitted to me that the area is way fancier than she's used to, but for my brother it's actually a step down; our family's penthouse is on the Upper East Side, making up the top three floors of our hotel, the Heyward Plaza. But Dean's new building is near the private school where he teaches, and since Allie has a lead role on a television show that shoots all over Manhattan, the location is convenient for both of them.

It must be so nice for them, having a place to live and all.

"Anyway, are you nice and settled at the Kappa house?"

"Not quite," I confess.

"For fuck's sake, Summer. What did you do?"

My jaw falls open in outrage. Why does my family always assume that *I'm* in the wrong?

"I didn't do anything," I answer stiffly. But then defeat weakens my voice. "They don't think someone like me is good for the sorority's reputation. One of them said I was an arsonist."

"Well," Dean says not so tactfully. "You kind of are."

"Fuck off, Dicky. It was an accident. Arsonists intentionally set fires."

"So you're an accidental arsonist. The Accidental Arsonist. That's a great name for a book."

"Awesome. Go write that." I don't care how snide I sound. I'm feeling snarky, and my nerves are shot. "Anyway, they kicked me out, and now I have to figure out where the heck I'm going to live this semester."

ABOUT THE AUTHOR

A *New York Times*, *USA Today*, and *Wall Street Journal* bestselling author, Elle Kennedy grew up in the suburbs of Toronto, Ontario, and holds a BA in English from York University. From an early age, she knew she wanted to be a writer and actively began pursuing that dream when she was a teenager. She loves strong heroines and sexy alpha heroes, and just enough heat, humor, and danger to keep things interesting!

Elle loves to hear from her readers. Visit her website ellekennedy.com or sign up for her newsletter to receive updates about upcoming books and exclusive excerpts. You can also find her on Facebook (ElleKennedyAuthor), Instagram (@ElleKennedy33), or TikTok (@ElleKennedyAuthor).